MW00444455

# The Mine

ISBN-21: 978-1-7923-6400-6
March 2021
Printed in the USA

Cover Design: Phoebe Hyder
Elemental Cover Designs

Dedicated to Nefi, Marley, and those that read this over and over again to help me make it what it is.

# Preface

"Hurry, baby," the woman said as she pulled the little girl along. The girl kept getting distracted by the hundreds of legs and shoes that surrounded her. She toddled after her mother on chubby legs, giggling when she was pulled so quickly her tiny legs were lifted off the ground.

"Momma," she smiled, waddling behind the tall, slender woman, "where go?"

"We have to leave, baby," her mother replied sharply. "We are going to live somewhere else."

"Why?"

"Because baby."

"Where, Dada?" the little girl looked around to find her father but couldn't see his smiling face anywhere.

"He went to go get tickets."

"Oh," the girl's mouth dropped open, and she let out a scream of delight when she saw where they were heading. "Twain!" she yelled.

"Yes, baby, we're going on the train. Keep up, please."

The girl's mother led her up to the boarding platform, where crowds of people shuffled anxiously around each other. They would look at their watches, mumble, look back towards the entrance to the station, and mumble some more. The little girl missed all the nervous mumbling; she was focused on the massive black locomotive puffing before her. To her, it sounded like the machine was breathing.

"Wanna go on twain!" the little girl cried, trying to tug her mother closer to the engine.

"Hang on," her mother said, "we have to wait for your father."

Just then, a frazzled-looking, bespectacled man came jogging up to them, holding a tiny bundle of cloth in one arm and several pieces of paper in his opposite hand.

"Made it," the man said, stopping before the girl and her mother.

"Dada!" the little girl cried out, reaching up for her father. Her father didn't notice; he was too busy transferring the squirmy bundle to her mother.

"Bubby!" the little girl squealed happily when she saw the baby.

"Any news?" her mother asked, her voice cracking.

"None," her father said sadly, shaking his head. "There are whispers of raids downtown—"

"But that's not legal!"

"The Chancellor made it *legal*," her father spat.

The little girl lost interest in all the talking. She turned her gaze to the massive train before her, her giddiness making her limbs tremble. She took a few steps towards the train, but her mother yanked her back.

"No, baby, this is not our train."

Another man came hurrying up to them. This man was trailed by a frantic-looking woman and two boys. The girl recognized these people; they had come over for dinner a lot.

They were all carrying large suitcases.

"We barely made it out," the man gasped as he approached. "The police are beginning to round everyone up."

"I don't understand," the girl's mother whispered, covering her mouth. "How could this happen?"

"Democracy," her father spat. "The masses are idiots."

"Don't say that," her mother looked around in fright.

"Idiot!" the little girl giggles.

4

"Hush!" her mother scowls at her father, but then they continue speaking quietly but quickly.

The little girl was getting bored. She looked longingly at the train.

Just then, the woman who had come with the man stumbled and dropped everything she was carrying. The girl's mother bent down to help her pick up her things, letting go of the girl's hand at the same time.

The little girl waited by her mother's side but watched with sad eyes as the train she had been looking at whistled and pulled away, making those delightful chugging noises.

While her mother was helping the woman and her father was speaking to the man, another train pulled up. This one was bright and shiny, the color of her mother's jewelry, and had a bunch of words on the side. Surely this was their train, the girl thought. It looked so beautiful.

The train hissed to a stop and opened its doors. The inside, the girl could see, was just as shiny as the outside. She took a step forward, wanting to see more.

She suddenly found herself on the train, touching the soft carpet and the nice seats. There were lots of children on this train, but they all looked sad, and no one looked at her when she walked in.

"Want play?" the little girl asked, walking up to a little boy sitting on a soft seat.

He looked at her with horror in his eyes and quickly turned away. He scared her, and she moved to the next child, but no one would look at her. She did not like this train; she turned around to go back and tell her mother that she did not want to go on this train.

She got to the entryway and could see her mother, who was still helping the lady when there was a quiet hiss, and the glass doors slid over the opening. She bumped into them, confused.

She started banging on them, yelling for her mother.

"Momma!" she screamed. "Momma!"

Her mother stood, then looked around frantically.

"Momma!" The little girl felt the train begin to move, and she began to cry.

"No!" her mother screamed, eyes locking with the little girl's. "NO!" She began chasing the train, which was gaining speed. "No, stop!"

"Momma!"

"What are you doing out of your seat?"

The little girl turned to see a large man, dressed in black, coming towards her. He looked angry.

She banged on the glass doors even harder, crying for her mother, who was still chasing the train, yelling something.

The man bent down and picked up the little girl. He stood, and from his height, the little girl got one last look at her mother before the train went into a tunnel, and her family was lost from view.

The Constitution for the Society of the Republic of the Colonies

"Democracy is the foundation of Society: Equality is the foundation of Life."

1.  Everyone must be equal, so anyone that would disrupt the equality must be put to other use or eliminated.
2.  Literacy is the most equalizing of all skills, so each citizen must acquire it.
3.  Each citizen must participate in Society for it to be equal.
4.  Participation includes:
    a.  Working at a designated occupation
    b.  Keeping the peace
    c.  Obeying Society Laws, both federal and colonial
    d.  Encouraging all citizens to be a participating member
5.  In order to ensure peaceful transitions of power, His Majesty the Chancellor will appoint colonial and federal leaders.
6.  The Thirteen Colonies will decide their own laws in accordance with Federal laws, to be approved and enforced by the people.

# Chapter One

The lift clunks and rattles up the shaft, moving from complete darkness to only somewhat darkness. I lean against the back wall, letting the shaky ride lull me. The smell of sweat and must permeate the air, but coal dust coats my nostrils so thickly that it masks the cloying, nauseating smell. During my first week, the stench nearly always made me vomit up what little food I could stomach, but now I can handle it and the food. After all, everyone tells the newbies that if they can't get past the smells, they won't make it a week.

The ride up is silent, like always. The others crowded into this creaky metal box are my fellow searchers of the western tunnels. Shashan, my partner, hangs his head low, worry thick on his brow. He's eighteen, so of course, he's worried. Everyone else, though, is quiet out of habit. Searching is a good job, not one of the back-breaking or mind-numbing ones, but it means going deeper than almost everyone else in the Mine. And deeper always means darker.

We're quiet because darkness breeds silence.

No one talks much in the Mine anyway, even those in other jobs. I didn't expect anyone to speak in the lift because it's always quiet. We work in silence, eat in silence, and ride in silence. Besides the darkness, I think we all just ran out of stuff to say a long time ago. I think I stopped caring about talking twelve years ago when I was five. Five-ish, anyway. I'd only been here for two years then.

I've known almost everyone in the lift for years or more. Years are tricky down here, but we keep track of them through Arrival Day. Today.

Shashan and I have been partners for five years, but we both know that's going to change today. We rarely speak in the tunnels, but for the last few weeks, he's stopped talking altogether.

That's fine by me. What are we supposed to talk about anyway? Rocks? It's not like either of us can change anything.

The elevator cranks to a sharp, jolting stop, jarring us a little. The door is heaved open by a small child covered in black smudge. I hate seeing them, the little ones. The kid is barely taller than the lever. He has to yank back and forth, but we're forbidden to help each other, and I don't want any more scars on my back, so I let him heave it by himself.

As I watch the little boy, I can't help but think he looks like two eyes floating in the blackness around him. All of us look like that--so covered in smudge and dirt that we blend in with the walls and stone and darkness--but it is hard to see the little kids like that. They're just...small and terrified eyes looking out from inches of black smear.

"B floor," the child says wearily as we all exit the elevator. The lift itself is little more than a metal box surrounded by chain-link walls and lit by a dangling lightbulb that occasionally flickers into existence. I really can't imagine spending all day long in the creaky box; running through the tunnels isn't exactly comforting, but at least the ground below me is stable.

As I walk out of the lift and into the Open Area of B floor, I take a deep breath and look up. The Overhang is empty, which isn't surprising for today; normally, there are a few in-charges milling about up there, watching us from on high, safe from our "dirtiness." The Open Area rises high up into the mountain, passing A floor and going up and up seemingly forever. There are string lights strung around the edges of the Open Area, illuminating the circular space. Even though it's not much brighter and not outside, it's nice to stand in the center of the Open Area; the air here doesn't quite seem to suffocate you.

The workers filing past me to the cafeteria are all slouched forward, faces downcast, eyes empty. The eyes are really the only thing about their faces you can see. Everything else is so covered in black smudge that we all look like walking shadows.

B floor is where we live and eat and everything. It has our barracks on one end of the Open Area, and on the other is the Cafeteria and the Gathering Room.

We continue walking in silence, our soft boots thudding against the stone floor. More and more workers file in line, all of us diggers and searchers, the last to leave our work, all of us heading to the cafeteria. I see Dirk mingled in with some other searchers to my left, but I don't try and get his attention, and he doesn't move to get mine. We all just keep walking, eager to eat and sit.

We pass a guard, and all of us naturally give him a wide berth, never even breaking stride. The guards are all dressed in black and are situated throughout the Mine. They can be seen everywhere, but their dark clothes make them hard to find sometimes. The only place they're not allowed in is the barracks, but I don't really trust that rule. The guard we pass stands stoic as always, arms to his sides, a thick plastic stick hitched around his waist. I have seen and felt those sticks leave bruises the size of my hand. The guards rarely speak and seem all the more sinister because of their silence. It seems they're bred by the darkness, materializing out of the stone to stand watch. They always make the hair on the back of my neck stand up, even if I'm not doing anything wrong.

I walk into the cafeteria, a large, dull room lined with gray tile and covered in metal tables and benches. When you walk in, you can turn left or right to go to a table or stay straight to get in the food line. I walk straight, lining up with everyone else, to get a tray of food. It's usually the same stuff--gray sludge that tastes salty and thick and gritty all at once, paired with a thin slice of bread.

The line moves fairly quickly. Everyone is used to the routine and not interested in lagging around. I grab a blue plastic tray, let the food workers slap a scoop of slop and a piece of bread onto it, grab my glass of water, and then walk to the table.

There is an especially depressed mood among the other workers today; it's Arrival Day.

In just a little while, the oldest workers will be gone, and new ones will Arrive.

I always sit at the same table, in the very back corner of the cafeteria, furthest from the tunnel and Open Area. It seems...quieter there.

"Evening."

I look up from my food to see a tall, slender girl slide onto the bench next to me. Krin.

"Food any good?" she asks, examining her slush.

"Is it ever?" I ask.

Krin gives a slight smile, a brief flash of teeth beneath her smudged face. She hitches her long legs over the bench and settles down next to me at the table.

Krin makes me very aware of my shortness and limited tendency to smile. Krin is one that everyone kind of stares at sometimes, and she can make people smile. I only make people scowl. For some reason, which probably has something to do with the fact that our beds are next to each other and have been since she Arrived, Krin has decided to hang around me. She rarely speaks to anyone, but she rarely shuts up with me. I got used to her eventually. We were probably around the same age when she came--I think maybe six or so--but sometimes she still acts like a little kid, all quiet and shy and needing someone to follow around. I have no idea why she decided to follow me.

A broad, stocky boy comes over and sits next to Krin. Without looking up, I know it's Hoss. Whenever they can, Krin and Hoss stay together. I've had this battle with Krin before; I have tried telling her how stupid it is to form attachments down here, but she won't listen. I've just given up; she knows how I feel.

Krin immediately sits straighter, and she kind of leans towards Hoss. I turn my gaze back to my slosh.

"Evin," Hoss says, his voice deep and grumbling from his chest, but I say nothing.

We eat for a few minutes in silence before more bodies and trays join our table.

"Evening all," comes the smirking tones of Duna. The others mumble a hello to her as she sits down. Over the top of my spoon, I can see the two curly bunches of black hair poking out from underneath Duna's hat.

"Dirk," Hoss nods as another boy sits down next to Duna. Dirk is smaller than Hoss by quite a bit, which is why he's a searcher and not a digger. He smiles a lot, too, like everything is secretly funny. I don't get it.

Duna picks up her fork and begins shoveling food into her mouth.

"What's the rush?" Krin asks.

"Want a good seat for the Arrival," Duna mumbles between mouthfuls.

The Arrival. My stomach knots.

"Do you know how old you are?" Krin asks Hoss quietly, but I still hear.

He heaves a sigh but says, "No. Old, though. I'm old."

12

And Hoss is starting to look old. He towers over the rest of the kids, and his face looks lined and...tired. He's older than is safe. I think we all are.

*Please let me be seventeen,* I think silently. *Please.*

The five of us finish our meal quickly, the despair in the air moving to our table and silencing any further conversation. We take our trays to the washing station, set them on the stack, and head back into the tunnels. From the cafeteria, we follow the tunnel back into the Open Area. Once there, we make a sharp right and head down the tunnel towards the Gathering Room.

The Gathering Room is the only place where everyone--in-charges and workers alike-can or do sit together all at once. It's a large room, fit with benches cut out of the stone going down to the floor below on a slant. The floor at the bottom is raised on a little platform, and on the platform are twelve chairs where the twelve main in-charges sit. On either side of the platform are doors. One door says, "Arrival," one door says, "Departure." At least, that's what the in-charges tell us they say. None of us can actually read. Everyone filing in to sit on the benches has come to this place through the "Arrival" door. It's terrifying and makes you want to cry, but despite how Arriving makes you feel, you absolutely do not want to go through the "Departure" door. But, after all, what choice do we really have?

I follow close behind the others as they pack in with the rest of the workers who sludge along into the Gathering Room.

We generally sit near the top, so I slide down the bench until I'm about halfway across it.

There are three sections of seats, flowing from the top to bottom. We sit in the middle one.

Looking down, I can see the empty seats at the bottom of our section. Three empty rows. Those are reserved for the Newbies.

I remember walking in, taking a seat on those benches, and not being able to control the shaking in my hands.

The room, just like everywhere else, is dark and lit by strings of dim lights. There are three brighter lights hanging over the stage, so the in-charges don't have to sit in darkness and so we can all see our "fearless leaders" clearly. The twelve chairs on the platform are empty right now, just like they always are until right before it all begins.

As the last stragglers are making their way into the room, Duna shoves hard against me, making room for Dirk and two others who slide onto our bench. Nolan and Mayla, always together, always just as obnoxious as Hoss and Krin. I have no idea why everyone down here is obsessed with being close to someone. Don't they know that closeness only leads to sadness?

Duna reaches across Dirk and gives Nolan's hand a squeeze. I know that Duna is worried about him; he is a year older than her, they think. They're pretty sure about that. It's dumb to be sure, but they're "sure." But, she's mostly worried because Nolan is her brother.

I can practically feel Duna's nervous energy as she straightens and faces forward.

Then, a tall, thin man steps onto the platform, seemingly materializing from thin air. He raises his hands and waves at the children sitting in the massive room. He is bald but has a thick mustache that he twirls on either end. His clothes are clean, and even though he must've been walking in the tunnels at least for a minute to get to this room, there is not an ounce of coal dust on him. He is Mr. Withers, one of the in-charges at the Mine. He is the only one that really ever smiles and looks *at* us instead of through us. The only time he's seen, though, is

14

today, Arrival Day, so everyone hates him. Maybe that's why he is so happy, though. If he only has to be here one day a year, he must not be completely drained by this darkness.

"Good evening, children!" Mr. Withers exclaims, making his mustache turn up even more. "It's so nice to see you all on this wonderful night!"

I roll my eyes; as if anyone in this Mine has ever had a wonderful night here. I'm not even sure what a wonderful night looks like; I've never seen one beyond the Mine's ceiling. At least, not one I can remember.

"Please welcome our cherished patrons, the Board of Executives!" Mr. Withers turns to gesture to a line of sharply dressed men and women who are making their way down the ramp to the platform. Like Withers, none of them are dirty. Not even a speck on their gray clothes. At all. I suddenly have an overwhelming urge to go and hug one of them, just to see what they would do. I have my eye on one of the women who is looking around in disgust. Her hair is pulled into a tight bun, and she is wearing spike shoes that make her walk kind of funny like she can't quite get her balance. I've never seen her before, and I bet she would absolutely scream if she received a hug from a dirty kid like me.

We half-heartedly clap as all the gray-clad in-charges of the Board of the Executives make their way down to the platform and take their seats in the twelve chairs. They are the twelve main in-charges. They are the ones who are rarely seen, and that's fine with me. They're all older, gray hair leaking out of their scalps. Their whole purpose is to make sure the Mine runs as smoothly as possible, and that means making sure that it produces enough coal and gold as possible. I hate them; they're the meanest in-charges out of any of them. When they inspect us, bruises show.

"Very good!" Mr. Withers smiles. "Now, per tradition, we will read the laws of our great nation to better understand our positions in life." He reaches into his pocket and pulls out a long, rolled piece of paper. He clears his throat and reads, "'Under the official order of his Majesty the High Chancellor of the Republic of the Colonies, it is a law that every citizen must be equal. To achieve perfect equality, sacrifices must be made. The first sacrifice is that every child between the ages of three and seventeen who is illiterate and therefore cannot contribute to society must be sent to work in order to be a contributing member of society. They can contribute to the Mines, the Ports, the Forests, or the Railroads. Their contribution will be most welcome and necessary. Then, every adult who reaches eighteen years of age and remains illiterate in our great society will provide the most basic of services: entertainment, for entertainment, relies on skill alone, not knowledge. Their contribution will be most welcome and necessary. For, after all, an equal society requires equal contribution from every one, no matter age, race, or gender. After all, 'Democracy is the foundation of Society: Equality is the backbone of Life.'"

"Democracy is the foundation of Society: Equality is the backbone of Life," we all mutter back to Mr. Withers. I hate saying that. Apparently, it's the "motto" of the Society, but I don't know what that is. I don't even know what the words mean, really. All I know is that it is drilled into our heads; we have to repeat it at breakfast each morning, at every Gathering, and sometimes the in-charges will stop us and make us recite it to make sure we're "willing members of society." Whatever that means.

I'm still not sure what all the rules Withers just said mean. They may as well read gibberish for us the good it does, especially for the littler kids.

"Lady Executor," Mr. Withers beams, gesturing for one of the in-charges seated on the platform to come forward.

The new woman, the one I didn't recognize, struts to the middle of the stage, her nose practically straight up in the air. Her mouth is crinkled in disgust as if she dares not breathe the air in front of her. My stomach knots; the Executors are in charge of the Mine. They don't just enforce the rules, like the regular in-charges. They *make* the rules. The previous Executor, a man, named Phortin, had increased the max number of workers here from 560 to 600. The meant cramped beds and less food for us, but more coal and gold getting cranked out for "the Nation."

Worry eats away at me; what is this clean woman going to do to us?

She gets to the middle of the platform, clasps her hands in front of her, and says in a high, clear voice that radiates authority, "You, the workers of the Northern Mine, have repeatedly stayed on-quota for this past year. You have supplied the Colonies with coal to power our trains and factories and gold to substantiate our currency. You should be very proud." She gives us a stern look and a slight raise of her head. I wonder if she knows most of us in the audience have no idea what half her words mean; I sure don't.

"My name is Lady Executor Jinade. Executor Phortin has retired, and so, under the direction of our wise Chancellor, I have decided to enforce a few changes to increase the effectiveness of this operation. The max allotment for workers in this Mine will be decreased from 600 to 500 in order to increase productivity and revenue. I have also decided to increase the quota for this year. The Societal Keepers of the Mine will inform you of your new tasks and responsibilities. You will also be required to do a formal check-in at each post--"

I stop listening. I'm too focused on the agitation now coursing through the crowd and through my own blood. I can almost hear everyone's frantic thoughts, surely matching my own. A limit of 500 means that at least 100 workers will be forced to leave today...and even more, since there will be newbies...

I may not be good with words, but I can do numbers. Almost everyone down here can do numbers. And the numbers only make sense one way: they're going to take seventeens. My stomach drops.

"What does that mean?" I hear Krin whisper.

"They're going to take seventeens," I whisper.

I feel her freeze next to me. "They can't," her voice shakes. "They can't do that. That's not the law!"

I shrug in response. When has anything been fair down here?

Krin's lip begins to tremble, and for a good reason. I have been in the Mine the longest out of any of us; I remember them all coming, but even I don't know how old any of them are *for sure*. I know I was three when I came because when the in-charges had asked, I had responded, "Three." I remember that. I can remember at least fourteen Arrivals since then because no one around here ever forgets an Arrival. But those numbers make my stomach clench. That would mean I'm 17. Most likely, anyway. The only way to be sure would be to ask an in-charge, and I am not about to do that.

"Don't worry," Hoss puts his arm around Krin's shoulders. "They can't do that."

"Of course they can," I scowl. "They can do whatever they want."

Duna doesn't say anything during all of this; she stares straight ahead, stone-faced and stoic.

From the corner of my eye, I see her glance down the row to Nolan and Mayla. Nolan has his mouth pressed against Mayla's ear and is speaking rapidly. She just nods, wide-eyed, lip trembling.

I turn my attention back to the Lady Executor Whatever-Her-Name-Is. She is still rambling on, never skipping a beat, about all the changes she's making, but it doesn't seem like anyone is really listening. Why do they make us listen to words we don't understand?

"Finally," Executor Jinade says with a cold smile, "We have decided that, due to the increase of illiterates in our great nation, it may sometimes be necessary to Depart workers from the Mines before Arrival Day, based on when they turn eighteen."

A low rumble goes through the workers, and I feel my hands go cold. It isn't enough that we have to live in fear of Arrival Day, but now we must *always* live in fear? Once you look older than the other workers, you dread the Arrival naturally. Getting older is not an exciting thing around here. But now, if you look older and know you're somewhere around seventeen, you must fear waking up every morning since it could very well be your last. Suddenly, the ceiling feels closer, and my hands start shaking.

"Evin," Krin whispers. "They can't do this. This isn't fair."

"Since when is anything fair down here?" I breathe back.

"Now," Jinade says coolly, "for the Arrivals." She waves her hand, and the Arrival door swings open. From it files the new workers, all clean and coal-dust free. They all look terrified. There are maybe fifty of them in all, led by two stiff guards.

With a sinking feeling, I see that most of the new workers are no older than about ten; a good chunk of them are tiny, maybe five. The uniforms on the tiny ones had to be rolled several times to even make walking a possibility. They clump together, trying to get comfort from each other.

My thoughts immediately go to my own Arrival. I was so small, and the memory itself is fuzzy, but I had clung to Maria's hand. She had been friendly, had smiled at me, and had helped me through the whole process. I had squeezed her hand so tightly on the platform, hoping she'd never let go, terrified of the hundreds of eyes staring at me from the seats. Maria had steadied me, had made me feel secure, but eventually, we had had to let go. I remember thinking all the coal-dust faces were monsters, creatures waiting to eat me. With a silent chuckle, I wonder now if the new kids think I look like a monster.

A few of the other Executives hurry forward to stand next to Jinade. They each hold clipboards. One hands a piece of paper to Jinade.

"When I call your number," Jinade says, looking at the newbies, "you will step forward and receive your assignment. Number NM1711." A small girl steps forward, clutching her left arm with her right hand. The sight makes my own arm ache; when you Arrive, you receive your number inked into your forearm with a sharp needle. I'm NM1448. I can still feel the needle blackening my skin with my new name. I have to resist the urge to reach down and scratch at it.

"Cafeteria," Lady Executor Jinade announces. The girl looks up with wide eyes. The other in-charge takes the piece of paper from Jinade and scribbles a note on it. "You will report to Number NM3255." A boy about my age stands and goes forward; I recognize him. Ruper. He runs the cafeteria. He helps the little girl down and leads her to the benches for Newbies. He sits with her and begins speaking quietly to her. Their heads bent together.

Jinade takes another paper from the in-charge. "Number NM1712."

The Arrival goes on as usual; it's almost as dreadful as the Departure itself because everyone is so anxious to see if they're here for much longer. I find myself, though, not being able to look away from Jinade's scowling face until Krin elbows me hard in the ribs.

"What?" I whisper, rubbing my now sore side.

"That girl, the one that was just called, she looks like you!" Krin says.

I look at the platform. A girl, maybe a few years younger than me, is standing next to Jinade. She is average height, has red-brown hair chopped off at her shoulders, and hugs her arms around her. I squint but don't see the resemblance.

"No, she doesn't," I whisper back to Krin.

"Yes, she does! Look at her face."

"I'm looking at her face, Krin. She doesn't look like me. Why does it matter? We all look the same down here," I scowl.

"Still," Krin shrugs. "Did you catch her assignment?

"No," I reply.

"Sorting," Lady Executor Jinade solves the problem for us. The girl is swept away by the tall girl in charge of a sorting group.

"Oh, she's with me," Krin says. "That was Annet."

I shrug but don't really think anything of it. Who cares if she looks like me? She'll be covered in coal dust soon enough, and then she'll *really* look like me.

"Number NM15266," Jinade announces, reading the number off of a new piece of paper. A small boy, painfully small, walks forward. I can't even age him because of how tiny he looks. He has huge eyes, though; I can see that even from my seat. He glances around the room in a quiet manner. He doesn't seem scared or nervous, more like he's just...here. He seems to almost have strength in his stance, a sort of steadying look about him.

"Searching," Jinade says. "You will be assigned to Number NM1448."

I sigh but stand. I think about trying to find Shashan in the crowd but don't. This is just proof that he really is eighteen, and he will be Departing in just a few minutes. However, it relieves me mostly because at least I will not be Departed today. They wouldn't assign a Newbie to someone who was just going to die. This may even mean I'm here for a while longer.

I make my way slowly down the benches until I reach the stage. The kid, whose number I've already forgotten, makes his way down the steps to me. We go and sit next to each other in the Newbie section. I don't say anything to him, and he doesn't to me. He'll figure it all out soon enough anyway.

There are a few more numbers called, but then every new kid is off the stage and sitting next to someone they hope will help them through all this. I hope the boy sitting next to me doesn't expect much. I also hope he's not stupid.

"Now," the Lady Executor says, "I will turn the time over to Head Reader Kevoc."

All the workers not sitting in the Newbie section seem to shrink a little as an old, frail man--the same old man who has been the Head Reader as long as I have been here and was ancient when I was little--stands and hobbles, all wrinkly and saggy and creaking, to where the Lady Executor is standing. He is practically bent in half, but his voice booms in a clear, even tone when he announces, "I will now call the names of those Departing from this, the Northern Mine."

From beneath his coat, he pulls out a massive roll of paper. There is a collective intake of breath, then anxious, heavy silence as everyone waits.

He unrolls the paper, clears his throat, and reads, "'Those who have turned eighteen in the last year will now be required to be a participating member of society, and so will be called down to the platform. At the platform, they will be asked to read a line of text. If they can read the line, they will accompany the Board to Level A, where they will be assigned a new position in society. If they cannot read, they will go through the Departure door where they will be taken and prepared for the Colosseum and their rightful place in the entertainment force of our great Nation.'"

I hold my breath out of habit as the in-charges come forward with clipboards for Kevoc to read from. I don't mean to--I'm not even holding my breath for myself since I know I'm still safe for now--but we all just seem to lose air when Kevoc speaks.

"Number NM1332," reads the Head Reader.

A tall, thin boy rises and makes his way down to the platform. I don't know him, but he looks familiar. Maybe loading?

The boy walks down to the platform, head held high. Like everyone else, he is covered in coal dust. He goes up to the stage and walks to where the Head Reader is standing.

Kevoc unrolls the scroll again and holds it in front of the boy. "Read the first line."

The boy looks at the paper held up to his eyes and then whispers, "I don't know what it says."

The Head Reader nods and then gestures for the guards standing by the Departure door.

They march forward, grab the boy's arms, and pull him towards the massive, foreboding door. They stop just in front of it, the boy's face still turned towards all the workers watching him from the seats. I hate this part. The guards don't ever *force* someone through the door; they wait for you to go through on your own.

Finally, after a long moment, the boy turns to the door. He takes a deep breath that, from my seat, I can see, shakes his whole body, and then he marches forward. He pushes open the Departure door walks through and lets it shut behind him without ever looking back.

"Number NM1345."

More and more workers disappear through the Departure door. With each one, I feel colder and colder, the air seeming to lose heat as more and more kids leave. I lose track after a while; it's all the same. I think maybe we're now in the sixties. A worker goes to the stage, can't read the writing, and then leaves through the dreaded door. I've never seen someone read the Head Reader's script, and I doubt I ever will. I doubt anyone ever will. That doesn't really seem to be the point down here.

"Number NM4457."

"No!"

I wince at the outburst; we aren't supposed to talk during the Reading. And I know who had. Without turning around, I know that voice, that fire. I know that Mayla will have slowly risen from her seat, face in her hands and that Nolan will be standing next to her, eyes alight. I never understood why Nolan chose Mayla to attach himself to. I mean, I don't really get the attachments at all, but if you must have someone, wouldn't you want someone who wasn't so small and timid and seemingly scared of her own shadow? That's no way to be down here; everything is a shadow. Nolan, on the other hand, is like Duna. Tough, stoney. Yet, he chose *Mayla*. I roll my eyes.

"You can't take her!" Nolan shouts. "She's not eighteen!"

If the audience was quiet before, we go dead silent.

24

"And how do you know?" the Head Reader asks.

"How do *you*?" Nolan shouts back.

*Shut up, Nolan.* I scold him in my mind. Does he think he can win? He's just making it worse for both of them.

"What is your number?" the Head Reader asks.

"NM4458," Nolan replies steadily.

The Head Reader makes a show of checking his list and then says, "You're on my list as well. Why don't you just come up together?" He smiles, but I don't think he means it.

"I'm not marching to my death!" Nolan shouts back.

"Very well," the Head Reader shrugs.

"Guards!" Lady Executor Jinade shouts.

From the corners of the room comes the sound of running feet. I look around and see the Mine guards, dressed in their usual black with their thick plastic sticks at their sides, hurrying towards Nolan and Mayla. I can't help turning around to watch at this point. Nolan doesn't flinch as two guards grab his arms and drag him up to the platform. One guard pulls a crying Mayla by her arm.

No one in the seats moves or even whispers. We just sit there. Watching.

"Number NM4457," the Head Reader says sternly, "read this." He holds up the scroll. She whispers something back, so low I can't even hear her, and I'm practically right next to the platform.

"Louder," Kevoc commands.

"I can't read it," Mayla sniffs, putting her face back in her hands. Nolan tries to move toward her, but the guards hold him back.

"Number NM4458, read this," the Head Reader turns to Nolan.

Without looking at the text, Nolan spits, "You know I can't." His body is rigid, and I can feel the heat of his gaze.

"Very well," the Head Reader smirks. "To the Colosseum." He jerks his head in the direction of the Departure door.

Mayla lets out a wailing cry, but Nolan remains stoic. The guards release Nolan's arms, and he goes to Mayla. He puts his arm around her protectively and draws her into his chest as they turn towards the Departure door. The guards remain close by their sides.

When they reach the door, Nolan turns and searches the crowd. His gaze goes straight for where I know Duna is sitting. Nolan's eyes find her, and he gives her a sad smile and quick nod. Then, his arm still protectively around Mayla, Nolan turns toward the door and calmly walks through.

Once they're through, I turn and glance back up at Duna. I can just see her head, but from my distance, I can't read her expression. I can see the gaping hole next to her, though, where Nolan and Mayla had, minutes ago, been sitting. I know that, within a year, that hole will be filled with some other coal-smudged body. It's suddenly like Nolan and Mayla were never even here, never filled that hole. That's how it always feels; a body goes through the door, leaving behind a hole that will be filled immediately. So, did that person ever really exist?

I shift back around, turning my attention to the platform.

Kevoc goes through more names, but I'm not really listening. If Nolan was 18, the rest of us most likely aren't. I know I'm safe, but it makes me feel better that I hopefully won't be seeing Krin or Hoss or Dirk go through that door.

Every year it's the same. Every year we watch more and more workers who I didn't bother getting to know march up the steps and out towards their death. Holes and bodies shifting around in the darkness.

I somewhat listen as they take a girl, screaming and clawing, all the way to the door. Sometimes workers break like that and try to beg or scream or cry their way out of Departure. I knew that girl a little; she won't make it ten minutes in the Colosseum.

My heart pounds, and I desperately want this day to be done. I've now lived through 14 Arrival Days, and I'm so tired. I don't want to watch this anymore.

Then Shashan is called. His number is familiar to me, having seen it on our crate every day for years now. But I don't watch. I don't know if I can't or just won't. I just stare at the floor until the next number is called.

Finally, the Head Reader calls the last number. "Number NM14365." A short, stooping boy is sent through the door just like all the others. None of them could read, and none had ever been given the chance to learn. The in-charges know this, which makes my mind race with this question: why do we have to go through this each year?

"Thank you all for your attendance," Head Executor Jinade smiles at all of us seated before her. The Head Reader makes his way back to his seat and sits with a smug smile on his face.

We all rise practically in unison, my legs almost creaking with the effort.

"Democracy is the foundation of Society: Equality is the foundation of Life." We mumble this in unison, and then Lady Executor Jinade waves us away. The sound of footsteps echoes around the dim room as we all begin shuffling for the tunnel out of here.

Arrival Days always seem to take forever, especially today's. They had Departed so many...and they are going to Depart even more.

The sight of Mayla weeping while Nolan waved to Duna is burned into my eyes; I saw their sadness up close, their desperation, and

Nolan's anger as they marched away. Those emotions are etched into me, making me twitch oddly every few seconds. Why had Nolan fought? It's pointless to fight. Everyone knows that, especially someone as experienced as Nolan. That image intermingled with all the new kids, the tiny ones with quivering lips and shaking hands, makes my stomach roil.

I've always been shaken after Arrival Days, but not like this. Not to the point where my hands are literally *shaking*.

I walk back up the tunnel, my new partner close behind me, but neither of us says anything. Eventually, I catch up to Krin and Duna as everyone emerges from the tunnel into the Open Area. They're quiet, but I don't expect anything else. Duna is crying soundlessly, and that seems to make my hands shake more, but out of annoyance. I grunt and quietly whisper, "Just forget him, Duna."

Duna doesn't even look at me.

Krin does, though. She raises her eyebrows at me, then shakes her head and looks away. She doesn't say anything, which is sort of odd for her. She usually has tons of stuff to say to me, but Arrival Day has a silencing effect. It's even more powerful than the darkness. Its power grew, too, since now we can be Departed at any time. It's a terrifying feeling to want to be anywhere but these tunnels, but knowing that leaving here will be worse. I'm doomed for the Colosseum. I know that. Everyone down here is. Just like everyone is stuck in this never-ending darkness until we walk through that door.

We all solemnly march into the tunnel that leads to the barracks, leaving the slightly less stale air of the Open Area behind us. Boys head down the right tunnel, girls to the left. My shadow of a partner finally leaves my side.

Krin eventually says something, but I don't hear her, nor do I really care for that matter.

She's used to not getting a response from me, so eventually, she just drops it.

We walk along the tunnel, the footsteps of hundreds of workers making the walls echo against the silence and sadness. I look around at the others; everyone has the same sad, beaten expression under a layer of black smudge and dust. I've always thought the coal-smudged faces were the worst part of looking at others, but now I decide that it's the eyes. The eyes of those around me are...gone. Blank and unfeeling. I wonder if my eyes look the same; the thought makes me catch my breath, but then I feel the heat of anger stilling the shaking in my hands. I don't want to die with blank eyes. Nolan's eyes weren't blank, and-

*And he died*, I remind myself. *Well, he's* going *to die.*

I sigh. What can I do? What can any of us do?

In the hallway to the girl's barracks, we pass a guard. He stands shrouded in darkness and silent, watching us. This is odd; they're not supposed to be in this tunnel. Once we get into this tunnel, the rule is they can't follow us. I know their rules aren't the same as our rules, but seeing him lurking there makes my arms prickle.

I hate him. I hate them all. I hate their cold, careless eyes beneath their shielded faces; their helmets mask their expressions.

I hate everything about this place.

And the worst thing about hating this place is knowing that you're stuck no matter what you do or want, so hating it is really pointless, but, for some reason, I can't stop myself from hating.

We reach the barracks and begin filing away into our rows. The barracks is a low-ceilinged room filled with rows and rows of bunks. There are seven rows with twenty bunks in each row. The bunks are

two beds, top, and bottom. String lights are strung around, but it's still dark and gray among the beds. However, knowing there are no guards helps us relax a little. I see shoulders drop and heads roll from side to side as we enter the room. I can't help thinking of the guard in the tunnel, though, and I don't let myself fully relax.

I follow Krin's tall form about halfway down the third row of beds. Krin hoists herself up onto the top bed of one bunk, and I climb up onto the bed next to her. Our beds are close enough that if I reach out, I can touch Krin's shoulder. The top beds are also incredibly close to the ceiling. If I'm lying on my back, I can reach up and touch it with my palm. I hate being so close to it, I hate feeling like the massive rock ceiling could just drop and squish me, but I love being able to lay down. However, if I lay on my back, I can't get my heart to calm down. So, most of the time, I sleep on my stomach. Sometimes, I can't sleep at all.

"Duna was still crying," Krin says softly, laying down and stretching out her long legs. Her toes dip off the end of the bed.

I sigh and rub the back of my neck. Somewhat guiltily, I remember what I said to Duna.

"We all saw it coming," I shrug. I feel the shame burn across my cheeks, but I squish it down. It was the truth, so why should I say different?

Krin frowns slightly, her bright blue eyes looking at my pillow instead of my face, which is still somewhat warm.

"I guess," Krin says after a moment. She begins pulling at the threads of her blanket.

"Still, though," she sighs, tugging a little harder.

"Still though, what?" I ask. "It's not like we could have done anything."

"I know we can't do anything, Evin," Krin scowls slightly. Her face is not built for scowling, so it looks more like a frown. "I just mean that it feels...odd. He's the first of us to be Departed."

"Of *us*?"

"You know what I mean," Krin shoots back.

"No," I reply. "I don't."

Krin rolls her eyes, "Uh-huh."

"What?"

"I don't think anyone can do this alone, Evin," Krin says softly, looking at me with wide eyes. "And down here, no one is really alone."

I roll my eyes now, tired of this same conversation. "Just because I'm being smart-"

"Is anyone down here really that smart?" Krin gives me a small smile.

"Well, at least I'm not being stupid," I say.

Krin's smile just grows. "Sure, Evin. Sure. All I meant was, each Arrival is worse than the last. And now, anyone could be Departed...anytime."

I shrug and say, "But, like you said, we can't do anything."

"No," Krin agrees. "We can't do anything." The tall girl gives a long, soft sigh before turning over.

I keep my eyes on Krin's back for a few minutes, wondering why this is suddenly bothering Krin so much. She came to the Mine a few years after me, but we figure we are around the same age. Ever since she was assigned to the bunk next to me, we have stuck together at mealtimes and in the tunnels, and at gatherings. She's okay; she's nice and talks enough that I don't have to. But now, I'm kind of annoyed at her. I mean, this happens every year, and yes, we had known Nolan somewhat, and Duna had cared for him, but how many times have I

31

told them all not to care about anyone? Maybe they'll finally start listening to me.

Not caring about anyone is hard sometimes, but it's necessary. After all, what else can I do? What else can anyone do down here? We're all just helpless bodies here in the dark.

# Chapter Two

It always takes a while after a Departure for everyone to fall asleep. The older workers are exhausted from being terrified all day, the younger ones are reliving their own Arrivals, and then there are the newbies. They cry.

I get it. It's hard, it's scary, but none of us can sleep with all their whimpering, and we *need* sleep.

Their sniffs and sobs echo off the walls, making their noise even louder. I eventually put my pillow on my head, trying to muffle the sounds, desperate for sleep.

"We all cry our first few nights, Evin," Krin whispers to me.

"I didn't," I spit back. I did, actually, but I barely remember it. I mostly remember the darkness and the feeling that I was going to be crushed by rocks at any moment.

"I did," Krin whispers. "A lot. Do you remember what you said to me?"

"No."

She chuckles a little and says, "You told me that it's okay to be afraid, but that crying won't help. You said I needed to sleep so I could work better so that I would be okay."

"Huh," I say, not really sure why she remembers that.

"It made me feel better," she continues. I pull my pillow off my head and look at her. I can see her eyes open, looking at the uncomfortably close ceiling, like two orbs of blue in the dimness around us.

"Okay," I reply, shrugging.

"I never said thanks for being nice back then," she replies, turning her eyes to me.

I roll my eyes. "Sure," I say.

She laughs, "Well, at least we know you used to be nice."

I can't help it; I smile a little.

"Do you still have your dreams?" she asks me.     I sigh, "Not as often. Sleeping on my stomach helps."

"Good," she says.

Krin knows I have bad dreams; she can hear them at night. She's even reached over and woken me up a few times, worried I was going to roll off the bed from thrashing or drown myself crying.

The crying is finally dying down; most newbies cry themselves out after a few hours, and then we can all get to sleep. My eyes are just getting heavy, grateful for the silence, when one voice starts ringing around the walls, singing:

*Stars shining bright above you,*
*Night breezes seem to whisper "I love you"*
*Birds singing in the sycamore tree*
*Dream a little dream of me.*

The voice is soft, sad, but clear. No one says anything, but I can tell most of us are still awake. There's an anticipation, a quiet interest, throughout the barracks.

The voice sings again:

*Stars fading, but I linger on, dear*
*Still craving your kiss.*
*I'm longing to linger till dawn, dear*
*Just saying this*

*Sweet dreams till sunbeams find you,*

*Sweet dreams that leave all worries behind you,*

*But in your dreams, whatever they be*

*Dream a little dream of me.*


Her voice rings a little bit around the room, echoing off the dark walls. I don't think the singer is too far away from me.

"Shut up!" someone hisses.

"Oh, you shut up!" someone growls back.

We all wait for a moment, but she doesn't sing anymore. I sigh and readjust my pillow. The words she sang are bouncing around in my head. Some kids sing a little down here, but not very often, and normally it sounds like nonsense; her song, though, makes me want her to keep singing. I want to know more about these sweet dreams.

I glance over at Krin and see her lying on her back, staring at the ceiling. She looks deep in thought, so I don't say anything. I don't really want to talk, anyway. Slowly, I let my eyelids close, the song still on my mind, and I hope for a dreamless sleep. Krin rustles around for a moment, and then I hear her drop to the floor and quickly pad away. I snort; of course, she's going to Hoss. It was Arrival Day. I'd be surprised if she didn't. I just hope the guard isn't in the tunnel anymore.

Yawning, I let my mind fall blank, and then I fall asleep.


The next morning, I feel groggy and slow. The worker bell whistles seemingly too early and much, much too loudly. I groan, throwing my feet over the side of my bed, eyes heavy. I rub them, trying to get them more open, but it just makes me more tired.

I lift my droopy head and look to see Krin's back, but still dead to the world. I sigh, reach over, and shake her roughly. She doesn't move.

I shake her again.

Nothing.

"Krin!" I say, shaking her harder. Now I'm awake, awake and worried. "Krin!" I practically shout, feeling like I might rip her shoulder off.

She sighs deeply and opens her eyes. "What?" she asks, rubbing her face.

I slump in relief and annoyance. I scowl at her and drop to the ground. "Come on," I mumble, grabbing my worker's cap and shoving it on my head. I stuff my ratted hair underneath it, trying to get all the little pieces to stay out of my eyes.

Krin drops to the ground a bit shakily; she puts a hand on the bedpost to steady herself. I raise an eyebrow at her, but she waves me off.

"Just tired," she says, then her eyes widen in urgency. "I have to use the toilet!" she says, and she hurries away.

I roll my eyes. The line for the toilet is probably already too long to wait.

I fall in line with all the girls heading off toward the cafeteria. As I thought, the line to the toilet is long, but I don't see Krin in it. I keep moving, knowing she will catch up.

The tunnel to the Open Area is packed with workers moving quickly but tiredly toward the morning meal.

As we emerge into the Open Area, the air feels lighter, and I feel some pressure in my chest lighten. I take a breath underneath the higher ceiling, looking up briefly to see the mountain stretch up above me. I can't see the top, and that comforts me.

We shuffle into the tunnel towards the cafeteria, hurrying forward to get our food.

I grab my tray and get in line; the workers give me my gray slop and slice of bread, and then I hurry off to the table in the back corner.

Dirk is the only one here, head propped up on his hand, scooping food into his mouth almost robotically.

I slide into the table, my tray clattering as it hits the top, and he jumps a little. He looks exhausted, eyes drooping. He rubs them but then gives me a small smile.

"Hey, Evin," he grumbles and then yawns so widely, I think he might swallow his face.

I roll my eyes but say, "You look bad."

"Aww," he smiles again, but then explains, "I was up late. Newbies, you know, and I was with-" but then he stops and begins shoveling food into his mouth with enthusiasm. I arch an eyebrow but don't ask. I don't care. Besides, then Hoss comes and sits down and starts talking to Dirk about the new kid assigned to the digging team--I guess he used to be a searcher Dirk knows--and I'm saved from having to speak.

The food is as gross as ever, but I choke it down; it's better than going hungry. Duna eventually shows up, but she hangs her head and doesn't even touch her food. She lets Dirk have it; you can't throw away food down here. Krin comes, too, but she looks a little unsteady on her feet, and she doesn't want to eat either. Hoss takes hers, and I suddenly want to ask why no one thinks *I* would want more food.

"What's wrong?" Hoss murmurs to Krin as she slides him her food.

"I think I'm just tired," she says with a weak smile. "We didn't get much sleep last night."

Dirk snorts into his plate, and Hoss shoots him a look, but I just roll my eyes. It's no secret Krin spends some nights with Hoss; everyone here knows. He's come to the girl's side a few times, too. I guess some people really like that there aren't guards allowed in the barracks.

"No," Krin rolls her eyes, "there were a lot of girls crying, and... singing…" she stares off for a moment. We all look at her, waiting for more, but then the whistle starts blowing.

We, all the workers, rise in unison and stand still for a minute until the loud whistle stops. I don't know where it comes from. It just kind of rings all through the cafeteria. When it stops, my ears still ring.

Then, we chant, "Democracy is the foundation of Society: Equality is the backbone of Life." We say it flatly, staring forward at the walls or at each other. I can see the guards around the room watching us, seeing if anyone dares not say it. The newbies learn quickly like they always do. They stood with us and spoke with us, even if they just mumbled the words or moved their mouths in silence. Whoever the newbies are assigned to generally explains the morning chant; I guess I forgot to tell my partner, whatever-his-name-is. Whoops.

The whistle chimes again, just one loud chirp, and then we move. Everyone scoops up their tray, lines up neatly, and flows out the tunnel towards the lifts.

As I'm setting my tray into the bin, I feel someone slide into the line right behind me. I turn and see my new partner; I guess he made it through the chant.

He doesn't say anything, just walks right behind me as we march into the tunnel that leads to the Open Area. Once in the Open Area, the line of workers begins separating for the levels they're going to. Usually, there's one lift on each level, but in the mornings, since we all are already on one level, they are all here except one. The furthest lift to the right is missing; it's on A Level, where the in-charges live. I turn my head and can see a bunch of them, gray-clad and sneering, standing on the Overhang, watching us. I look away, focusing forward; I don't want them to see me looking up there.

I get in the line of the furthest left elevator. That's the one that will go down to the Tunnel Room. Krin and Duna, who were in front of me, head to the elevator to my right, the one going to C Level; that's where the sorters work. Hoss and Dirk stay in line with me and what's-his-name.

The lifts board about twenty people and then go down. The one I'm in line for makes a great, creaking shudder as it begins to descend. I can hear it dropping...dropping. It lowers itself on squeaky wheels into the earth below, diving further under the mountain. I can already feel the pressing dark, the suffocating lack-of-air. I can see the stone and dirt walls sliding upward around me… I suck in a breath and hold it, forcing the image out of my head.

We all wait in line, completely silent, waiting for our turn.

Finally, the lift comes back up and twenty more file in, a great clump of black bodies huddled together in a square. Dirk and Hoss crowd on, but the lift worker stops me from boarding.

"Full," he grunts, even though he's maybe seven. Then he hauls the gates shut, throws the lever, and down they go. Dirk and Hoss watch me as they descend, their faces getting more and more shadowed as they go down until finally even the tips of their heads go below the ground, and I can't see them anymore. I can hear them, though; the lifts rattle and clank and echo all throughout the Open Area; it feels like the rattling is inside my chest.

I sigh and glance around; the lines are pretty short now. My gaze goes farther, and I find myself glancing back up at the Overhang, curious and angry all the time about the in-charges who just stand up there and watch.

The lift creaks back up, and my little partner and I climb aboard with the rest of the searchers, diggers, and track-layers bound for the tunnels.

When our lift is full, the worker throws the lever, and down we go.

I hold my breath as the darkness creeps up my body, sliding up my legs and onto my stomach as we go down. My chest feels tight, and I squeeze my eyes shut, not wanting to watch the black rock slide past my nose with only a thin layer of chain-link fence between us. Slowly, I count in my head, knowing the ride takes about a minute.

I'm just hitting 63 in my mind when the lift shakes to a stop.

"D Level," the worker says, and he gives a slight cough. I open my eyes to see the Tunnel Room before me, and I hurry out with the other workers.

The track-layers move to the center of the room, where there are piles and piles of metal rods for them to place throughout the Tunnels. The diggers push their carts along the rods, making it easier to get the coal back to the Tunnel Room, where they dump it into a large hole in one corner of the room, behind where the in-charges sit. The hole has a moving belt in it that slides the coal up to C Level, where it will be sorted and then put back on the belt moving up to A Level to be loaded.

I see some diggers grab a cart and load it with their digging supplies. Then they move off into a Tunnel. I can't see Hoss or his team, so they must already be in theirs. I search Hoss' Tunnel at the moment, so we will pass each other from time to time when he helps push his cart of coal back to the Tunnel Room.

My new partner follows me to one side of the room, where there are a bunch of shelves and crates. I pull my crate off the shelf--I know it's mine because it has NM1448 written on it--and set it on the table. I notice Shashan's number is gone, and in its place is NM15266. I sigh but then begin explaining:

"Every morning, we will come down here and get our supplies. Ours will always be in this crate. Don't *ever* touch another crate. We each have a lantern. You turn it on like this. No, twist the button on the bottom. There. Then, we each get a pouch. Always check to make sure your pouch has the hole-digger tool, this one with the handle and the sharp end, and then a couple of red lights and blue lights. I will show you how to use them later. We each need a timer, but we get those from the in-charges. Come on."

We walk back to the table where two in-charges sit, and they look absolutely thrilled to be here. I've noticed none of them like being in the Tunnel Room, even though it's well-lit with bright bulbs strung all the way around the room.

"Number NM1448," I say flatly. The in-charge on the right, a tall woman with graying hair, scribbles on her clipboard. The one next to her, a shorter woman with massive, pouty lips and watery eyes, hands me a strap with a timer on it. I quickly strap it on.

They turn their eyes to my partner.

"NM15266," he says quietly. I almost sigh in relief; if he hadn't known what to do, they would've blamed me, too. They hand him a timer, and he puts it on.

"Begin," the shorter in-charge croaks.

I show my partner which button to push on the timer, and he copies me. The timer has a little screen on it that counts down from 10:00 hours. It also counts your steps. Once our timers are counting down, I hurry over to our Tunnel to get going, knowing the in-charges are watching us.

Taking a deep breath, I enter our Tunnel and let the darkness wash over me. I hold my lantern up high, trying to get the light to shine as brightly as it can, and then walk forward. We have to hurry to get to where Shashan and I ended yesterday.

Yesterday. Shashan was here yesterday, and he might be dead today.

Shashan was a good partner; he didn't really say much, and he worked fast. I can see his wide, brown-black eyes looking at me in his lantern's glow. I can hear his deep, rumbling voice humming softly as we walked. I didn't so much mind the humming; Shashan's humming, at least.

He said he was about ten when he came here, that he had had a mother and a father, but that his father was taken away by people, and he and his mother had been living in the woods for a long time. He said his mother used to tickle him when he was sad and that she had blue eyes. His eyes were dark brown, so that seemed weird, but I believed him. He said that his parents didn't like the way the world was, and they got in trouble for that. I don't know what that means. The only world I know is the Mine, and I don't know what trouble they could give me that would be worse than this.

Sometimes I wonder if I'm here because my parents were in trouble. Sometimes I wonder if they brought me here. I don't know, and I never will. That's the thing: my whole world is down here, in this darkness. I will only live to be eighteen, and I've known that since I was little. I have one year at most left in this world, down in this giant hole, and I think I would give anything to know what is beyond it.

I wonder if Shashan got to see any more of it. He told me, once, the day after last year's Arrival, how much he loved the way the sun hit the trees in the morning. He described how the leaves would only let in so much light, but the world was lit all around you.

"Why are you telling me this?" I had asked him. He rarely told me anything about his past, and when he did, I hadn't asked.

He had shrugged and replied softly in his thick, deep voice, "You haven't seen it. I want to try and let you see it through my eyes."

Suddenly, my throat feels tight, and I feel hot tears threatening to spill over. I don't want to think about Shashan anymore.

To distract myself, I clear my throat and ask, "What's your name?" I should probably know it.

"NM15266," he says without hesitation. My heart feels heavy. I glance down at him and notice again just how *small* he is. He barely comes to my chest, and I'm not exactly tall. For a moment, I feel annoyed that he might slow me down being so short. His eyes are wide and watchful, though, and he's quiet. Not shy or timid or nervous, just quiet.

"No, your *name*," I say softly. "Your real one. Not the one they gave you."

He looks around, and I understand: he's worried someone might overhear.

"There's none of them down here," I say. "If there were, we'd know. They're not quiet, and they hate the Tunnels, even the guards. So what's your name?"

"Coden," he says, looking at me with a completely empty face.

"Do you know how old you are?" I ask.

"Ten," he responds without hesitation.

"Okay, then," and we move on in silence. Ten. He's ten. So he has at least eight more years of his life, eight more years in the dark. A grim smile touches my lips as I think that I at least won't have to train anyone else. I'll be dead long before Coden gets Departed.

We hurry along until we get to a bright, flashing blue. We stop at the flashing, and I dig out the stick with the bulb on the end.

"Blue marks where we get each day," I say quietly as I stuff the bulb into my pack. "Now, we search."

# Chapter Three

"See this?" I say, pointing to the tunnel wall. "Tell me about it." Coden looks up with bright eyes under his worker's cap, his gaze moving to the thin line of brighter rock I'm pointing to. It's only been a few days since the Arrival, but he is already coal-stained, nearly blending into the rock behind him.

"That rock is kind of lighter," he replies quietly, "so there's something different about it. We mark it so the diggers can explore behind it." He steps over the tracks for the carts to get a closer look.

"Yes," I say. Honestly, I don't really know how we are expected to find clues like this when the tunnels are barely lighter than pitch black. We have to scan each tunnel as it's dug with our lanterns, looking for clues of any kind for gold or anything else odd or valuable down here.

And you do not want to miss any gold. Ever. We have to search after the diggers because they're either too focused on digging things out to look for gold, or they keep digging after they found it and can't remember where it was. If any gold gets dug out by accident, then the sorters get it out.

The rock we are looking at has a slight silver sheen to it when compared to the brown and gray and black rock around it.

"So how do we mark it?" I ask, looking down at Coden. Really, the top of his head barely reaches my chest.

Without speaking--I actually haven't heard much beyond his name or repeating instructions when told to--Coden reaches into the pack at his belt and pulls out a small red bulb attached to a white stick. The white part holds some sort of battery, but I've never dared break one open to see.

Coden pulls out the tiny chipper (that's what the searchers call the pointy tool we have to dig out of the dirt) and digs out a small hole next to the mismatched rock. He then wiggles the stick into the Tunnel wall, so only the bulb is showing. Then, he twists the bulb once to the right, so it begins flashing.

"Okay," I nod. "Let's go." I step back over the tracks and hold my lantern high. Back to searching.

We continue deeper into the Tunnel, our lanterns creating dancing figures on the walls. We don't speak, and that seems to suit us both just fine. My second searching partner, Fredia, had spoken *nonstop,* and it had driven me crazy. Fredia had Departed, though, and was replaced by Shashan, and now Coden. Coden, whose pants have to be rolled several times just so he won't trip over them.

I scan the right wall and ceiling, and Coden scans the left and ground. Even though he is new, I trust him to spot anything worth marking. He's quiet and serious and doesn't cry as we walk, which is good. He's picked this up quickly.

We continue on in silence for a while. Despite Coden being quiet and quick and overall looking to be a good partner, I feel bad for him. Ten years old and confined to darkness for the rest of his life. I wonder what he thought when he came through the Arrival door, looking at all of us with our black faces and sad, broken expressions.

Suddenly, I remember myself walking through those doors and being forced to learn everything about this place so quickly.

Those days had been a blur, but I remember Hannah, my very first searching partner-- before Fredia--and her warm, kind smile. Hannah had been much older than me-- I was only six at the time-- but she was so kind and patient. Hannah had taught me how to search as efficiently, quickly, and quietly as possible. We moved fast, she and I, even though

I couldn't see even halfway up the walls. She did the tall stuff. I searched the bottom. It worked.

I remember her, the way her bright eyes shined on you and kind of made you feel special. I can see that day so clearly.

"Hi," Hannah said, looking down at me. For some reason, her face wasn't as black as everyone else's was, and I could see her nose.

"You have dots on your nose," I said quietly. She laughed, and I flinched, stepping backward, away from her.

"Oh, sorry!" she smiled, bending down, so we were the same height. "I'm so sorry. I didn't mean to scare you. I thought it was very funny. You see the dots on my nose?"

I nodded.

"What do you think they are?" she asked, scooching closer so I could get a better look.

She was sort of crouching in front of me, her knees sticking out awkwardly.

I shrugged, and she smiled. I smiled back for some reason.

"Well, they're called freckles," she said. "Do you know what freckles are?"

I shook my head. She reached out a hand, and I took it, letting my tiny hand get wrapped up in her bigger but softer one.

"Freckles hold happy thoughts," she said quietly, giving my hand a gentle squeeze. "Each time you have a happy thought, you get a freckle."

I quickly touched my cheeks, curious.

She gave a small laugh and said, "You can't feel them. They just show up. But I bet you have some beautiful freckles."

Then she did something that I will never forget. Still bending down, she grabbed a chunk of her shirt with her free hand and flipped it, so the inside was showing on the outside. It was slightly less black than the outside of her shirt. She pulled the shirt up and wiped my face gently. After a few moments, she pulled the shirt away and looked at me, eyes focused. Then, her whole face beamed.

"Yes!" she said. "I see little freckles here," she touched my cheek, "and here," my nose, "and here!" she tickled my chin, making me giggle and playfully pull away.

"You have happy thoughts," Hannah told me, smiling.

"Hey!" a harsh voice yelled at us. We were in the Tunnel Room, over by the crates.

"Why haven't you two gotten to work yet?"

Hannah's face darkened, and she stood, kind of pushing me behind her as she did. I peeked out from behind her legs to see an in-charge walking toward us, holding a clipboard, face seething.

"She's new," Hannah said calmly. "I was just explaining how searching works."

"You can explain while you work!" the in-charge growled, and then he swung his clipboard and smacked Hannah across the face with it. She went sprawling into the dirt from the force.

I stood there, chest heaving, frantically glancing from Hannah to the in-charge whose eyes were now on me. The scars on my back still stung from the lady in-charge who oversaw the sorters, and my legs shook terribly as the in-charge lifted his clipboard again.

He made to hit me, but Hannah quickly got to her feet and let the blow land on her shoulder, but she kept her eyes locked on mine.

"We're going," she said evenly, loud enough for the in-charge to hear. "We're going now."

"Hurry up!" he yelled and then stalked away, back to the table.

Hannah stood and grabbed my hand, pulling me hard into the Tunnel.

We walked quickly until the light of the Tunnel Room was far behind us. Hannah handed me a lantern, but I could barely lift it above my head.

Hannah's breath was quick, and I could hear the shakiness in it. Suddenly, she stopped. She sighed and dropped back down to me, looking at me with kind but urgent eyes.

"I didn't ask your name," she said softly. "Do you know your name?"

I nodded and whispered, "Evin."

She smiled, "Do you know how old you are, Evin?"

I nodded again but didn't say anything.

She reached out and took my hand and said, "You can tell me, Evin. I won't tell anyone else."

"Six," I squeaked. "They said I was too little to be here, so I told them I was eight." I sniffed, tears beginning to fall. "I didn't want to sort anymore," I sobbed out. "The lady...the mean lady...she said I was too dumb to be a sorter, too dumb to do anything. She said if I couldn't sort, she'd...she'd... " I dropped my head, not wanting to look at Hannah. "So when another in-charge asked how old I am, I said eight."

"Evin," Hannah said, lifting my chin up so she could see my eyes. "You did so good, Evin. *So* good. It was smart to say you were older. It's okay to be older than you are now, but not later. You don't want to get to be my age, okay?" She smiled, but I didn't understand. Not then, anyway.

I looked down again, ashamed that I was still crying.

"Evin?" Hannah lifted my chin again, and then she touched my cheeks and my nose softly. "You have happy thoughts, Evin. You don't have to tell me what they are, but don't forget them. Okay?"

I nodded, feeling the tears finally stopping.

"Okay," she smiled, then stood. "We have to work fast down here. Are you ready?" I nodded again, and we walked deeper into the Tunnel.

Remembering Hannah makes me feel guilty for how I've treated Coden. I should've explained more to him on Arrival Day, comforted him a little. I roll my eyes, but mostly it's at myself.

I hold up my lantern to the wall, slowly scanning every inch, looking for something that might hint towards gold. I find gold every so often down here, often enough that the in-charges leave me alone for the most part. Gold is shiny and yellow and pretty, so different than the usual gray and black rocks I stare at all day. The in-charges obsess over it, flocking to a find as if it were a feast. They would gather around it and murmur about how "valuable" and "precious" it is.

I guess they're right. I mean, it *looks* nice, but to me, it just seems like a shinier rock.

Once, a searcher cut out gold and took it to an in-charge, offering it to him secretly in exchange for freedom. The in-charge had been thrilled and taken the gold, promising to let the worker out the next day, but instead, the worker was taken outside and shot, accused of stealing.

So, there's that.

A little while later, the little timer strapped to my wrist starts beeping. I look at it and see our ten hours in the Tunnel are up. I press a little button on the side of it, which freezes the time, but I don't stop the one that counts my steps; the in-charges want every single step accounted for. They sometimes will follow us through the Tunnels, observing us, but not often. Thankfully, most in-charges seem scared of the Tunnels and seem just fine to let us use the timers.

"Let's go," I say, quickly marking our spot with a blue light, then turning on my heels and hurrying back up the Tunnel toward the lifts. Being a searcher or a digger, there is one major drawback: you have to get back out. The fastest way is to run, which we all do, but sometimes, depending on how far you went that day, you may have to run for at least an hour to get out. Our timers actually go off an hour earlier than anyone else's--they all work 11 hours--so we have time to get back to Level B for food. Even with that and running, we're usually the last of the workers to the cafeteria. However, we all know how to use the Tunnels and can cut down that time. If you take the digger's tunnels instead of the main Tunnels, you can get out faster and have more time to sit and eat.

The main Tunnels are the ones we search; they're wide and tall and lead to the Hive. The digger's tunnels are the smaller, less straight and uniform, side tunnels where the diggers wheel out piles of dirt, rock, and coal to the lifts to send to the sorters. The track-layers lay the metal rods in the main Tunnels and the side tunnels, so you have to watch your feet wherever you go, or you might twist an ankle. The side tunnels are the quickest way back to the Tunnel Room, but you have to memorize them. You have to know which side tunnel connects to which main Tunnel and keep your sense of direction. At all times, you must know which way the Tunnel Room is.

Eventually, direction becomes second nature. I've only gotten lost once down here, and a pack of diggers found me and got me out before I was too terrified. That was years ago when I was still little. Now, I just know that the side tunnel to our right will help us move faster.

So, Coden and I dip to the right and emerge into a low-ceiled tunnel with a bumpy floor. We hurry along it, Coden almost faster because he doesn't have to duck. He follows closely on my heels as we jog back. We were pretty deep when we stopped; I guess we will be at the Hive in just a few days.

The tunnel forks, one to the left that goes on a slight incline and one to the right that stays level.

"Left," I say between quick breaths. I'm not tired; I've been running these tunnels for years, but talking and running is not easy. We're now going uphill but still moving quickly.

Eventually, this tunnel levels off, and we move faster.

I can see dim light ahead of us now and slow to a walk. I don't want the in-charges to think we left early.

Coden slows down behind me; I can hear his panting. I almost tell him that it gets easier, but then I stop myself. Why would I tell him that? It doesn't really get easier. You just can run faster.

But then I think of Hannah.

I open my mouth but can't think of any words to say, so what comes out is, "Good...uh...good." I look away from his wide eyes, feeling heat burn my cheeks, and I'm grateful we're at the Tunnel Room, so we don't have to talk anymore.

The Tunnel ends abruptly in a large round hole. When we reach the opening, we have to kind of slide down the slope that leads to the floor.

The Tunnel Room itself is a wide and tall room, almost as large as the Open Area on Level B. There are five Tunnel openings on the east side of the room and five on the west. I work on the west side, same as Dirk and his partner Hannel, both of whom I see emerging from the Tunnel to my right. Each Tunnel eventually leads to the Hive, a great spiraling hole deep in the Mine, but the searchers rarely go there. There is nothing to search in the Hive but darkness.

I make my way over to the wall with the crates. I pull out the crate with the tag, "14448" and "32766," written on it and sigh as I untie my pouch and drop it, along with my lantern, into the crate. Moving aside, I let Coden do the same.

We walk to the in-charge table, and I hand them my timer.

"NM1448," I say dully.

"NM15266," Coden says softly.

The in-charges take our timers, scribble down the time and steps, and then wave us along, not bothering to question or scold us. Lots of searchers and diggers are emerging from the Tunnels now, there's nearly a hundred filling up the room, and the in-charges will want to go fast; they don't like waiting for dinner either.

We hurry to the lift and board it together. There are already about fifteen people on board, so it'll go up soon. I'm glad I don't have to wait for the other lift.

I spot Dirk on this lift, and I scoot over closer to him. We're packed pretty tightly, so I'd rather stand by someone I know.

"How's it going, little man?" Dirk asks Coden, smiling.

Coden just shrugs and looks forward. To my surprise, I'm beginning to like Coden. He doesn't talk much, and he doesn't tease me like Hoss or Dirk.

"Aw, has she taken away all your fun already?" Hannel asks, making his lower lip pout. "You know, I heard she eats worms she finds in the tunnel!" Hannel laughs. "Has she made you eat a worm yet, kid?"

I turn and scowl at Hannel; I've never liked him.

"Shut up, Hannel," Dirk sighs, rolling his eyes. I know Dirk doesn't like him either.

"Oh, come on," Hannel smirks, "you said yourself she never talks or smiles."

Dirk's eyes go wide as he looks at me. Hannel's words sting a little, especially since it seems they really were originally Dirk's. I didn't know they talked about me. I can feel my cheeks beginning to burn.

"At least she's not mean," Coden says softly, still staring forward. Dirk lets out a chuckle, and I actually smile a little, surprised. For Coden, that was quite a speech.

Hannel opens his mouth but doesn't say anything.

A few more kids board the lift. One is extremely tall and shoves a few little kids out of the way to stand by Hannel. I notice the tall kid has a long, thin nose. I haven't seen him down here before, but I think I've seen him with Hannel before.

"How was searching?" Hannel grunts, giving the tall kid a crooked, toothy smile.

The tall kid shrugs and replies in a voice that seems too high for him, "Better than loading."

The lift worker slams the gate shut, and we begin moving upward with a bone-grating squeal and a shudder.

I keep my eyes down, not daring to look to the side as we move up.

"Do they let anyone be a searcher?" the tall kid whispers, but loudly. "This one looks barely bigger than the lanterns." Hannel and the kid laugh thickly, and I feel heat in my cheeks. I don't like the way they're laughing.

"What about it, Tiny?" Hannel asks, and I see him give Coden's shoulder a light shove out of the corner of my eye.

"Leave him alone, Hannel," Dirk sighs. "He's just a kid."

"Ya," Hannel laughs. "Doesn't seem like this kid will last long, does it? Too small."

Hannel shakes Coden's shoulder.

The light from the Tunnel Room is quickly disappearing, the lift almost solely lit by the shuddering bulb above us. I resist the urge to close my eyes, though; I won't do that to Coden.

"Can't you speak, Tiny?" Hannel asks in a leering voice. "You stupid?"

"Stop, Hannel," Dirk says again. My fists clench.

Hannel just laughs, and I see him reach out to grab Coden again, and I suddenly find myself stepping forward to stand between the two of them. Hannel's hand grazes my hip, but he pulls it back quickly.

We're completely in the shaft, the vertical tunnel where the lift moves up and down. The walls feel like they're closing in on us; the chain-link of the lift clatters against them and scrapes some of the rock as we move upward. The air feels dead and heavy and stale, and I tell myself not to breathe deeply, even though I feel like I can't at all. I don't need Hannel making even more fun of me.

"Hey!" he whines, straightening to look at me, but I keep my gaze forward. "You do take all the fun, don't you?" Hannel laughs, but I don't look at him.

"Hey!" Hannel says again, but angrier. He reaches out and shoves my shoulder.

I whip around, fuming, glaring at him, unable to stop myself. Then I see the expression of the tall kid, the one Hannel knows. He's watching this whole thing hungrily, eyes wide and unblinking. His stare startles me, and I turn back to face forward, but then I see how close the stone wall is and feel my knees shake.

Finally, thankfully, I can see a little glow of light.

Once at B Level, the tiny kid yanks open the door, saying, "B Level," in a raspy voice. I'm somewhat in the back of the lift, so I have to wait for the other kids to get off before I can mercifully step from the lift to solid ground. But Hannel and the other kid are there, too.

I push forward, wanting to get away from them. I shove between two other kids and find myself at the edge of the lift. There's about a one-foot gap between the edge of the lift and the edge of the floor, and I hop it without risking to look down; I know what's down there, and it isn't easy to look at.

My legs, shaky from getting off the lift, carry me slowly into the Open Area. The Open Area lets me breathe a little deeper. Looking up, I see that there are only two in-charges on the Overhang, so I allow myself to pause and look up; a feeling of lightness chases away the pressure in my chest as I see the high ceiling above me. I take my time and try to breathe.

*Why aren't you used to this?* I growl to myself, angry at this weakness.

I feel someone at my side and almost jump when I look and see Coden standing right next to me. He looks at me with big eyes but doesn't say anything.

Hannel and Dirk, and the other kid make their way off the lift, and I see them walking up to us. Hannel gives me a nasty smile over his shoulder as he walks to the cafeteria, but the tall friend doesn't look at me at all. Dirk hangs back with us.

I finally feel better, and I walk to the cafeteria, letting Coden stay at my elbow.

"I'm sorry," Dirk says quietly. "I didn't mean what I said in a bad way. He was asking about you, you know."

"Why?" I ask, annoyed.

Dirk shrugs, "I don't know. Just wanted to know what you were like. I just said that you're quiet and keep to yourself. He asked why you never smile, and I just told him that I didn't know. That's it."

"Well, I don't really care," I say, and I don't. Not about Hannel, anyway. "It doesn't matter."

"You're not mad?" Dirk asks, his face so wounded, so pitiful, that I relax and roll my eyes at him.

"No," I say. "Let's go."

We continue walking, but I feel like I need to explain something to Coden.

"I don't eat worms," I tell him. "Just so you know."

I look down at him and find he's actually smiling a little bit.

"Too bad," he gives a small shrug. "They're actually pretty good."

My eyebrows shoot up, and I don't know what to say. Dirk starts laughing, and he reaches down and gives Coden's shoulder a playful shove, much different than Hannel's.

We reach the tunnel to the cafeteria and find it buzzing with quiet conversations and workers.

We hurry forward; my stomach feels tight and knotted and keeps rumbling.

I'm just about to grab my tray when I see them: two in-charges, standing at the beginning of the line with clipboards in hand and scowls on faces. They scribble on their pads, almost ferociously, and whisper something to the workers through disgusted expressions.

"Hey!" Dirk says, turning to smile at me. "Bath Day!"

My shoulders relax a little, and I find I'm actually happy to see these in-charges. Bath Days are almost as good as Sun Days. We get one Sun Day a month; at least, that's what they tell us, but I'm not sure how long a month is, really.

I grab my tray as one looks at me.

"Female?" he asks.

"Yes," I resist the urge to roll my eyes.

"Number?" he asks. He's tall with a thin mustache that is twirled up at either end, kind of like Mr. Withers.

"NM1448," I say. He searches his list and scribbles something on it with his pencil.

"You're in group 6," he says. "You will bathe before breakfast at 0600. Listen for your group number to be called."

I nod and move on, letting the next worker in line get their bathing assignment. My skin is already crawling, ready to get rid of a few layers of coal dust that seem to almost make up my flesh. Despite everything bad down here, Bath Day is alright. It makes me feel more...human, less like a thing that crawled out of the dirt one day to be bossed around by people in shining, clacking, polished boots.

The gray slop and bread are tossed onto my tray, and I grab my water before moving off to the usual table. I can see Duna is there already. Dirk is right behind me as we walk across the cafeteria. I notice Coden quietly slip away to sit by a few kids that look about his size. That's good: if he sat with me, he'd be sitting alone soon.

I slide onto the bench, ready to eat when I hear Dirk ask Duna if she's alright.

Looking up, I see the girl who usually has a smirk plastered on her lips and bright eyes piercing you, looking down at her food with a broken expression. She's been quiet for these past few weeks, unusually so, but I guess I understand why. But, really, she's hanging onto Nolan too hard. She needs to just let him go and stop being an idiot. Acting like this won't do any good. If the in-charges think she's moving too slowly, they may consider her unfit.

Duna just shrugs in response to Dirk's question, not looking up, and Dirk looks at me. I shrug back and then pick up my fork. He looks at her, his eyes worried.

Hoss sits down then, his massive frame takes up almost half of our bench, but he's looking around at all the other tables and workers.

"You lost?" Dirk asks.

"Seen Krin?" he asks, still looking around. "I can't find her. We normally meet at the lifts…"

We shake our heads no. I still think it's stupid for them to be so attached to each other down here, but no one ever listens to me about that. I get Duna being sad, somewhat, because he was her brother. She didn't choose him. But why would you dare choose someone down here?

"Maybe they Departed her," Duna says flatly, not looking up.

I stop my fork in midair and look at Duna. Then, my eyes flick to Hoss. His eyes go wide with panic, and he starts looking around with more desperation.

"They couldn't," he says, but almost like he's trying to convince himself. "She's not eighteen."

"Ya, well, neither was Mayla," Duna scowls.

I say nothing. I don't want to tell Hoss it'll be alright, and Lady Executor What's-Her-Name *did* just tell us that they would be taking kids out randomly when they turned eighteen instead of waiting for Arrival Day. I think for a second how I would feel if Krin really did get Departed…

I keep eating, telling myself that I wouldn't care, but every once in a while, my eyes flick up, and I quickly scan the entrance to the cafeteria.

Time seems to go slower as Hoss rakes his gaze back and forth. I notice how his giant fist is curled around his fork, and his back is rigidly straight.

"You're going to break your fork, Hoss," I say after a moment of watching the metal sweat in his palm.

Hoss drops the utensil without turning his gaze away from the crowd and takes a deep breath, but I can see the desperation and panic in his eyes. Krin is a sorter and usually among the first to the cafeteria, being on C Level and all. And, not many workers are coming in anymore; most of the tables are full, which means most if not all of the workers are here.

I look once more toward the cafeteria entrance, and a sigh escapes my lips. "There she is," I nod to where Krin's head has just appeared. Krin goes to the line and gets a tray, but someone else follows close behind her, too close to be casual. I don't recognize the worker, but they're still pretty far away.

Finally, they both come and join the table.

Hoss lets out a pent-up breath and seems like he might pass out.

"Where were you?" he asks, his tone sharp and worried.

"I had to go to the bathroom," Krin shrugs. Her hands are kind of shaking, and her eyes, which are normally soft and kind, look sad and...scared?

I don't have time to look too closely at her, though, because Dirk cuts in and asks,

"Who's the new girl?"

The new girl sits across from new, next to Dirk, and we all turn to look at her.

"Oh," Krin says, a ghost of a smile returning to her face, "this is Aila. We met on the way here. She's the one who I said looks like you, Evin."

I look at the coal-smudged face sitting across from me. Besides seeing that the girl has two eyes, a nose, and a mouth, I can't make out any resemblance. She's only been here a few days, and already the girl is as black as the rest of us.

"Whatever," I shrug, returning to my food.

"How old are you, Aila?" Hoss asks, finally devouring his food now that Krin is safely next to him.

"I'm fifteen," the new girl says, giving a slight smile, revealing perfectly straight white teeth. Her voice is soft and kind, and I notice that she really seems to believe in her smile like she knows it's a good smile. I roll my eyes; the Mine will take that smile soon enough.

"You know? For sure?" Hoss asks. The others stare at her. It's not terribly odd to know how old you are, but generally, only the little ones do. The ones who are five or six. To be fifteen and know how old you are and *just* be coming to the Mine, that is odd.

Odd enough that I stop eating and really look at this girl. The older kids that come here are usually angry and silent or terrified of everything. She seems...calm. I don't like it.

"Yes," she nods. "My family used to celebrate my birthday." Everyone stares at her, including me, not quite understanding.

Dirk finally asks, "What does 'celebrate' mean?"

"Oh...uh," Aila gives another smile, but this one seems nervous or confused, "it means to be happy about something, I guess. It's like a party. Everyone, friends and family, gather together and throw a party because, well, they're celebrating something."

"What's a party?" Dirk asks.

"You know, you eat food and get gifts. There's music and dancing and fun, and everybody is just happy. Stuff like that," Aila gives a small shrug like it was no big deal.

"No, we don't," I say evenly. "We don't know any of that." I can hear the snap in my own voice, and I don't really know if I meant to put it there, but I don't care. I don't care what this girl who had friends and family thinks of me.

"What's a birthday?" Hoss asks.

Aila raises her eyebrows but still smiles as she says, "It's the day you were born, and each birthday you get one year older."

"And people like them?" Dirk asks, looking shocked.

"Yes," she says. "Birthdays are times for fun, for parties."

I snort into my food but don't say anything. Everyone else looks at Aila with wide eyes. Aila's smile wavers for a moment, but it never fades.

"So, you know when your birthday is?" Hoss asks.

"Oh, yes," Aila replies. "It's January 27th."

"January?" Krin asks.

"It's a month in the year," Aila replies. "The first month, actually."

"Months have names?" Dirk asks, a smile on his disbelieving face. "Wow, people have parties when you get older, and months have names. Who knew?"

"You didn't know?" Aila asks.

"Most of us came here when we were little," Dirk shrugs. "We're not really that smart." He gives a laugh and shovels some food in his mouth.

We all get to eating, Aila looking somewhat awkward at us like we're some strange bug she just found crawling on her bed, and she's not sure if we're dangerous. As I look at her, watching her almost daintily lift her fork and examine the food on it, I feel a question burning inside me: "So, why are you here then?"

"What do you mean?" Aila asks, her brow furrowing.

"It sounds like your family cared about you," I say, almost darkly. "You had parties and birthdays and all. If they cared, why are you here?"

"Oh," Aila hesitates, then replies, "My parents couldn't afford me anymore. So, they traded me to the Nation to pay off their debts. I was sent here. They got to go home." She shrugs, but I can see something in her eyes. Worry?

"What do you mean, they couldn't afford you anymore?" I ask. I don't like this girl, and I can't exactly explain why, but her story isn't new. Lots of kids' parents send them here, and I know that's not fair, but I still don't like her. She doesn't quite seem like she's supposed to be here.

"They couldn't pay for me. They didn't have enough money," Aila replies, and I notice how she glances around the table quickly. Is she scared of us? I can't tell.

"So, they got money for bringing you here?" Hoss asks, his eyebrows raised.

"Yes," Aila says slowly, as if confused why we don't understand her. Then, a light seems to come on in her eyes.

"How old are you?" she asks me.

I scowl back but reply, "Somewhere around seventeen."

"Somewhere?"

"Not everyone has or had a family who has a stupid thing for their age," I shoot back.

"When did you come here?"

My cheeks burn slightly, not sure why, but I say, "I'm pretty sure I was three. Why?"

"That explains it. You don't really know anything about the Nation, the Republic of the Colonies, how all this works," she gestures around her at the cafeteria, like its gray walls hold all the answers.

I look around at the blank faces at the table and reply, "So? None of us really do. Besides what the in-charges tell us."

"Interesting," Aila looks excited and pitiful at the same time, which infuriates me. She looks at me with big eyes, almost as if she is extremely happy about something. "Do you want me to explain it?"

*No,* I want to spit in her face, but it comes out as, "Yes." The others nod as well.

"Well, I will explain it as simply as possible. Basically, about twenty years ago, a man was elected into government. At that time, America was a Democratic Republic, and he was voted into office-"

"Smaller words, please," Dirk says, a bashful grin on his face.

Aila blushes, noticeable even under the lay of smudge on her face, and continues, "He became in charge of the nation, what was then called the United States of America. Within a few years, he completely changed everything and gave himself all this power to do whatever he wanted. He goes by the name of High Chancellor. I don't know his real name. But anyway, there was this big war, and half the Nation agreed with him, and half didn't. So the half that didn't went to the west and the half that did stayed in the east. The High Chancellor created a new nation called the Society of the Republic of the Colonies, or the New Nation. He made new states, a new system of government. It's a place where everyone is supposed to be equal and everyone work together, but--"

"What does 'equal' mean?" Dirk asks.

"The same," Aila replies without missing a beat. "Everyone gets the same stuff and has the same rights. But it's not that way."

"You're telling us," Hoss huffs.

"Exactly," Aila continues. "One of the laws in the New Nation is that everyone has to be able to read to contribute to society. If you can't read, you can't participate, and therefore, you aren't equal, and you make society 'imbalanced,' which means you basically throw off the whole plan. So, the illiterates, or people who can't read, are sent to work in mines, on ships, in forests, until they're eighteen. People can also trade in family members to pay off debts, even if those family members can read. When the kids in the mines, or on the ships, or in the forests turn eighteen, they are deemed 'dangerous' and must be taken out of society altogether and used for entertainment or slave labor. They go to the Colosseum, are sent to the army, or are sold."

"We know about the Colosseum," Duna says angrily, looking down.

"Everyone goes to the Colosseum first," Aila explains, "but they don't always stay there."

"Ya, because they die," Duna scowls.

"Or are sold or put in the army," Aila explains calmly. "Have you seen the Colosseum?"

"Once during an Arrival," Hoss replies quietly. "A few years ago."

"They put up things they called pictures on a big sheet of paper, so everyone could see," I say evenly, staring at Aila's eyes. I hate that she knows so much, and I hate that I don't understand even half of it. "They said we should get to 'experience the entertainment we will help create.' They showed us pictures of what happens in the arena." Duna looks down, and I can hear her sniff. Dirk scoots closer to her.

"Huh," she replies, "well, not everyone dies there. In fact, very few die there. Like I said, most are put in the army or are sold."

We're quiet for a moment, and then Hoss breaks the silence.

"What's an army?" he asks.

"It's a really big group of people who fight for their country," Aila explains.

"Fight?" Dirk raises an eyebrow. "Why do they have to fight?"

"Well, sometimes they have to fight other countries," Aila says. "Not everyone was happy about the New Nation, so the High Chancellor had to make an army. Mostly they fight those that went to the west."

"Is it fighting like in the Colosseum?" Hoss asks.

"I don't know," Aila shrugs. "I haven't seen the Colosseum, and I've never seen war. I've only ever heard about them."

"War?" Dirk asks.

"Where the armies fight."

"Sh!" I quickly hush them all, noticing a dark figure slinking towards us from across the room. We all shut up immediately, but Aila looks slightly confused. We look down at our plates and pretend to take a sudden, urgent interest in our food.

The guard reaches our table, walks by us, and positions himself against the wall near our table. We must've looked too engaged in the conversation; we're supposed to eat and leave.

The guard is too close to continue talking, so we eat, stand--almost all at the same time-- and then turn to leave. I naturally fall in next to Krin, who is glued to Hoss's side. Aila sidles up close to Krin, too, though, which bugs me. Duna and Dirk walk a few steps behind us. Looking around, I notice that our table is one of the last in the cafeteria. No wonder the guard came closer.

We walk down the tunnel to the Open Area in silence, guards still occasionally posted like shadows against the tunnel walls. It isn't until we've crossed the Open Area, eyes automatically gazing upwards to see if there are any in-charges looking down on us from the Overhang, and safely reach the tunnel to the barracks that we begin talking again. No guards are positioned past the Open Area. Or, at least, they're not supposed to be. I don't really trust it, but we don't see any guards in sight, so it feels safe to talk. At least, safer.

66

"So," Duna says softly, "not everyone goes to the Colosseum?

"No, they do go to the Colosseum," Aila replies quietly, all of us gathering closer to hear her. "They take the strongest from the Colosseum into the army. They use that place as a kind of training test for war. Some of the other ones that survive are sold."

"Sold?" Duna asks.

"People buy them to work as slaves or personal soldiers," Aila shrugs like it's no big deal.

Duna looks hopeful and horrified at the same time, her chest rising and falling rapidly. I can't tell if she took this as good or bad news.

"How many illit...illiot... uh, people who can't read, are there?" Dirk asks.

"Lots," Aila says simply. "I don't know for sure."

"So how come your parents couldn't afford you anymore?" I ask.

Aila hesitates like she's trying to get her words right, then says, "I'm not really sure. One morning they took me to the train station, told me goodbye, and sent me on my way. They said it was them or me."

"That seems harsh," Hoss says.

"It's a harsh world," Aila shrugs. For a moment, I think I see a tear form in Aila's eyes. The others look at her sadly, but I don't. Her whole story, whole...*everything* feels wrong to me. I can't explain it, but I want her to go away.

"What is it like?" Krin asks her gaze far away. "Out in the world. Outside the Mine. What is it like?"

"Well," Aila sighs, looking past them as if the world was laid out just at the end of the tunnel, as if there were rows of the world instead of rows of beds and stones. "Everyone lives in cities, and the cities are surrounded by tall walls. Each city is made up of tons of buildings, some for living, some for working, and they all look the same, tall and gray.

67

Some are so tall they seem to kiss the sky. The cities are always busy, full of people hurrying back and forth. Everyone has to work, and no one can be late. If you're late, you're not a good citizen." She smiles like that is funny. "All the kids are taught to read and write at home until they are six, and then they're sent to training facilities to be taught a certain skill, like cleaning or driving or something."

"So how are there newbies down here if kids are supposed to learn to read at home? There are tons of older kids, like you," I say.

"Not every kid has a parent. Some parents die, some kids are caught in the wilderness, and some parents just don't teach their kids," Aila explains. "I had a friend whose parents refused to teach her, so I taught her."

"That's horrible," Krin says, her mouth shaking. "How could you not teach your own children?" She flicks her eyes to Hoss.

I am about to say something snarky about parents just not caring about their kids in general, but the words suddenly freeze in my mouth. I stare at Aila. We have just reached the end of the tunnel where we're supposed to split, girls to the left, boys to the right, but I can't move.

Dirk asked something, but I hold out my hand, stopping everyone.

"You can read?" I ask Aila, mouth still hanging open, voice quavering. I glance around quickly, making sure no in-charges or guards or even other workers are around.

Aila gives a confused, half-smile, then quietly replies, "Yes. I can read."

The breath leaks out of me in a fast gasp, and I look around at the others. Hoss is clearly shocked, his eyebrows raised; Krin's eyes are huge, and she holds a slender hand over her mouth; Dirk looks confused, but that isn't necessarily odd for him; and then there is Duna, who looks like she is starving and Aila is all the food she would ever need.

I turn my focus back to Aila.

"What?" she asks, clearly confused by our reactions.

"You can read," Duna explains, her lips parting in an almost hungry smile.

Aila just shrugs, but inside my mind, there are conflicting emotions. The strongest among them are jealousy and curiosity. What must it be like to read? And how come Aila can do it and I can't? I realize it's stupid to think this way. Obviously, it's not my fault I can't read. But it crosses my mind that Aila will not have to go to the Colosseum. She will stand before the Head Reader in a few years, he will ask her to read the scroll, and she will. She'll be the first worker ever to get out of here, to join the in-charges on their level, and then go out into the world. My blood boils at that. She will only have to spend a few years down here, and then she'll get out. Out! Meanwhile, I'll have been dead for years, or worse, if what Aila says is true. I want to scream at her, tell her how unfair this all is. But there's no point.

I think I hate this girl.

Workers come into the tunnel, talking softly, which makes us stop. We all turn and head into the rows of barracks, not wanting to draw more attention to ourselves. I turn and robotically make my way to my bunk. Krin is silent next to me as we walk, even as we get ourselves onto our beds.

After a few minutes, while girls are still talking softly all around us, Krin breaks the silence.

"What do you think?" she asks. I can just barely see her in the dim glow from the string lights around the room and across the ceiling.

"What do I think about what?" I sigh.

"About Aila?" she whispers. "About her being able to read?"

There are others talking around us, but it's still good to whisper. I wouldn't put it past the other workers to rat us out to the in-charges.

"So?" I shrug. I don't want to talk about it.

"So maybe she would teach us," Krin says, her eyes alight with excitement and hope. She swings herself into a sitting position, apparently too excited to remain lying down.

"Do you really think that'll do any good?" I search Krin's face, trying to keep my face and voice empty.

"You can't tell me you aren't thinking the same thing!" Krin sighs in exasperation.

I shrug. "I don't know, Krin. I don't think it'll do any good. Is it worth it to spend what little free time we have to risk our lives to read when we could be Departed tomorrow anyway?"

"That's exactly why we should!" Krin says. She stares at me with her intense blue eyes. She squints as if trying to figure something out on my face, then asks, "Shouldn't we at least try?"

I heave a sigh and say nothing for a moment. I want to yell at her, to demand why she wants me to try and have hope for anything because that's all it means. If we try to read, we're trying to have hope to get out of here, and there's no point in that. Besides, I don't really want to hang out with Aila. And I especially don't want her teaching me to read. I don't want to stare at that smile while I'm trying to eat any longer.

Krin's eyes are wide as she waits for my response.

As if she can read my mind, she softly says, "It would be nice, you know, to hope for something."

I raise my eyebrows at her; I'm not really sure if learning to read is against the rules, but I think there's an unspoken rule against it. If we read, who will go to the Colosseum? But what if I didn't have to go to the Colosseum? What if I learned to read fast enough and was able to walk out into the sunshine without being chained or kept behind a wall? What if this really actually helps? But, what if it gets us all Departed faster?

Krin looks pathetically hopeful, so I roll my eyes. "Fine. Ask her."

"Evin!" she almost squeals with excitement.

"I'm not saying I'm going to do it," I say, "but you can ask her. We'll see what she says."

"Thank you, Evin," Krin gives a soft smile and then lays back down.

I grumble a little, annoyed that she feels the need to thank me. I didn't do anything; in fact, I really don't know if I will do it if Aila agrees. But Krin can do whatever she wants, I guess.

For a moment, I close my eyes and let myself imagine what it would be like to walk out of here a free person, not someone destined for the Colosseum. But to walk out and just...keep walking. *Outside.*

We've all been outside on Sun Days, but only for a few hours, and even then, we're stuck inside a high metal fence that blocks any of the world outside it. The field where we spend Sun Days is long and has some grass and a few trees. Mostly it's rocks and dirt, but it's still outside. And to be able to be out there, all the time, and not have rocks constantly inches from my face threatening to crush me forever would be incredible. I can almost feel the grass beneath my fingers, the cool wind on my face; I imagine outside feels so much better beyond the fence. I can almost hear the birds chirping around me, singing their sweet songs, welcoming me to the worlds.

The chirping starts to get louder.

The chirping starts to get annoying.

Suddenly, there's one really long, loud, shrill chirp, and I sit up, rubbing my eyes, realizing I've been dreaming.

Then the chirp registers as what it really is: a whistle.

I groan and hear the stomping of boots accompanying the whistle and know that we're getting an inspection.

Rolling my eyes, I scoot to the side of my bed and jump down next to Krin, who's rubbing her eyes and yawning. Her hair is always kept neatly tied in a cloth on top of her head. My hair is loose and messy, tangled around my shoulders and down my back like it always is until I shove it up and under my worker's cap each morning. The cap itself hangs on my bedpost each night.

The inspections are random, but we've noticed they fall closely around Bath Days and Sun Days. They always happen in the middle of the night. We're awakened by a whistle, we have to get up and line up in front of our row of beds, and then in-charges and guards come in to make sure we're keeping everything clean and following the rules.

The group of inspectors is noisy, ripping apart everyone's beds, but they're two rows ahead and still at the beginning. We just have to stand still until they reach us. I wish I could fall asleep standing up.

Krin gives a big stretch as she moves into line next to me. "Why do they always inspect us before Bath Day? They'll just inspect us again tomorrow."

I shrug, but we all know they're looking for food or something worse. No food is allowed outside the cafeteria, and if you hide food in your bed, you become a problem. Not just a messy problem, but a problem for bugs and rodents. The in-charges don't want problems, and so they will beat you until you're no longer a problem. Now, I figure, they will just Depart you, put you in the one place where you'll never be a problem again: the Colosseum. No matter what Aila says, the Colosseum is where we go to die. Everyone knows that.

The inspection moves fairly quickly. The in-charges rip apart the beds while the workers and guards watch. I have only ever seen two people get punished during an inspection; one had food, the other had taken a piece of gold. The one with the food was beaten in front of us, but the one with the gold was taken outside and shot.

The group of in-charges and guards is in the second row. I can see them pulling off mattresses, searching through blankets and pillows, all to make sure nothing bad was there. Then we have to put it all back immediately; messes are not tolerated down here.

A sniffle makes me pause in watching the in-charges and turn to look at Krin. She's trembling beside me.

I catch her eye and make a questioning look. She just shakes her head in response, her bottom lip quivering.

"What?" I breathe out of the corner of my mouth; we're technically not supposed to talk to each other or move while we wait to be inspected.

Krin says nothing, just keeps her head bowed and her eyes shut. I think I spot a tear rolling down the tall girl's cheek.

I stare at her for a moment, eyebrows arched. What's with her? She's never cried during an inspection before. Is she worried she's eighteen? I don't think she is... Maybe. Maybe that's what it is.

"I don't think you're eighteen," I whisper.

Krin shakes her head, more tears rolling down her face.

"Sh!" the girl next to me hisses. I turn and scowl at her. She's like, what, 12? Calm down.

"Krin," I whisper.

She shoots me a look, and I see true terror in her eyes. But it's an inspection! Why would they bother inspecting us if they were just going to Depart us? Maybe she's not worried about her age...but then what is she crying about?

My heart quickens without permission, worried, wanting to know what's upset Krin. I think hard; she's quiet and does her job, I didn't see her take anything from the cafeteria, and she's not dumb enough to do that. Then what?!

Then, I freeze: she has something, she has to, and that must be why she's acting this way. And my guess is it isn't bread. My stomach churns. I try not to let myself care. Whatever Krin did wrong is her fault, not mine.

But maybe I have enough time to dart to Krin's bed and grab whatever it is she's hiding.

I'm so much shorter than Krin and have darker hair. Maybe they won't see me.

But what if they do see me? They'd Depart me for sure, or just kill me here for disobeying rules and possessing whatever it is that Krin has. Plus, I have no idea what or where it is! Or if she even has anything!

How could Krin be so stupid?!

My palms sweat as the in-charges, now on our row, begin to make their way toward us. Tears are now flowing freely down Krin's cheeks, and her chin shakes as she tries to stifle her sobs.

I'm panicking and furious at myself for feeling this way. I. Do. Not. Care! I'm not responsible for Krin or her stupid choices.

The in-charges finally get to our bunks. Two go past us and begin tearing the beds apart while another takes notes on a clipboard. One holds a bright lantern and the whistle, and a fifth watches them all work. Two guards stand stoically behind them. These in-charges are not as important as the ones at the Arrival; they don't announce themselves or give speeches, and they have to work at night and in the dark and touch our stuff. If there's one thing about in-charges, they do *not* like to touch us or anything we touch. The two who are ripping apart our beds are scowling and huffing as they do so.

I watch Krin out of the corner of my eye. Her head is bowed, and she does not look up; I know she's just trying to hide the tears and how her chin is shaking. She'll give herself away if she keeps crying.

Turning around to watch the in-charge search Krin's bed would just earn me a whack from a guard's stick, so I resist the impulse. I can hear it, though.

I hear him step onto the ladder leading up to her bed, and then there's an odd sliding sound and a big thud. There's also a quiet, almost distant clinking sound. The in-charge swears and mumbles under his breath. I realize he must've lost his balance and fell.

None of the other in-charges seem to care that much or even notice he fell. They don't say anything or offer to help him to his feet. I secretly hope he fell on his face.

I hear him get up and grumble his way back to where the in-charge with the clipboard is standing.

"Nothing," he grunts and then moves to the next bunk on the row.

We have to stand completely still, completely silent, while they move down our row and onto the next one. We aren't allowed to move until the entire barrack has been searched and the whistle blown again.

Looking next to me, I see that Krin has relaxed a little; she's lifted her head and keeps trying to nervously peer over her shoulder, but she doesn't dare. Her fists are clenched, though.

Finally, after what seems like forever because of my burning curiosity and urge to scream at Krin, the in-charges finish. The whistle blows, and they march away. One in-charge and the guards pause just inside the tunnel, watching us.

We scurry to our possessions, quickly trying to get them in order. Laziness is not tolerated down here, and if you don't put your things back together quickly, you're lazy.

I heave my thin mattress back onto the top bunk and then go in search of my blanket and pillow. My blanket is threadbare and barely offers any warmth, but it's *my* blanket. I find it and my pillow just to the side of my bed, along with my hat that someone so graciously stepped on; there's a boot-print on it. Krin, I notice with a roll of my eyes, hasn't even begun to set up her bed. In fact, she's not even by her bed.

Groaning in exasperation, I grab Krin's mattress and toss it unceremoniously onto her bed. Her blanket and pillow are just on the floor, and the girl who sleeps under Krin has already gathered her things, so these must be Krin's. Curiosity getting the better of me, I quickly run my fingers through the blanket and reach my hand into the pillow. Nothing. Even more annoyed than when I started cleaning up after Krin, I toss her things up and then climb onto my bed, fuming.

Krin finally comes back, slinking through the shadows as quickly as she can.

I say nothing to her as she climbs onto her bed, hoisting her long legs up and over without really even needing the ladder's help.

"Thank you," she mutters quickly, laying down facing away from me.

"Where did you go?" I demand, glaring at her back.

She sighs, rolls over, and stares at me with her big, blue eyes.

"I went to—" but I don't let her finish.

"What do you have in your bunk?" I ask in a harsh whisper. Girls are still talking around us, but I don't want anyone else knowing Krin has something. Besides, I think I see the shadows of the guards still hovering in the tunnel.

She looks at me guiltily. Then, she reaches her hand up to her makeshift headscarf.

Slowly, with shaky hands, she pulls something out and opens her fist, letting me see.

My insides turn to ice.

"Are you insane?" I ask, heart racing, peering around nervously, just knowing that charges are going to pop up out of nowhere...

In Krin's hands is a small, clear stone. It's so clear it's almost blue, and it shines in even the dim light, giving off a soft glow. I've seen a few of them, and the in-charges love them more than the gold. We don't search for them specifically, but if you find any, you are to immediately go report it to an in-charge. They don't even want you to waste time marking it.

There was one time when Shashan and I found one. It was last year, maybe. We had run back through the tunnel and got an in-charge. He followed us to where it was and then sent me ahead to go get a digger. By the time I made it back with part of a digging team, the in-charge was screaming at Shashan, yelling at him to get the stone out of the wall. Shashan didn't have any way to, so the incharge slapped him across his face. Shashan's nose bled for hours after that. Once the diggers had gotten the stone out of the wall, the in-charge took it and hurried back up the tunnel, leaving us to get back to work.

I wish Krin had just been hiding food.

"Where did you get that?" I ask, my voice trembling as I look around for anyone watching us. Most of the other girls seem to have fallen asleep.

"Hoss," Krin whispers, a ghost of a smile on her trembling lips. "He found it while digging. He said his team was focused on pulling rock, and they weren't looking...so…" She closes her palm and clutches the stone to her chest.

"Krin, if they find it-"

"I know," Krin spits back, a flash of anger in her eyes. Anger and...pleading? "Don't you think I know? I thought for sure they were going to find it tonight. I forgot to grab it out from under my mattress before the inspection. If that in-charge hadn't slipped...But I can't give it up. It's Hoss' promise to me."

"Promise?" I almost scoff.

Krin nods sadly. "Yes. He promised that, somehow, we'll be together, even after we leave this place." She looks around at the gloom that surrounds us.

"Krin," I sigh, "you can't make promises to people down here. Especially not a promise like that." I don't know what's dumber, the promise or the rock.

"Well, I did," Krin just shrugs. "And it's not your promise, so why do you care?"

"I don't," I scowl back.

"Good," Krin flips over to her other side.

A few moments pass, but curiosity wins over inside me. "What's your promise, then?" I whisper at her back.

Slowly, Krin reaches up and pulls her headwrap off, revealing her hair. I gasp as I realize what I'm looking at. Krin's hair, which usually flows like sunshine to her hips, which has made every single girl down here jealous and reach up to tenderly finger their own hair (including me), which she keeps tightly wrapped so it won't ever get dirty, is chopped in uneven, clumsy bunches, reaching only to just above her

78

shoulders. Her long blonde locks are gone, with only a stupid promise left behind.

# Chapter Four

It's all dark, and there's pressure on my chest, and I can't breathe. Then, I see a small light out in the distance. I run towards it, but my feet feel heavy. I fall, and it feels like I fall forever. Finally, I land, and the ground is soft. I look around, and I'm just outside a circle of light that illuminates a few figures crouching down. I can't see their faces, but I know they're facing away from me. There are three of them. Their figures are shadowy and blurred, but then they must hear me behind walking towards them, and they turn.

"Hello?" I call out to them. My voice is louder than normal.

They don't answer, but they stand and fully turn to look at me. Their faces are bright white, and I can't see any features.

"Who are you?" I ask.

No answer, but I hear them start to laugh, cruelly.

"What is this place?" I ask. They continue to laugh.

Then, hands grab me from all around and start dragging me backward.

"No!" I scream, but they continue to pull me. "Help!" I cry to the people in the light, but they don't move. Instead, they turn back around and crouch back down, leaning on each other.

"Help!" I plead with them, tears streaming down my face as icy cold hands pull me further and further into the darkness. As it gets darker, more and more hands grab me, gripping my arms, my legs. Hands cover my face, dripping something sticky and wet all over me. I scream as I realize that its blood.

The light is eventually lost, the three people with it. I can still hear them laughing.

There's a loud shrieking in the distance, and something big seems to be coming.

The hands holding me drag me to the mouth of a Tunnel and then throw me inside. I can hear growling, feel hot, sticky breath on my face as I stand, unable to make my feet move.

I see the eyes. Wide, red circles, full of hate and anger. It seems to mold from the darkness, built of shadow and fear. Vaporish-feet form, terrible white claws extended from the swirling mist. It walks toward me.

"NO!" I scream, falling to my knees.


"NO!" I gasp. I'm soaked with sweat and shaking, gasping for breath. I take a deep breath, in through my nose and out through my mouth. I push myself onto my elbows and look around, making sure I'm in my familiar darkness. There are rows of bunks in front of me, and I'm lying on my own with my blanket and pillow. My shoulders shake, and I press my face into my pillow, silently crying.

Hannah's face forms in front of my eyes.


"They're not real, Evin," she said softly, taking my hand and gently pulling me into the Tunnel. I could see the sadness in her eyes as she forced me to take tiny step after tiny step.

I didn't say anything, just held her warm hand with my shaky, clammy one.

"I know what those kids said," she whispered as we entered the Tunnel. I felt like my chest was going to explode from my pounding heart. "I know that they told you there are monsters here. There aren't any. I promise."

We were completely inside the Tunnel, the in-charges out of sight. She knelt down in front of me, taking both my hands and looking at me tenderly, but firmly.

"Evin," she said, "listen. They're not real."

My chin shook as I said, "But they told me there are monsters, mean things, that eat little kids because we're not fast. They said that I will be dead in a week because of how small I am."

Tears streamed down my face.

Hannah gently wiped them off my cheeks.

"I dream about them," I whimpered. "I dream they drag me here." I was sobbing, Hannah still wiping my cheeks softly.

"They're just dreams," Hannah assured me. "Dreams can't hurt you. Dreams make them even less real."

"But--"

"Evin," she took my face in her hands, "look at me. There are no monsters in these tunnels. Nothing will get you."

"But--"

"I'm with you, Evin," she said softly, staring into my eyes with intensity. "I'm not going to leave you down here. I promise."

I looked at her through my watery eyes, paused for a moment, and then nodded. I let her pull me deeper into the Tunnel, less frightened when my hand was safely in hers.

"When you have bad dreams," Hannah said, "just think of your freckles."

I honestly don't know if I have any freckles left, but I touch my wet cheek anyway. I can't remember the dream, not all of it, but I do remember the darkness and the fear, and I know there was a monster in it.

*I used to have freckles,* I think. *What made those freckles?*

Sun Days, Hannah, maybe Krin. I can't think of anything else, but my breathing has slowed, and I feel okay enough to lift my face out of my pillow.

I look over at Krin, but she's sleeping heavily, her face barely visible with the dim string lights around the edges of the room. I'm tempted to reach out and wake her up, but I stop my hand midair and pull it back in. Krin normally wakes up with me after these dreams; I mean, my screaming wakes her up, but she's never complained. Maybe she doesn't want to hear about my dreams anymore.

*No,* I think, *she's just tired.*

At least, that's what I hope for.

Taking another deep breath, I lay back down on my stomach and close my eyes, willing myself to fall back asleep. It takes a few minutes, but I do go back to sleep.


They blow the whistle, waking us all up.

Groggy, eyes heavy, I lift my head and look up. Three in-charges have entered the barracks, along with at least five guards, but it's not as easy to see them in their black uniforms. I sigh; I'm happy that it's Bath Day and all, but it's early. The breakfast signal hasn't even sounded yet, and they're already here.

The pack walks about halfway up the big hallway in the barracks and stops. The girl's Bath Room is at the back end of the barracks, a straight shot across from the tunnel to get to the barracks. They set up their folding table, then a few of the guards set up some chairs for them before retreating to stand to the sides and behind the table.

There's a new sound at the tunnel, and I turn my head to see a few workers pushing in a couple of massive carts loaded with clothing. I sigh and lay back down. I'm in group 6, and we won't be bathing for a few hours at least, but I will be awake. Why are the in-charges so loud?

I lift my head and then am surprised when I see Krin is *still* sound asleep. Will anything wake her up? She didn't wake up to my screaming or to the whistling. How tired is she? She's laying on her back, her arm over her eyes, snoring deeply. I shake my head, annoyed that she can sleep through all of this. Normally, she sleeps lighter than me and wakes up with the slightest noise.

The workers push the carts over to the table, and then they stand to the side. These workers aren't as coal-dusted as the rest of us, so I figure they must be the cleaners, the ones who basically live in the in-charges' offices. Their faces are drawn and tired, but I still don't feel as bad for them; their cheeks aren't sunken, and I can see their actual skin. I look down and see my own arm, black as the darkness around me. Jealousy runs through me, and I realize that I don't think those kids have it so bad. So, there's that.

Once they apparently finish getting everything set up, one of the in-charges stands on a chair and picks something up. I've seen it before; it's this cone-shaped thing that makes him louder. The in-charge holds the cone-thing to his mouth, and there's a loud buzzing sound, but then he says, "Group 1, please approach the table."

I hear shuffling around me, and a few girls straggle out of bed and begin making their way to the table.

Krin is still asleep. I roll my eyes; I don't know which group she's in. What if she's in 1?

I reach over and shake her shoulder. She sighs and rolls over.

"Krin!" I whisper, shaking her harder. "Krin?" What's with her? She's been sleeping like the dead and not eating. If she's sick, she's in trouble.

"Krin!" I almost hiss as I shake her even harder. "Wake up!"

"What?" she mumbles, turning to face me, eyes barely open a crack.

"Are you in group 1?" I ask, annoyed.

"What?" she asks again, rubbing her face as she props herself onto her elbows.

"Are you in group 1?" I ask again, pointing at the table where the in-charges sit, writing down numbers, and handing out clothes.

"Oh," Krin sighs and lays back down. "6." She says, then rolls back over and is almost immediately asleep again.

I stare at her still form, annoyed and yet relieved. Then, I follow her example and lay back down. I know I won't sleep, but it's nice to be awake and not have to be doing something.


Finally, they call group six. I jump down, ready to feel clean. Well, *cleaner.* I reach up and shake Krin roughly.

She wakes up easier this time and looks down at me.

"Our turn," I say. I turn and grab my cap from my bedpost, but I don't put it on. There's not really any point yet.

Krin jumps down beside me, and we hurry over to the in-charge table. There are only about five girls ahead of us, but to my annoyance, one of them is Aila.

She gives us a small smile as we approach and get in line behind her. We don't talk, though; in-charges don't like it if you talk in line. We can talk in the Bath Room. I wonder if

Krin is still going to ask her to teach us to read. I hope not.

Aila reaches the table first and gets through fairly quickly, as does Krin. Then I approach.

"NM1448," I say.

"Wait to be asked," the in-charge drawls, his voice high and nasally as he looks at me over his clipboard. He shakes his head, clicks his pen, and then asks with huge emphasis, "What is your number?" I notice his mustache is twirled up at either end, and I realize I've seen this in-charge before. I also realize that I already told him my number but must now tell it to him again.

I force myself to speak evenly when I reply, "NM1448."

He writes something on his clipboard and then waves me over to his companion.

"Any exchanges?" the next in-charge asks. This one is small, looking like a child in his chair. He has a beard, though, so I know he's not a child.

"No," I say. If our shoes or cap have holes or are too small or big, we can exchange them on Bath Day. No guarantee that you'll get a better replacement, though. Actually, my boots are a little big, but I'd rather have them too big than too small, so I don't risk the exchange. I have to scrunch my extra socks in the toes of my boots to help them fit better, but at least I never lose my socks.

He waves me to the next in-charge sitting at the table, the one closest to the carts full of clothes.

This in-charge waves forward the workers behind him, who bring forward small bundles and set them on the table.

He stands, disgust clear on his face, as he gives me my new clothes. "One shirt." It's gray, long-sleeved, and will soon be black. "One pair of pants." Black, fairly thick, that fall to my ankles. "Two pairs of socks." Gray, large and scruffy. They also will soon be black.

I take the clothes from him, but then I feel my fingers graze his. His eyes widen, and my mouth drops open as I stare at him.

"I...I'm sorry..." I stutter out, horrified. My heart begins to pound as the other in-charges rise out of their chairs. I can't breathe.

"Did you just touch me?" the in-charge asks, lifting up his hand in his other hand as if it's broken.

"I...I didn't mean--"

"She touched me!" the in-charge roars, holding up his hand to display to the others.

"How dare you!" His eyes darken, and he sneers at me. My knees shake.

"Guard!" he says, turning around. I can't breathe.

A black-clad guard materializes next to the table, standing rigid before me. The in-charge reaches out his hand, and the guard places his plastic stick in it.

"You. Do. Not. Touch. Us!" the in-charge sneers.

"I...I..." I gasp, but I can't find the words. I barely touched him! It was an accident!

The stick hits my shoulder hard. I stumble, catching myself, and then turn and face the in-charge again, shoulder burning. He lifts the stick again, but then something strange happens.

"I think that's enough, Keeper Jones," says the middle in-charge, the short one with the beard. My chest heaves as I turn and look at the bearded in-charge. He looks bored, rolling his eyes at the in-charge wielding the stick.

"Really," the bearded one continues, "isn't it obvious she didn't mean to? Go sanitize your hand and come back."

The angry in-charge, Jones or whatever, scowls at his bearded companion. But, he then thrusts the stick back into the guard's hands and storms off, heading for the tunnel that leads to the Open Area.

I look at the bearded in-charge, unsure what to do.

He looks back at me, then raises his eyebrows and says, "You can go."

Not needing to be told twice, I gather up my clothes, which I'd accidentally dropped on the floor, and hurry past the table, not looking back.

Tears are burning in my eyes, but I don't want to cry. My shoulder burns, but I still don't want to cry. Krin and Aila are at the back of the line, staring. So are most of the other workers.

*Don't cry*, I command myself as I take my place behind Krin, head held high.

"You okay?" Krin asks softly as everyone slowly turns back around, facing the Bath Room. Her eyes look red; I'm suddenly furious, thinking that she was crying because *I* was getting beaten.

"'Course," I shrug, then wince. My shoulder.

"Why did you touch him?" Aila asks, eyes wide. I could punch her. I wish I had a stick to hit *her* shoulder.

"I didn't mean to," I scowl at her.

She purses her lips at me, then turns back around. Krin gives me one more look, then copies Aila.

I take a deep breath quietly, trying to get my heart to stop pounding. All I did was accidentally touch his fingers. He was going to beat me for that. I haven't been hit like that in a while, at least not for a few years, and never for something that stupid.

Pushing it from my mind, I focus on the Bath. The line moves fairly quickly, and I'm ready to get into the water and rinse off as much darkness as I can.

Aila enters the tunnel when a girl comes out, and then a few minutes later, Krin goes in.

I wait for someone to come out so I can go in. We only have ten minutes in the Bath Room and only four in the actual water. Then, back to work.

Finally, a girl comes out, smiling because her skin is back to a pale cream color for the most part. I hurry in.

The tunnel is damp and feels thick but only lasts for maybe twenty feet. Then, I emerge into a low-lit room about thirty feet long.

The room itself is like a long hallway with benches stretched all down it. In the very middle of the room, where a few girls are gathered, is a large hole in the ground called the Chute. The Chute is where we drop our dirty clothes to get washed or burned or whatever. We only keep our cap and our boots each time. Then, on either side of the room are six little stalls, separated by a stone wall about five feet high. Each stall has a shelf cut into the wall, a little stone bench, and then a spout.

I hurry to the Chute and begin undressing. The light in the Bath Room is kind of reddish, giving the stone and the water a rusty glow. I toss my clothes into the big hole and then look up to find Krin and Aila, hugging my new clothes close to my chest.

The two girls are all the way at the end of the room on the right side, and there's an empty stall next to Krin.

The floor is cold against my bare feet, and I take quick steps, trying not to shiver. My skin thrills at the idea of water, but my mind is focused on Krin and Aila. The water and the fact that guards aren't allowed in here should make it so we won't be overheard, but I still don't want to talk, especially to Aila. It's so risky and seems like there won't be any reward.

My shoulder is stinging, reminding me that so much worse could be in store if we're caught reading.

The other girls around us are chatting loudly, all of us feeling free to speak amidst the trickling water and echoey floor and lack of guards. Krin sees me approach out of the corner of her eye and smiles. She then raises her eyebrows and nods toward Aila. Surprised, I frown at her and shake my head. She rolls her eyes and then nods again.

"You okay?" Aila asks, looking at Krin like Krin might suddenly vomit. Krin scowls at me. I sigh.

"Aila, there's something that Krin and I would like to ask you," I say, trying to keep the snarl out of my voice.

Aila looks over at me, arching a lean eyebrow. She has already gotten some coal dust off her face, and up-close without coal and hair in her face, I notice how startling green her eyes are. They are like the leaves in the trees in the workers' field. We see the trees on Sun Days, and when it's warm, the trees have leaves, sometimes green and sometimes yellow. I feel a sudden pang of envy, but I shake it off, furious that I'm getting distracted at something so stupid.

"Yes?" Aila asks, leaning back to wash out her dark brown hair. I try not to notice that Aila's hair has the same softness and wave that Krin's does--*did*--as it tumbles around her shoulders. It seems to shine despite the dirt in it.

I shake my head, annoyed, again, that I got distracted by this stupid girl. I try to begin the words to ask what Krin and I had discussed, but I can't think what to say. Wasn't Krin supposed to ask this? Why is she making me? To buy time, I turn on the water and sigh as the cool liquid spreads across my limbs. I can almost hear my skin sighing, too.

"Yes, Evin?" Aila presses, giving one of her kind smiles. I hate that smile; it was like Aila thinks she's so much smarter than the rest of us. I know Aila really *is* smarter than us, but why does she have to act like it?

I swallow hard before I speak, but then Aila gives a sort of squeak of alarm and nearly shouts, "Krin! What did you do to your hair?"

Krin has taken off her head wrap and is washing out her jaggedly-chopped, shoulder-length hair.

"Shh!" I automatically hush Aila, looking around suspiciously, but the other girls don't seem to be paying attention to us.

Krin, meanwhile, gives a soft smile, stands tall, and replies, "I gave it to Hoss."

"But your hair…" Aila says as if it had been her own hair and not Krin's. Aila even reaches up and gently touches her own hair as if to make sure it is still there.

"I'd do it again," Krin says softly, drenching her short hair in the water.

Aila opens her mouth to say something, but I shoot her a look that makes her flinch. In a second, her smile is back, and she says, "Did you have a question, Evin?"

"Well," I sigh, fighting the scowl, "Krin and I are wondering if…well…maybe you would be willing to, I mean, if you *can*, we were wondering if you could teach us to…read." The last word drops in volume, but I know Aila still heard it. Her eyes widen quite a bit, her mouth hangs open, but then she smiles again.

"Read?" Aila asks. "Why?"

My cheeks flush, and I almost spit. *Why? You don't know why?* but Krin saves me by saying, "Because we want a chance."

Aila's eyes stay focused on Krin for a moment, but then they slide to my face. She looks at me *hard*, but her smile stays plastered on her cheeks.

"Sure," Aila says, almost shrugging slightly like it's nothing. "Why not?"

My eyes bulge, and I want to shout at her about how dangerous this is, but Krin silences me with a look. So, instead of yelling, I turn back to the water, grab the soap, and start scrubbing myself vigorously.

For the next few seconds, we wash in silence. Then, Aila's water trickles out, and she hurries to dress and move on. We're not supposed to linger in the Bathing Room.

Krin turns and beams at me, but then her smile falters. I can see she's staring at my shoulder. Bracing myself, I turn and look at it, washed and ready to be assessed. There's a large red blotch that almost encompasses my whole shoulder, and the skin is split slightly in the very center. There's a thin line of blood trickling down my arm. I look back at her and shrug and then wince. I've got to stop doing that. She keeps looking at me, though, expectantly.

"What?" I ask, almost snapping.

"She agreed!" Krin said.

"Yay," I roll my eyes. The water is getting colder, a signal that my time is running out.

"Thank you," Krin says.

"For what?"

"For agreeing to try."

"You could have tried without me," I say.

"I could," Krin says, her water shutting off. She turns to go but quickly says, "I could, but I wouldn't."

"Why?" I scoff.

"Because if anyone is getting out of here, it'll be you," Krin says, so matter-of-factly that I don't even notice my water shutting off before I can finish getting the soap off.

I'm so furious with Krin that I almost don't notice Coden has stopped to mark a spot. The whole idea of learning to read feels stupider and stupider the further I go into the Tunnels. Reading will not keep us out of the Colosseum. If anything, it just seems like it might get us there faster. And Krin has the *nerve* to tell me that *I* will get out? I scoff and roll my eyes at the black ceiling; ya, I'm really going places.

How can she put that on me? How can she tell me that she believes in *me*? Idiot. I stand, hands on my hips, behind Coden, and try to hide my anger.

What really annoys me is how much time we're going to have to spend with Aila. I don't want to be close to Aila, and I don't want to feel dumber than her. I mean, I already do, but I don't want Aila to have the satisfaction of knowing-

"Evin?" Coden calls softly.

I turn and roll my eyes in frustration when I realize how far Coden made it along the Tunnel without me noticing he had finished marking.

"Sorry," I say as I hurry and search my section of the Tunnel separating me and Coden. I catch up with him, and he just shrugs. I give a slight smile in spite of myself.

Coden must've had his bath earlier, too. His big eyes look up at me from a spotless, pale face. I notice how long his brown, curly hair is getting; the curls bounce around his ears. He looks so small.

Unable to stop myself, I ask, "Why are you here?" I don't even know if I meant to ask the question, but after talking with Aila about birthdays and families, I actually want to know. I want to know what brings so many kids here.

He shrugs and says, "My parents died when I was really little. My sister tried to take care of me, but she never really learned to read, and eventually, people figured it out. They came one day and took her away and brought me here. I don't know what happened to her." He says it so evenly, so quietly, that I can only stare at him.

"What?" he asks, turning to continue.

"I don't know," I reply honestly, turning to accompany him deeper into the dark. We had to run for almost an hour to get down to where we stopped yesterday; I know we won't be in this Tunnel much longer. I expect we will emerge into the Hive any time now. Maybe tomorrow.

We search on in silence, scanning the walls with our lanterns, but my thoughts are not on gold or coal or dirt. I keep wondering what kind of a world waits outside the Mine. Aila described tall buildings, but I'm not sure what those look like. She said it's gray, and I do know what that looks like. I've always imagined an endless blue sky, a bright sun, and just open stretches of cool, green grass. I think in my picture of the world, I forgot that there are other people out there, people who might be worse than in-charges. I mean, if parents leave their children, give them up, can't afford them, and basically condemn them by not teaching them to read, do I really want to be in that world? I've already been given up once…

I wonder how people can be okay with all of it; the thought of parents just not wanting their children makes my cheeks burn. My parents had apparently not wanted me, throwing me into the Mine when I was just three. I can't remember anything about them besides I know that I had parents. Their faces are fuzzy in my memory, but I know they're there, and I think I hate them. Why didn't they want me? Doesn't anyone out there care that parents are deserting their children to suffer in darkness? It makes me think that maybe it's a world full of in-charges, and that's not any different than my world now.

As we continue searching, I can't help but stare at Coden. He is so small. I wonder what sort of life he would have lived if he had been taught to read, if he was still with his sister. Maybe he would have grown to have a family of his own and loved his children enough to save them, enough to give them the gift of reading.

Looking at Coden, watching the little boy hold a light up to a rock wall looking for gold to give to the in-charges, is when I decide. I decide that I don't care if it's pointless. I'm still going to try to learn to read. I'm going to try to prove to my careless parents that I can take care of myself. I'm going to prove to the in-charges and to the Society itself that I'm not worthless. I will learn to read with Aila. I'm going to show them all, even if I can only read one word. Even if I still march to the Colosseum, I'm going to march with that one word on my lips.

The table is empty as I sit down, sliding my tray in front of me. The glob of gray goo looks horribly unappetizing, but I pick up my spoon and begin eating it anyway. It's better than going hungry and trying to sleep with those sharp pangs of hunger in your stomach.

After a few minutes, Duna comes and sits across from me, keeping her eyes down as is usual for her these days. I can remember a forceful and lively Duna, a girl that had bright brown eyes and a comment for everything, but this Duna is different. She's broken. She *let* herself get broken, though. Neither of us speaks to each other, but I notice that she's mostly clean, just a light sheen of coal dust brushing her cheeks. Duna, like quite a few kids down here, is still dark even after Bath Day. Her skin glows creamy brown in the yellow light of the cafeteria, and her black hair is springy and looks soft in its tight curls. I know I have brown hair and brown eyes and that I'm pale and short, but I wonder what other people notice when they look at me, especially today.

"Evening," Hoss says as he slides in on the same side as me. Hoss somehow looks bigger when he's clean, but his shirt seems just as filthy as before. He must've dug through a lot of coal today.

I nod toward him as a response. I don't need to look up to know that Dirk has just clambered in next to Duna.

Without a word, Duna moves in next to Dirk, almost so close that she's leaning on him. They begin speaking quietly to one another. I notice Dirk is eating, but Duna isn't. In fact, Duna looks *skinny*, more so than usual. Dirk puts his arm around Duna, but she doesn't even lift her head to look at her food. She better hurry and eat it; the in-charges don't like us to waste food.

"Where's Krin?" Dirk asks between mouthfuls.

Hoss shrugs but looks around. I roll my eyes. For two people making promises to each other, I figure they'd at least know where the other one is.

Mostly because I'm annoyed, I turn around to look at the entrance. Hoss's shoulders lower as Krin enters, followed closely by Aila. Minutes later, Krin climbs in between me and Hoss, and Aila slides in next to Duna.

"Good, we're all here," Aila says, smiling like normal. I want to punch her already.

"Whoa," Dirk says, looking between Aila and me.

"What?" I almost spit at him.

"She looks kind of like you," Dirk says, giving a confused smile. Dirk's smile crinkles at the edges, and his bright brown eyes look happy and stupid at the same time.

"Right?" Krin smiles, looking almost triumphant. "It's the eyes."

"Her eyes are green," I say evenly, not looking at Aila. "Mine are brown."

"Still," Dirk says, shoveling in more food.

Desperately wanting to not discuss any similarities Aila and I have, and already regretting wondering what people see when they look at me, I turn my attention back to my tray and quickly mumble out, "What do you mean 'we're all here'?" Despite myself, my eyes flick up to Aila's. I crinkle my nose, not finding anything that makes us look alike. She's short like me, sure, but her face seems kind of pointy, and her eyes slant upwards a little. I don't think my eyes do that; I mean, I haven't seen them in a long time, but I'm pretty sure they're big and round. Aila's lips have a weird curve to them, too, like she constantly is grinning. I *know* my lips don't do that. Again, I feel a rush of anger at this girl.

"I mean, everyone who wanted to learn to read," Aila smiles slightly.

"*All* of us?" I ask. My stomach twists with nerves; the more who learn to read, the more likely it is that we will be caught and Departed immediately. I thought it was going to just be Krin and me. But I should've seen this coming. Krin wouldn't do it without Hoss, and Hoss undoubtedly told Dirk, and Dirk told Duna. I let out a small groan.

"You don't want me to read?" Dirk raises an eyebrow, but I can see the smile pulling up the corners of his mouth.

I roll my eyes, "No, I just don't want to get caught."

"We're going to be very careful," Aila gives me what I assume is a reassuring smile, and I have a sudden urge to spit in her face.

"So, what's the plan?" Krin asks, her voice full of hope.

"We have very few moments when we're all together," Aila says, glancing around at the other workers and at the guards lined along the walls. "We can learn at meals, in the barracks, and on Sun Days. So, I figured I would teach you letters first, then move on words. Once you know letters, I can give you words to practice on your own."

"How are you going to give us words?" I ask, my tone harsh without necessarily meaning for it to be.

"We...uh...well, we're going to have to collect paper," Aila replies softly, eyes flitting around, making sure no one is listening. If she was offended by my tone, she doesn't show it.

"How are we supposed to do that?" Hoss asks. I just scowl; paper down here is very rare.

The in-charges have some on their clipboards, but that is all I've ever seen.

"Well..." Aila gives a sheepish smile. She reaches down the neck of her shirt and pulls out something that makes my jaw drop: a small sheet of paper. It has some words scribbled on it already, is crumbled and a weird brown color, but still. I've never even touched paper, and yet Aila somehow has some stowed down her shirt.

"Where did you get that?" Hoss asks, similarly amazed.

"One of the in-charges kind of threw their clipboard at me while she got after two small kids who were working too slow," Aila replies quietly. "I guess she needed both of her hands to...talk...to those kids. So I figured I would lighten her load and take a piece of paper." She gives a small smile, but I think I see a flash of fear in her eyes.

*Good,* I think. *Let her learn to fear this place.*

"You better not let them catch you with that," I warn.

"Yes, because I've been waving it around in everyone's faces," Aila scowls, finally showing some annoyance at my comments. I smirk in satisfaction as she hides the paper back down her shirt. I'm glad I finally got something out of her besides a smile.

"Anyway," Krin says, giving me a warning stare, "how are you going to teach us letters? Don't you need something to write with?"

"Yes," Aila says, "that's the next issue. We need a pen or pencil, but I'm not sure how to get one away from the in-charges without them noticing. Pieces of paper here and there are one thing, but they'll be sure to notice if their pen goes missing. Pens are pretty valuable, even outside of here."

"Do we know anyone who works in the offices?" Dirk asks. "Maybe one of the cleaning kids? They might be able to snag one?"

"But then we'd have to let them in on the plan," Hoss says quickly.

"I'm not talking to those kids," I snort, thinking how their cheeks don't sink into their face and that we can all see the actual color of their skin.

"I agree. The smaller the group, the better," Aila nods her head.

Everyone slips into thoughtful silence as we try and come up with a way to get a pen. Out of everything, I don't want this not to work because we can't find a *pen*. Surprisingly, it's Duna who keeps the plan going.

"We don't need a pen," she says softly, looking up from her tray for the first time.

We all look at the somber girl. Her black curls are sticking out from underneath her worker's cap, and her large brown eyes still look watery, but there is steel in them that I haven't seen for weeks.

"We don't?" Dirk asks, raising an eyebrow at Duna.

"No," Duna gives the ghost of a smile. "Look." She rubs a finger on her coal-smudged shirt. Then, she reaches out her slender arm and draws her finger across the tabletop. An excited smile spreads across all of our faces as we watch the black streak form across the gray table.

"Duna," Aila whispers, smiling at the girl. "Brilliant!"

Duna begins to frown, but Aila quickly says, "It means very smart." Aila reaches across the table and gives Duna's hand a gentle squeeze.

"It'll be better if we have a piece of it, instead of using what's on us," Duna shrugs, "but at least we won't get in trouble for stealing a pen. We're basically walking pens." She gives a small laugh, but then the smile drops from her face like it was ashamed to be there. Her eyes flick back to her tray, and she looks deep in thought.

I hold back my eye roll. I'm glad she spoke--that's the most she's said in weeks--but she's still so sad. She needs to let it go. She needs to let *him* go.

"I can get us a piece," Hoss says. Everyone nods; he is a digger, so picking up a stray piece of coal shouldn't be a problem for him. I mean, he picked up that clear stone without getting caught, so coal can't be much harder, right?

"Good," Aila says, "then we can start tomorrow."

Everyone around the table nods, and then we quickly turn to our food. We've been talking too long; it's a wonder guards didn't come over. I notice Krin quickly slides her food to Hoss again, but I don't think much of it. If she doesn't want to eat, that's not my problem.

My mind is racing, though, making it hard to eat. Suddenly, it feels very real and very terrifying. I can almost feel the hope radiating around us, and I want to run away from it. I can see the light in Krin's eyes, and it makes it hard to breathe. I want to do this; I *need* to do this to prove all the in-charges and all the parents wrong. But what happens if it goes wrong? What happens if nothing comes of it? What happens if we're all Departed tomorrow?

Despite all those thoughts, there is a spark of warmth in my chest, too. I can't help but hope that I will feel sunshine on my shoulders without facing the inside of a fence, that I will be able to walk without having to be in line. I take a quick, shuddering breath, trying not to let the others hear. We're going to learn, I tell myself, we're going to learn because we have to try. If we don't try, then the in-charges win. I don't want them to win anymore.

# Chapter Five

"Say it again," Aila whispers as we hurry down the hallway.

I sigh, frustrated, desperately wanting to punch the smile off her face, but I whisper, "A...B...C...uh..."

Our heads are low together. I can see Aila smile, almost in pity, then say, "Think about it."

Then she turns her head towards Krin, who is walking on the other side of her. "Now you."

I faintly hear Krin whisper, "A, B, C, D." *D*! Ugh! Stupid letter.

Jealousy burns on my cheeks; Krin is confident with the first four letters of what Aila calls the alphabet. We have been learning them the past few days. Apparently, the letters are in a stupid order that you have to keep straight. Why do they have to be in an order? Aila taught us the sound and shape of those four letters, and we've been practicing reading and writing them. She had passed around a small paper that had tiny, delicate lines drawn with the sharp coal rock Hoss had stolen.

The letters confuse me. Each one is different, and I don't understand how writing lines in different ways forms sound. The others are much more confident, except for Dirk maybe, and I have to hide my embarrassment as much as I can. Aila says it's fine, that reading is hard, but what does she know? She can already read!

Aila quizzes Krin again. Out of the corner of my eyes, I see Krin's lips form a smile as she repeats the letters with ease.

"Good, Krin!" Aila whispers, smiling back.

She turns back to me. We don't have much longer to walk down the tunnel, so I try to hurry.

"A...B...D...C," I scowl, trying to remember how Krin said them.

"Close," Aila smiles. "A, B, *C*, *D*. You mixed up the last two."

"Did I?" I whisper under my breath, rolling my eyes.

"What?" Aila asks.

"I asked how many letters are there?" I quickly say, rubbing a hand across my face.

"Twenty-six."

I groan, but Aila quickly rearranges her face into a reassuring smile. "You'll get it," she adds softly, but I see a look of...impatience? cross her face.

Krin told me to be nice to Aila, but she wouldn't believe me when I told her that I don't think Aila is as nice as she lets on.

"That's because you're mean to her," Krin had said, rolling her eyes. "She's perfectly nice to me and the others. Just stop scowling and rolling your eyes at her, and it'll be fine."

"Krin, don't you think her story is weird? Her parents just dump her here after years of caring about her?" I had asked, almost pleading with her to believe me.

"No," Krin had shrugged. "Lots of kids end up here like that."

"But she can read!"

"And she's going to help us. Just try to be nice to her, Evin. She's helping us."

The conversation rings in my ears as we walk, making me want to hurry away from Krin and Aila and all of them.

We reach the end of the tunnel and part ways; Dirk and Hoss head to the right while we all go left. Once inside the girl's barracks, we split again. Aila and Duna don't sleep in the same barrack section as Krin and me, so they head off to the right while we head straight toward our bunks. We had talked about continuing reading in the barracks, but Aila was worried about how many of the other works would notice.

"We could do it after everyone falls asleep," Dirk had suggested. "The guards won't see. They're not allowed in the barracks."

"No," Aila had replied, shaking her head fiercely. "The last thing we need is someone seeing us out of bed and learning to read. We're safer in the cafeteria." I wanted to point out that we aren't really safe anywhere, but I had kept my mouth shut.

Krin says nothing as we walk to our beds, which is somewhat odd of her. Now that I was thinking about it, Krin had seemed...*off*, lately. She was quieter, especially to me. I have a sinking feeling in my stomach that Aila might have something to do with that. Maybe Krin is thinking that Aila is better to talk to. Maybe I should start responding more to Krin.

I peer over at Krin; her face seems paler, but it's hard to tell in the dim light and under all the coal dirt coating her skin. Her cheeks seem a little more sunken, but she's always been skinny. Maybe her clothes are looser? Her shirt seems much baggier now that I am looking at it, and it hangs down further. Maybe she had just been given a bigger one during Bath Day.

I'm tempted to shrug it off, but my stomach clenches and the words are out before I can stop them. "Krin, are you okay?"

The tall girl turns to look at me but then stops, panic suddenly in her eyes. "I have to go," she says and then turns and runs back toward the entrance of the tunnel.

I stare after her in wonder but then sigh. Maybe Krin had forgotten to tell Hoss just how much she loves him and needs to go find him. The guards don't keep the girls and boys from going into each other's barracks. But then I feel my cheeks rush with heat when I think that maybe Krin ran off to go talk to Aila.

I tell myself that it doesn't matter, that I don't care. Krin and I have stuck together because it was easy to; we sleep next to each other, so it was almost convenient to eat and walk with her.

It doesn't matter if she ran off to talk to Aila; that's fine. At least she won't be bugging me all night.

That's what I tell myself, anyway.

I push those thoughts away and climb into bed. A sigh of relief escapes me. Excitement prickles through me, a feeling that even not being able to repeat letters correctly can wipe away.

At dinner, two in-charges had come in with an announcement.

"Attention," the taller of the two had shouted. He looked like one of the in-charges who inspected our bunks.

The cafeteria had quieted down immediately, and all eyes turned to fix on the two men who help control all our lives.

"Tomorrow will be this month's Sun Day," the short one had said evenly.

The very air in the cafeteria had seemed to lighten, and my chest had felt not so tight. Sun Days are even better than Bath Days. On Sun Days, we get to go outside.

The workers murmured excitedly, much to the obvious displeasure of the in-charges. They seemed angry at the little whispers.

Aila looked confused the whole time, making me want to laugh. "It means we get to go outside tomorrow," I explained to her.

"I know," Aila said quietly, looking around at the excitement. "But why is everyone suddenly so excited? It's only for a few hours, right?"

That had infuriated me, making my cheeks burn in frustration. This girl just didn't *know*.

Aila. Why does Krin like her so much? Thinking of Aila makes my mind wander to those stupid four letters. I imagine how they form, the delicate lines scratching the paper to form A, B, C, D. I wonder what my letters will look like. Aila said we'd all need to learn writing. Hers is so neat, though, so straight and even. Mine will probably just look stupid. Maybe if my parents had given me birthdays, then I could write letters, too. Jealousy burns inside me.

Krin doesn't return for at least ten more minutes, and when she does, she seems shaky and lost in thought. I hear her approach and open one eye to see the tall girl reach a trembling hand up to her bunk and climb the ladder to her bed.

Once I hear her settle with a sigh onto her mattress, I open my eyes and fully look at her. Krin sees me looking at her but then turns her head, so she's looking at the looming ceiling above us. Then, she rolls to be on her side, her back to me. She rolls weird, though, slowly, like she's in pain or trying not to squish something delicate underneath her. She settles softly and then sighs.

"It's nothing," she says softly, so softly the girls below us won't hear. "I'm just tired and...tired." She sighs at the end, rubbing her eyes with her hands.

I wait, not saying anything, just looking at her. I expect her to say more. She never rolls to face me, though, or says anything else. I roll my eyes and turn over, so my back is facing Krin, then close my eyes and try for sleep. If Krin doesn't want to talk, then that's her problem. I won't complain; I never want to talk anyway. She can go talk to Aila for all I care.

Sleep, for me, is always hard-in-coming; I have to take deep breaths and push all thoughts from my mind, which is proving extremely difficult at the moment. My mind races with reading, the upcoming Sun Day, Krin's odd behavior, and *Aila*. I sneer at just the thought of her. I don't know why, but I just don't like her. It almost feels like I *can't* like her.

Readjusting my pillow brings my eyes to the ceiling, which is an immediate mistake. My heart starts hammering, and the air feels stuffier. I have to shut my eyes and will myself to believe that the rock ceiling is not right above me. I know I need to roll onto my stomach, but for some reason, I can't.

*It's fine*, I tell myself. *It's not going to collapse. You're fine.*

"Evin," Krin says softly, "deep breaths."

I take several deep breaths, keeping my eyes shut tightly.

Eventually, the frantic pumping of my heart slows, and I'm able to breathe normally, but I refuse to open my eyes.

"Deep breaths," Krin says again, and I follow her instruction, albeit somewhat angrily. My breathing begins to slow, and I feel myself sinking into my bed.

The inside of my eyelids dance with images of Aila's smiling face, and everyone else's faces lighting up as they read and say letters. I can almost picture tomorrow, sitting underneath the scraggly tree at the very end of the field where we had agreed to meet, watching Aila draw letters and hearing her sound them out for us. Everyone is so happy and laughing in the sunlight.

Suddenly, Aila looks up at me and says, "Evin, I'm sorry, you're just too stupid. No wonder your parents didn't want you."

"Ha!" Krin's laugh rings out.

"I don't think you should learn anymore," Aila says with a sharp smile, but her eyes are cold. "I don't want to waste my time."

"I can learn!" I scream at her.

"Ha!" everyone around us laughs. I feel panicky.

"Read this," Aila smiles smugly. She draws some letters in the dirt and backs away.

I look at them, but I can't understand what it says. I think the first letter is a "D," but I'm not sure about the other four.

My throat closes, and I feel like I'm choking.

"See?" Aila grins an evil glint in her eye now. "You can't even read what you are. 'Dirt.'

Idiot. You will never be fit for Society."

Aila is suddenly standing next to Head Reader Kevoc.

"Through the door," Kevoc says, his wrinkled hand lifting from his side to point at the Departure door.

"No!" I scream. "I'm not stupid! I can learn! NO!" I fall to my knees, shaking terribly; I can hear the guards storming up to the platform.

Their storming feet ring and echo all around, and there are whispers filling the room.

"Evin?" I hear Krin's voice through all the whispers. I turn and see her standing on the platform, too. She reaches out to me, but I'm furious that she laughed at me, so I push her arm away.

"Evin!" she yells a little louder.

I feel her grab my arm now, and I sit up quickly, panting. I almost bump my head on the ceiling in my haste.

"What?" I ask, looking around frantically for Kevoc and the guards. But I'm in the barracks. I'm in bed. I heave a sigh, but I can still hear the stomping guards.

"What's happening?" I ask groggily, looking toward Krin. Her eyes are wide and worried, but she shakes her head.

"I don't know," she says. "I just got back from the toilet and heard them."

The dim glow in the barracks offers just enough light for me to see that all the other girls are sitting up and looking to the tunnel that leads out of the barracks. Suddenly, people start emerging into the barracks. From this far away, they all seem to be guards.

A pit of fear forms in my stomach, and ice creeps through my limbs. I look over to see Krin, frozen in her bed, fingers clutching her blanket so hard her knuckles are white and her face a still sheet of terror as the footsteps grow closer. I watch her, quickly but shakily, reach under her thin mattress, grab something, and then stuff it quickly under the wrap holding her chopped hair. I know it's the tiny, clear stone. My throat suddenly feels tight as the guards march closer.

I want her to throw it and throw it now, but I can't find my voice. What if they hear me?

The stone has to be why they're here. Why else would they come in the middle of the night? Why else would there be so many guards? Someone found out about it, and now Hoss and Krin are both doomed.

Finally, I swallow and manage to whisper out, "Throw it, Krin."

She looks at me, her chest rising and falling rapidly, but she shakes her head defiantly.

The guards have turned down our row. We have seconds.

"Throw it!" I hiss.

"No!" she says through gritted teeth, but I see a tear in the corner of her eye.

I want to scream at her, hit her, throw things, but the guards are almost here. Why is she being so stupid?!

"Give it to me," I whisper frantically.

She begins to open her mouth, but I scowl and say as quietly as I can, "I'm not going to throw it! Give it to me!"

They were almost to us! I reach out my hand, my heart pounding.

With tears now falling, Krin reaches up, yanks it out from under her headscarf, and shoves the stone into my outstretched hand. I copy her and hastily put the stone in my hair and slam my worker's cap on. I can feel the tiny stone pressing painfully and heavily into my scalp, almost like it weighs 100 pounds and is made of sharp corners.

Just as I lower my hands from my head, the guards stop in front of our bunks. I feel cold and sweaty and try to hide my shaking hands in my blanket.

The black-clad guards part, and three in-charges push to the front of them. My heart drops as I see who the in-charges are. Jinade and Head Reader Kevoc are right below my bunk, next to an in-charge holding a clipboard and looking excited. Jinade looks like she did at the Arrival: gray, clean, and cold. Kevoc looks as ancient as ever. Up this close, though, Jinade looks older, lines crinkling the skin around her eyes. Her gray hair is pulled into a tight bun, no hair standing up or out of place.

I can barely breathe. The guards fan out from behind the in-charges to form a solid line in between the two rows of the barracks.

Kevoc is clutching that rolled-up piece of paper in his hands.

Chancing a glance at Krin, I peer over to see that Krin looks like she needs to vomit.

"According to law," Lady Jinade says, chin up and eyes steely, "we must clear the Mines routinely, instead of once a year. Therefore, we have come to collect-" she looks over at the clipboard the nameless in-charge is holding- "numbers 8478 and 8497 for Departure or entrance into Society."

A gasp escapes me before I can stop it; it's not us, but it's starting. The random Departures are starting. It's been maybe three weeks since the Arrival. I almost forgot about these Departures. For a moment, I wish I knew when my birthday is, like Aila; that way, I'd know when my

Departure was coming. They didn't call my number this time, but what if it was the next time? What if it's tomorrow?

There is rustling beneath me. I watch as two figures rise, one that sleeps beneath me and one that sleeps diagonally down from Krin. Both girls walk slowly towards Jinade and the Head Reader. I recognize them as Affa and Lorna, both sorters. They're visibly shaking.

The Head Reader lifts his wrinkled head as the two girls approach. I don't really know either of the girls, but Affa, poor Affa, has always had a bad cough that she has to hide. No one really notices it anymore, but she has to try and not cough in front of the guards or in-charges. It is an unspoken rule that if Affa's cheeks are puffed out and her eyes look strained, you have to make some sort of noise so she can cough without being noticed. I once dropped my tray of food in the cafeteria because her cheeks had been puffed out and her whole body trembling. The in-charges wanted workers, but sick workers are of no use to them. The guards would have dragged her straight through the Departure doors. It's funny, Jinade made it seem like suddenly we can be Departed at any time, but people have been Departed like that forever. Sure, it has never been in the middle of the night before, and a worker would've had to have dropped something or made an in-charge mad or stole something, but Departure has always been hanging over us like a massive rock about to crush us into the dirt.

Now that I can see Affa, I can see how her face is strained, and her hands are shaking. She has to cough. I suddenly have an urge to pretend to fall out of bed, but that wouldn't help; they'd probably just take me, too.

The Head Reader unfurls the rolled-up paper and holds it out to Affa.

"Read this," he says in his old, gravelly voice.

Affa opens her mouth, but before she can say anything, she begins coughing, horrible, deep coughs that shake her whole body. I cringe with each cough and then groan when I see the pitiless smile cross Jinade's face as she watches Affa hack.

"Sorry," Affa whimpers, but the coughs keep coming. She puts a hand on her chest and starts wheezing. The coughs now sound like grating rocks.

"It would seem this one is unfit to work," Jinade says evenly. "Someone unfit to work is unfit for Society. Guards." She flicks her hand at Affa, and two guards hurry forward to grab the girl's arms. Sobs emerge between the coughs.

The Head Reader turns his attention to Lorna, who is wringing her hands in panic, her gaze flying between the guards and Jinade and Kevoc.

"Wait," she says, holding up her hands as Kevoc holds up the paper. "Wait. There's been some mistake. I'm not eighteen. I'm only seventeen!" She adds this last with a breathy smile.

The entire barrack is silent except for Aila's coughs. I can see heads poking out from every bunk.

Jinade clasps her hands and gives Lorna a horrible, cold smile. "We don't make mistakes," Jinade says slowly, evenly. "And if someone thinks that their government makes mistakes, then that someone is unfit for Society. Guards." I see true cruelty, and possibly hatred, in Jinade's eyes as she watches two guards come forward and grab a now screaming Lorna.

"No!" Lorna screams. "I...I was just explaining! I'm not eighteen!"

The guards begin to haul her down the row.

"You didn't give me a chance to read!" Lorna sobs. "I have to have a chance! I'm not eighteen! I have one more year!"

She continues screaming, and Affa continues coughing as the guards and the in-charges march away, leaving only echoes of screams and marching footsteps behind. It all had only taken about five minutes.

Silence comes back to the barracks, quickly followed by frantic whispers and murmurs.

I realize that I'm holding fistfuls of blankets in my hands. I release the blanket, as well as my pent-up breath. Then I turn to Krin.

She's visibly shaking, sitting on her knees and leaning forward on her elbows. Her face is in her hands, and she's quietly sobbing.

"Krin?" I whisper. I reach out a hand to comfort her but then think better of it and pull it away before Krin sees.

I wait for a moment, a little confused at Krin's reaction before I remember that I have her stone. I reach up and yank the stone from my tangled mess of hair.

"Here," I say, reaching over and shoving Krin's side. Krin looks up, eyes wet with tears, sees the stone, and grabs it, a look of relief spreading across her face. She nods at me and then replaces the stone under her mattress.

"You didn't have to do that," Krin says, still propped on her knees with her face on her pillow.

I shrug, but I glare at her. She looks back, and I raise an eyebrow.

"What's wrong?" I don't mean it to sound as mean as it does.

"I thought...well...I thought..." Krin sniffs and buries her face in her pillow.

"I told you," I hiss out. "I told you to get rid of it."

She shoots me a scowl, then turns back into her pillow.

"You going to tell on me?" she grumbles, finally rolling onto her side and off her knees.

I roll my eyes, "No, but--"

"Then why do you care?" she says, eyes red but shining with something beyond tears.

I throw my hands up and say, "I don't! I just don't see why that stone is more important than your life!"

"It's not the stone," Krin whispers, her lips barely moving. "It's what it means."

"Ohh!" I roll my eyes. "That's even stupider. You could have gotten us in trouble!"

"You didn't have to take it!" Krin hisses back.

I open my mouth, but nothing comes out. She has a point. But still, I *had* to. Right? Instead of telling her that, I scowl at her and lay down hard, hitting my head on the hard bunk when I miss my pillow. I hiss in pain and roll over to face away from Krin.

"You didn't have to take it," Krin says again, but softer. "Thank you."

I shrug, not rolling over.

"We knew them, Evin," Krin whispers. "We *knew* them."

"No, we didn't," I say, unable to stop myself. "They just slept under us."

"I knew them," Krin says. "They were sorters."

"They told us this was going to happen," I say, trying to soften my voice. "They told us at the Arrival--"

"That doesn't make it any better!" Krin says, exasperation clear in her voice. "Knowing it's happening doesn't make it easier! They took them from their *beds*, Evin! Their *beds*!"

I roll back over, looking at her. Her eyes are swimming with tears again.

"And we knew Nolan and Mayla, and they had to march away in front of all of us. How is it any different?"

114

"How can you be so dumb!" Krin's chin begins to shake. "How can you just not care?"

"Because I don't want to sit and cry every time someone gets taken," I reply angrily. "I'm not going to cry about people when the only thing I knew about them was their name."

"What if it had been me or Duna?" Krin asks. "What then?"

"I told you it was stupid to care down here," I scowl. "I told you not to like people."

"So you don't like me?" Krin asks, steel in her eyes.

I just shrug. I really don't know.

"Then why did you take the stone, Evin?" Krin asks, her voice full of accusation. "Why risk it instead of just letting me get in trouble?"

I open my mouth, but again, no words come out. I don't know.

"That's different," I finally say.

"How?" Krin asks, her face smug.

"They wouldn't have searched me if they didn't find it on you," I spit back. "I would have been fine."

"You sure? It's still a risk."

"Not a very big one."

"You're right. A *huge* one."

A smile seems to be playing at Krin's lips.

"What?" I ask, folding my arms. "What's so funny? One minute you're sad, then you're yelling at me, and now you're laughing. What?"

"You," Krin shakes her head, then reaches up to readjust her hair wrap. "You yell at all of us to 'not care,' 'don't care,' but I think you care most of all."

"I don't care," I growl.

"Sure, Evin," Krin chuckles softly, wiping tears off her face. "Sure."

Krin rolls over so I'm looking at her back.

115

Too mad to say anything else, I roll over, too, Krin's words burning in my mind. I don't care about anyone; I decided that a long time ago. I had taken the stone because the in-charges wouldn't have searched me, but if Krin wants to make fun of me about it, fine, I will just let her take *all* the risk next time. I won't help her next time the in-charges come.

An image of Krin being led away to the Departure door flashes across my mind and my stomach tightens. I roll my eyes and then close them tight, willing sleep to come back. I don't know what time it is, only that we've lost precious sleep with all this, and now I am going to have to calm myself back down.

The chatter around the barracks eventually dies down, everyone settling into what little sleep we have left. Me, however, I keep seeing guards marching in and dragging us away. I grip my blanket a little tighter and force my mind to clear.


Morning arrives too early, and even the knowledge that it's a Sun Day can't make me wake up faster. I feel like my eyelids weigh as much as boulders. I groan as the worker bell sounds through barracks and the girls begin shuffling around, everyone trying to wake up enough to get to work.

I try to force myself up quickly, though; there's always a long line for the toilet, and I need to go this morning.

Glancing over, I see Krin is gone already. She probably snuck over to Hoss in the middle of the night, which isn't unusual. I hurry down to the ground and then walk as quickly as possible to the small room just inside our barracks, next to the opening of the tunnel, where the toilet is. Most days, I can wait until after eating, just before going down to the tunnels, but today it's urgent.

116

There are only about three girls in line, so I hop in behind them. I stand in the back of the line and hop a little from foot to foot to distract myself. Finally, thankfully, I'm next. I smile in relief when the door opens, but then a tall figure rushes past me and slams the door behind themselves, shutting me out.

"Hey!" I shout, pounding on the wooden door with my fist, but then I hear retching sounds from inside. *Great,* I sigh. *Someone's sick.*

A few moments later, the door opens, and I take a step back in confusion. It's Krin.

"Krin?" I ask. "You sick?"

Being sick here is terrible; you have to hide it from the in-charges and guards. People are pretty good to help, like with Affa, but no one can do anything if you vomit all over a cafeteria table.

Krin's forehead looks sweaty, and she's shaking slightly. She steps out of the toilet and says, "Sorry, Evin, I didn't want to make a mess on the floor."

"Don't let the in-charges see," I scoff, and then I walk into the little room.

*Great,* I think. *Now it smells like vomit in here.*

The tiny, dark room is lit by a single lightbulb that flickers ominously from the ceiling, dangling on a long, skinny string. The walls are dark stone, cold to the touch. The only thing in this room besides the lightbulb is a hole in the middle of the floor. You kind of have to squat over it. The hole is deep, deep enough that no one knows how long it goes on or where it leads to. I don't really care. All anyone cares about when they're in here is how fast you can get out; it stinks in here, even without the vomit smell.

I quickly finish and then leave the room to find a long line waiting to get in. Turning, I go into the tunnel heading to the Open Area.

There are lots of girls heading through the tunnel, and I can hear the occasional whisper about what happened last night. I roll my eyes and walk faster. We eventually merge with the boys' tunnel, and they all seem deep in conversation as well. Why is everyone talking so much all of a sudden?

Finally, I emerge from the tunnel and into the Open Area. Everyone is heading steadily towards the tunnel that leads to the cafeteria, but for some reason, I stop in the middle of the big space. I take a deep breath and throw my head back to let it out, feeling the air hiss through my teeth.

Looking up, I see the empty space hanging above me, going up and up and up for who knows how far. Then, my eyes tilt to the Overhang.

There are in-charges up there, their gray uniforms standing out from the dark stone behind them. They are chatting amongst themselves, even occasionally laughing, gesturing down at us. I suddenly feel like throwing a rock at them.

But then I see her. *Jinade.*

She's standing in a group of four or five in-charges, but she's not talking to any of them. She's staring down into the Open Area. No. She's staring at *me*. I can't explain how I know--she's far enough away that the only way I know it's her is because of the gray bun at the base of her neck and the overwhelming look of *clean*-ness about her--but I know her steely gray eyes are focused on me.

My breathing quickens, but I feel rooted to the spot. The other workers slide around me, no one really noticing that I've stopped, but I can't move. My hands feel cold, I want to hurry away from her stare, but I can't. I can't get my legs to move! Finally, one of the in-charges says something to her, and Jinade turns her attention to them.

I take a deep breath and force my eyes away, force my legs to move. I feel kind of shaky, and I can't explain it. I hope I'm never close enough to feel the cold ice of her stare right in front of my face.

The cafeteria is buzzing with conversation and the sounds of eating when I get in line to get my tray. We all tend to talk a little more on Sun Days, but this feels ridiculous. The workers are talking a lot and loud enough that I worry we might get in trouble.

The line moves fairly quickly, and then I head over to our usual table in the far corner. I sit down, everyone here except for Krin and, well, Aila. I briefly wonder if they're together, the thought kind of annoying to me, but then I notice everyone else around the table has stopped talking and is looking at me.

"What?" I ask, picking up my fork.

Hoss leans toward me and whispers, "The in-charges came to the barracks last night. They took three boys."

I nod and say, "That happened in ours. Two girls were taken."

"So they're actually doing it," Dirk shakes his head, almost sadly.

"We knew they would," I shrug, shoveling gray sludge into my mouth.

"But now they are," he whispers, staring at his food.

"We need to hurry," Duna says. "We need to be able to read."

"We're working on it," Hoss grumbles. "It's hard, and we don't have much time together."

"We need to work harder," Duna glares at him, her words harsh. Hoss stares at her, clearly confused, and then her expression clears, and she goes back to eating. I sigh, annoyed at this new Duna. She's snippy and angry and sad and annoying. And stupid. She used to be funny.

"Where's Aila and Krin?" I ask, wanting to break the awkward tension. I look around. I still don't like that our only hope rests on the shoulders of that stupid, know-it-all, little-

"Hey," Krin sighs, sinking onto the bench between me and Hoss. She sets her tray down but looks at it like it might crawl towards her. Aila is right behind her, and she plops down next to Duna, across from me. She smiles at me; I scowl but make sure only my food can see it.

"Why aren't you eating?" Hoss asks, looking at her with frantic eyes.

"I'm not feeling well," Krin replies, leaning against Hoss's shoulder. I have to admit, Krin does not look good. I'm starting to worry she might seriously be sick, not just kind of sick like most of us get at some point down here. Her clothes look baggy like they're starting to drown her, and her cheeks are sunken. The cafeteria lights are brighter than the barracks, and they emphasize the circles under her eyes.

"Krin, you need to eat," Hoss says softly. Krin takes one look at the food on Hoss's plate and turns quickly away, a hand covering her mouth.

"Well, at least it's not a full day's work," Aila says with a bright smile. "It's a Sun Day, right? They said we just have to do a bit of cleaning?"

"Yes," I try to keep the sneer out of my voice.

"So, how long do we work?" Aila asks.

"Two hours," Hoss replies. "Everyone cleans for two hours, and then we get to go out."

"How wonderful," Aila smiles. I roll my eyes. Wasn't she just saying last night that she didn't think it was that big of a deal?

"Aila," Duna says quietly, looking up from her food, "we need to read faster. Five people were taken last night that we know of, and most of us are at least seventeen. We need to go faster." There was desperation in Duna's voice.

Aila thinks for a minute and then asks, "How much time do we get outside?"

"About four hours," Hoss answers.

"Are we watched very closely?"

"Not really," Dirk shrugs. "We're kind of released into this open space, but it's fenced in, so we can't escape. The guards watch from a balcony above the Field."

"Okay," Aila says, "that'll work fine. We will get through the rest of the alphabet today. It'll be tough to go so fast, but I agree with Duna. We need to go faster."

"The rest?" I scoff. "How many letters did you say there are?"

"Twenty-six," Aila smiles at me.

I choke on my food slightly, then wipe my chin with the back of my hand. "Twenty-six?"

I ask, trying not to shout. "It took us days just to learn four!"

"Well," Duna smirks, "it took *you* days just to learn four."

I turn my head slowly to look at her, to see her sneering face. "What is that supposed to mean?" I ask her, my hands beginning to form fists.

"Hey, those four letters are hard!" Dirk says, smiling but looking quickly from me to Duna.

"They're not hard for all of us," Duna kind of snorts and turns back to her food. My vision turns red, and my cheeks burn; what, exactly, did Duna mean?

"We'll all do our best," Aila says reassuringly, reaching across the table to give my hand a slight pat. I yank my hand back, forcing myself not to growl at her. She looks surprised but continues to say, "It's going to be fine. We will see how it goes today and then decide where to go from there."

Everyone seems happy with this and goes back to eating, except Krin, who slides her tray to Hoss.

I'm furious; when did Duna become so...mean? My dream rushes back to me; they *do* all think I'm stupid. Well, fine. I'm still going to learn to read, and I will just have to try harder, harder than all of them. I'm nervous, though, and I feel the urge to cry pressing heavily on my eyes. I hold the tears in, though, determined not to be stupid *and* weak. I'll show them. I'll show Aila and Duna and the in-charges and the parents and everyone. I'm not stupid.

I'm soaked from my knees down. I have just mopped underneath all the bunks on my row by hand, the gray stone floor now gleaming gray in the light.

Whenever we have to clean, and the in-charges have to be in here for a longer time, the lights get brighter. There are lights in the ceiling that are only turned on for these occasions, and the string lights seem much brighter than normal so we can actually see what we're cleaning and the in-charges can inspect us properly.

The light makes me think it should be warmer in this cold, stone room, but it's still chilly. I hope it's warm outside; I'm shivering. The last Sun Day was pretty warm, but windy, and there are normally about seven really nice Sun Days in a row before we stop having them for a while. The in-charges tell us that it's too cold outside, that we'll freeze. I don't believe them; I just think they don't like us getting outside too much. Makes us too happy, too...hopeful.

Krin is leaning against a bunk, her head against the top bed. She is supposed to be helping me, but I do not want to have to mop under the beds *and* clean up Krin's vomit if she throws up again. I just move the tall girl from bunk to bunk as I mop, letting her lean and look like she is helping. I just hope no one looks too closely. Krin herself isn't talking, just breathing deeply, eyes focused on the ground as I work. She really does look terrible. I rack my brain and try to remember when she started acting like this, started being sick. I can't remember. I don't really care, but I realize how little attention I actually give Krin.

The barrack is a hive of activity as all the girls try to work as quickly as possible so we can get outside. I'm just thankful I wasn't assigned to clean the toilet and that Krin wasn't either. I've had to do it once before. You have to wipe down the whole room with a strong-smelling liquid and down the hole as far as you can reach. The in-charges even give you long sticks to wipe further down the hole. Whoever cleans it stinks for days afterward.

But Krin and I, since we were standing next to each other in line, got assigned together and assigned to mopping under the beds. Not a bad job, really. And, Aila got assigned to cleaning the Bath Room, so it's nice not to have to see her face while I'm trying to make it look like Krin is being helpful.

"Finished," I sigh, rising to stand next to Krin. Krin's eyes seem glassy, and her hands are kind of shaking, and she stands like she's hugging herself.

"Krin," I whisper, "what is going on?"

"I'm sick," Krin replies feebly, still staring at the ground.

"I can see that," I try not to roll my eyes. "But besides that. You've been...odd lately."

Hurt flashes across Krin's face, momentarily making me regret my words, but Krin says,

"Well, it shouldn't worry you since you don't care."

With that, Krin storms away, going to report to the in-charges who are overseeing the cleaning of the barracks. I roll my eyes but follow her. I don't think I'm wrong, though.

Normally, Krin is quite happy and friendly, albeit quiet. Well, quiet around everyone else. Lately, she's been constantly sad, tired, and almost always crying or on the verge of tears. And now she's sick.

I shrug; she's right, I don't care. I get in line behind Krin to check in with the in-charges.

"Number?" the in-charge sitting behind the desk at the opening of the tunnel asks. The desk itself is covered in sheets of paper with numbers and assignments detailed in neat rows of ink. I jealously wonder if I might be able to read any of them. I squint my eyes and tilt my head, lost in the idea of trying, but then the in-charge clears his throat, and I snap back to attention.

"NM4267," Krin says evenly.

"NM1448," I grumble.

"Ah...yes," he says, glasses on the very tip of his nose as he pours over the papers. "Floor duty. You will be checked off by Societal Keeper of the Mine Kredit."

I see a tall, thin man step forward from the line of in-charges behind the one at the desk. He is skinny, almost painfully so, and he carries a clipboard in his gloved hand. I've never really seen in-charges wear gloves, except for the main ones, like Jinade. He looks at me in disgust as he steps forward, so I have no doubt what he thinks of us. He has beady eyes set deep in his pale face. His nose is long and hooked and reminds me of a bird I saw on a Sun Day a while ago.

Then I see his twirled mustache and realize that I've seen him quite often in the last little while.

124

"Follow me," he says in a snivelly, whiney voice. I feel a shiver go down me at his voice, but we turn and follow the twig-like man back towards the row of bunks we had been assigned to.

When we reach the first bed, Kredit produces a white cloth from his pocket. Bending, he quickly wipes it underneath the bed and stands, almost in one fluid movement, and holds up the still-white rag in front of his pointed face. He smirks but puts a check on the paper on his clipboard. He moves on.

This continues for each bed down the row, and Kredit's scowl seems to grow deeper and deeper as the rag stays white through them all. I wonder if he secretly wants us to fail.

We finally reach the end of the row. Kredit stands, the rag still white, and turns to frown at us. He looks from my face to Krin's, and I hope she doesn't look as terrible to him as she does to me. His eyes linger over her, though, and I swallow hard.

His eyes turn back to me like he knows his words will mean nothing to her.

"It would seem you've passed," Kredit almost hisses.

"Thank you," I reply, keeping my voice as flat as possible, my face blank.

"You're free to go get in line for Sun Day," he rolls his eyes and walks back to the in-charges clustered around the desk.

I grab Krin's fairly limp arm and pull her towards the tunnel entrance, but a painful yell makes us turn and look back.

My heart drops when I see an in-charge push a small girl, no older than ten, to the floor. They're only about two beds away from the entrance, so we can see the fear on the girl's face and the fury on the in-charge's.

125

"Look at this!" the in-charge yells. She's a massive woman with a thin bundle of hair slicked to the top of her head. She is waving a rag at the girl on the floor.

"Look at this!" she screams again. By now, everyone in the barracks has stopped to watch the scene. I flick my eyes quickly to the in-charges around the table. They look excited; my fists clench.

"Do you expect the Nation to be satisfied with *this*?" she throws the rag at the girl on the ground. The girl is sobbing. I can't really see anything, even with how close we are to the scene, but I bet the rag has just a tiny bit of dirt on it. I want to yell at this woman that since we are covered in dirt, how do they expect us to clean very well, but of course, I hold my tongue.

"I'm sorry!" the girl sobs, turning to get on her knees. "I'll clean it again!"

"Of course you will!" the woman thunders. She picks the girl up by her shoulders and throws her hard into the bunks.

The girl cries out in pain and slides to the floor.

"Evin," Krin whispers, a hand covering her mouth.

"What?" I ask, not looking away. My stomach is clenched, and my fists are shaking slightly, but I'm frozen to the spot. I want nothing more than to run away from what's happening, but I can't seem to find my feet.

"We've got to do something, Evin," Krin's chin is trembling.

"What?" I finally look at her, disbelief burning in my expression. She's crying. Of course.

Krin doesn't respond, her eyes glued in horror at the scene before us.

The in-charge woman keeps picking up and throwing the little girl, yelling at her the whole time.

"You pathetic waste!" she bellows. "How can you be proud, turning in work like this?"

The girl just sobs.

Finally, almost thankfully, the woman stops. She stands up, straightens her gray shirt, and then turns to face the little girl.

"Clean it again," she spits.

The little girl pitifully gets to her knees. I can see her trembling, even from this distance.

The girl rises to her feet but clings desperately to the ladder on the bunk next to her.

She reaches down to get her cleaning supplies, but she falls over with the motion, having had to let go of the bunk. She tries to stand again, and I notice she can't put her left leg down. It seems every worker in the barrack is holding a collective breath.

The girl tries to reach down again and just falls with a painful cry.

"Get up," the in-charge sneers, and I swear I hear laughter in her voice.

The girl tries and falls hard.

"Get up," the in-charge now smiles.

Once again, the girl falls.

"Oh dear," the in-charge gives a slight laugh, "it would seem you are unfit to work. And anyone unfit to work for the Nation is unfit to be in the Nation."

No one makes a sound, but I know we all gasp and then groan in our heads. We all know what this means.

"Guards!" the woman yells.

From the edges of the room, guards emerge, seeming to mold right out of the stone wall, their black uniforms the same color as the Mine itself. They're allowed in here today since the in-charges are here. The

127

in-charges never go anywhere without their precious guards. They march up to the broken girl who is now sobbing in a curled-up pile on the floor.

Two guards step forward, and each grabs underneath the girl's arms.

"Departure," the in-charge woman says, a wide smile on her face.

The entire barrack is silent except for the young girl's cries. The guards pass right by us, dragging the girl between them, and I catch a glimpse of the already black and purple bruises forming on her tiny face.

No one speaks until the guards' marching echoes into silence further down the tunnel. Finally, the in-charge behind the desks seems to notice no one is working, so he shouts, "Back to work!"

Everyone hurries to get back to what they were doing, so I grab Krin's arm and pull her into the tunnel. I can't shake the sounds of the girl's body flying against the barracks from my ears. I can't escape her cries or the woman's shouts no matter how fast I walk. I tug a reluctant Krin after me into the Open Area and take a quick breath.

We stop for a moment, and I look around. Workers are hurrying over to the lifts where in-charges with clipboards are marking numbers and sending them up in batches. I just...need a minute before we go over there. I look up, trying to find comfort in the big, empty space above me, but I'm having trouble getting my breath to slow down.

I look at Krin, but she's staring at the ground and crying. I want to roll my eyes at her stupid reaction, but I don't. I don't want to argue with her right now, and I don't want to talk about what just happened. So, I grab her arm again and tug her over to the lifts.

We get in line for the middle lift.

"Can you see Hoss anywhere?" Krin whimpers, not even looking up.

"No," my tone is somewhat harsh, but I don't really care. "We'll find him outside like we planned."

Krin nods and wipes her face with the back of her sleeve, making her cheek blacker and smudgier.

More and more workers pour into the Open Area as they finish their Sun Day chores.

We're almost to the front of the line. Now, my breath is quickening because of excitement, of desperation.

We're going *outside*! I can almost feel the wind on my face, taste the fresh, open air. I think of the birds sitting and chirping in the trees, but then the sound turns deeper into screams. The image of the girl being thrown around and around and yelled at slides before my eyes, making me squeeze them shut. I beg the image to go away; I just want to enjoy the sunshine.     Finally, we get to the lift and the in-charge there, flanked by two guards, holds up his clipboard to us.

"Number?" he asks in a dull, bored voice.

"NM1448," I say quickly. He scribbles it down and then nods for me to board the half-full lift.

Krin gives her number quietly, not looking up, not letting them see that she is crying. She slides into the lift next to me and then stands in silence.

A few more workers squish into the lift. I hear two voices that I recognize, and I glance up. Hannel and his friend have just boarded. I shrink a little, pressing myself against Krin, hoping her height will hide me.

The lift is finally full, and then the tiny lift worker slides the gate closed, throwing the lever forward to move us upward.

The lift jerks and shudders as we begin to move. I can't help it; I look up and see the crushing darkness, the absolute blackness that we are moving towards. My vision swims, and I lean against Krin harder. The pressure throws her off balance, and she stumbles into the kid next to her.

"Hey!" he grumbles.

"Sorry," Krin mumbles as she straightens. "You okay?" she whispers in my ear. I nod and inch my eyes back open.

I immediately see Hannel and his friend looking straight at me from over their shoulders. Hannel scowls and turns back around, but his friend (I can't remember his name or even if he said it) stares at me for a moment. A slow smile spreads across his face, a smile that makes my stomach knot and my heart beat faster, and then he eventually turns back around. I don't know what scares me more: the darkness or the way that kid looked at me.

Slowly, the light begins inching into the lift.

Finally, the lift stops, the little worker grunts out, "A Level," and we all clamber out. I hold back a little, letting Hannel and his friend get off and away from me until I get out. I don't know why, but Hannel's friend makes my skin crawl.

Guards line the tunnel here. This is A Level, where the in-charges live. I don't know exactly where they live, only the cleaning workers do. All we ever see of A Level is a long, tall tunnel. It's tall enough that three of me stacked on top of each other could walk down it easily and wide enough for at least four workers at once with room to skirt around the guards. The guards themselves stand maybe six feet apart from each other, snug up against the stone wall, hands on their weapons. We, the workers, all crowd together into the center of the tunnel as we walk along, not wanting to get anywhere near the ominous, black-clad guards.

It's no secret why there are so many guards up here or why they look so threatening.

Last year, on a Sun Day, two boys had gotten it in their heads that they could sneak out of the Mine. Their thinking sort of made sense: Sun Days are the only days when we're permitted on A Level, and A Level is where the two doors to the outside are. One is the door that leads to the Field, where we spend our few glorious hours in the sun each month. The other is to the Loading Bay (at least that's what I've heard it called). It's where the coal goes out to the train and where workers come and go. I don't know exactly how to get to that door, but these boys were loaders and figured it would work. So, instead of following the rest of the workers to the Field door, they went towards the other door. I don't know what happened exactly, but they were eventually caught and shot. The guards on A Level don't carry the plastic sticks at their hips like all the other guards do; they carry little metal things called guns. Sticks bruise; guns kill. We all heard the shots-- most of us were in this tunnel when it happened--and the guards made some of the other workers drag the two bodies out of the Mine. Those workers told us what had happened.

They told us about all the blood. The memory still gives me chills.

The guards don't flinch as we walk by, and I give them a wide berth, trying to stay towards the middle of the tunnel. I'm still pulling Krin along by her arm, her face down and her feet dragging slightly. I'm okay that she is walking slower; Hannel and his friend aren't that far ahead of me, and I don't want to catch up to them.

A Level is well lit compared to the rest of the Mine. The string lights up here have more bulbs and are a bright yellow-white color compared to our dim, dull yellow bulbs that sometimes flicker and die and don't get replaced for months. In this tunnel, you can see all the way up the walls to the ceiling without needing to squint.

We all shuffle forward, moving as quickly as we can. Finally, Krin and I come to the staircase. The staircase is split in half, with a waist-high stone wall dividing it. If you go down the left side, the stairs lead to a big green door that opens onto the Field. The right side's stairs lead further down and then turn to go even lower. That's the way to the loading bay, but I don't know what happens after the stairs turn, how many rooms or guards there are before the actual door to the outside.

The coal and gold ride moving belts from C Level to A Level. Belts from D Level (the Tunnels) take the stuff to C Level where it's sorted, then it all keeps moving on different belts up to A Level where loaders put it onto a big train in the sorted piles. That's what we work so hard for: filling up train after train with coal and gold. The thought makes me angry; the coal and gold get to ride away from here, far away, and I'm stuck here, deep in the Tunnels.

Scowling, I tug Krin's arm hard, and we move quickly down the left staircase. It's about twenty steps to the bottom, and I feel my feet can't move fast enough. I have to get outside, even if only for a minute. I need air.

At the bottom of the stairs, we all gather tightly together, packed at the door. The bright sun leaking through the open door is already starting to make me squint. The green door is tall and wide, and we push through as fast as we can.

Finally, I'm outside. I have to shut my eyes as I take the first steps through the door, and then I can only open them a tiny bit, just enough to stare at the ground as we hurry forward. The ground is dusty and brown with scraggly bits of green grass growing here and there, but I love it.

Outside dirt is so much better than Mine dirt.

My eyes eventually adjust enough to where I can lift my head as we move forward. The sun is still blinding enough that I can only really see straight forward, eyes watering, but that's enough. The tree we're meeting at is at the edge of the Field, next to the fence. It's really a straight shot. The Field itself is long and wide, sloping downward slightly. There are a few trees and some patches of green grass, but mainly it's just flat and dry and dusty. The fence keeps us all from running away or seeing what's beyond the Mine. It's tall, tall enough that not even Hoss could jump and reach the top. And it's solid, just a thick slab of gray rock. It's kind of a threatening wall, but at least we're outside.

Krin is still sniffling as we move, but I don't care or try to talk to her. We're outside, and I don't want to think about the inside right now.

Finally, we reach the end of the Field. It's warm out here, the sun already burning my cheeks, and I'm sweating a little, but I love it.

Duna and Dirk are sitting beneath a skinny tree. It isn't very tall, and its limbs are thin with a few patches of leaves. It offers a little shade, and Krin and I stand close to Duna and Dirk, letting the cool shadow sweep the sweat from our foreheads. The ground beneath the tree is thick dirt, just what Aila wanted.

"You made it," Dirk smiles up at us, but then his face frowns as he sees Krin. "What's wrong? You okay?" Duna even looks up from staring blankly at the ground to see Krin's tear-stained face. She's cried so much today that the tears left deep tracks in the coal smudge on her face.

When Krin doesn't reply, I roll my eyes and say, "A girl got taken from our barracks just barely."

"Not just taken," Krin stares at me with almost accusing eyes.

Just then, Hoss and Aila stroll up. Aila looks happy. She's even taken off her cap to reveal thick, red-brown hair that falls in soft waves around her face. Her hair looks shiny and pretty, like Krin's used to, even after being shoved up in a cap all day. I feel jealousy worm into my stomach as I watch it lift gently in the wind. She brushes it out of her eyes as she approaches us and gives an even wider smile. But then she sees Krin's face.

"What is it?" Aila asks, rushing to Krin's side and taking her hands in hers. Hoss goes too, reaching out and rubbing Krin's arms. I stare at them in confusion. Aila's only been here a few weeks. Why is she comforting Krin? When did they become so close?

"What's wrong?" Hoss asks, looking Krin up and down with so much intensity that I have to look away.

"Evin said a girl got taken," Dirk replies softly when neither Krin nor I respond.

"She wasn't just taken!" Krin sobs and drops her face into her hands.

Through her crying, she says, "An i-in-ch-charge b-beat her, and then d-declared her unfit t-to work! Unfit b-because of wh-what the incharge d-did! Just think--" but then she suddenly looks up, looks at me, and then looks away.

"What?" I ask, confused and getting angry now, even in the sunshine. "Just think what?"

Aila, Hoss, and Krin look at each other, almost guiltily, and then look away. None of them will meet my eyes.

Suddenly, I'm furious. I'm so mad at Krin; she's keeping something from me. After all this time over the years I've spent listening to her, now she's gone and told everything to *Aila*. I want to punch Aila in the face.

"What?" I ask through gritted teeth. Krin starts crying even harder.

I feel a burn in my cheeks, and it's not the sun. I open my mouth to yell and scream at Krin for being stupid, for ruining Sun Day, and at Aila for just...just being here. But then Krin opens her mouth shakily and says something that stops all my words.

"Evin," she sniffs, "I'm going to have a baby."

# Chapter Six

I stop and swallow my words. I swallow a few more times for good measure. Suddenly, the sun does not feel warm anymore.

"What?" I hiss out, not sure there's even air out here anymore.

I look at Krin, my chest hurting with each breath. I look at her, her coal-smudged face and wide, sad eyes.

"Hoss is the dad?" Dirk asks from behind me.

"Of course!" Hoss scowls. "Who else?"

I look from Hoss to Krin. Hoss, with his massive muscles built from years of being a digger, puts his arm protectively around Krin's shaking shoulders.

"Huh," Dirk cracks a little smile. "So that's what's been up. Well, okay!" He leans against the tree, face beaming. How can he be happy? I feel like I can't breathe. Duna looks horrified, a hand over her mouth.

Krin finally looks at me. We just lock eyes for a moment.

Then, she says, "Say something."

For a moment, I don't. Everything seems to be going really fast; I can't really see the ground or the sky. *Not Krin* is all I can think. *Not this.*

"Evin?" Krin asks again.

"Are you stupid?" I finally breathe out.

Krin's lip shakes.

"Hey--" Hoss tries to interject, but I won't be stopped.

"What were you thinking, Krin? How could you do this? And you, Hoss? It's bad enough that you two make *promises* to each other, but now this?" My fists are clenched in rage. "Do you know what's going to happen? Do you know what they'll do--"

"Yes," Krin snaps, her chin finally stops shaking. "Don't you think we *know*? Don't you think that's what I think about every...single...day?

Don't you think we're terrified? Don't you think I know what will happen if they find out?"

I don't care what she says. I'm just so mad. How could they be so stupid?

"Are you sure? Sure that's what it is?" I spit out, thinking of how odd she's been lately, how tired and sad and...odd.

Krin shrugs and shuffles her feet as she says, "I didn't know what was wrong with me. I just felt...sick. All the time. It's been going on for months. Aila found me puking in a corner, and I told her everything. She told me...well...she knows about this, I guess. She's seen it all..." Krin looks longingly at Aila, who picks up the story.

"My aunt had a baby not long before I came here," she says, looking all-knowing. "I knew pretty much right away what was happening with Krin when she told me how she felt and what was going on."

"Oh, did you?" I can't help myself sneering at her.

Aila flinches but doesn't drop her gaze. She tosses her hair over her shoulder and says, "Yes. And I think I remember how everything goes, so we should be able to--"

"What?" I roll my eyes and cross my arms so hard my chest hurts. I even laugh emptily. "We should be able to *what?*" Krin is not the first one that this happened to in the Mine. There have been two others that I know of. I don't know much about...well...*it*, but I know it has something to do with the boys and that the girls get sick. I know they start to look bigger and bigger until they can't hide their stomachs anymore, and then the in-charges find out, and they are taken away through the Departure door. That is going to be Krin now.

Krin's chin is shaking again, and she turns and hides her face in Hoss's shoulder. Hoss is glaring at me, and it seems Aila is trying to keep her face even. Dirk and Duna aren't saying anything.

I sigh, take a deep breath, and then ask as evenly as I can, "What? What will we be able to do?" I look at Aila and try to keep the glare off my face.

"Well," Aila replies quietly, glancing around at all of us and then around us to make sure no one else is listening, "Krin's is getting bigger. That's why she's been wearing Hoss' shirts." I look at Krin and realize that her clothes are big on her because they are big clothes. Hoss must've not sent his old shirt down the chute on Bath Day. His shirt does look dirtier and blacker than normal. And, looking closely, it does look like Krin's stomach is a little rounder. Actually, quite a bit rounder. How did I miss all this?

"Okay?" I say, trying not to sound impatient.

"She's going to have a hard time working," Aila says, casting a worried look at Krin.

"She already is with how sick she's been, but the next problem is going to be how big she'll be. And then, well, she's going to have to deliver..."

"What?" Dirk asks, confused.

"It means have the baby," Aila explains.

"What happens then?" I ask.

"It's...it's not pretty," Aila almost whispers. "There's...uh...a lot of blood." Aila shivers, almost unnoticeably. "And then there's the baby..."

For a while, no one says anything. I feel panicked, still like I can't catch my breath. I know the in-charges will Depart Krin when they find out about her, and they'll probably Depart all of us if we try to help. Even if we can somehow manage to hide all of it until the baby comes, what then? We can't really be expected to hide a baby. It's bad enough for us to hide bread. And I don't even really know what babies do! I have a vague picture of a baby in my mind like I dreamed of one once, but I can't remember anything about it.

I want to walk away; I want to *run* away. But my feet won't move. Looking at Krin, looking at how she and Hoss are looking at each other, terrified and in love, I can't convince my feet to run. I look at them and see how Krin is already cradling her stomach, probably already in love with what is growing inside her, and I can't leave. Hoss and Krin will be parents; they will have a child, and that child already seems to be condemned. Somehow, that doesn't seem quite fair, and I wonder if maybe there is something we could do.

"Krin," I ask softly, looking up at Krin huddled in Hoss' arms. "Krin, do you want this baby?"

Krin looks at me for a moment, then looks up at Hoss. They smile at each other, and then she looks back at me and gives a small nod.

"Yes," she replies firmly. "Yes, we do." I see the steel in her eyes, and I make my decision.

"Okay," I say, turning to look at the others. "Okay. Then we have to escape."

They're stunned.

"Are you stupid?" Duna asks, finally rising to her feet. "You're going to kill yourself for a baby that's not even yours?"

"Well, none of our parents tried to save us," I shrug, not turning to look at her. "I don't think this baby should die just because of where it's born."

"You're going to die!" Duna spits.

I round on her, eyes burning. "We're going to die anyway, Duna."

"But the reading--" Duna begins, but I cut her off.

"Reading isn't enough anymore!" I nearly shout. I glance around to make sure no one hears or is paying attention. Quieter, I say, "Don't you get it? Reading won't save Krin now."

"It might save us," Duna crosses her arms.

"Duna," Dirk says, reaching out to grab her arm, but she pulls it free.

"That's enough for you?" I ask.

"It used to be enough for you," Duna spits. "Don't you always say we shouldn't care, shouldn't like others, that it'll only hurt more?"

"Since when did you listen to me, huh?" My hands are shaking. "You're still sad about Nolan and that was weeks ago! You can't save him, but you can help us save Krin!"

Duna's eyes fill with tears, and she just says, "You're stupid, and you're going to die."

"I'd rather die than get Departed," I stand straight as I say it.

"At least I have a chance of seeing Nolan if I'm just Departed," Duna sniffs.

I shrug, "If he's still alive."

"Evin!" Krin gasps.

"It's true," I say, folding my arms. "Come on, Duna. You can't be this dumb. He's been there for a long time. It might be months until you get there. What chance do you have of seeing him? Aila said most kids aren't there long, anyway, remember? So, you could wait and see, or you could help us save the baby."

"That baby is not my problem," Duna says, but I notice she won't look at Krin.

"Then don't come," I say simply.

She glowers at me, her dark eyes burning.

"Come on, Duna," Dirk says softly, putting a hand on her shoulder. "We'll all be together. It'll be fun." He gives her a wide smile. I roll my eyes, thinking that only Dirk would smile at a time like this.

Duna doesn't reply. She just looks away.

"So, no more reading?" Hoss asks, somewhat awkwardly.

"No, we should still read," Aila says. "If we do get out, we will need to blend in with Society. We will learn as fast as we can, but I agree with Evin. Reading alone isn't enough for Krin."

I don't really like that Aila agrees with me, but whatever.

"So what do we do?" Hoss asks.

"I don't really know," Aila says, for once her smile fading. "You all know this place better than I do. But," Aila flicks her eyes to Krin, "the sooner, the better. I don't really know how far along she is, so we need to move fast. We will want to be far away from here when the baby comes."

"How long do you think we have?" I ask, my teeth clenched to keep in my scowl. I hate that Aila is now in charge of Krin's survival.

"I don't know," Aila shrugs. "I'm not a baby expert."

"You said you knew what was happening!" I sigh exasperatedly.

"Evin," Krin sighs.

"What?" Evin asks. "It was just a question. She seems to know the answers to all the other ones."

Aila glares at me, making me satisfied that she is no longer smiling, but she says, "If I had to guess, I'd say she has at least three more months until the baby comes. But it very well could be sooner."

"So three more Sun Days?" I ask, not really asking Aila, more just thinking out loud, but Aila nods anyway.

"But," Aila adds, "we will want to leave sooner than that. The shirts won't hide the baby forever, and we will need to travel away from here, and the sooner we do that, the better. When Krin gets closer to having the baby, it will be hard for her to walk very far."

I suddenly am relieved that Krin is a sorter. Sorters sit all day.

Then her words sink in a little more.

"Walk?" I ask. "Where are we walking to? Where can we go? Do you know where to go?"

"There's a place," Aila says quietly, eyes flicking around the Field. All the other workers are relaxing in the sun, the shade, playing games with rocks and sticks, or just standing around and talking. I suddenly find it odd that they're not all feeling this sense of panic and urgency.

How can they all just sit around when all this is happening?

"What place?" Hoss asks, his face full of desperation and hope.

"I only heard rumors of it when we lived in the city," Aila says quietly, wringing her hands together and glancing around. "There are some people who got away from the Nation and the new government before it really rose to power. They ran away from all the cities and got to the mountains."

I swallow hard; I know what mountains are. I live in one. They're massive mounds of rock and dirt that rise high into the sky and fall deep into the ground. They're full of dark tunnels, deep shadows, and mean people. I don't really want to escape this mountain just to go to another one.

"Why did they leave?" Hoss asks.

"Some people didn't like what the Chancellor was doing, and so they got away. There was even a small war," Aila says quietly. "That's what my dad said."

"What's a war?" Dirk asks.

"It's like a big fight," Aila answers. "People die, or go away..." She looks away.

"Where are these mountains?" Duna asks, raising an eyebrow.

"Thought you didn't care," I scowl at Duna.

Duna sneers and says, "I was only asking."

But Aila answers her question anyway and says, "I'm not sure. I just know they're west of here."

"West?" Dirk asks.

"That way," Aila says, pointing to the fence, but beyond it as well.

"That's it?" I ask. "You just know it's *that* way? That's not much."

"It's all I have," Aila shrugs.

"Better than nothing," Hoss says in his deep voice. "At least we have something."

"Something?" Duna scoffs. "*Something?* You have *nothing.*"

"Yes, we do," Krin says, looking Duna in the eye. "We have hope."

I want to roll my eyes, but Krin looks so certain, so determined, that I don't have an eye roll in me. I want to hope, too. Really. I just don't know if I dare. I want to save the baby and Krin, but there's some truth in what Duna is saying. We have nothing. No one has ever gotten out of here unless it was through the Departure door. How can we do this? How can we *hope* for this?

But I have to do this. At least, I have to try.

No one really talks about escaping for a few minutes. We just stand there, letting it hang over us. All I wanted today was to feel the sun on my shoulders, but now I only feel the icy chill of hand-trembling terror.

Eventually, we decide to spend the next few days looking for possible ways out. Seeing as how the Mine is designed to keep us all *in*, this will be the impossible part. After that, after we somehow miraculously get out of here, we just have to walk...somewhere.

We spend the rest of the Sun Day listening to Aila finish the alphabet. She draws letters in the soft dirt with a stick and makes us repeat them after her. Then, we have to take turns copying her. My brain hurts after just four letters, but she makes us keep going. I can't decide if I hate Aila or reading more. I keep getting the stupid letter "q" wrong. I can't get the sound right and drawing it is even harder. Well, I know I hate writing more than reading. Aila makes the lines so straight and neat. My lines look crooked and sloppy, all wriggly and slanted. And then the letters that have "curves" or whatever are downright impossible. No one even recognizes my "g." They all thought it was really bad "d."

It would have been better if the others struggled, too, but they keep getting it so fast, all the while Duna's sneering face telling me that I'm the stupid one keeps flashing in my mind even though she won't look at me. Krin and Duna can repeat everything after hearing it once, and Hoss is nearly as good. Dirk's writing is even better than mine! Hoss, with the stick looking tiny in his massive hand, writes evenly and neatly, and Krin's is just as good as Aila! Meanwhile, Aila can't even read what my stick writes. I hate the alphabet.

Finally, almost to my relief, the whistle starts blowing, telling the workers it is time to go back inside.

Suddenly, I realize that I spent the entire Sun Day, this one glorious day each month, to breathe clean air, arguing and sitting, and drawing in the dirt. I'm upset. I had just wanted sun and warmth and air, and now I'm worried and tired, and my back hurts from sitting hunched over.

We rise together, brushing off our pants as best we can, not that it really matters. My heart starts doing the thing it always does when Sun Day is over. I feel the steady beats speeding up, feel the stream of fear and anger as I walk back to the darkness. The grass seems softer with each step, the sun warmer, the air cleaner, almost like it's beckoning me to stay outside. The Mine looms before me, and I already feel tight and closed-in.

Each step makes me feel colder and colder, but I keep going, the others walking around me. I straighten my worker's cap and take a deep breath as we approach the door. Two guards stand on either side of it, stoic and rock-like as ever. The workers file in. I turn and give the sun one last look before marching in after Krin.

I breathe slowly, trying to calm my heart as the sun gets further and further away. It's almost like coming into the Mine for the first time again. I remember marching through the darkness, then getting handed to a tall, skinny, thin-lipped woman who yelled at me and made me sit on piles of coal, checking for any gold. I still have the scars from the mean lady's stick. That's what sorting used to be like all the little kids sitting on piles of coal looking for anything shiny. Now, they have the moving belts and decided the older kids might be better at it, and I was moved to searching. My scars wish they would've figured that out sooner.

I remember the first time Hannah saw my scars. She was furious.

"Where did you get these?" she asked, her eyes wide. It was Bath Day, and we were in the same group. I was seven then, having been with her for a year.

I just shrugged and went back to washing myself.

Later, in the Tunnel, she paused and looked at me, making me stop. She held her lantern up to my face and really stared at me like she was trying to memorize everything about me. So, I stared at her.

I followed her wide, soft eyes and realized that her eyebrows were a light shade of brown. Her lips were full and round and red, and her cheeks, though sunken, looked like they should have been round and

145

full. She had a soft face, a kind face, and I can still see it when I close my eyes.

"Listen to me, Evin," she said, "what they're doing isn't right. It's not nice to treat people like this."

"Okay," I said and moved to keep working.

"I know you're little," Hannah said, putting a strong hand on my shoulder, "but you need to understand that all of this is wrong."

"So what can I do?" I asked, looking up at her, not really understanding.

"You can be kind," Hannah gave me a small smile. "We can all be kind. That way, the in-charges don't really win."

I looked at her and shrugged.

"They don't treat us well," Hannah said. "But if we're kind to one another, we can show them that what they do can't change us."

"How can being nice do anything?" I asked, thinking of the scars on my back. I'm pretty sure that lady would've whipped me more if I smiled at her.

"It's not really being nice," Hannah shook her head, "it's about caring. You need to care about the other kids."

"Why?" I asked.

"Because the in-charges don't care about us," she said, standing. "They don't care about me. They don't care about you. But if we care about each other, it doesn't really matter what they think, does it?" She gave me one of those big smiles, the ones that made me feel good about myself. Then, she got down on her knees and opened her arms. I hurried into them, so used to her arms and so needing them that I didn't notice the force of my hug knocked her slightly off balance. She laughed a little as she straightened, tightening her arms around me.

"This is caring," Hannah whispered in my ear. "I will never stop caring about you, Evin."

"I love you, Hannah," I whispered back, my tiny voice sounding shaky and small. She gave me a final squeeze and then rose, towering over my little, seven-year-old self.

Hannah sighed, brushed the dirt off her knees. She didn't look at me for a while, but when she finally did, I noticed she was crying.

"That's good," she said, wiping her clean face. "Thank you, Evin. I love you, too." I smiled at her, and she smiled back. She wiped her face one more time, and then we got back to work.

I don't like thinking of that memory. It makes my stomach clench and makes my eyes sting with tears. I push them and the memory away, forcing myself to pay attention to where I'm going.

The line of workers trudges forward. No one smiles or walks excitedly anymore; Sun Day is over, and it will be for a while.

I also feel the slightly crushing weight of trying to save Krin and her baby. I still think she and Hoss are so stupid that it makes my teeth hurt, but that's not fair to the baby.

How are we supposed to get out of here? Why did I say we need to escape? There's no way out of this stinking place. I'm so frustrated at Aila and Krin and Hoss and so sad I'm walking away from the sun that I almost miss it.

As we're walking back toward the lifts, I see movement out of the corner of my eye. I almost gasp but manage not to. There is an open door! I have never seen doors in this hallway, and I see why. The door is colored like the stone wall it sits in and looks like it would fit right into the wall. There is a gray-clad in-charge walking through the doorway, and I catch a glimpse of the inside. It must be the in-charges' offices because I can see several of them inside, but what catches my eye is higher up on the wall. I have to crane my neck and look backward to see it clearly, but it looks like a little square of light, and the light looks like sunlight. I only have two breaths to take this in, and I frantically try to memorize this room before the in-charge quickly shuts the door behind him, a look of embarrassment and worry on his face. He stands awkwardly in the hallway now, pressed up against the wall away from all of us. He watches us go with wide eyes like he's scared of something. His cheeks are a deep red color, and he sways slightly on his feet like the ground is tilting beneath him.

I keep my eye on him until I've passed him, hoping he will open the door again, but he doesn't.

My mind is racing as I cram into the lifts next to Krin and Hoss, and the others. I want to tell them what I saw, but I can't here. There are at least twenty workers in here total; someone will hear.

I barely register that we begin moving down, and, for once, the descent into darkness doesn't make me panic. I'm not even really paying attention as we move out of the lift. I'm still trying to hold the picture of that little square of light in my mind.

Krin suddenly elbows me in the ribs, hard, and I look up. We're in the cafeteria, and I'm holding up the line. I hurry and grab my tray and let them slap a spoonful of sludge on it, followed by a thick piece of bread that actually looks kind of warm before I hustle after Krin.

I'm excited to tell them what I saw, even Aila, which makes me a little angry.

Duna and Dirk are already sitting, whispering close together, as the rest of us slide in. As I sit, Duna's eyes flick to me, then she straightens up and suddenly seems interested in her food.

Dirk slowly straightens but looks worried.

"What?" I ask, arching an eyebrow at them.

"Nothing," Duna mumbles, scowling and looking away.

I roll my eyes but don't press it. Let her be angry. What does she have to be angry about? That we're trying to get out? Trying to have a better life? Trying to save a little kid? Those are stupid reasons to be angry.

"Whoa, slow down!" Dirk laughs, looking at Krin. Krin is shoveling food in her mouth so fast it's as if the food is air and she can't breathe.

"I haven't seen you eat in weeks," I say, turning back to my own food.

"I'm starving," Krin mumbles through a mouthful of food.

We all eat in silence for a moment. I see Krin drop her fork on her now spotless plate and stare, longing at it as if more food will magically appear. My own food suddenly sticks in my throat, but then I see Hoss give a small smile and slide his half-full plate on her empty one. Krin looks at Hoss in surprise and gratitude, but then she lifts his plate, slides half of what's left onto her own, and replaces his plate back in front of him. He smiles back and resumes eating. I roll my eyes.

Suddenly, I remember why I was so anxious to get back to the cafeteria.

"Aila!" I almost shout, making the others jump. "Sorry, but, um, I have a question for, uh, for you."

"Fine," Aila smiles, "but next time, just ask it." Dirk laughs, and I shoot him a scowl.

"Have you ever seen something that's kind of square and is in a wall, and it lets in light? Light that looks like sunlight?" I try to keep the excitement out of my voice.

Aila scrunches up her face but then nods and says, "I think what you're describing is a window."

"A window?" I ask.

"Yes," Aila nods. "They're generally made of glass and can be opened to let in fresh air. People have them in their houses, and they're all over buildings. They let you see the outside when you're inside, and you can open it when it's hot--" she stops suddenly and looks at me. She had been speaking without much thought, almost like she was verbally shrugging, but now her eyes get wide. "Where did you see a window?"

"In the in-charges' office," I give a slight smile, feeling a source of pride.

"You were in their offices?" Dirk asks, mouth agape. "When?"

"No," I scowl, "I just saw *into* them. An in-charge opened the door as we were walking through the tunnel. He was coming out when we walked by, and I saw the, uh, window. I don't think he was supposed to open the door while we were there. He looked kind of worried."

Aila's mouth forms a small "o" as she stares at me. Everyone else is looking at Aila, which kind of annoys me. I'm the one who found the window. She just knew what it was.

"You said the window could be opened, right?" Hoss asks Aila.

Aila blinks once, slowly, and replies, "Normally, to let in the air. Where, exactly, was the office?"

"A Level, about halfway down the tunnel. The door fits right into the wall, but I think I could find it again," I say, loving that Aila suddenly needs a question answered, and I'm the only one that can give it.

I can see the excitement, the intensity, in everyone's eyes.

"Well, that was easy," Dirk gives a big smile. I guess they're all thinking along the same lines as me.

"What was easy?" Aila asks, finally looking away from me to turn and look at him.

He shrugs and says, "Well, that's our way out, right?"

Duna just snorts.

"I don't know," Aila says calmly. She spoons up some sludge and eats it.

"You don't know?" I ask, raising my eyebrows and enunciating every word. "What don't you know? That's the only way out I've ever seen that isn't surrounded by guards--"

"No, guards *and* in-charges, I would think," Aila says evenly. "We need to look for something more accessible."

"What?" Dirk asks.

"Something easier to get to," Aila explains. "But we will for sure keep this in mind." She gives me a nod and a smile, then turns her full attention to her food.

I think my stomach might actually be on fire, and my cheeks definitely are. Everyone follows Aila's example, and it's like the window no longer matters. How could it not matter? Two seconds ago, everyone was thrilled, and now, because of what Aila said, my idea no longer matters? It's almost like I no longer matter to them.

"What do you mean 'keep it in mind'? I found our way out!" I whisper furiously.

Aila opens her mouth to speak, but then we hear the familiar, bone-chilling sound of stomping boots.

We all turn to look and see guards marching into the cafeteria. Behind them are Lady Executor Jinade and the Head Reader, and two other in-charges. There are at least ten guards with them, and there might be more in the tunnel; sometimes, it's hard to distinguish the guards from the walls. My heart begins racing. I don't dare look at the others; I don't want to see their panic, too. If someone overheard what we're trying to do and told the in-charges...

Besides that, I know everyone sitting around me, minus Aila, is most likely seventeen.

What if they Depart us all before we can even make a plan? I let out a low groan.

I glance to my left and see Krin squeezing Hoss's hand, staring at her plate with a burning intensity. She isn't even looking at the in-charges. Her hands are shaking.

Jinade looks around the cafeteria with a scowl, her lips a thin line on her pale face. The Head Reader stands next to her, hunched over and as wrinkled as ever. He holds a roll of paper in his hands. In a way, I'm glad he's here. If they're planning on making whoever is called try to read, then it can't be because of Krin's baby or our plan; they would Depart us flat out for those things.

The entire cafeteria silences the instant they walked in. Everyone watches them, and the older ones hold their breath, me included. I know we're all hoping it isn't us, that it can't be us. We're all hoping that we can live this miserable life for just one more day.

Holding up a clipboard, Jinade clears her throat and announces, "The following workers have turned eighteen and will be tested to see if they are fit for Society. NM3490, NM4368, NM2390, and NM1470. Come forward."

I let out a slow breath, and next to me, I feel Krin relax a little. But we don't know if it's over.

Those four kids rise from their benches and walk forward to Jinade and the Head Reader. My heart pounds painfully when I see who one of the boys is. I don't know his name, but he came to the Mine with me. He had been on the train, had Arrived with me. He had been assigned a digger around the same time I was told I was a searcher. I have never spoken to him, nor him to me, but we would always kind of nod to each

152

other in the tunnels. I've never bothered to ask him his name, but I *know* we're the same age. We were even the same height when we first came here, but now he's tall and muscular, a testament to his years digging and hauling coal through the tunnels. My stomach feels like a rock, and I suddenly feel like I might be sick all over the floor.

One by one, those called approach the Head Reader, and of course, each fails without even beginning to start.

The boy I know is the last one.

"NM1470," he says in a deep, growly voice. I've never heard him speak.

"Axel," Hoss says quietly, and I can hear the sadness in his voice. "We used to be on the same digging team."

"Read this," the Head Reader holds up the paper with a shaky hand.

"I can't," the boy called Axel says evenly.

"Very well," the Head Reader nods and steps back.

Lady Executor Jinade steps forward and says in a clear, ringing voice, "These workers have been found unfit to enter Society. They will be Departed."

The guards step forward and surround the four workers. They start marching them to the tunnels, and we all know they will go to the Gathering Room and then through the Departure door.

*Goodbye, Axel*, I think, watching the back of his head until it is so far down the tunnel that I can no longer see it.

I can't decide how I feel. There are too many feelings inside me. I'm terrified, and kind of sad, and furious, and worried. We had all just sat there, sat and watched them be marched away. I came to this place with that boy, and now I'm here without him. And I just barely learned his name.

Axel.

There is a sudden, burning desire inside me to escape, and yet a panic of leaving the darkness that now surrounds me. I want to leave this place on my terms, not surrounded by guards. That's how I came. That's not how I want to leave. I know it's almost my time, and I feel as though these days are getting shorter and shorter, the in-charges' hands already closing around my throat. My hands are cold and sweaty at the same time, and I feel slightly dizzy. I can't breathe.

"Are you alright, Evin?" Krin asks quietly. I nod, not trusting myself to speak. What could I tell her? What could I say? And I really don't want to make her cry. I'm so tired of her crying.

The cafeteria is still silent, so I look up. Jinade, an in-charge, and two guards stayed behind, but the Head Reader seems to have left with the others.

Jinade gives us all a wide, cold smile, almost as if her tight silver bun pulls her cheeks farther back than normal to allow all her teeth to show at once. Then, she says, "In one month, we will be visited by His Majesty, our beloved High Chancellor. Until then, we will be doing intensive cleaning, regular inspections, and nightly Departures to prepare for him. We hope you all enjoyed your Sun Day." She scans the room once more with her unnatural smile, and her eyes seem to find my face for a second longer than anyone else. Maybe I just imagine it, but it definitely feels like she *saw* me. My cheeks burn under her gaze, but then she gives a nod, turns on her heel, and goes back through the tunnel, sharp shoes clacking against the smooth stone floor.

No one moves for a little while as her words and echoes hang in the air. The pit in my stomach is now the size of a rock, and I feel like I can't swallow. Nightly Departures... Jinade said *nightly* Departures. That means that every night more and more will go, and with every passing day, it's more likely that it will be me, or Hoss, or Krin...

154

"I hate her," Krin hisses when the echoing footsteps had stopped, and the workers had resumed eating and talking in low, worried voices.

Looking around, I see horrified and sad faces, but I also hear the word 'Chancellor' thrown around a lot. This won't be the first time he's visited the Mine. He's been here twice before since I've been here. The last time he came, we cleaned and cleaned until our fingers bled and were inspected so often most people didn't even bother sleeping with their blanket on. I'm terrified about the Departures, though…

"We need to leave," I say, turning to look at the others.

"We're working on it," Aila reminds me, sounding slightly annoyed. "As you've mentioned, it's not exactly easy to get out of here."

"We have to," I say, "before the Chancellor gets here."

"Why?" Aila asks. "Krin has longer than a month before-"

"You don't get it!" I try to keep my voice down. "If the Chancellor is coming, there's going to be nightly inspections, nightly Departures, do you really think they won't eventually notice Krin? And even if they don't Depart any of us before then, when the Chancellor is here, he is going to go through every inch of the Mine with the in-charges. They follow us around all day. You said Krin is going to have a harder time working. What will happen when they see her? If the Chancellor sees her?

"And sure, she may have more than a month before the baby comes, but I don't think any of us have more than a month down here. That kid, Axel, Arrived with me, and we were the same age. We were *three*. If he just turned eighteen, and we're all close to the same age…"

I can see panic flicker in everyone's eyes, even Aila's, even though she is only fifteen.

"Okay," Aila said, wringing her hands, "okay. So we have a month."

"Less," I say sternly.

155

"*Less* than a month," Aila shoots me a look. "We need a way to get out. Tomorrow, tomorrow, we need to all have an idea for how to get out."

"I already came up with an idea!" my hands curl into fists.

"*If* no one can come up with anything better, we will go for the window," Aila says nicely, but I can see the strain in her smile, the anger flashing in her eyes. I have to keep from smiling at knowing I'm finally getting underneath the niceness. Nonetheless, my cheeks burn a little bit; I feel like the window is already a good idea.

I glare at Aila as we all continue eating, everyone else simply accepting her words without argument. Why can't they see how stupid she is? I don't want to be around Aila, even though Krin tells me how nice and helpful she is, that she and I should be friends. *Friends.* That word is death down here. Why can't they see that? Why can't *Krin* see that?

We all finish eating and stand to go to the tunnel. I don't say anything. I don't even look up as we walk. I'm still mad at Aila for tossing out my idea, and I'm still mad at Krin for loving Aila so much. More, though, I still feel empty, remembering Axel walking down the tunnel. I just...I never spoke to him. Not that I care, but he's gone now. Gone. I glance at Krin--walking arm in arm with Hoss, a ghost of a smile on her face-- and I feel cold. I don't want to watch anyone else be taken away. I have had a lifetime of that.

# Chapter Seven

"Coden," I ask softly, "what is the world like?"

I have been wondering this ever since we decided to get out. I know I should be focusing on finding a way out, but I still think my window is a good idea. I keep thinking about what everything looks like beyond the darkness and beyond the fence. Aila told us a few things, the buildings and some of the rules, but what is it like for everyone? And I don't really want to go to Aila's mountains. I don't know if it would really feel like leaving if I just go to another mountain. I want to know if there was anywhere else to go. But I can't ask Aila. No. I *refuse* to ask Aila. So, I figured my next best option is Coden. He doesn't talk much, so I think he won't go and tell everyone what we talked about. And, I'm a little curious about what the world is like from Coden's eyes.

Coden looks up at me from under his low-hanging cap, gives a small shrug, and replies, "It's nothing special. Everything is gray and boring, and you have to be nice and not do anything bad. And there are lots of guards everywhere."

"Guards like down here?" I ask.

"Kind of. They don't hit, though, since that's not polite, and they're not silent. They talk to you sometimes, and if you do something bad, they take you away."

We are scanning the Tunnel, going deeper and deeper; we still haven't made it to the Hive with this Tunnel, which annoys me. I'm tired of going so far into the darkness each day; I want to get to the Hive and start a new Tunnel. The diggers reached the Hive two days ago. Normally, I'm only a day behind them.

I don't like being so deep. Even though I'm older, the stories about the monsters waiting in the dark still terrify me. I imagine they're always waiting just outside my ring of light, ready to squeeze and claw me. Hannah told me not to be afraid of them, and I trusted Hannah. I try not to be afraid.

"Where do they take you?" I ask, trying to pull my mind away from monsters lurking in the dark.

He shrugs again and says, "Here. Somewhere else like here. Just...away."

"What else is out there?" I ask quietly, turning back to my wall.

"We used to live in a green place," Coden says softly. "I was really little, and it was before my parents died, but it was big and green, and there were lots of trees. We had a dog. She was yellow, but I can't remember her name. Our house had a big set of stairs. Every night when it was warm, we'd sit outside and look at the stars. My sister liked to tell me about pictures in the stars. She had yellow hair, like the dog. Then, my parents died. Anna took us to the city to try and work, but nothing happened. She was little, too. We lived in the city, in boxes, under bridges for a while. But then the guards talked to us and knew we couldn't read. They took us."

"Oh," I say, mostly because I really don't know what to say. I don't know what half his words mean, but I could hear how evenly he said it all, even though it sounded like he should be sad. He just...said it. Like it was nothing. So I don't know what to say.

Something stuck out to me, though. A word that girl had been singing about the night of the Arrival.

So, I ask, "What are stars?"

"They're like little lights in the sky," he says. "There are lots of them. Too many to count. They come out every night with the moon."

"Moon?"

"It's like a less bright sun. Instead of yellow light, it's like gray light."

"And the stars are like string lights in the sky?" For some reason, I really want to see these stars. I like the idea of little lights in the sky that come out every night.

"Kind of," Coden says, but he doesn't say anything else. Already, this is the most we've spoken to each other since he came here a few weeks ago.

We continue looking in silence, the only sound being our boots scuffing the stone floor.

Suddenly, I have the urge to tell Coden about the plan. I want him to get back to the green place again and see the stars again with his yellow dog. I want to ask him what a dog is, but I don't. I want to ask him more about the stars, but I don't. I want to tell him about the plan, but I don't.

I don't want to leave him down here to die; no child should live down here, and especially no child should live down here knowing they're going to die. But then I think of Krin's baby; I can't save every kid in the Mine.

I hear Hannah's voice telling me to care, that I have to care. But I *am* caring! I've been trying to think of a way to save Krin's baby all day. I can't come up with anything besides the stupid window that Aila hates.

Aila with all her words and letters and knowing how to read and being so smart all the time. Why does everyone like her so much? She hasn't even been here long; I mean, she Arrived with Coden and-

Suddenly, I have an idea.

"Coden, do you remember anything about Arriving?" I ask. I was so young when I came that I don't remember anything much besides the crowds, the darkness, and clinging desperately to Maria's hand.

Coden actually stops walking with this question. He holds up his lantern to my face, making me squint and turn away.

"What?" I ask.

"You don't normally talk so much," he shrugs, then continues walking. "I remember being on a train with others. We were all chained to our seats and couldn't talk. It was a long ride. Then the train stopped, and we got off. We were in a dark room on a tall platform. Then we got to a big door and went through it. There were some in-charges sitting at a desk, and they gave us our...numbers." He scratches at his left arm, almost subconsciously. "Then, they made us stand in a line in this long hallway. We had to stand there for a long time, and then another door opened, and we walked out into the Gathering Room. And now I'm here."

As Coden speaks, I think how much older than ten he seems. His eyes look...deep, like his mind is somewhere else. He has the eyes like those kids that have been here for years. I wonder if my eyes look like his.

I nod, and we walk on in silence for a while. His answer, though it fills me with dreaded memories and makes me feel sad for him, gives me an idea: what if we go through the Arrival door? I'm not sure how heavily guarded it is, but if Coden remembers correctly, it sounds like on the other side of the Arrival door is a hallway (so, a tunnel), and then a big room with a door that leads outside. *Outside!* I don't know for sure, but it sounds like it could work. And it sounds easier than getting to the in-charges' offices. But I won't admit that to Aila. And, I'm convinced she will think what Coden said makes sense.

I pause in my thoughts. Coden. I glance over my shoulder and see him scanning the wall with his lantern. Guilt worms inside me. This is technically Coden's idea, and he doesn't deserve this.

Hannah told me to care. I swallow hard.

"Coden?" I ask quietly.

"Hmm?"

"I...well, I wanted to ask you...well--"

"Evin!"

I jump slightly and then hold my lantern up higher to see Hoss and a few other diggers emerging from the darkness behind us. Really, the only way I can see them is because of the lamps on their heads; other than that, their eyes look like little floating lights in the tunnel.

Diggers are always the most coal-covered and so hardest to distinguish from the stone walls.

"Thought you finished this tunnel?" I ask as they approach.

"Did," Hoss says, pausing in front of me and leaning against the tunnel wall. "We were coming to see if you marked anything in the last section. I thought you'd have got to the end by now." He says it in a teasing way, and I shoot a scowl at him, which only makes him and the two diggers on either side of him chuckle.

"How much further?" I ask, ignoring their laughter.

"Ten more minutes to the Hive," he says. "You gettin' slow in your old age?" He gives a small smile.

"Ha," I say, smirking back at him.

"We've got to get back to our Tunnel," Hoss says. "Let me know if you mark anything?"

"Ya," I wave a hand at him. He and the others nod at us as they turn and hurry back up the tunnel. They'll take a side tunnel to where they're digging now and get right back to loading up carts to haul to the Tunnel Room.

I sigh, and we continue walking. Ten minutes at a digger's pace is going to take us three times as long searching. Then, we have to hurry back to the Tunnel Room just to get assigned a new Tunnel. And they'd know if we didn't hurry since our timers count our steps as well as time.

161

"What did you want to ask me?" Coden asks a few moments later.

"Do you want to get out of here, Coden?" I ask, looking at him over my shoulder.

He pauses in his searching, and looks at me, eyes widening.

"How?" he asks, glancing around. I smile a little; it's already habit for him, a tiny ten-year-old who's been here a little over a month, to immediately look for in-charges.

"I'm not sure," I admit, shrugging. "All we know is that we're getting out before the

Chancellor comes. I have a few ideas, but we haven't...well...we don't..."

He looks at me, almost as if sizing me up with his massive brown eyes, then shrugs and says, "Sure."


I fill him in on what we've been doing as we continue on. I tell him about the reading, Aila's mountain people, and her ideas to get out. I leave out Krin, though; I don't know if she wants me to tell Coden about the baby, and I don't know if I want to say it out loud to someone else yet. Coden remains silent through all of it. The only sound is his feet scuffing against the rock floor.

"So that's it," I say, lifting my lantern up and down to quickly scan the wall in front of me, worried about looking at his face. What if he thinks we're stupid. What if he thinks *I'm* stupid?

Coden is silent for a moment, but then he says, "Better than being down here. But I don't want to go to the mountains."

I smile, even though I'm facing away from Coden and he can't see it. He is already on my side about the stupid mountain people, and he's going to come with us. With any luck, I can save two kids: Coden and Krin's baby. Maybe.

Despite my excitement, I still have to ask, "Why don't you want to go to the mountains?"

"Why don't you like Aila?" he asks evenly.

The question startles me. "What makes you say that?"

He shrugs and says, "Just the way you talk about her."

I roll my eyes and respond, "It's not that I don't like her. She's just...stupid."

"Why?"

"Because she just...she just *knows* everything."

"And that makes her stupid?"

I scowl, "I don't know. She's just...smart, I guess."

"Is that bad?"

"I don't know," I sigh. "Does it matter?"

"Yes," he says. "I'm not going to put my life in the hands of someone you don't like."

"She's fine, it's fine, we just...I just...we don't..." I stammer. I growl and come to a halt, rounding to face Coden. The little boy stops and stares up at me with his big, knowing eyes. He doesn't look at me with unkindness or suspicion or any sort of anger, just innocence. His expression makes me pause, and again I see just how young he is.

I sigh and let my shoulders drop. I'm tired. "Look," I say, lifting my lantern so I can see him better, "I really don't like anyone, so going off how I feel isn't the best plan."

"I don't really think any of this is a good plan," he says very simply.

I roll my eyes, "Well, neither is waiting around to die."

"I didn't say no," Coden gives me a small smile, which casts odd shadows on his face. "I just wanted to know why you don't like her."

I look at him for a moment and then say, "So you're coming then?"

"Yes," he says, "but not to the mountains."

I nod, "I don't want to go there, either. Aila doesn't even know how to find them!"

Coden is still smiling at me.

"What?" I ask, crossing my arms in front of me.

"You're funny, I guess," he says.

"Why?" I scowl.

"Well, you don't like anyone, but you want me to escape with you."

"You don't have to-"

Now Coden rolls his eyes and says, "Come on, Evin. I don't want to have to sleep here tonight."

He turns and keeps scanning the wall and ground with his lantern. He is so short that he has to step back a little to hold the lantern up as high as he can to see the top of his wall.

I like Coden enough, we work well together, and he doesn't ask stupid questions or anything, but I don't know why helping him escape makes me funny. I'm not completely sure what funny means, but Hoss and Duna sometimes called Dirk funny, and I don't really want to be anything that Dirk is. He's stupid.

Despite my brief annoyance at Coden, I'm quite glad he's going to come with us. At least, the pit in my stomach that was forming into a guilty rock now feels better.

We search the rest of the time in silence, and I'm fine with that. I prefer it, really, but part of me wants to bug Coden more about the outside world and why he doesn't want to go to the mountains. He must know more about them since he just came from the outside, and his not wanting to go makes me want to not let Krin go, but I know she'll do whatever Aila wants. Aila knows *everything*, after all.

The Tunnel begins to slope uphill, and I know we must be getting to the end of it. The loose dirt kicks around my feet; not many people have walked on this floor yet. I don't envy the diggers; they have to slice the stone and haul it away in big, heavy carts back to the Tunnel Room. Once they dump the coal and rocks onto the belts, it all goes to C Level where it's sorted and then put on more belts destined for A Level, where loaders put it all on trains.

Up ahead, I can see a dark hole just at the edge of my lantern light. I know that is a turnoff point for the diggers. I hope Coden is getting the hang of the Tunnels; it can get confusing between the main Tunnels and the turn-off tunnels. There have been workers who never made it out of the Tunnels, and no one ever found them. But no one ever really looked for them, either.

The thought makes me shudder.

We pass the turn-off tunnel, and my eyes flick into the thick darkness it holds. My shudder deepens, and I hurry past it.

Our Tunnel goes almost harshly uphill for a few moments. My legs start burning as we climb, but I take that as a good sign that this Tunnel is almost done.

Glancing down at my timer, I see that we have two hours left until the end of the day. I almost smile at that; it's going to take us at least two hours to run back up to the Tunnel Room from the Hive, which means we won't have to go down another Tunnel once we get there. We won't have to search anymore today.

I push on, scanning quickly but thoroughly, hoping to get to the Hive soon. Coden keeps up with me, like always. I'm still a little bothered by him, but I try not to care; I kind of like Coden, despite myself.

Finally, I feel cool air kiss my cheeks, not the hot, stuffy air that clings to the Tunnels. The ground beneath my feet feels softer, and then, all at once, we're at the end of the Tunnel.

I sigh as we step through a small opening into a huge, open space. I hear Coden gasp beside me. I look down to see his eyes are wide and somewhat fearful. He clings tightly to the wall, and for good reason.

"This is the Hive, Coden," I say.

The Hive is the place where all Tunnels eventually meet. The walls are dotted with holes opening to the twisting Tunnels that will lead throughout the lower levels of the Mine. It's a massive cavern, empty except for air, making the inside of the Mine a hollow mass stretching from the bottom of the mountain to the top. You can't see the bottom, and you can't see the top. You can only see darkness. Our light shows nothingness in front of us, and I'm thinking that's why Coden is trembling. You can just *feel* that there's nothing there.

The diggers created paths and steps in the Hive so you can get to the tunnels above and below, but the paths are cut into the rock and very narrow; you have to walk in a single-file line and cannot misstep.

Our lanterns cast creepy shadows across the walls, making the holes appear sinister, like there are creatures just inside them, waiting for us to walk by so they can reach out their terrible claws and grab us. I hold mine up a little, casting a glow around us so we can sort of see the expanse of the Hive. It seems to go up and down forever, and you can't see the other side. There are more holes over there, but it's too far away for my weak light to see. I can feel the emptiness, though, and it feels strange after so long in a Tunnel. It's not the same emptiness as the Open Area. That emptiness makes me feel less...crushed. This emptiness makes me feel like I can't quite breathe right, as if the whole world has suddenly been sucked away, leaving only holes behind.

Coden's breath seems to have sped up quite a bit, too.

"Just stay close to the wall," I say softly, looking down to see his wide eyes staring out at the great big empty before us. I stifle a laugh--I know my first time I was just as scared--and say, "Come on, let's go back."

When I first saw the Hive, I wouldn't let go of Hannah's hand.

"It's okay, Evin," she said, "just stay close to the wall."

I couldn't breathe. It was like all the air was in the center of the Hive, and I couldn't get any of it. The darkness was crushing me; it was even worse than sleeping on my bunk. Not knowing what was out there, not being able to see the great big nothingness in front of me, was so much worse than a rock ceiling.

"H-H-Hannah," I wheezed out, clinging to her hand like a lifeline and pressing myself against the stone wall. It felt like the Hive was sucking me in, pulling me inch by inch towards the emptiness. I kept scooting back, pressing harder and harder against the stone wall.

Hannah yanked me into the Tunnel, keeping a tight hold of my hands.

"Evin," she said, getting down on her knees and grabbing my face with her free hand, "Evin, look at me."

Her face was swimming before me, making me dizzy.

"Evin," she said, "breathe, Evin. Close your eyes and take a breath."

I closed my eyes and sucked in a shaky breath.

"Good. Let it out."

I did, and tears streaked down my face with it.

"It's okay to be scared, Evin," Hannah whispered. "It's okay to be scared of this place. But that doesn't stop us from being strong, okay?" I didn't open my eyes, didn't say anything.

"Did I ever tell you about my parents?" Hannah asked, pulling me back up the Tunnel. I still didn't open my eyes, but I shook my head.

"My dad could sing really well. He used to come home after work and pick up the guitar. He'd sing for my mom and me. He'd sing funny songs and happy songs, some love songs for my mom. Those always made her smile. She loved flowers. She had the prettiest garden you could ever imagine! She was really good with sunflowers. She could grow them to be all different sizes. I like the little ones because I could make bouquets out of them."

I didn't know what any of these words meant, but it calmed me down.

"My parents loved each other, and they loved me," Hannah said quietly. "It's hard to remember them. It is. But I have to. They're my biggest freckles."

I touched my cheeks without thinking.

"That's right," Hannah said. "Don't forget your freckles."

"What happened to them?" I asked softly, finally opening my eyes. We were hurrying pretty quickly back up the tunnel, hands still locked together.

Hannah heaved a sigh, then looked down at me. She almost whispered, "They were taken. They didn't like the Chancellor. I was brought here. Four years ago. I was fourteen."

I didn't say anything.

"I used to read, Evin," Hannah whispered, tears in her eyes. "I loved to read. I liked poetry. But…now…I haven't done it for so long. I can't even remember what the alphabet looks like."

I gave her hand a squeeze, and she looked down and gave me a teary smile.

"It's okay," she said, wiping her eyes with her free hand. "Don't you worry, Evin. It's all going to be okay."

If only Hannah could see me now, standing at the brink of the Hive, next to a little kid. Nothing is okay.

Before I can get back into the Tunnel, Coden grabs my arm in a tight grip that seems much too strong for his age.

"You asked why I don't want to go to the mountains," he says softly, not taking his eyes away from the empty darkness before us. "There are people there. And if they're who Aila wants to get to, I don't want to go."

"What?" I ask. Coden sounds a little scared.

"They're not good people, Evin," he says. "I mean, the Society isn't good, either. But the mountain people aren't any better."

"Why?" I ask, my mind racing.

"We would hear stories about them all the time. They hate the Chancellor, and the Nation, so they would kill people, set fires, take kids and make them join their army. Stuff like that."

Aila had told them about 'army'; she had said it is a big group of people who fight other people. The mountain people do that, too?

To be sure, I ask, "What's an army?" I want to see if Aila and Coden's definitions are the same.

"A big group of people who have weapons, and they go and fight and kill other people," he says.

I'm kind of relieved and annoyed Aila was telling the truth when she told us what an army was.

"Why do the mountain people make you join their army?" I ask quietly.

Coden heaves a sigh and says, "Same reason as the Nation. They want you to fight for them. We call them the Shadows. They're always fighting the Nation. Lots of people die...I'm not going to the mountains, Evin."

"Me neither," I say, giving him a small smile, but inside I'm terrified. Should I tell the others? Should I tell Krin? What can I tell Krin? Will she believe me?

"Then where do we go?" I ask softly.

Coden looks up at me, still pressed against the wall as tightly as he can, and says, "West. That's where everyone else who doesn't like the Nation, who doesn't like war, tries to get to."

"What's West?" I ask. I think Aila said something about it.

"It's a direction," he explains. "We go west until we find it."

"Find what?" I ask.

"Home," he says softly, turning to gaze back out into the Hive.

I like the sound of that word. I pull on Coden's arm to lead him back into the Tunnel.

"We'll find it," I say as we duck back into the tunnel. "We will."

# Chapter Eight

We hurry back up the tunnel. We have to run fast; we'd stayed too long at the Hive, and now our timers are against us.

We're both out of breath when our timers start beeping; we race faster. My legs are burning, and I can't seem to get enough air, but we can't be too late back to the Tunnel Room.

I'm glad we talked, though, even though we have to run now. My mind is racing with everything Coden told me, and I'm trying to think of a way to tell Krin. I don't dare confront Aila about it until I have Krin on my side. I know Krin trusts Aila, but she has known me for so long; she trusts me, too, right?

We finally emerge, panting, into the Tunnel Room, and it looks like we're the last ones. I quickly try and control my breath; I don't want the in-charges asking why we're so tired.

We hurry over to the table to where the in-charges, blatantly annoyed at us, sit waiting.

"Timers," one of the in-charges reaches out her hand. I unhook my timer from around my wrist and hand it to her.

"Numbers?" she asks.

"NM1448," I say flatly.

"NM15266," Coden says.

"14,512 steps, 5.2 miles, 10.42 hours," she reads off my timer, and the other in-charge writes it on a clipboard.

"We reached the Hive," I inform them.

"Congratulations," the in-charge scowls without looking up. "You did your job."

I hold back my eye-roll and say, "I'm just reporting it so we can be assigned a new Tunnel tomorrow."

Both in-charges stop writing and checking our timers and look up at me. They look simultaneously surprised and furious.

"Do you think we don't know that?" the in-charge with the clipboard asks. "Do you suppose we don't understand?"

I take a second before I respond, but then I say, "No. I was just telling you-"

"How to do our jobs?" the in-charge asks, his eyes narrowing. I notice now how fat he is; he doesn't really have a neck. "Do you think you could do it better?"

"She just wanted to make sure we reported it," Coden says softly. "That way, your jobs are easier."

The lady in-charge sticks her nose in the air and smirks, "Let them go, Keeper Nelson. She obviously is trying to make herself look better."

"You better watch yourself, NM1448," Keeper Nelson scowls at me.

I nod, and then Coden and I hurry to our crate to deposit our packs and lanterns. I'm not sure how I feel. Annoyed, obviously, but also a little worried. Why are in-charges suddenly getting so angry at me?

"Idiots," Coden mumbles under his breath as he sets his lantern in the crate.

"Coden!" I hiss, looking up quickly, but the in-charges are busily marking things on their clipboards. I see a few more searchers emerge from a tunnel and sigh in relief. I don't want to be the last ones anymore; I don't want to be the focus of the in-charges' anger at having to wait for dinner.

Coden just shrugs, and then we move off toward the lifts. I'm surprised at him, but grateful, I guess. I didn't really need his help, but I guess he made the in-charges see that I wasn't being stupid. He's right, though; those in-charges are idiots.

We get on the lift, alone beside the kid who operates it, and wait for the other workers. They hurry on, and the lift worker throws the lever before the in-charges come walking over. If they were ready to go up, we'd all have to get off and wait for a lift to come back down.

The ride up is as terrifying as always, and I squeeze my eyes shut, not caring if the other workers or even Coden sees. The lift grates to a shuddering stop. "B Level," says the kid, and we get out, our footsteps echoing in the empty space. We hurry across the Open Area, the Overhang empty of in-charges, and into the tunnel leading to the cafeteria.

By the time we get there, the line is almost gone, and all the tables are full. We grab trays quickly, and I mutter under my breath, "Come sit with me."

I lead him to our usual table, where I see everyone is already sitting. I slide in next to Krin, and Coden sits next to me. He immediately starts eating, seemingly comfortable with the new arrangement.

Everyone stops eating and whispering and looks at Coden. Then they look at me.

"Who's this?" Duna asks, eyeing the little boy.

"Coden," I reply, beginning to eat. "He's, uh, with us now." I see everyone's eyes widen, but Duna's narrow.

I shrug their looks away and keep lifting sludge to my mouth.

"You're stupid," Duna finally says.

"Since when do you care?" I ask, glaring at her.

"I don't," Duna sneers.

I'm still amazed at the anger inside Duna. Something must've really snapped when Nolan got Departed to make her act this way.

"Good," I say.

"Oh, Evin," Krin sighs, pushing around her food on her plate.

173

"What?" I scoff.

"Why me? Duna's the one arguing." Krin rolls her eyes.

Aila finally breaks the tension by turning towards Coden.

"Hi Coden," Aila smiles. Coden looks up and sees her, and I see him look nervously at her before looking down and enthusiastically scooping food into his mouth. I'm suddenly annoyed at the boy. Maybe I don't like him after all.

"We Arrived together, didn't we?" Aila asks sweetly. I want to punch her in her face.

Coden nods, risking a glance up at Aila. He looks down quickly again, a ghost of a smile spreading across his lips. I want to hit him now. He knows I don't exactly love Aila, and now he's all nervous because she *smiled* at him?

"Anyway," I say, "back to the plan."

"Right," Aila said. "What are everyone's ideas?" She looks around at us with bright eyes.

We look at each other, not speaking.

"We could use the belts," Hoss grumbles quietly.

"The belts?" Aila asks. I roll my eyes; isn't she a sorter?

"The belts that move the coal and rocks and gold," Krin says.

"Oh!" Aila says, giving Hoss a big smile. "Those belts. They lead outside?"

"Eventually," Hoss says. "They go to the loading bay, where the train is. But I know there's always a lot of guards there." He kind of ducks his head like he's embarrassed by his idea.

"It's a start," Aila says, giving Hoss another wide smile.

*A start?* I want to shout. *Wasn't the window a start?*

"How could we get on the belts?" Aila asks. "They aren't very big. Maybe two feet wide?"

"And when do they get to the loading bay?" Dirk asks. "All we know is that they eventually go up."

I don't want to get on the belts. I don't want to be in a tunnel that's only two feet wide and *hope* it leads out somewhere. I suddenly can't breathe just thinking about it.

"True," Aila says. "But it's the best idea we have so far."

I scowl into my food.

"I don't know if I'd be able to crawl up those," Krin says softly. "They stop moving when we finish sorting for the day, and I don't know how to turn them on, so we'd have to crawl. I don't know…" she looks desperately at Hoss. Her hands go to her already round stomach. Now that I know it's there, it seems too big not to notice.

"You could do it," he reassures her. "You'd do it." He leans forward and presses his forehead against hers. I try not to gag but then decide I better tell them my plan.

"Coden gave me an idea," I say, and all eyes turn to me. "He said that on the other side of the Arrival door is a hallway, and then a big, empty room. He's pretty sure that room leads outside because the train came into it."

Everyone moves to look at Coden, who glances up and returns their stares blankly. He doesn't react to their expressions at all.

"Huh," Aila finally says. "He's right." Her expression is hard to read, but I can tell she's kind of annoyed.

I shrug, but I feel a warm glow knowing that *Aila* hadn't thought of it.

"That might work," Aila said, smiling, but I can see it's not a real smile. "I remember that. It was dark, though, so it was hard to be sure. We'd need to get to the Gathering Room and then through the door. I wonder if it locks...I didn't notice…" I can practically see Aila's mind working furiously.

"How would you get there?" Duna snorts. "How will you get past the guards and in-charges. That's one of the main rooms in this place!"

"It's not as risky as the window," Aila replies quietly. I want to slap her now. "I doubt it's as guarded as the offices. It's probably less guarded than the loading bay, too, since there's nothing valuable there."

"Still," Duna scowls.

"Again, why do you care?" I sneer.

I hear Krin sigh and want to yell at her. Why is everyone so against me?

"It's all we have," Aila shrugs, giving Duna a soft smile. Then she turns to the rest of us.

"All those in favor of escaping through the Arrival door?"

Looking around the table, I see everyone is as confused as I feel. I don't know what "favor" means, and it looks like no one else does either.

I see a quick flash of impatience cross Aila's face, but she quickly hides it and says, "Favor means you agree. Does everyone think getting out through the Arrival door is the best idea?"

No one says anything, but we all nod, and I'm relieved we now have our exit. I just wish Aila would stop using stupid words.

"Good," Aila says, "then we have to start planning. I will decide how to get out, but I need all of you to watch guards and in-charges. Where are they? When do they move? All that stuff."

"So you're making the plan?" I ask, arching an eyebrow. "You don't want us to help? We've been here longer."

Aila flashes her bright green eyes, looking at me from beneath a coal-smudged face, and replies, "But I've been in that room more recently. I know Coden has, too, but I'm older and know more about the outside world. Please, just trust me. I will come up with an idea that will get us out."

"Do you really know more about the outside?" I ask, feeling anger flash through me. I want to yell at her about the mountain people, but I hold it in. I want to tell Krin first.

"I'm sure I know more than you," she says evenly, and I can hear the anger in her voice. I raise my eyebrow, but Krin whispers, "Just drop it, Evin. Please?"

"Krin!" I hiss out, but she won't look at me.

"We'll talk tomorrow," Aila gives one more half-hearted smile and then gets up to leave. She rises gracefully, pulling her legs over the bench with ease, and says, "Goodnight." She picks up her tray and flits away to the tray station. I watch her go, glaring at her back.

"Oh Evin," Krin sighs, pushing her empty tray away from her as she rises to stand.

"What?" I round on Krin. "Why are you on her side?"

"We're all on the same side," Krin says patiently. "You just seem to not want to be on anyone's side."

"But Aila-"

"Is our best chance," Krin replies, swinging her long legs over the bench. I suddenly feel very self-conscious about the way I walk after watching Aila and Krin. "And you're the only one that doesn't like that." Krin strides away, Hoss hurrying after her. Duna smirks at me as she rises, Dirk immediately following her. Soon, it's only me and Coden at the table.

"Well?" I ask him, my cheeks still hot.

Coden shakes his head and mutters something that sounds dangerously close to, "She's okay." Then he, too, gets up and leaves.

I'm furious, and I grumble as I get up. I know Aila had only seemed nice because she was all smiles for Coden and nice to him, but didn't he see how Aila shot down everything I said?

Didn't he feel that she's hiding something?

I think I hate Aila.


I get to the bunks and find Krin isn't here. Of course. She's probably with Hoss. Maybe she's talking to Aila. I'm fuming as I climb up and throw my blankets on me. I lay on my stomach, willing myself to forget how close the ceiling is.

For a moment, I try to picture what Coden calls "stars." I close my eyes and imagine tiny string lights covering the dark sky and a softer, less yellow sun. I desperately want it to be real, desperately want to see it. Want to sleep somewhere other than under a mountain.

I hear a sound across from me and crack open my eyes to see Krin climbing into her bed.

She lays down and rolls over to face me. I open my eyes fully.

"What?" she asks.

"Oh, you want me to talk now?" I ask, not hiding my scowl.

She rolls her eyes and says, "Come on, Evin. You were being mean."

"She's being stupid," I say.

"She's trying help-"

"Do you know that, Krin?" I ask, urgency in my voice. "Do you *know* that?"

Krin looks at me for a few minutes, then sighs. "Why don't you like her?"

"Coden told me about the people in the mountains," I say quietly. "He says they're just as bad as the people in the Nation. They kill people and make them fight, too! They attack people,

Krin, same as the Nation! You really want to go to them?"

"Why didn't you say anything to Aila?" Krin asks. "Maybe she doesn't know. She just said she knows the mountains are out of the Nation-"

"Aila doesn't believe anything I say!" I try to keep my voice to a whisper. "Why would she believe this?"

I look at Krin for a moment, who looks at me with...sadness?

"Krin," I ask. "Do *you* believe me? About what Coden said?"

"I believe Coden said that," she says softly.

"Do you believe it?" I ask. "That the mountain people are bad? That we shouldn't go there?"

"Where else, Evin?" Krin asks. "Where else? Aila thinks it's okay-"

I scoff and roll my eyes. "Of course, if *Aila* says it-"

"Stop, Evin," Krin scowls at me. "That's the problem! Why do you hate her?"

"Because she's not real!" I say. "Something's wrong about her, can't you see that?"

"What's wrong about her?"

"She just...*knows* everything, and she thinks she's so smart, and...and…"

"Do you just want something to be wrong with her?" Krin asks softly.

"Why would I want that?"

"I don't know, Evin," Krin sounds tired. "But I wish you would just trust her. Please? For me?"

I look at Krin and feel so empty inside. I'm so mad, but the madness feels cold and just...empty. She talked to me just like Aila does; she didn't even really listen to what I said, and she definitely didn't believe me.

"Fine," I say, then roll onto my stomach and look the other way.

"Thank you," Krin whispers, but then we stop talking.

I'm so...I just...I don't know. I can't get a hold of my thoughts. Fine. If Krin wants me to play along with whatever Aila says and does, then fine, I will. But, as soon as we get out, Coden and I are heading as far from the mountains as we can. We're going to the West. We're just going to run, and then Krin can save her own baby and do whatever Aila says without me.

Softly, suddenly, the echoing voice returns, after having been silent for a while:

*Stars shining bright above you,*
*Night breezes seem to whisper "I love you,*
*Bird singing in the sycamore tree*
*Dream a little dream of me.*

*Stars fading, but I linger on, dear*
*Still craving your kiss.*
*I'm longing to linger till dawn, dear*
*Just saying this*

*Sweet dreams till sunbeams find you,*
*Sweet dreams that leave all worries behind you,*
*But in your dreams, whatever they be*
*Dream a little dream of me.*

Suddenly, I imagine I'm lying on my back in a grassy field, looking up at the sky. Coden is with me, and he's pointing up to the dark night, telling me all about the stars. The grass is soft beneath us and tickling my bare feet. Krin comes over and sits down next to us, hand-in-hand with Hoss and smiling so big at her baby in her arms. We all just sit and look at the stars, soaking in the fresh air and clean night.

Quickly, I wipe my eyes with my blanket, annoyed that I'm crying. I hadn't realized that I started until the thick drops dripped down my chin. Rolling over, I squish my pillow over my head, begging the singing to stop.


I have a hard time sleeping that night. I toss and turn in my bunk, listening to the snores and breathing of all the other girls. I can't turn my mind or my emotions off; it feels hotter than normal, the air thicker, so I eventually have to pull my pillow off my head just so I can breathe.

The ceiling seems closer, and I can almost feel it pressing on my back.

After what must have been hours and hours of tossing and turning, I sit up, grumbling. I rub my eyes, wishing they felt heavy, knowing they will feel heavy once the worker bell rings and I have to go to the Tunnels.

Krin is snoring lightly beside me, but I don't feel like waking her up. She'd be okay with it--well, she *used* to be okay with it-- like when I sometimes wake her up to tell her about my dreams, but I don't feel like it. And, I would feel kind of bad waking her up now. So, instead, I throw my legs over the side of my bunk and drop lightly to the ground.

The air feels cooler the further I get from my bunk, and it's filled with the soft sighs and snores of the girls around me. The dim lights never go out, even at night, so there is a yellowish glow around the edges of the room. If the in-charges didn't tell us when to sleep and when to wake, it would always seem like night down here. But this night doesn't have stars. I must've seen the stars before I came here, but I don't remember them. I wish I had Coden's memories; I wish I could remember things about my parents, whether or not they told me about stars and dogs and everything. But, mostly, I wish they'd wanted me.

I pause in my thoughts; maybe it's better I don't have those memories. That way, I have nothing to make me miss the outside world. I bet Coden misses his parents, his sister. I don't. I can't even remember my parents' faces beyond the fuzzy images that sometimes pop up in my dreams. Maybe it's better this way.

But now I have hope, or whatever. It seems like hope might be as bad as memories. Now I hope to see the sky full of stars, hope to see the darkness full of light. I want to see that so badly, and I don't know if that's good.

I weave my way through the bunks toward the toilet. I don't know what time it is, but I think it's getting close to morning, so I might as well get an early start and go before everyone else wakes up.

The toilet is next to the tunnel entrance that leads to the Open Area, and I don't really like being this close to any tunnel at night. The dark, gaping hole looks foreboding without anyone walking in it, without the echoing sound of footsteps. It just seems...emptier, darker. I shiver but force myself to walk on.

I go into the small room and shut the door behind me, hurrying to pull the string to turn on the light. The light bulb swings back and forth for a moment, casting odd shadows around the tiny space.

I go quickly, the ceiling seeming to shrink closer and closer the longer I'm in here. I pull my pants on, reach up, click the light off, and have just inched the door open when I freeze: voices. It's not that odd, I'm right next to the tunnel, but it's so late--or early?-- and I'm far enough from the bunks for it to be anyone over there, so I'm nervous. The voices are definitely coming from the tunnel. Workers aren't supposed to leave the bunks at night, so it can't be them; guards never speak, so it's not them; that leaves in-charges.

I leave the door open a crack and press my ear to the opening. I do not want to be caught out of bed; in-charges coming down to the barracks during the night can only mean Departures, and why not grab the worker sitting in the bathroom when they're supposed to be sleeping?

My heart is racing, and I try to keep my breathing quiet. The voices are quiet, whispering. Why would in-charges whisper? They're getting closer. I press my ear harder. It seems like there might only be two people. I can hear their footsteps now. In-charges only ever travel in pairs and with guards, but there aren't enough footsteps. So, who is it?

"...I will get them all down there," one of the voices says. I freeze. I know that voice. I know *her*. It's *Jinade*.

My heart is pounding. If Jinade finds me here, I'm Departed for sure. I can just imagine her gray eyes smiling as she orders the guards to haul me away.

But...there are no guards. At least, I didn't hear any.

The other person says something back, but I can't hear them. Either they're speaking too softly, or my heart is too loud in my ears.

"Very well," Jinade whispers. "Go on."

Suddenly, the whispering stops. I hear one pair of footsteps walking closer, and I squeeze the door as shut as I can and still peek out.

I see someone walk right by me and move quickly toward the bunks. It's a worker. A worker talking to Jinade? Not even the cleaners are allowed to talk to in-charges, and who on earth would Jinade come all the way down here for?

The worker walks under a flickering bulb and looks back over their shoulder. I almost scream.

It's *Aila*.

# Chapter Nine

My mouth drops open, and all the air seems to suck out of my chest at once.

*Aila. I knew it.*

Satisfaction and terror fight inside me; I was right about her, but I don't know what that means. Did she tell Jinade everything?

Did she tell Jinade about Krin?

If she did, I'll kill her. I'll kill her, and I don't care what it means for me.

Suddenly, I want to run to Krin and tell her everything that I just saw. She has to believe me now; I *saw* Aila talking to Jinade.

For a long time, I can't move. I feel like my legs have melted into the dirt beneath me, and I can't pick them up. Finally, I steel myself and step out of the toilet, half-expecting an in-charge to reach out and grab me. My heart is pounding, even though I haven't done anything wrong, and I know that, but I hurry back to my bed nonetheless.

I have to wake Krin up, *now*.

I've just hauled myself back onto my mattress and am about to reach out and shake her awake when I hear the boots. I lay down quickly, my heart pounding. Aila must've told them. She told them, and now they're coming for us. *Jinade* is coming for us.

Peeking out over the top of my bed, I see a group of guards trailing Jinade, Kevoc, and two other in-charges. They walk in, boots hitting the ground like stone against stone, marching into our beds, waking us all up.

Krin lifts her head and looks at me, eyes wide. I give her a slight shake of the head, hoping she won't move.

We watch with wide eyes as they pound their way in. However, the group passes our row. The in-charges eventually stop three rows behind us. I can just see them if I look over my shoulder. I can kind of hear their voices, and I'm suddenly worried about Duna. Where is Duna's bed again? Are they going to get Duna first?

I hear crying, one girl is screaming, and then the guards and in-charges are leaving. Leaving? It only takes about five minutes, and even the echoes of the guards' boots disappear through the tunnel.

My heart slows down, my breathing evens.

"It wasn't Duna's row," Krin whispers to me. I shrug, shaking her off, but my shoulders relax a little. "I don't think it was Aila's either," Krin adds.

I feel my expression darken, and I see Krin's face get tired.

"Evin-" she starts, but I interrupt in a harsh whisper.

"Aila was talking to Jinade," I hiss out, the words grinding against my teeth as they make their way to Krin.

Krin frowns and asks, "When?"

"Just now," I say, "just before the Departure. I was in the toilet, and I heard voices. One was Jinade's, and when I looked out, I saw Aila walk past me toward the bunks!" I can hear the desperation in my voice, the excitement; Krin and I will finally agree about Aila!

"So you didn't see her actually talk to Jinade?" Krin asks, face still puzzled.

My excitement falters a little, but I say, "No, but who else could it have been? There were only two voices, and then I see Aila come in from that tunnel? Come on, Krin."

"But you didn't see her actually talking?" Krin asks again.

"No!" I growl. "But it was her! It had to be!"

"Evin…" Krin shakes her head, and I can't believe my ears.

"You don't believe me?" I ask, feeling my cheeks burn and tears sting my eyes.

She looks at me hard and then shrugs. She says, "I believe you saw Aila."

I open my mouth, but nothing comes out. Krin doesn't believe me.

"Evin, I know you don't like her-"

"Stop," I whisper, laying back down. "Just stop."

"It's not that I don't believe you-"

"You don't."

"But you didn't see her-"

"I saw enough, Krin," I scowl at the ceiling, not caring if it crushes me right now. "I saw enough."

Sleep feels heavy on my eyelids when, suddenly, the worker bell dings. I groan; they couldn't have Departed those girls after we had to wake up? They couldn't have done it before we fell asleep last night?

We drop down to the ground; I refuse to even look at Krin. We begin making our way to the tunnel, girls' bodies shuffling all around us.

"Evin," Krin says softly, reaching out to touch my arm, but I jerk it back. I'm furious. I'm so furious I could scream. But I don't. It doesn't matter that she doesn't believe me. I don't care.

"Evin," Krin says again. We're in the Open Area. I can see in-charges looking down at us from the Overhang. I feel like I might explode. I see tiny black dots at the edge of my vision.

"Evin, it's not that I don't believe you. It's that we don't know for sure, and we really need Aila. *Please*, Evin." I can hear the desperation in her voice.

We turn and head to the cafeteria. It looks like Krin wants to say something else to me, but I don't care. I'm too angry.

We arrive in the cafeteria and get our food. We sit at the table with the others who are already there, and they immediately start talking about escaping. Aila is smiling and nodding, and talking like normal. I don't look at her; I can't. I might hit her if I do. I don't say a word about what I heard last night to the others. Krin didn't believe me, so why would they?

Coden eats silently next to me, and I'm secretly relieved he and I have already planned not to go to the mountains.

"Aila," Krin says softly, breaking up the other conversation about whether or not we should try and steal food on our way out, "Aila, I was in the toilet last night and saw you out of bed, in the tunnel. Where were you going?"

Everyone stops eating and talking and looks at Aila. I even glance up to glare at her. Aila looks surprised, and she even flicks her eyes to me before looking back at Krin. She plasters on her smile and says, "An in-charge came and got me last night, told me I had been summoned by the Lady Executor." I see Aila's hand shaking. "It was terrifying, obviously, but I went up with the in-charge and a guard to A Level. Lady Executor Jinade was there, and she told me that she had been watching me and that she wants me as her personal cleaner." I roll my eyes. Aila's gaze turns to me, and I see suspicion and fear in them. *Good.*

"Personal cleaner?" Dirk asks. "What does that mean?"

"I'd clean specifically for Jinade," Aila replies. "I guess her old one just got Departed."

She shrugs like it's no big deal.

"And you said yes?" Dirk asks again.

"Did I have a choice?" Aila gives a smile, but it's weak.

"Then why are you still here?" I ask harshly.

"What?" Aila asks, looking surprised.

"Cleaners eat and work and do everything separate from us," I nod, gesturing generally at the workers that surround us. "Why are you here?"

Aila shrugs, "I was told to stay with the regular routine, but just head up to A Level when the worker bell rings."

"So you can still teach us to read?" Krin asks.

Aila nods. I roll my eyes.

"And," Aila adds, "I figured me working up there is really good for us. I will be able to look around the offices and see if there is anything that will help us escape." She adds this with a smile, and the others look totally convinced. My stomach churns, and I feel like I might vomit.

"Are you alright, Evin?" Aila asks, turning to look at me. So does everyone else, including Krin.

"Yep," I scowl at my food, moving to shovel as much into my mouth as I can. Working with Jinade will let Aila look around the offices, sure, but it is also going to give her plenty of opportunities to rat us out.

Everyone at the table goes back to eating, goes back to being completely happy with another one of Aila's explanations. Another clear lie.

Krin is even smiling at Hoss; she smacks him playfully on the arm, and he smiles back at her. Dirk is talking to Aila about something, and Duna is actually listening. I turn my head to look at Coden, hoping to see some suspicion in his eyes, but he just shrugs and goes back to eating.

When did everyone at this table get so stupid?

The worker bell rings, and we all stand in unison, forming a silent, solid wall of black smudged workers.

"Democracy is the foundation of Society: Equality is the backbone of Life," we lifelessly chant, and then everyone begins moving off.

Those words fill me with anger, my face burning, my hands shaking. I hate repeating them, and I hate repeating all the words Aila makes me say. How is saying what she tells me to say different than saying what the in-charges force me to say?

I look at her back as all the workers head for the lifts. I watch her walk with ease, talking softly to Krin as they make their way, shoulder to shoulder, into the tunnel, and across the Open Area.

If Krin is trusting Aila more than me, fine. Who cares? Not me.

I look up and see that Krin has stopped; she lets me catch up to her and then walks next to me.

"See?" Krin says, smiling slightly. "That's all it was."

"You believe her?" I ask, scoffing.

"You don't?" Krin raises an eyebrow.

"Since when have you heard of an in-charge having a 'personal cleaner,' and since when does the Head Executor walk around at night with workers?" I fold my arms across my chest hard and stare at her as we walk toward the lift lines.

Krin shrugs and says, "Jinade is new. Maybe she's doing new things."

"Come on, Krin," I roll my eyes. "You can't be this stupid."

Krin suddenly rounds on me, eyes wide and terrified, and asks, "What choice do we have,

Evin?"

I stare at her, shocked. I open my mouth, but then I hear a voice behind me.

"You should be in line."

I turn around and see Hannel's friend, the tall, skinny one, the one who makes my skin crawl, standing just behind me.

"So should you," I shoot back at him. He laughs, winks at me, and then passes me to get into the left line, the one going to the Tunnels.

Krin and I watch him go and then turn back to each other.

"Who's that?" she asks.

"Who knows," I shrug. The hairs on my arms are still standing up.

"Evin," Krin rubs a hand across her face, and I realize how tired she looks. "Evin, I need your help. Please? I can't do this without you, and we can't do it without Aila."

I sigh. Aila can read. We need to read. We need to read so that if we do get out of her, we're not caught right away. Aila also knows the outside; she has to guide us once we're out of here. Coden is too little.

All of this makes sense to me. I know that that is how this is going to work, but I can't get past how I feel about Aila.

"I don't trust her, Krin," I whisper, hoping the kids around us don't hear.

Krin gives me a tiny smile and says, "I know. I trust you, Evin, I do. But I have to do this." She gently pats her stomach and then gets into the line heading for C Level.

I sigh and get into my own line. Deep down, I know this isn't going to work. I know Aila is not what she says she is, and I can't trust her. But Krin is right; we have to try. I'd rather try than just wait around to be Departed, and I couldn't live with myself if I didn't try for Krin.

I said I'd help her get out to save the baby, and I will. I will go along with whatever Aila comes up with, even though I don't trust her as far as I could throw her. I'm going to do whatever it takes to save Krin's baby. Then, I'm going to leave. I'm going to take Coden, and we are going to go somewhere where there is no Nation, where there are no mountains, and most importantly, where there is no Aila.

# Chapter Ten

Days begin melting into weeks of repetition. The in-charges are working us to the bone to get ready for the Chancellor.

After we finish our regular work, we spend an extra hour each evening cleaning before we're allowed to eat. I have scrubbed the stone floors of the Tunnel Room, polished the bunks in the barracks, and am now helping clean the Bathing Room.

In the back of my mind, all I can think is, *Why would the Chancellor want to see where we bathe?*

Aila has been keeping track of the days and reminds us each day how much time we have left. The reminders make the hairs on my arms prickle. Krin has been so happy with me lately; I haven't scowled at or gotten angry with Aila in weeks. Mostly because I don't look at her, but also because I'm forming my own plan as she forms the plan for all of us. I need to listen carefully, and I can't do that if I'm arguing with her. And, I really don't have anything left to say to Krin or Aila or any of them.

A few days after I'd heard her talking to Jinade, Aila had told us the plan.

"We're going to leave the night the Chancellor comes," she had said.

"Won't there be extra guards?" Hoss asked. "The last time he was here, there were tons more guards."

I said nothing, just looked at my food.

"They'll be with the Chancellor," Aila said with a knowing smile. "And in the middle of the night, where will the Chancellor be? Up on A Level, sleeping. So, we will sneak down the tunnel to the Arrival room and out the door, hopefully with no one the wiser."

"How are we all going to get there without anyone seeing us?" Dirk asked. "We'd have to cross the Open Area."

"If we go one at a time and keep to the shadows," Aila shrugged, "it shouldn't be a problem."

"That's it?" I said in disbelief, looking at my food. I couldn't believe this is what she had come up with.

"I figure the easier, the better," Aila gave me a wide smile. I held in my eye roll and scowl and just shrugged.

Every night since then, for about two weeks, we go over the plan at dinner. There isn't much to memorize, but Aila says it's important to know each piece. We have to know who is meeting where, who goes first, and all that. She said we couldn't talk much, hopefully not at all, so we have to get everything mapped out here, at the table. I keep my mouth shut and my face blank as best I can through it all. Krin has asked me a few times over the past few weeks what's wrong, but I just shrug and tell her I'm tired of thinking or something. She always looks like she wants to say something, but she never does. But, she did have the nerve to thank me for being so nice and understanding towards Aila. I cringed, but said nothing.

Besides going over the plan every night, Aila has been making us read almost constantly. We've all learned the alphabet--me and Dirk just barely-- and have now moved onto actual words. I hate words. I don't understand how to put all the sounds together, and sometimes letters make different sounds if they're next to a certain letter. I just can't keep it all straight.

Duna and Krin understand it so easily, and Hoss gets most of the words right on the first try. Dirk and I have difficulty reading even the shortest, simplest words. It infuriates me when I have to ask Aila what a word says. I only ask her because I'm determined to read. Once we're

194

out and Coden and I leave, we're going to have to pass as "fit for Society," and that means we have to read. Coden, however, doesn't seem interested in reading; he sits and watches and listens, but he never repeats the words or sounds. I worry that once he and I are on our own, he will be caught or give us away, but I don't press it. I have to worry about one thing at a time, and maybe we will be able to find someplace where it won't matter that he can't read.

I have no idea how this plan will work; it seems too easy to me. And I don't know where Coden and I will go if we do miraculously get out, but I don't care, as long as it's far away from Aila.

"Here," Krin says, setting a bucket of soapy water down next to me. The water splashes onto my hand, bringing me out of my own thoughts. I hiss, not at Krin, but at the water hitting my fingers. They're chapped and bleeding in between the knuckles, and the soap in the water makes it sting.

"Sorry," Krin says softly. "Didn't mean to scare you."

I don't say anything, just dip my rag into the sudsy water and continue scrubbing the Bathing Room floor, wincing when the soap gets into my dry, cracked skin. The only benefit to cleaning is that I can see my skin from my wrists down. My pale, cracked skin almost glows in the dim light around us.

Krin and I have been tasked with cleaning the floor, but getting on hands and knees is now hard for Krin. I think Aila's counting is wrong; Krin seems huge to me. I know I don't understand how all the baby stuff works, but I can't see how she could get any bigger or go for months more like this. So, I told Krin I'd take over on the floor. She just needs to move the bucket and make sure it's full of water. To make her look busy while I'm scrubbing, Krin puts a rag under her boot and wipes it around where I have just washed to make it look shinier. Well, as shiny as gray stone can get in dim lighting. But, most of all, I'd made sure Krin was assigned to work with me. I practically dove around another worker to get next to her when she reached the in-charge table.

There are other pairs of workers cleaning the walls, the benches, and polishing the spouts where the water pours out. I desperately want to sneak over there, turn the water on, and scrub my face clean, but I know it's against the rules, and the in-charges are not to be tested these days; one had Departed a young boy for dropping his food tray two nights ago. The in-charge, a fat man with little neck, had called the boy "unfit to do even simple tasks, and would therefore never be fit for Society." It was unsettling, especially since in-charges are rarely seen in the cafeteria. They've been watching us closer these days, but still. Dropping a food tray? I remember dropping that food tray for Affa and realize I never would've done it if it meant Departure.

There are two guards and an in-charge standing in the doorway to the Bathing Room. Ever since coming up with the plan, I've become hyper-aware of guards and in-charges, especially if they're stationed in the same place every day. The in-charges are rarely down in the Tunnels, the cafeteria, or barracks, but they're almost always in the Open Area, the Overhang, the Tunnel Room, and by the lifts. I know there are more of them in sorting, where Krin and Duna work, and Aila practically crawls through them when she cleans for Jinade.

Aila won't, however, tell us about her new job.

"It's quiet and pretty clean," she shrugged. "I basically wait until Jinade is done using something, and then I hurry in."

But Aila doesn't look like the other cleaners. The other cleaners are rarely seen, look so much cleaner than the rest of us (they don't want coal trails in their clean offices), and generally get more food. Aila still eats with us. She is still covered in coal dust and just as skinny as we all are.

I don't trust it for one minute.

She's been telling us all about the in-charge rotations and everything she's learned about being on A Level and all that stupidness. Well, as long as the in-charges leave me alone, I don't care what she learns.

The guards, however, are everywhere. There is one every twenty steps or so along every tunnel, by the lifts, in the cafeteria, everywhere. The only places they're not are the barracks and the Tunnels; we don't see even them when we're searching. I have never really paid attention to them because they seem to blend into the stone. Now, though, I see them, every one of them, and they all make my skin itch in fear. Whenever I pass them, I'm worried they'll read my thoughts.

I keep as far from them as I can, and whenever one comes near, I can't seem to take my eyes off the plastic stick on his hip.

"Evin?" Krin whispers, kneeling down to pretend she is helping me. I know Krin can't do the work, but I'm sometimes--like right now-- bothered that it means more work for me. I know I chose this, I chose to help her, and it's fine, but my knees don't think it's fine right now.

"Hmm?" I ask, not taking my eyes off the floor. I wipe sweat out of my eyes. The Bathing Room always seems a little...sweaty.

"Do you really think we'll get out?" I can feel her looking at me, so I glance up. Up close, I can see the dark circles under her eyes and the hollowness to her cheeks even though Hoss gives her most of his food at every meal, and her stomach is practically exploding out of Hoss's shirt.

I want to yell at her, demand why she all of a sudden wants to know how I feel or what I think, but I just sigh and say, "Yes." I do mean it. I know we'll get out of here. I just don't know if it'll be through the Arrival door or the Departure door. I try not to think about Krin getting Departed. Despite how angry I still am with her, despite it all, I force myself not to picture her back walking through that big, metal door, turning and giving me one last look...

"I'm glad you're my friend, Evin," Krin whispers, reaching over and giving my hand a little squeeze.

I freeze for a second. Friend? I look up at Krin, at the tall girl's hopeful, smiling eyes, but then my gaze drifts towards Krin's tummy, at the bump that is now impossible to hide even under the massive shirt. A fierce need to protect this baby burns inside me; I have to save it from the in-charges and the guards and the people who don't think it has any worth. Krin and Hoss think the baby has worth, and, really, so do I.

I'm still furious with Krin, but I suddenly miss her and don't want her to know how bad she's made me feel. I know this isn't easy for her. So, I give a small smile and reply, "Okay."

Krin laughs a little and shakes her head.

"What?" I ask before I can stop myself, angry that now she's laughing at me.

"Well, a month ago, you would've yelled at me and gotten mad for saying the word, 'friend.' Now, you're almost admitting we're friends," Krin gives me a smile.

I shrug and roll my eyes, not wanting to talk about it. I shoo her hand away from mine and get back to work. The last thing I need is for Krin to get declared "unfit" now that we're just weeks away from escaping.

Krin stands and continues "shining" the floor. I think about that word, "friend." I wonder what friends really are. I don't know, but whatever it is, it can't be Krin. Right? She didn't, *wouldn't,* believe me. She believes Aila. That's fine. She can believe whatever she wants, I guess, and when we're out, she'll realize the only friend she has is Aila, and I don't think Aila is anyone's friend. But, then again, I don't really think I'm anyone's friend, either.

With a hiss of pain, I realize the water has chapped my hands again, and little drops of blood roll off my skin onto the floor.

*Great*, I think, *now I have to mop that, too.*

# Chapter Eleven

"Come on," Aila whispers, urging me on with a gentle smile. I want to smack that smile off her black-smudged face, but I don't. I have to do this.

"Cuh-at," I stutter out, squinting at the tiny writing on the paper Aila always keeps tucked away in her clothes.

"Good," Aila says, "but you need to put the sounds together. It's 'cat.' One word. If you break them apart, they'll know you can't really read."

"They're going to know we can't really read as soon as they give us a three-letter word," Dirk smirks to me, and I give a little laugh, despite myself. Yes, he's making fun of me, but he's making fun of himself at the same time. He and I haven't managed to get past the simple three-letter words. Krin and Duna are already on four-letter words, Hoss right behind them.

"They're going to know you can't read if they ask you to read a single letter," Duna smirks at me, leaving Dirk out of her insult. I scowl back, furious, cheeks burning in shame.

"What's cat anyway?" Dirk asks.

"A cat is a small animal," Aila replies. "It's got four legs, a long tail, and fur."

"Sometimes, I think you just make these words up," Dirk laughs.

"Again," Aila whispers, ignoring Dirk.

While she's quizzing Dirk, I glance around the cafeteria. I see the regular four guards standing, one against each wall. They're unmoving, so it seems we're still safe. If a guard moves, that generally means they think they've seen something suspicious or an in-charge wants them to do something.

I focus back on the words Dirk is saying, listening to how Aila corrects him, thinking of how all the sounds blend together. Krin and Duna are helping Hoss with a different paper, one with harder words. It turns out Aila is very good at stealing paper. Well, isn't that just good for her. Another thing she's just super great at.

Maybe we'd all be super good at stealing paper when we have Jinade as our friend.

Coden, as always, watches us all with a blank expression.

Aila turns back to me and nods, holding out the paper.

"The...see...bed...yes...dog...cat," I say slowly, focusing on each sound. I peek over at Krin and Duna, watching them sound out words on their own. I feel a pang of jealousy and embarrassment ripple through me, making me double my efforts to memorize the sounds and words.

We can only read for maybe twenty minutes each night during dinner. The workers generally eat for half an hour, and we still have to make it seem like we're intent on our food, so the guards don't get suspicious. One time, a guard walked by us. I hadn't noticed, I was too busy looking at words, but Coden had seen. He tapped the table twice next to my wrist, and I glanced up. The guard was too close to try and hide the list, so I picked it up and wiped my face with it like it was the napkin that comes on our tray. The guard hadn't done anything, just kept walking, but Aila was furious at me for ruining one of our lists. We couldn't save it: the coal dust from my face had smudged everything and turned the paper almost wholly black. I countered that we hadn't been Departed, but Aila was still annoyed.

"Good," Aila says, scooping up the word lists and replacing them under her shirt. "You're making progress. You said them all right today." She gives me an encouraging smile. I grind my teeth but smile back. Aila beams.

*I need to learn to read. I need to learn to read.* Only that thought prevents me from reaching across the table and punching Aila in the face.

"Okay," Aila says, looking around at all of us. "We have four more days until the Chancellor gets here. That means, in four days, we are going to get out."

I look at everyone around the table. They all seem excited, but I feel like I might vomit. Krin looks huge and exhausted. I'm not sure how the in-charges and guards haven't noticed her yet. We do all we can to hide her belly, but it's just so noticeable. Then my eyes find Duna.

She looks...different. Lately, she's been rolling her eyes and scowling at us and only talking to Dirk or to Aila when we're reading, but now...she seems almost nervous. She keeps biting her lip and looking at the ground, and her eyes seem watery. No one else seems to be paying too much attention to her. She insulted me just like normal, but now with the idea of the Chancellor in the air, she's all trembling.

Weird.

Aila continues on, making us repeat the plan over and over again until she's satisfied.

Then, we all rise to go to bed.

I'm exhausted. The new Tunnel I'm assigned to, the one Hoss' team is digging, is at a consistent uphill, which makes my legs ache angrily. And, the in-charges made us clean the Tunnel Room shelves today, so my arms are sore from lifting and moving crates around to clean around and behind them.

All of us naturally form a kind of circle around Krin when we rise from the bench, hiding her stomach as we walk through the tunnels.

There are a lot of workers packed into the tunnel right now, though, so the guards can't see her well.

When we reach the Open Area, Hoss puts his arm around Krin, and she leans into him. She puts her head on his shoulder and sighs softly, and I look away. I still just...I don't know how I feel about Krin. Mostly, I'm just angry and hurt. I'm risking everything to save her stupid baby, and she wouldn't listen to me. We haven't really talked since I told her about Aila and Jinade. Sure, she called us friends, but I don't believe that. How can I, right? How can friends not believe each other?

My eyes drift over to Duna, and I see her glance up, hands shaking slightly. My eyes follow her gaze, and again, I find myself looking at the gray, cold form of Jinade peering down at us from the Overhang. I force myself to keep walking this time, but I swear I see Jinade *smile* at us. At Duna? I look back at Duna, my heart speeding up knowing Jinade is above us, and see her lip tremble and her eyes fill with tears. I instinctively look at Krin, but she and Hoss are still walking steadily forward. I hope Jinade didn't notice anything. I feel sort of bad for Duna, knowing how scared she must be of Jinade. For a moment, I almost want to tell her that I tend to freeze up when Jinade is around, too, but I don't. Duna's been too stupid for me to want to tell her that, and what good would it do?

We get into the tunnel that leads to the barracks. We're all quiet, either too tired or too preoccupied with our own thoughts to say anything. We get to the end, where the tunnel splits. Dirk waves and heads to the right. Hoss follows him after kissing the top of Krin's head. She looks after him with a sad smile on her face. I roll my eyes, and the four of us head down the girl's tunnel.

We emerge in the barracks, and Aila and Duna hurry off towards their beds. We thought, once, about trying to practice reading at night, but we didn't want any of the other workers seeing what we were doing.

Krin and I move to our row and then turn to head to our beds. We say nothing.

I climb up my bunk and lay down, my back to Krin.

A couple of minutes pass and my breathing starts to slow. I desperately want to sleep, so I try to clear my mind. Seeing Jinade hasn't helped me feel like I can calm down. Seeing her brings back all thoughts of Departure, of seeing Krin walking through that door, and then my fight with Krin, and my terror that Aila is not really with us, and--

"Evin?" Krin asks softly.

I sigh and try to pretend that I'm asleep.

"I know you're not asleep, Evin," Krin gives a small laugh.

I turn over and look at her. "What?" I ask.

"We just haven't...talked for a while. You okay?" she asks me.

"Okay?" I scoff, but then I see her face. She's tired; she looks even more tired than I feel.

"I'm fine," I finally say.

"Uh-huh," Krin sighs and lays down, grunting as she lowers herself onto her back.

Curiosity overcomes me, and I ask, "What's it like?"

She looks at me, one eyebrow raised, and then replies, "It's weird. I can feel it moving. It moves more when I'm sitting or lying down, and sometimes I think it moves when I'm speaking like it's saying 'hello' or something." She smiles lovingly at her round belly.

I give a small laugh, and Krin looks at me and smiles.

"You haven't laughed for a while," she says softly. "Evin...I just...I know you don't like

Aila, but I promise it's not that I don't believe you or anything, but-
"

"Krin," I say, closing my eyes, "no. Don't. Okay? It's fine. Let's just focus on getting out." It's not fine, not at all, but I don't want to talk about it. I don't want to talk about Aila or how I'm convinced she's going to get us all killed with her stupid, easy plan and night wanderings. But Krin won't believe me, so what does it matter, really? When the time comes, Krin will have to choose Aila or me to listen to, and not even my need to save the baby can stop her from choosing Aila.

"I meant what I said," Krin says.

"What?" I ask, opening my eyes to look at her.

"That if anyone is going to get out, it's going to be you, Evin," she replies. It's like she suddenly can read my mind. "You're strong. Not like Hoss strong, but a different strong. Stronger than any of us. Even Aila."

That surprises me. What kind of strong is stronger than Aila? What kind of strength can beat words?

I can feel my face softening as I look at her, and she gives me a smile.

Krin lets out a long sigh and then says, "I'm really glad you're my friend, Evin."

I don't say anything, and then Krin slowly falls asleep, her breathing becoming deep and even. The barracks are silent now; no singing tonight, I guess. I kind of wish whoever sings would start singing, just to distract me from how I feel right now. Maybe Krin would choose to listen to me if it came down to it.

Suddenly, I'm in the Arrival room, sitting on one of the long benches, but I'm alone. None of the other workers are in here.

Up on the stage, Lady Executor Jinade is standing next to someone, but I can't tell who it is. I know it's a worker because of the cap and coal-covered clothing, but I'm too far away to see their face.

Jinade unrolls a piece of paper and reads with a cold, clear voice, "NM1448."

My stomach drops. I want to run, but for some reason, my feet go obediently to the stage.

I walk slowly, watching a satisfied smile spread across Jinade's face.

When I reach the stage, I climb up the few steps and cross over to the woman and worker.

"Where is everyone else?" I ask. "Where are the workers? The Head Reader?"

"You're the only one left," Jinade laughs. "Everyone has already been Departed. And here is your Head Reader."

I'm finally close enough to them to see that the other person is Aila, her bright green eyes flashing from a clean, shining face; there's no coal dust on her face. She gives me a wide smile as she lifts the paper in front of my eyes.

"Read this," she tells me.

I look at the paper, but the letters look wrong. I can't recognize any of them from the alphabet.

"I can't," I whisper. "It's wrong. They're not letters."

"Yes, they are," Aila whispers quietly, leaning in towards me with a cruel smile on her lips. "You're just stupid."

Cold creeps through me as two guards appear and grab my arms.

"No," I say. "No! You taught us wrong!"

Aila and Jinade start laughing as the guards pull me toward the Departure door. I try and push against them, try to yank my arms free, but their grips are too tight.

"You can't do this!" I scream. "I can read!"

"No, you can't," Aila calls to me, waving the paper.

"No!" I cry. The door opens, and a thousand screams seem to erupt from the opening.

"Goodbye, Evin," Aila says.


"No!" I gasp and sit up. I feel like I can't breathe, and I'm covered in sweat. My blanket is tangled around my legs. My hair hangs in my face, sticking to my forehead in clumps.

Slowly, I take deep breaths, trying to control the shaking in my hands. Glancing around, I see that no one else woke up, or if they did, they didn't bother to see what was wrong.

Sometimes girls scream or talk or call out in their sleep; no one really cares. Well, it's either they don't care, or their own dreams are worse.

Krin is sleeping like the dead, her belly making a small mound under the blankets. I doubt even if the ceiling fell on us that Krin would wake up.

I hate when I dream. In fact, I think I prefer dreams that I can't remember. I sit up and put my head on my knees, wrapping my arms around me. *In...out...*I breathe.

I sit in the darkness for a moment, bent over my knees to keep my head from scraping the ceiling and focus on the wall across from my bed. Even though it's a little ways away with two rows of beds between us, I'd rather look at the wall than the ceiling or even the inside of my eyelids right now. It's dark gray stone, and the string lights above it cast shadows down it. I look at the lights; one of the bulbs is out. Huh. The bulbs are clear when the light is gone; I've never noticed that before. My searching bulbs are always faintly red or blue even when their light is off. I wonder what color I am when my light is out.

207

Shaking off an image of clear bodies in my mind, I lay back down. I recite the alphabet a few times in my mind, not caring even if it *is* fake right now, just needing something to fill my mind. I take even breaths, but instead of dreams, a memory comes to me:

I was curled up in a corner, crying. No, *sobbing*. I had messed up on marking, hadn't marked something properly. I didn't really understand what I did. How could I? I was seven.

Seven and crying because I had been so scared.

The in-charges had stood above me, bringing plastic guard sticks down again and again on my back until Hannah stepped forward.

"Stop!" she shouted, throwing her hands up. "Stop! She's new. She won't do it again!"

"This is your fault!" one of the in-charges shouted at Hannah, and he raised the stick to point at her. "You didn't make her fit!" The guards took a step forward. "This is your fault!"

"No!" I sobbed, seeing what was going to happen. It was my fault, and they were going to take her from me.

I stood, shakily getting to my feet, and Hannah drew me against her, burying my face into her chest.

"She's new," Hannah said, almost pleadingly. "She's new. She hasn't marked anything yet. I will fix it, and it won't happen again."

"Do you think the Chancellor would approve of this?" the in-charge pointed at the wall.

I had put the blue marker to mark gold instead of the red marker. During an inspection.

Hannah said nothing; I couldn't see the in-charges, but I could feel Hannah's panting.

"Do you realize what tonight is?" the other in-charge asked, his voice soft and silky, almost hiss-like.

Hannah shuddered.

But then, I heard footsteps. They were running.

"Keeper Mellon, Keeper Grimes!" came a voice. I didn't try to see. "The Chancellor has arrived early! He's here! We must report to A Level immediately for his welcoming!"

The in-charges made surprised sounds, and then I heard them all running away, leaving Hannah and I trembling in the darkness.

We stood there for a long while, Hannah cradling me, both of us crying silently. My back ached from being hit with the sticks, and I never wanted to leave the safety of Hannah's arms.

"Evin," Hannah finally whispered. "We'd better get back to work, Evin." I could feel her arms trembling.

"I'm sorry," I whispered, sobbing into her shoulder. I clung to her shirt tightly, my little fists holding wads of the fabric. "I'm so sorry."

"It's okay, Evin," she said softly, calmly. "It was a tiny mistake. And you won't do it again, right?"

I nodded against her shoulder.

"Good. You can't do it again, okay? You must be so careful," she said, and then she set me down. I hung on, refusing to let go. She laughed quietly.

"Evin," she whispered, prying me off her to look into my face. "Evin, we need to talk about something."

I wiped my eyes and looked at her; we were kneeling on the ground, so I could see her eyes more easily. Her bright, kind, loving eyes.

"Evin," Hannah's chin shook, "Evin, baby, listen to me. Tonight is the Arrival. Do you know what that means?"

"New kids come," I said, crying again because she was crying.

209

"That's right," she smiled, but it didn't last long. "That's right. New kids come. But kids leave, Evin. Lots."

"Are they going to take me because I messed up?"

"No, baby. They take the big kids."

"Am I big?" I asked.

She smiled again but said, "You're big in a different way. I mean big like tall."

"You're tall," I said, my chest suddenly falling and rising rapidly. "But you're tall!"

"Yes, I'm tall," Hannah dropped her gaze to look at the ground. "I'm tall."

"You can't leave!" I said, panting, chest hurting from breathing so hard. "You can't leave me!"

"I might have to," Hannah said. "I don't know for sure."

"Don't leave!" I threw myself into her arms again, pressing myself as tightly as I could against her.

She just held me for a minute, rubbing my back softly where the in-charges had hit me.

"Is it because of me? Would they take you because of me?"

She didn't answer for a long time.

"Evin," she said, "listen, Evin. You need to remember what I told you, okay? Just in case. Do you remember?"

"Freckles," I choked against her chest.

"That's right," she said, "remember your freckles. What else?"

I didn't say anything; what mattered if Hannah left?

"You have to care, Evin," she whispered. "You have to care about the other kids."

"I care about you!" I cried out, thick tears rolling down my tiny cheeks.

"I care about you, too," Hannah's voice shook. "I love you, Evin."

"Hannah," I whispered, burying my face in her shirt.

I wish I'd never had to come out of her arms.


*Three more days, three more days, three more days,* I chant in my mind as we work. Coden and I are in the new tunnel, legs burning from going uphill for the last few hours, closely searching the new stone.

As I work, I review the plan, the alphabet and just try and not think about Aila.

A low rumbling ahead makes me stop. Sighing, I step to the very right side of the tunnel, pressing myself against the wall as flat as I can go. Coden does the same but on the left side.

The rumbling gets louder and louder, and eventually, a light appears in front of us, accompanied by voices.

Coden and I wait until the diggers are right in front of us, pushing their cart full of dirt and rocks on the track that runs through the center of the Tunnel. Since it's a new Tunnel, there aren't any turn-offs yet, and there won't be until diggers dig them, so they have to cart all the stuff through the main Tunnels. The cart itself is almost as wide as the Tunnel, and it squeaks and moans as it's pushed along. I don't envy them having to push that load up and down in this dark. It's no wonder the diggers are all huge and strong.

*Not Hoss strong, a different kind of strong,* Krin had said.

"Watch it," says one of the diggers, but not unkindly. He's big and has a grumbling voice like all the diggers do. I don't see Hoss, so I don't pay attention to any of them as they pass.

One stops, though, and looks at me. The others stop, waiting for him. They're like three massive trees in the shadows. I think I've seen him before, the one that stopped first. He and Hoss are often together in the Tunnels, but I don't know or care for his name.

"There's a mark up ahead," he says evenly, nodding over his shoulder. "Big one."

"Okay," I shrug. Why did he bother telling me? I know how to do my job. Maybe I should tell him he needs to dig up ahead. I know the diggers almost always find gold before we do. We basically mark it for them so they and the gold diggers can find it easier once they start extracting it.

"Do you want us to tell the in-charges?" he asks. "We'll be there anyway."

"No," I scowl a little bit. "Do you want me to dig for you?"

He rolls his eyes but says, "Fine. Just trying to help."

"Don't need it," I grumble as they move on. I don't know if he heard me, and I don't care. If he tells the in-charges, they will think I'm either too lazy or too dumb to report it right.

There's cause for my Departure right there.

*He's just trying to help himself*, I think sourly, sneering at the stone as I lift my lantern.

Once they're gone, Coden and I continue searching. We walk in silence for a while, and again I lose myself in my thoughts.

"Evin," comes Coden's quiet voice.

I stop and turn to see the small boy is a few steps behind me, holding his lantern up to the stone wall. His eyes are wide, and as I get closer, and I see why. The digger wasn't kidding.

The entire wall is veined with gold, specks of bright flecks glinting in the lantern light. They twist and cross each other, creating intricate designs among the stone. It twines from the bottom of the tunnel to the top, weaving around each other to make thick drops and small spindles.

I choose one arm of gold and follow it deeper along the tunnel. It keeps going, even after ten steps. I gape. It is the single biggest gold spot I have ever seen in all my years of searching the tunnels.

"Whoa," I whisper, turning and walking back to Coden. "It just keeps going." I gesture down the tunnel.

Coden and I stare at it for a few minutes, overcome by the mass and shininess of the golden wall.

"It's beautiful," Coden says finally, reaching out and almost reverently touching the wall.

I nod, and then begin rifling through my searcher's pack to find the marking tools.

"Wait," Coden says, placing a soft hand on my arm. "What...what if we...take some?"

I gape at Coden, eyes wide. "What? Are you stupid? We'd. Be. Killed." I say it slowly.

"Maybe," Coden says, "but we're getting out of here in a few days. We're going to need money. Wherever you and I go, we will need money. Maybe Hoss could even dig some out for us. We'd have money..." He is gasping he is so excited. A small smile is spreading across his face.

"Coden," I say evenly, taking his shoulders and turning him to face me. "We can't. The diggers will notice if some of it has been dug out. They already know it's here. They'll notice, Coden. They cut main Tunnels smoothly, with special tools. See? Feel the wall. We couldn't cut it the same. They'd have to tell the in-charges. It's not worth it."

"But what if we got Hoss and the other diggers on our side? Shared some with them?" he asks, almost pleadingly.

"Coden, no," I shake my head. "It's too risky."

"But learning to read every night and planning to escape isn't? You could be killed for either of those, too!" I've never heard Coden angry before. For the first time, he seems his actual age.

"Coden, that's different," I say, shaking my head. "Reading is something we can hide and escaping, we have to do that. We're too old. *I'm* too old. You'd understand it better if you'd been here longer."

"And for Krin," he says darkly.

I flinch and look down at him, suddenly worried about this boy, but I can't explain why.

"I'm not stupid, Evin," he says. "I know what's wrong with her."

"You going to tell?" I ask, scowling at him.

He rolls his eyes and says, "No. But having gold on our side when we get, when *she* gets out, will only help. Don't you see that?"

He glares at me, big eyes slanted down by furious eyebrows. His lips pout out, and he crosses his arms. I feel nervous. It's like he might...explode.

"Coden," I say quietly, "we just can't. We have to mark it and move on." I slowly reach down and pull out the marking tools from my bag. After creating a deep enough hole, I screw the bulb into the wall. I finish and twist the bulb, making it glow red, and then I turn around to see Coden standing behind me, facing the opposite wall. He keeps flexing and unflexing his fist.

"Come on," I say, picking up my lantern and continuing to scan my wall. After a few moments, I hear Coden move and continue scanning the other wall.

The gold Coden found stretches far along the tunnel. We scan for nearly thirty minutes before we reach the end of it. I won't take that risk. I won't. I know how taking the gold will end.

I want to at least try and escape before I'm taken outside and shot.

We finally hear the beeping from the wrist timers that mark the end of the day. I sigh and stretch my tired back. I'm glad we're done; I can hear the echoing sounds of diggers in front of us, and I was worried we were going to overtake them before the end of the day. If that happens, we're supposed to help them dig.

I look behind me to see Coden standing there, glaring down the dark Tunnel like he's waiting for a monster to come and eat him. Coden sets down his lantern and pulls out a blue bulb. He sticks it in the wall and twists it to mark where we got for the day.

"Let's go eat," I say, giving him a small smile. He doesn't even look at me as we begin walking back up the tunnel. I roll my eyes; he just doesn't understand. He's too young. The longer you're here, the more you know the types of risk you can take, like dropping your tray to hide someone's coughing (but only if the in-charges aren't worried about the Chancellor coming). But, this is not worth it. We'd be lying on the floor in a puddle of our own blood before we'd even get to do anything with the gold. I have tried to tell Krin this when Hoss gave her that clear stone, but she wouldn't listen, and now Coden can't or won't understand why we can't even take a fleck of gold.

Besides, what, exactly, is *money* anyway?

Ahead, I hear the squeaking of a cart on the tracks. The three diggers from Hoss's team reappear, pushing their now empty cart. I don't envy them; they will have walked this Tunnel four times today. We pass each other without comment. I think the one digger tries to look at me, but I look away angrily, not wanting to meet his eyes.

We pass the gold, the red bulb flickering in our lantern light. That's when I notice something; Coden doesn't have his lantern.

"Coden?" I ask. "Where's your lantern?"

He stops suddenly, looks at his empty hand, throws his head back, and growls angrily.

"It must be back there," he grumbles, pointing back up the tunnel. "I set it down when I put the blue bulb in." He practically spits the words.

I sigh. "The diggers might notice and get it for you," I say, my stomach grumbling.

Coden looks at me, his eyes burning, and says, "Not after you yelled at them. They'll probably throw it further down the tunnel."

I'm surprised, my mouth opens to say something, but nothing comes out.

"Besides, I don't want to get in trouble," Coden says, but it sounds like he's mocking me.

"Well, I don't want to go back," I say, folding my arms angrily. I know I sound kind of whiney, but that's kind of how I feel. It was a stupid mistake, and why is he acting like it's my fault? Hoss really would grab it. Probably. If he sees it.

"Then don't," Coden shrugs. "Wouldn't want you to miss a meal, anyway." He starts walking.

"How are you going to find your way in the dark?" I call after him; I already can't see him.

"It's a straight Tunnel, Evin," he calls back. "Not all of us are scared of the dark."

His footsteps echo away, and I'm alone.

I roll my eyes, and then I turn and head back for the lifts. If he wants to wander around in the dark alone, fine, but I don't want to, and I don't have to. I want to eat, and he was dumb enough to leave his light behind. It's not my fault.

The light from my lantern casts eerie shadows along the walls as I walk, my feet echoing in the long tunnel. Alone, I notice how empty and big the Tunnel feels; it's so dark. My lantern only casts a small circle of light in front of me. I shiver thinking about Coden walking all that way in the dark. I turn and see creeping darkness behind me, the air cooler and more pressing, and I walk faster, my heart racing a little. I hate the dark, I hate the stone, and I hate the Tunnels! I want to scream, but my throat feels tight. I want to run, but my legs feel wobbly as I will them to go faster. I feel tears come to my eyes, and I take a shuddering breath. I hate this place. I want to get out.

Then I laugh at myself. Kind of. I've been here for almost fifteen years, and I'm still not used to the darkness, the *closeness* that feels like emptiness. I slow my breathing down by trying to picture a dark sky filled with little lights in the sky.

"I will see the stars," I whisper to myself. "I *will* see the stars. I will not die under this mountain."

It takes me a while to reach the end of the Tunnel; even though we've only been searching this tunnel for a few days, the diggers are fast, and we must already be a little over a mile in this tunnel. The end of the tunnel leads out into the Tunnel Room. The large, circular room is dotted with five tunnel openings along the left side of the room and five openings on the right side. My tunnel is on the left side.

I emerge and let out a quick breath, relieved that I'm one less layer in the darkness. The Tunnel Room is well-lit, the bulbs of the string lights much brighter than in the cafeteria or barracks.

Once in the Tunnel Room, I walk over to the table where the in-charges wait with scowls.

"NM1448," I say, handing over my timer.

"Wait until you're asked," the in-charge snaps. I have to stop myself from rolling my eyes. It's difficult, but I know if I did, I would either end up beaten or Departed these days.

"Number?" the other in-charge asks, looking at a clipboard.

"NM1448," I say as evenly as I can.

"Where's your partner?" he asks.

"He's coming," is all I say. I don't want to point out that Coden left his lantern in the Tunnel; they might punish him for that. Then I remember why I'm angry at Coden in the first place. "We marked a find today. The gold diggers will need to go to the Tunnel tomorrow."

"Very well," they wave me on.

I go to the shelves, pull out mine and Coden's crate, and set my gear inside it. As I'm turning to head to the lift, I see Dirk and Hannel emerge from the tunnel to my right. There are only five openings to the Tunnels on either side of this circular room, so each Tunnel opening is wide and tall. Once inside, you can take any number of Tunnels. There is only one live Tunnel in each of the openings at a time, meaning only one Tunnel that is currently being dug.

Dirk gives me a nod and a smile as he and Hannel move to the in-charge table. I go to the lifts and find myself the only one inside besides the lift-worker. Naturally, we have to wait for others. My stomach growls.

"Well, if it isn't Miss Smile herself," Hannel laughs his big, loud laugh as he and Dirk enter the lift. I don't like Hannel; he's stupid and loud. I'm glad he doesn't hang around Dirk in the cafeteria. He Arrived a few years ago and was assigned to searching; Dirk says his parents sold him to the Mine, but I don't think that gives him the right to be so stupid.

I stare straight ahead.

"Where's your little friend, sunshine?" Hannel asks in his smirking, laughing way. "The little kid with the dopey look?"

I don't answer. I'm not in the mood.

"Shut up, Hannel," Dirk sighs. I can tell from Dirk's tone that Hannel must've had a lot to say that day. Hannel is one of the few down here that actually talks when he doesn't have to.

Hannel just shrugs and leans against one of the chain walls of the lift. Dirk scoots a little closer to me, even though the lift isn't that big, to begin with.

"Where is Coden?" he asks.

"Had to go back to get his lantern," I reply. "He left it in the Tunnel."

"And you didn't go with him?" Dirk sounds shocked.

"No," I reply firmly. "It's not my lantern."

"Huh," Dirk says. He looks away from my face. I'm instantly annoyed by this, and my cheeks burn.

"It's not my job to hold his hand!" I almost hiss. Why does everyone get upset at me when I do things that everyone else does down here? Partners have left me in the Tunnels before!

"I didn't say it was," Dirk shrugs.

"Then what?" I ask. Hannel is looking at us greedily, but I don't care. I'm fed up with everyone getting mad at me over stupid things that aren't my fault. It's not my fault Coden left his lantern, it's not my fault we can't take the gold we found, and it's not my fault that Krin is having a stupid baby!

"Well, you seem to like the little kid. I kind of like the little kid. I'm just...it was weird that you left him alone, that's all," Dirk says softly.

"I don't like *anyone*," I grumble.

"Uh-huh," Dirk sighs, reaching up to scratch his smudgy cheek. This close, I notice he has prickly hairs growing on his chin, under that layer of coal.

The digging team that works in the same Tunnel as Dirk joins our lift and the lift worker moves to close the gate. I'm relieved. I don't want to talk to Dirk anymore, and I want to eat.

Before the gate is all the way shut, a small voice yells out, "Wait! I'm coming!"

Dirk and I look up to see Coden running from the Tunnel to the table. He practically throws his timer at the in-charges, who look so annoyed I'm a little worried for the boy. He tosses his stuff in the crate and then races to the lift. I don't blame him; the lift worker will take us up, and then the other lift currently stationed at Level B will drop down here. The lift has to wait until so many people get on or until so much has gone by. Coden could be waiting in the next lift for a while unless he catches ours.

The lift worker grunts as Coden jumps on, out of breath.

"You made it," Dirk gives the boy a smile. "Evin was worried sick about you."

Coden rolls his eyes but says nothing. I smirk, and I feel another feeling of liking toward the boy, despite how stupid he's been today. He can keep his mouth shut, unlike some people, like Hannel. I still don't know if I've fully forgiven him for blushing at Aila or suggesting we steal gold, but he's okay. At least, I will still let him escape with us.

The ride up is quiet after that, besides the rattling and shaking of the machine itself. I watch the black rock walls slide by. We move into total darkness, all except for the single light that swings from the lift ceiling. My chest constricts a little; looking around, there's only darkness. I look down and focus on my boots, waiting until we get to Level B to look up.

*Three more days*, I think at my boots, and I take deep breaths. Coden, much to my annoyance and relief, slides closer to me, close enough to be touching my arm. He doesn't say anything, but I know he's trying to comfort me. I know now that he knows how much I don't like the darkness. He's much more observant than I thought.

We finally reach B Level, and the worker heaves open the gate. I try and not focus on how little the lift worker is, so I hurry out. The lift to the right of the one we came up in goes down. I wonder if running the lifts is better or worse than running in the Tunnels. To me, it just seems like an endless stream of darkness. At least in the Tunnels, I feel like I can run away from it. In the lifts, you're trapped in a cage. I shake my head; no job down here is good.

There are in-charges waiting in the Open Area to give us our nightly assignments. I'm assigned to clean the floor in the Open Area. This will be awful; the in-charges are watching on the floor, but also from the Overhang. I hope Krin got an easy job or that someone was with her to take her load of the work. Dirk is assigned with me, as is Coden. But so are Hannel and, much to my increasing annoyance, that tall kid that hangs around Hannel.

We get the cleaning buckets, rags, and soap from a table over to the side and begin wiping the floor.

We work in silence for a while, but then I hear Hannel and the other kid whispering something to each other. I glance up and find they're looking at me, but then their eyes quickly flick away. My cheeks burn.

Dirk and Coden are a little ways away from me and the other two, cleaning the floor quickly. Dirk says something softly, and Coden gives a small smile in reply. I clean even faster, my arms burning from the motion.

It doesn't take too long, especially since there are about fifty of us cleaning the massive floor. But, by the time we're done, my knees and elbows are soaked, and I'm even hungrier.

Plus, my fingers are cracked again. They're at least not bleeding, but they're dry and painful.

Dirk and I walk side by side towards the cafeteria, but Coden hangs back a little. I figure he's still mad at me, but I don't move to speak to him. If he wants to act stupid, let him.

We get our trays, our food (I almost smile when the workers slap an extra thick piece of bread on our trays for today), and go to the usual table in the back corner of the low-ceilinged cafeteria. Aila and Krin are there, but Hoss and Duna aren't.

"Evening," Aila smiles at us as we sit down. Coden sits with a larger-than-normal space between us and doesn't look at anyone. Aila gives him an odd look but doesn't say anything.

Krin, I notice, looks exhausted. Her eyes are bloodshot, her cheeks sunken, and even though her face is smudged black like everyone else's, I can see dark circles under her eyes. She's sitting awkwardly on the bench, leaning slightly to the left like she can't quite hold herself up.

"Krin….?" I say, not really knowing how to form the words. She didn't look nearly this bad this morning. Tired, for sure, but not this. I know I've been mad at her, but she looks awful. I feel instantly worried this isn't going to work and that it has to work at the same time.

"I'm fine," Krin gives a weak smile, but she doesn't turn to look at me. "Just a little tired."

Aila flashes a look at me; her eyes are wide with worry. For a moment, I'm surprised and annoyed that she's sharing this emotion with me of all people, but then, I realize that if Aila is showing *me* worry, she must be *really* worried.

Hoss and Duna eventually make their way over. Duna slides in next to Dirk and Hoss next to Krin. Hoss puts his arm around Krin and talks to her in a low voice. Duna, meanwhile, stares at the floor and doesn't touch her food. She seems just as sad and empty as when Nolan was Departed. Over the past few weeks, she's been angry and commenting on everything. Now, she's...like this. I don't know which is worse, and I don't know what made her change again. I remember how she reacted when she saw Jinade; maybe the in-charges gave her a hard time today.

Speaking of in-charges, we hear the all-too-familiar stomp of boots echoing down the tunnel. Krin puts her face in her hands and leans into Hoss's chest. Aila sucks in a breath and watches the tunnel opening. I don't want to turn around. These nights, when they Depart us, have been torture. It's even worse that it's sometimes at dinner, sometimes at night, sometimes right before we have to wake up and go to work.

Sure enough, Jinade comes sauntering in, nose high in the air, followed closely by Kevoc, a few other in-charges, and at least a dozen guards. We haven't even really started eating, and they're already coming in. Can't they let us be Departed on a full stomach?

The cafeteria instantly quiets down, and everyone turns to look at Jinade and Kevoc, and the guards. They're a gray and black line blocking us from the tunnel.

Jinade smiles at us all, cold and sneering, and then she takes a rolled-up paper from an in-charge when he hands it to her.

She unrolls the paper and says, "The following workers have turned 18 and will be required to be reassigned in Society. When your number is called, step forward to be tested. NM3487, NM2355, NM1299, NM1278, NM4488, NM3267, and NM3184."

Seven kids shakily rise from their benches and make their way to the in-charges. They line up in order, and, in order, each one is taken by the guards and marched to Departure. It doesn't even take that long. I feel a little relieved when I watch the guards leave with the kids, knowing that, at least for tonight, I am safe, and so is Krin. Both she and Hoss slump a little, just as relieved as I am.

I wonder how much longer our luck can last. Hopefully for at least three more days.

Jinade lingers behind, like she has before, and keeps our silent attention for several minutes before she finally speaks.

"Tomorrow will be your monthly Sun Day," she says. I feel an immense weight suddenly leave my shoulders. I am going outside again. At least one more time.

"The following day, we will have Bath Day," Jinade continues. "And, the day after that, is the day our beloved leader, His Majesty the Chancellor will be visiting us." She beams as she says this and clasps her hands in front of her. "His inspection is most important, and we expect you all to be on your best behavior. To not be would be most unwise. Enjoy your Sun Day." Then she turns on her heel and leaves, followed closely by two guards.

"Of course," Duna rolls her eyes, "they'll want us all clean for when the Chancellor comes."

I shrug. At least we get a bath. Who cares if it's just to impress the Chancellor? That just means I will be taking less of this place with me when we leave the next day.

"We'll get some good reading done tomorrow," Aila says brightly.

My stomach rumbles, and I dig into my food now that the nightly activities are over.

Hoss slides half his food onto Krin's tray and gives her half his bread. Looking at him, I find him looking more tired than usual as well.

"Okay," Aila whispers, pulling the papers from underneath her shirt. "Let's get going."

I brace myself for this nightly round of humiliation and wait for Aila to give me the words that always seem impossible to pronounce and understand. I still can't picture what the stupid cuh-at is or a lake. Maybe if I could picture the words, it'd be easier to understand them. But I just can't imagine water big enough that it stretches miles before you and miles beneath you. The only water I've ever seen is the puddles that form in the Bath Room. "Ready, Evin?" Aila asks. She slides a list of words over to me. The words written in the coal smudge on the crumpled piece of paper taunt me as I look at them.

I take a deep breath, then begin to whisper what I read to Aila: "And...lot...r-run...dog…"

# Chapter Twelve

The Sun Day passes normally, except for the reading. We get new blankets and pillows to make our beds with (no doubt to impress the Chancellor. I've had my blanket since he came last time, about ten years ago, and now I get a new one. I almost wish I could take the old one with me), and then we scrub all the tunnels on B Level. Krin, Aila, and I are assigned to the same team, so Aila and I help Krin along. I don't like working with Aila, but she cleans quickly and instinctively helps Krin move to make it less obvious she isn't doing anything, so it's alright, I guess.

And, she's actually silent for once. No words or talking about her new cleaning job or the outside world. So, it's *really* okay.

We get checked off and then head to the lifts and ride up together. Krin's face seems brighter and less haggard as we ride up, and I feel my chest lightening, too.

Once outside, we squint against the bright sun as we hurry to the same tree as last time. It feels much cooler than the previous Sun Day, and the leaves on our tree have a red tint around their edges.

Again, we sit in the dirt and read the words Aila draws with a stick. The words seem especially hard today: *men, can, row, see.* Maybe it's just because I'm having trouble focusing. We're outside, the air is crisp and clean, and we will hopefully be rid of this place in just a few more days.

Aila hands me a stick and tells me to write some letters in the dirt. I'm kind of angry that she's pushed me back to letters--I thought I'd been doing okay with writing some words--but when I finish, she reads over the letters and then smiles at me.

"What?" I ask, folding my arms angrily over my chest.

"That's you, Evin," she says softly. "E-V-I-N. Evin."

My eyes widen in surprise, and I look back at the dirt. The letters are scraggly and uneven, but I sound them out to myself.

"Evin," I whisper under my breath, looking at the letters, feeling pride and hope bubble in my chest. I wrote my own name! It's odd; I feel suddenly more...real. I feel like the numbers etched into my skin don't matter anymore. No matter what the in-charges call me, these letters in the dirt are who I am.

*Evin.*

The time outside ends quickly, and we hustle back inside to the cafeteria. In-charges wait at the entrance to give us our group numbers for Bath Day tomorrow. Krin and I are, again, in group six together. Aila is in group five this time.

More gray slop, more words written on crumpled paper.

More Departures.

Three more kids go, all of them sorters.

We make our way back to our bunks, all evidence of a day in the sun washed from our faces after watching three more kids march away to their death.

It's hard to sleep that night, but I eventually do.

I wake to the sound of the in-charges and guards coming in, setting up their table and carts full of clothes.

*Tomorrow*, I think. *Tomorrow I will be gone.*

Group six is called after a few hours, and Krin and I make our way to the table.

"Make sure to get a stall near the back," I whisper to Krin. "Try not to let anyone see you."

She nods, casting worried glances around at the other workers. Who knows who will try and use Krin's secret to gain advantage with the in-charges?

227

But, Bath Day goes smoothly. I'm careful not to touch the in-charge's hand as I receive my new clothes, and Krin is careful not to let anyone see her stomach. I don't look myself; I don't want to. Her hair, though, looks less choppy and now sits just below her shoulders. This makes her so happy that she smiles. I smile, too but add an eye roll.

In the cafeteria afterward, Hoss passes her a clean shirt, having kept his one from last month. It looks filthy, compared to everyone else's, but after today, no one will notice. Mine already has a nice layer of coal dust coating the sleeves, so it's alright.

For some reason, I feel okay, like everything's alright. I'm clean. I'm somewhat hopeful. Everyone is sitting around the table, reading, eating, and I see Krin and Hoss smiling and laughing quietly at each other. This morning just feels good.

I wish that feeling could have lasted longer.


*One more day, one more day, one more day,* I chant to myself in the Tunnels.

We passed Coden's gold to get to where we left off yesterday, and he looked furious as we walked by it. He still hasn't said anything to me. Silence is fine with me, and I eventually forget he's with me at all; I'm too focused on my side of the Tunnel and on the chant in my head.

I review the plan again, even though there isn't much to review. I still want to argue with Aila that the plan seems too simple, but I don't. I want to save Krin--*have* to save Krin--but I don't want to argue with Aila to do it. I don't want to be reminded that everyone likes her so much more. I don't trust her, so I'm just going to have to do whatever it takes to save Krin and the baby.

The sound of footsteps echoing behind me makes me stop and turn around, Coden copying my actions. I hold up my light and wait for whomever the footsteps belong to. A brief flutter of nervousness makes my stomach feel tingly, but I know it's normal for in-charges to come and observe us before the Chancellor comes. I've actually been waiting for it. I hope that's all this is. Well, I hope, and I don't hope. I hate being observed.

A few seconds later, two men appear, carrying lights of their own. They're in-charges, holding clipboards and wearing their crisp gray suits. I smirk a little when I see their clothes have coal dust on them. One guard follows closely behind them, seemingly a third shadow cast by the lanterns' light.

All three of them stop about five feet away from us. It's like a standoff of lanterns for a few moments. I take them in as we look at each other. One in-charge is tall, his mustache curled on either end. It's Kredit!

The other in-charge is quite short and fat; I know I've seen him before, too. He is in the Tunnel Room quite often. He's the one who yells at you if you tell him your number too quickly.

"We're here to observe you," the Kredit announces. He's older, with gray in his hair and wrinkles around his eyes. His mustache is a crisp black, though, and wiggles when he talks.

He lifts up his clipboard as if to prove that's why they're really here. "Numbers?" he asks.

"NM1448," I say.

"NM15266," Coden replies.

The in-charge scribbles on his clipboard and then says, "Go ahead."

I turn and begin scanning the wall again. Just before I do, I see Coden's face. He seems to have shrunk before the in-charges, and he looks sweaty and wide-eyed. I know he's never been observed before. I wish I could tell him that it's alright, that it's no big deal as long as we do our work. I maybe should've told him this might happen. Oh well.

The last time the Chancellor came, we'd all been observed the days leading up to his coming. The in-charges watch us work, make notes, and then show the Chancellor the best, hardest working ones in the Mine. I don't want to be the best; I don't want the Chancellor coming to observe me and then not finding me or Coden where we're supposed to be. However, we still have to work hard; I don't want the in-charges thinking we're unfit before tomorrow.

I can hear the in-charges walking behind us as we work, occasionally scribbling something on their clipboards. Their scribbling makes me think of Aila, how she can just pull out paper and *write*. It annoys me. Why do we need to write anyway? And writing is just one step beyond reading. I hate that I'm determined fit or unfit based on words and whether or not I can read or write them.

"How many steps so far today?" one of them asks.

I don't turn around to see which one, but I look at my timer and answer, "4,058."

"How many hours?"

I look at my timer. "Three."

They mumble something between themselves, but I don't care. Let them mumble. We're on a good pace today.

A long silence passes, and I'm starting to hope they'll get bored and leave, but then one asks, "When is the last time you actually marked something."

I can hear the sneer in his voice, but I reply calmly, "Yesterday. We found a large amount of gold in this Tunnel and marked it. We reported it in the Tunnel Room yesterday." Was the fat one in the Tunnel Room then? I honestly can't remember. I just remember being furious at Coden; I hadn't paid attention.

"Really?" he sounds disbelieving. "The gold diggers were not sent here. No gold has been extracted today."

I stop for a moment, my heart beginning to pound. I told the in-charges yesterday. I'm sure I did; in fact, I'm sure the fat one was there. Why else would he sound so smug, so...greedy?

But Coden wasn't there. He can't back me up.

Suddenly, all my air rushes out of my lungs in a silent panic. I know what they're doing. They're catching a mistake, trapping an "unfit" so they can prove to the Chancellor that they keep us in line.

I'm going to get Departed. Just so they look good.

I turn and look at the in-charges, trying to keep my face somewhat calm. Both of them are looking at me expectantly, but more like they're expecting (or hoping) for me to fail.

"We marked it," I say evenly. "I told the in-ch--uh--the Keepers in the Tunnel Room yesterday."

"So now you're blaming us?" the fat in-charge smirks, his cheeks almost smacking his shoulder when he talks. He writes something on his clipboard. He has a horrible, nasally voice that normally would sound kind of funny.

"No," I say, trying to keep my voice above a panicked whisper. "No. I'm just saying we only marked it yesterday, so maybe the gold diggers haven't made it yet--"

"We didn't pass anyone on the way in," the in-charge says.

Suddenly, I realize that I didn't see the flashing red light of the marker when we passed by the gold. I saw the gold, but not the marker. Why didn't I see the marker?

I open my mouth to speak, but no words come out.

Surprisingly, Coden speaks up and says, "Would it be alright if we go and check? I marked it myself. I remember it. We wouldn't hide it from you." He says it very evenly; his words almost sound authoritative.

The in-charges raise their eyebrows at Coden, but the older one shrugs and says, "If you insist, but you will be expected to make up for the lost distance."

I nod, my legs heavy as I turn and start walking back up the Tunnel. I'm grateful Coden spoke up, but I'm not sure what we will find when we reach the gold. I'm not really sure what the in-charges did to make us fail.

I can hear the in-charges scribbling on their clipboards as they follow us, and it almost seems they are walking closer, which makes me think the guard must be closer as well. I gulp silently.

Coden and I walk quickly; I don't want to get accused of going too slowly.

It takes us a while to get back to where the gold marker should be, and I arrive slightly out of breath from walking so fast. I arrive first, and I quickly start scanning the wall for the marker, but the wall is so full of gold, I'm not sure where it should be exactly.

I hear the in-charges and guard approaching from behind. The Tunnel fills with light as they hold their lanterns up to the wall. They gasp. I look at them and see them staring at the gold, eyes wide and mouths open. The gold shimmers in the light, reflecting in their eyes.

"How much is here, Kredit?" the shorter one whispers to the taller one.

"I don't know, but enough to get us noticed," the tall one, Kredit, replies quietly. "If we bring him down here, can you even imagine the praise? Especially if the worker was unfit..."

232

I know they mean the me, and I feel sick. Now the Chancellor will be here, possibly on the day we're planning to escape. He usually stays for about a week. I try and hide the shaking in my hands and knees. They're going to Depart us-- or kill us-- for sure for not marking this properly. I'm going to die to make them look good, even though I did my job correctly.

*What happened to the marker?*

I look frantically along the wall, but I can't see the marker. I think my heart is in my throat.

"Where's the marker?" one of the in-charges asks in a sickly sweet voice. I can practically hear their minds screaming for my Departure. They're hoping to get double praise: find this much gold and punish the worker who overlooked marking it.

My heart is racing, and I can feel sweat on my forehead. I can't believe it: after everything, all the reading and planning and putting up with Aila, after being only one day away from getting out of here, I'm going to be Departed. I open my mouth, but again, no words come out.

Again, Coden speaks up. "Look!" he says.

I turn, fighting back tears, and sigh in relief as I see Coden holding his lantern to the wall, a marker in place among the gold. It just isn't flashing.

"Why isn't it flashing?" the shorter in-charge asks, folding his arms.

"Did you turn it on?" the taller one sneers. "How many finds have been missed because you can't use the markers correctly?" He leans down toward me, his eyes piercing from above his pointed nose, his mustache almost more intense up close.

"I-I-" I stammer.

"I marked it," Coden reminds them quietly. "But look." He gently pulls the marker out of the wall. He holds it up to the in-charges, so it's in the light, and then I see what he's seeing. Looking closely, I see that the tiny bulb inside the marker looks weird; it looks black and no longer has a red glow.

I've never seen that before," I say softly, almost pleadingly to the in-charges.

"Hmm," the shorter one replies, scribbling on his clipboard. "It appears the bulb burned out. Why didn't you report this? Why didn't you mark it with a different marker?" He glares at me.

"It was flashing when we marked it--"

"Why didn't you notice it this morning?"

"I didn't see--"

"You didn't see?" the in-charge asks.

"I saw it," Coden says softly. "It must've burned out just before you got here."

"And we're just supposed to take your word?" the in-charge asks, scowling at Coden now.

"True members of Society always have proof," Kredit adds. "They are trustworthy because of proof. Guard!"

The black-clad guard seems to materialize into the lantern light. I feel my stomach drop. I have nothing to say to defend myself; even the few words I can read won't save me now. He steps forward menacingly, and I squeeze my eyes shut, willing it all to go away when the sudden sound of laughter echoes from further down the tunnel.

I open my eyes a tiny bit, looking towards the laughter. Everyone, including the guard, looks, too.

A few moments later-- my heart taking painful counts of the seconds-- three diggers materialize into the lantern light; I recognize them from Hoss's team. In fact, I think they're the same three from yesterday. They're pushing a big cart full of coal.

"Whoa," one says, stopping and lifting his arms to slightly block his face. Four lanterns must be suddenly very bright to their one, and digger lanterns are pretty dim anyway since they only need to see a few feet in front of them at a time.

"Why have you three left your post?" the short in-charge snaps. "It is not time to stop yet!" I notice his face turns red as he sees the diggers.

"Cart's full," the one who spoke to me yesterday says deeply, gesturing at the cart, which is bulging with coal. "And our team lead told us to come help the gold diggers with this find since it's so big. They were finishing up an extraction this morning, so we had time to fill a cart."

The in-charges quickly scribble something on their clipboards.

"Did you take the marker out?" the worker asks, looking at the wall. "There was a marker in the wall this morning."

"It burned out," Coden says softly, holding the bulb up for the workers to see. "We'll put in a new one so you can find it."

The digger nods at Coden then looks at the in-charges expectantly; he even has the guts to lift an eyebrow at them, as if challenging them to say something. He's even taller than Kredit and twice as broad.

The tall in-charge stares at the digger, then says, "What's your number?"

"NM6148," the boy says, folding his arms over his massive chest.

"And your team lead?" the in-charge asks.

The digger's scowl falters a little, but he replies, "NM3490."

"Thank you for the information," the taller in-charge smiles cruelly at the big digger. "Be assured that we will investigate this matter further. We wouldn't want the Chancellor thinking things like this went...unnoticed." He smiles even broader at the digger, but the tall boy doesn't even flinch. In fact, his face darkens to a deep scowl; my stomach twists for him. The shorter one is writing so quickly on his clipboard, his face so close to the paper, that I'm not sure whether he will break his pen or bump his fat nose first.

Then the in-charges turn back and face me.

"We expect you to make up for this lost time," the taller one scowls. "Don't think this goes unnoticed for you, either. Go." He nods over his shoulder. I don't need telling twice, I grab Coden's arm, and we hurry past them, the cart, and the diggers back down the Tunnel. My guess is that the in-charges are now going to observe the diggers extract the gold. I'm not sad, but the way that big digger talked to the in-charges made me nervous; how could he be so calm and so obviously hateful of the in-charges? He looked old, too. He needs to be careful.

Before we go too far, I hear the in-charges begin asking questions to the diggers. I can hear that boy's rumbling voice answer one of them, but we're too far to hear what's said.

We hurry on, desperate to get back to where we were and make up for the lost time. We have to get as many steps in as we can in the next four hours, or we'll be marked "unfit" for sure. I know we will be watched closely now. Any tiny mistake will lead us straight through the Departure door.

Since we didn't mark where we had stopped and turned around (thankfully, the in-charges hadn't noticed this), we have to guess where we stopped. I'm pretty sure we searched much of the same area today, but I can't be sure, and I'd rather search something twice than miss a section altogether.

We search in silence, and I'm still shaking. My lantern light shimmers along the wall, and I can't get my hand to hold still. We came so close--I came so close--to being Departed. All because of a burned-out bulb and the in-charges' need to catch us being "unfit."

Finally, my wrist timer begins beeping. I check how many steps we have gone today, and I feel satisfied with the 17,456 steps. It's about three thousand more than we regularly get, which is due to having to backtrack, but I think we made up the time. Hopefully.

Without speaking, we turn and begin hurrying back up the Tunnel. This Tunnel is still at a gradual slant, so running back to the Tunnel Room is easier since it's pretty much downhill.

We're able to keep a good pace, and I'm able to block out my terrified thoughts by focusing on the jarring impact of each foot on the dirt floor. I'm just hoping that the in-charges aren't waiting for us to emerge, aren't waiting to see our timers, and declare us unfit for not making up the time.

After nearly an hour, I see light ahead, but not the bright light of the Tunnel Room. This is a single, dim lantern sitting on the floor of the tunnel. I see shadows moving around it and realize that it must be the diggers. That confuses me, though, since they should've been back to the Tunnel Room by now.

I stop in front of them and see them working at extracting the gold. There's more of them now, six in total, but Hoss isn't with them, so the extras must be the gold diggers. Their cart is over half-full of differing-sized chunks of gold. I see Coden's eyes go to them, and I step in front of him, not allowing him within arm's reach of the cart.

There are tiny, almost delicate tools on the ground; I can't imagine how long this wall will take to extract, especially using those tools.

The one digger, the one who spoke to me and the in-charges, lifts his head as we approach. I'm confused why they're still working.

"Timers went off," I say, holding up my wrist.

The boy rolls his eyes and hauls himself to his feet. He stands head and shoulders above me, forcing me to look up as he speaks.

"The idiots decided we should have an extra hour today since we didn't start actually extracting until later," he grumbles.

I nod, feeling sorry for them but also not knowing what to say. Besides, my stomach is rumbling, and *I* wasn't given an extra hour. At least, not yet.

"They're waiting in the Tunnel Room," the boy adds, "to make sure we don't leave early. You better watch out, sis."

"Sis?" I ask, annoyed at that. What does that mean?

He rolls his eyes again, "Just trying to help, you know, warn you, or whatever."

"I don't need-" I start, but then Coden grabs my arm and pulls hard.

"Come on, Evin," he whispers, continuing to tug on my sleeve. "Let's go."

"So you're Evin?" the boy asks suddenly, still standing so close to me that I can look up and into his pale blue eyes.

I don't reply.

"You're Hoss' friend," he says. It's not a question.

I shrug, but, again, don't say anything.

"Huh," he unfolds his arms, but his eyes turn stern. "Take care of him." Then he gives me a knowing look before turning back to hammer away at the gold.

I stand there for a moment, stunned. It isn't until Coden tugs on my arm again, making me jump, that I turn and continue running back up the Tunnel.

Now, not even the pounding of my feet can block out my thoughts. I'm confused and getting more and more terrified, thinking of what that boy said. What had Hoss told him? If Hoss had told *him* what we're planning, who else knew? My frustration at Hoss is turning to fury; how could he be so dumb to tell someone? He had to have, right? Otherwise, why would that massive boy tell me to take care of him? I want to scream; can I trust anyone?

I'm so caught up in my thoughts, I don't even see the light in front of me until I almost crash into it.

"Are you so dumb you can't even walk?" It's the in-charges, the same ones from earlier.

My insides turn to ice. They stand in front of us, looking angry but also hurried.

"Get out of my way," the taller one growls, and then he steps forward and shoves me in the stomach, hard. I fall, clumsily, to the ground below, landing heavily on my elbow and side.

The air rushes out of me, and I gasp, groaning.

"Get up," the short one sneers, excitement in his voice.

I don't hesitate. I rise quickly, staying just out of reach of the two of them, but I keep my eyes on the floor.

They growl as they walk by, mumbling to each other under their breath. Coden and I slide to the side of the Tunnel and press ourselves against the wall until they've walked by. We wait until their boots' echoes have died away before continuing on.

"Where are they going?" Coden asks quietly.

"Check on the gold, most likely," I say, my chin trembling a little bit, almost like I'm shivering. I can't help but glance over my shoulder to make sure there's no light coming up on me from behind. I stretch my arm, trying to loosen my aching elbow. I must've hit a rock on the way down.

My mind is a mess of thoughts and emotions as we hurry through the tunnel. I hate today.

We're almost to the Tunnel Room. I can see the circle of light and feel a touch of relief when Coden stops. He stops so short that I almost crash into him, which makes me even madder.

"What?" I ask, not hiding my annoyance.

"I just...Evin...I..." he stutters, sucking in big breaths. His chest is heaving. "I'm sorry. Today, I didn't think-"

"What?" I ask, a little softer. I look down at him and see tears brimming in his massive brown eyes. He looks panicked. I didn't realize how much the in-charges had shaken him; he had seemed so calm.

"Coden," I say quietly, leaning down to look him in the eye, "it's fine. It was just the bulb. We're okay." Saying it out loud actually makes me feel a little better.

"But Evin, I just...I don't know what to do," the tears start falling.

I open my mouth to say something, but before I can, Coden rushes forward and throws his arms around me. It surprises me enough that I fall all the way to my knees, making us the same height. He squeezes me, and I feel his fear as he clings to me.

Hesitantly, I reach up and put my arms around his thin shoulders. He's so small and, I know, so scared.

*"You have to care, Evin," Hannah's voice rings in my head.*

Suddenly, I'm angry again and shove all thoughts of Hannah away.

Coden clings on for several more minutes until he gives a shaky breath and pulls away, looking at my face as he does. His eyes seem heavy like they've seen a hundred years.

"Sorry," he says quietly. Then he turns, picks up his lantern, and marches towards the Tunnel Room.

I stay back for a moment, still stunned by the embrace, still burning with anger and fear and confusion. I sigh, then rise and hurry after him.

We return our tools and get to the lifts. Dirk catches our lift, and we all walk to the cafeteria together. None of us speak, not even Dirk. He seems quiet and...worried?

It's not until we're in line for our food that I hear him say something.

"What?" I ask.

"Did you have any in-charges observe you today?" he asks quietly.

"Yeah," I reply, walking with my tray to the table. Duna is the only one there so far.

"Us too," Dirk replies. "They didn't say much, just wanted to know how fast we go and how often we find stuff." He shrugs like it's no big deal, but I can see worry in his eyes. It's normal; after observations, we all worry we're going to be "unfit." Especially now. Especially with how old we are.

"Same," I say quietly, but my stomach is in knots. It feels like I ate rocks. I clench my tray so tightly that my knuckles turn white. I'm exhausted from all the emotions I felt today.

We sit down, Dirk next to Duna, Coden next to me. The empty space to the left of me will be replaced by Krin and Hoss on her other side. Then, Aila will come and sit across from me. I feel a sudden pang of familiarity and wonder what, in one day, we will do for dinner. I know we won't be sitting at this table, one way or another.

Suddenly, I feel like throwing up.

I try to eat while Dirk and Duna whisper quietly to each other. I haven't spoken to Duna for the last few days; she has seemed sadder and sadder each day and won't really speak to anyone but Dirk. A part of me still hopes that Duna will come with us; I don't want to leave her to rot by herself until her Departure day.

The gray slop tastes thick today, and I have to take sips of water between each bite. The bread is oddly gritty, but it mops up the slop nicely.

Then, Krin and Aila appear at the table. Krin is breathing heavily, and she sort of heaves herself onto the bench. Hoss's shirt looks stretched. I look away; just a month ago, the bump was barely noticeable. Now, you can't miss it. Seeing her makes me panicked; how are we going to do this?

"You okay?" I ask, arching an eyebrow. I don't want to say what I'm really thinking, but Krin is *huge,* and she looks absolutely exhausted with sunken cheeks and heavy eyes. It's almost like her stomach is eating her.

"She's fine," Aila says through a tight smile. "You're fine. We still have time." She says this to Krin, giving her a little nod. Krin nods back as if she's reassuring herself. I want to roll my eyes at Aila; Krin is obviously not fine. And since when does Krin need Aila's reassurance?

"Where's Hoss?" Krin practically whispers, still out of breath. She looks around but half-heartedly.

"He and the other diggers will probably miss dinner," I say. "There was...uh...some confusion in the tunnel, and now they're digging out gold."

All eyes immediately turn to me, which makes my cheeks burn. I want Hoss to be here so

I can ask him what that other digger meant, but now I'm the one being asked questions.

"Confusion?" Krin's eyes are wide. "What do you mean?"

From the other side of the table, I see Duna, Dirk, and Aila looking at me expectantly. Only Coden keeps his eyes on his food. I almost ask him to explain, but I don't. His eyes still look a little teary.

I sigh and then explain, starting with how Coden basically found a wall full of gold. I explain how we marked it, the in-charges coming, going back, everything. I end with seeing the diggers extracting it and bumping into the in-charges on our way back out. "Hoss wasn't with them, though," I say. "He might not have to stay behind."

They're all staring at me.

"What?" I ask, shrinking a little under their expressions.

"You almost got Departed," Aila whispers, leaning in closer. "Do you realize that?"

"I'm not stupid!" I scowl back.

"Oh, Evin," Krin says, her eyes shining with tears.

"Krin, don't cry," I sigh, rolling my eyes at her. I try to hide the shaking in my hands; I feel all my panic coming back from their expressions.

"What if you had been Departed?" Krin sniffs. "What would we have done?

"You'd be fine!" I said, annoyed. "That's the point. That's why we can't care!" I whisper it, but I know the others feel the force of what I say.

"Evin," Krin says evenly, wiping at her wet cheeks, "I don't know why you're like this, after everything, after all of this!" She gestures around us. "But I care about you. So you will let me be sad at the thought of you getting Departed, especially...well...especially after everything." This is the first time in weeks that anything Krin says has any strength behind it. I stare at her for a moment, at a loss for words.

"Stop being stupid," Dirk rolls his eyes. "You'd be sad if we got Departed, even if you won't say it. We're just glad you're okay."

My eyes slide to Aila for some reason, and I see her staring at me with intense green eyes.

"Don't wait until you get Departed to realize you need friends," Aila says quietly.

They all quietly go back to eating and whispering to each other.

I'm surprised by all of them; they've never said anything about caring about me before. I look down at my plate, somewhat ashamed of myself, but I don't think it's for the reason I should be. Inside, I'm trying to decide if I care about them as much as they say they care about me. Deep down, maybe, but I really think I would be okay without them. I mean, I'm planning to leave them once we're out of here. I'm grateful that they're happy I'm okay, but I'm embarrassed that I don't know how I feel about them. I decide the best thing is to not say anything. What would I say?

Suddenly, I don't feel like eating. Suddenly, I wish I was alone.

# Chapter Thirteen

"So the bulb had burned out?" Dirk asks, spooning mush into his mouth. "I've never seen that before. Surprised they didn't blame you for that, too." He laughs, but there's a hard edge to his laugh that I've never heard from him. He's usually so happy, but now...I don't know how to describe it.

I shrug, still not trusting my words. I cast a sideways glance at Coden. He's scooted a little way away from me, and I can see his hands shaking as he eats. Kind of suddenly, he rises and leaves, dumping his tray and then heading for the tunnel. I watch him leave and see that he almost bumps into Hoss as the big kid comes nearly racing into the cafeteria.

Hoss hurries over to our table, out of breath and without food.

"Hoss?" Krin asks, looking him over. "What's wrong?"

"Evin," he says, not even looking at Krin. "The gold, the gold that you marked, did you do something to it? Did you touch it?"

I look up at him, dread filling me. His expression is pure terror.

"No," I say. "No, we just marked it. Why?"

"We came up on Hugo and Kern and Jack, and the gold diggers," Hoss says, trying to catch his breath. "Hugo told us about everything, so we started to help them. Then, two in-charges came to watch us. While we were digging, Travis found something weird and pointed it out to Gethry, our team lead. The in-charges heard and went to look."

"What was it?" I ask, fear rising in my chest.

"Part of the gold, near the floor, a big vein, looked like someone had chipped away at it with something sharp, and a chunk of it looked like it was missing. We weren't sure, but it was a different enough cut than how we shape the tunnels that Travis pointed out. The in-charges are furious, Evin. They're sure someone stole some."

I go cold.

It won't matter what I say. Who else could it have been? The only ones in that tunnel, the only ones who saw the gold, were me, the diggers, and...Coden. I look over to my right, the space where he normally sits, which is empty now.

I can hear his small voice in my head: *"What if we took some?"*

He left. He left because he knew, somehow, that he was going to get caught. My only hope is that he is going to get rid of it. If they *think* we stole, we might just go to the Colosseum.

If they *know* we (meaning he) stole some, they'll shoot us.

"Coden," I say, turning back to face the others. Then I look at Dirk. "He went back yesterday." The words are barely a whisper. Dirk's eyes widen. "I didn't go with him..." It feels like a confession, like I'm admitting my guilt. How could I have been so stupid? Of course he left his lantern on purpose!

"What do we do?" Dirk asks me.

"He has to get rid of it!" I say, feeling tears threatening to fall. It feels like I'm shouting, but I can barely hear myself. "Now! We have to find him! He has to throw it down the toilet before the in-charges get to him!"

"Come on, Hoss," Dirk says.

He rises, but Duna catches his arm. "If they see you helping him, they'll take you, too!"

He gives her a firm look, then hurries off towards the tunnel, Hoss close on his heels.

I feel cold, empty, like I can't move.

"This is your fault."

I look up to see Duna glaring at me, saying the words that are playing over and over in my mind.

"Duna!" Krin hisses.

"It is!" Duna doesn't take her eyes off me. "You brought him here, and now we're all in danger."

I don't say anything. She's right. What could I say?

The worker bell starts ringing, signaling the end of dinner.

"Come on," Aila says quickly, rising. She grabs Dirk's tray and stacks it on top of hers.

"Let's go see if they found him. Maybe it's not too late."

We all rise, but I can't feel my legs. Krin actually grabs my hand and pulls me towards the tunnel, and I'm grateful. All the workers crowd in close as we head for the tunnel, and I feel like I can't breathe, smothered by all the bodies around me.

"You don't have any, right?" Krin asks, whispering the question in my ear.

I shake my head, but I feel somewhat annoyed. Who is she to ask if *I* have something I shouldn't?

"They're going to search you," she adds slowly, looking at me with worried eyes.

"I know," I hiss back, heart racing. Those in-charges already hate me; is it even going to matter that I didn't take any gold? At this point, the best I can hope for is the Colosseum.

We hurry through the tunnel to the Open Area. We're about halfway across when a lift stops, opens, and spews out a group of in-charges and guards.

Jinade is with them. Kevoc isn't.

They head for the barracks.

I try and speed up but feel like I can't pick up my feet. Why am I just walking towards them? Krin squeezes my hand like she knows what I'm thinking.

We get into the tunnel towards the barracks. At the split, there's a group of boys huddled in the mouth of the tunnel towards their barracks. So, they went after Coden first.

We get into the barrack and hurry to our bunks. Part of me wants to go to Coden, wants to be with him…Krin grabs my hand harder, though, and tugs me mercilessly toward our own side.

"It won't help. Come on," Krin says. "Let's go to bed."

Why? I want to ask. What's the point?

We get to our beds, Aila hurrying off toward her own with a worried look tossed over her shoulder.

Krin climbs up, heaving herself up and onto her mattress, and I climb shakily to my own. My limbs are quivering, my chin shaking, making my teeth clack painfully together. Krin lays on her mattress, looking up at the ceiling. I can't lay down. I'm sitting on my mattress, cold and terrified. I clutch my blanket with icy fingers.


The Gathering Room was dimly lit, except for the platform. I was huddled next to Hannah, gripping her hand with all the force a seven-year-old could muster. She holds it tightly back, but she doesn't look at me. She stares stonily ahead, eyes fixed forward.

The in-charges walked down to the platform in their single-file line. They were all clean, all gray, and all angry looking.

This wasn't my first Arrival, and, being seven, I knew it wouldn't be my last. Yet, my heart was pounding. Everyone was so quiet, and Hannah seemed so sad.

A bunch of new kids filed in from the Arrival door. They seemed terrified, shaking and clutching their left arms. They all sat when their numbers were called.

An old man, wrinkled and bent, eventually went to the center of the platform and unrolled a big piece of paper. Then, he started calling numbers.

I didn't listen, didn't hear.

"NM1352," the Head Reader called.

Hannah tensed, her hand like stone, and then she started to rise.

"No!" I hissed out, tears springing to my cheeks. "No! Hannah, no!" I whispered the words, but kids began looking our way. I didn't care.

"Evin," Hannah said, softly but firmly, "don't forget, Evin." She ripped her hand out of mine, sending me to the floor.

I stayed on the floor, waiting. I heard her tell the Head Reader that she couldn't recognize the letters, even though I knew that she used to be able to.

I didn't look as the guards' boots echoed across the floor, guiding Hannah to the door.

I didn't look.

I didn't look, but I know she looked back. I know she did. She was Departed because of me. I knew it even then. She stood up for me because she cared about me, and it sent her through the Departure doors.

I stayed on the floor, crying, too cowardly, too sad to look up and say goodbye to the only person that I'm certain I ever loved.

The marching finally enters our barracks.

I know they're coming for me, but I can't move.

249

The boots stop in front of my bed. I turn my head and see Jinade flanked by two other in-charges, surrounded by at least ten guards. The in-charges are the ones from the Tunnel. They look extremely pleased with themselves. The short, fat one still has his clipboard, looking ready to write down the need for my death.

Then, two of the guards shuffle forward, and I see that they're dragging Coden's limp form between them. The sight of him sucks out any breath I have remaining.

"NM1448," Jinade says coolly, glaring at me.

I slide off my bed, missing the bottom rung of the ladder and slipping to the floor. I have to grip my bed to keep from falling over. I refuse to look at Krin's face; I won't look at her. But I know she's looking at me.

My feet carry me forward, and I can feel the eyes of everyone in the barracks looking at me. I force myself not to look at Coden, to see his head hanging down and his feet dragging on the floor. I don't even know if he's still alive.

Jinade watches me approach with a cool glare. She finally speaks when I stop in front of her.

"NM1448," she says, her voice carrying to everyone's eyes, "you are accused of stealing gold from this, the Northern Mine of the New Nation."

She stares at me like I'm going to confess. I don't say anything.

"You will be searched," she finally says and then snaps her fingers.

Two guards hurry forward and grab my arms, dragging me forward until I'm level with Coden. I can see him breathing, and relief rushes through me. He doesn't look up, though; I think he's passed out. Another pair of guards hurry to my bed and begin ripping it apart. Unlike a regular inspection, they actually rip my mattress, sending pieces of fluff flying all around. They rake my blanket apart, destroy my pillow, pat down every inch of splintery wood to see if there is gold.

The guards' grips on my arms are tight and painful, but I don't make a sound. I tell myself not to make a sound.

"There's nothing here, Lady Executor," one of the guards finally says.

I heave a sigh, and the guards heave me to my feet. I didn't realize I'd fallen to my knees.

They turn me around and face me to Jinade. Her cool expression makes my knees shake.

Her gray eyes are ice cold and relentless.

"But her partner!" the tall in-charge, Kredit, hisses out. "What about that?" He gestures to Coden, who seems to be stirring.

Tears well up in my eyes. *Coden, you idiot.*

Jinade looks me up and down, her gaze steely, and asks, "Did you steal gold?"

My knees are shaking, but I look her in the eyes when I say, "Does it matter what I say?"

The Lady Executor smirks. "Drop him," she says to the guards. The two holding Coden let him fall heavily to the floor. He groans.

"Did you steal gold?" Jinade asks me again.

"No," I say flatly.

She snaps her fingers, and one of the guards kicks Coden fiercely in the ribs. He moans in pain and coughs horribly. I flinch, my chin shaking, but I turn my gaze back to Jinade.

"Where is the gold you took?" Jinade asks, a smile still on her face.

"I didn't take any," I say, my voice barely more than a whisper.

She nods at the guards, and I hear them kick Coden again, making me jump, but I refuse to look. This isn't my fault. This isn't like Hannah.

The guard kicks him again, and Coden starts crying; I feel a tear slide down my cheek.

"Where is the gold you took?!" Jinade asks, her voice rising.

"I didn't take any," I say evenly, but my voice catches, and I have to clear my throat.

A guard draws his plastic stick and whacks Coden.

"Ah!" Coden screams, now fully awake.

"Where's the gold?!

*Whack!*

"I didn't take any!" I say, tears now flowing down my cheeks.

*Whack!*

"She doesn't...have any!" Coden coughs out, chest heaving. He's lying on his side, curled into a ball, but he's looking at Jinade. "She doesn't." Jinade turns her gaze back to me.

"Where is the gold?" she asks, but more calmly.

I sink to my knees. "I don't have any," I sob out. I almost wish I did; then they'd stop hitting Coden and just let us both die.

*Whack!*

"I don't!" I say, looking up at her pleadingly. "Please! Please! I don't!"

*Whack! Whack! Whack!*

I'm sobbing, my head in my hands, unable to make this stop. I have nothing to give Jinade to make this *stop*.

*Whack!*

"Stop," Jinade says.

The guards move away from Coden, but I don't look up. I can't look at Coden; I can't see his pain.

"She doesn't have any," Jinade says.

"Your Ladyship, for all we know, she could have hidden it-" the fat in-charge begins, but Jinade cuts him off.

"She would've given it up by now," Jinade says. "Still." She snaps her fingers, and I wait to hear Corden's cries of pain, but, instead, I feel the stick crash into my own ribs, sending me flying backward onto my back, gasping in pain.

"Get up," Jinade spits.

Shakily, I rise to my feet, cradling my ribs, breathing heavily.

Jinade steps forward until she's just in front of me, and she smiles. Her eyes are steely gray and ice cold, her lips tight and cruel. Then, she slaps me across the cheek, *hard*. I go whirling, falling back to the ground, eyes watering, cheek stinging.

"Get up," Jinade says again. I do as she commands, my knees shaking as I do. I tell myself not to cry out, but the second slap sends me down again, and I hit my head against my bunk's post.

I can't see for the tears in my eyes, but I don't cry out; I won't.

"Get up," Jinade says again, but now she sounds almost bored.

I rise, my whole body shaking, my face on fire.

"Hmm," Jinade says, pursing her dark red lips. "I think an adequate lesson has been learned, especially since she wasn't the only one who learned it."

The in-charges look furious. They cast each other a glance and then focus back on me.

She looks at Coden, then at the guards, and waves them away. They stoop down, grab his underarms, and begin dragging him away. I watch him, the little boy who loved stars and used to have a dog and parents and a sister, be pulled toward the tunnel. Briefly, he looks up at me, gives a small smile, and then lets his head droop.

I can't breathe.

Jinade says loudly, "A friendly reminder that our beloved Chancellor will be arriving tomorrow evening. Sleep well."

Then, they all leave. The two in-charges throw me furious looks over their shoulders, but they follow Jinade out of the barracks.

Once they're gone, the last footstep swallowed by darkness, I collapse on the ground. I'm lying on my side, curled into a ball. I put my stinging face in my hands and begin shaking.

I heave my breath in and out, just letting the tears come.

"Evin," Krin says, kneeling down beside me. She carefully lays a hand on my arm, and I can hear that she's crying. "Oh, Evin."

Then there are more feet coming quickly over.

"Let's help her up," Aila says softly. "Quickly. They can't come back and find her like this."

"But her bed?" Krin says.

"Here," a voice I don't recognize says. "There's an empty bunk down the row. She can use this one."

I hear some girls moving around, but I don't lift my head. I don't even open my eyes.

"Evin," Krin says softly, "come on." Hands lift me from under my arms, but I don't look up. They drag me to my bed and then lift and shove me up onto the borrowed mattress.

I fall on the mattress heavily, struggling to breathe. The girls all hurry away, all except Krin who hoists herself onto her bed.

"I'm so sorry, Evin," she says softly.

I don't say anything.

What is there to say?

The morning hurts. I wake up crying, having had the dream that I can't ever remember, but I'm shaking and sweaty and sore. My ribs ache, and my cheek feels puffy and hot. Krin wakes without me needing to shake her, and she lowers herself slowly down. Then, she reaches up to help me.

"How are you?" she asks softly. I don't answer because I really don't know.

We hurry to the cafeteria, and I try not to look around. I don't want to see pity or smugness painted on the other girls' faces this morning.

We get in line, Krin helps me get food, and we get to the table. I never even lift my gaze from the floor.

"Evin?" Aila asks quietly. "How are you?"

I don't answer.

Then, I hear Hoss and Dirk slide onto the bench. I look up, finally, and look at Dirk. His eyes widen as he takes in my face, but I shake my head and look at my tray. I know the bump must be noticeable even through the dirt.

"I'm so sorry, Evin," Dirk whispers. "We didn't find him in time..."

I nod but don't look up. It's not Dirk's fault, and I should tell him that, but if it's not Dirk's fault, whose is it? Coden was just too little. I really don't want it to be my fault, and it kind of feels like it is.

"Will they Depart him?" Aila asks the others quietly.

Anger bubbles inside me. Aila is stupid, and she didn't care about Coden.

"No," Dirk finally says. "They'll take him outside."

"Why-?" Aila begins, but I explain with tears in my eyes and anger in my voice.

"You're taken outside for stealing," I say, "and shot. It's too messy to shoot anyone inside the Mine if they can avoid it."

Aila opens her mouth, seemingly surprised at my anger. She looks down, averting her eyes, and I'm satisfied.

The others say nothing for a while. They just pick at their food. Krin keeps her arm around me, and eventually, I lean over and drop my head against her shoulder. I feel exhausted. I have felt too many emotions and too much pain.

I'm so mad at myself. Coden had gone back that night. He'd gone back for a lantern that he'd left behind on purpose. I can just imagine him, once we'd escaped, showing me the gold proudly, eyes shining.

Why hadn't I gone back with him? Then I could've stopped him. I could've saved him...

"I'm sorry," I whisper, loud enough for only Krin to hear.

"For what?" Krin whispers just as quietly back. I'm so grateful for that, grateful that she knows I don't want anyone else to hear.

"For not believing you," I say.

"What do you mean?"

"It hurts," I sigh, feeling the hot tears fall on my cheeks and being completely incapable of stopping them. "I knew losing people hurt. I knew it, but I didn't want to. It would hurt to lose you."

# Chapter Fourteen

*Today*, I think. *Today, today, today.*

It has happened several times before, but this time seems the most awkward and annoying. As my new partner approaches me, my heart fills with rage and sadness. Rage at the in-charges who had taken Coden, rage at Coden himself for being stupid enough to take the gold, and sadness that it had all happened to a small boy who liked to look at stars, had parents, but then died in the Mine. In darkness.

*I hope he got to see the stars one last time*, I think sadly. If I die tonight, I hope they take me outside, so I can see the sky. I want to see the lights in the darkness. I want to see Coden's stars and know why they're so important in that stupid song that stupid girl sings sometimes.

My new partner comes up to me just outside the lifts. He is tall and so, so skinny; his clothes hang off him and look like they're swallowing him. He has the standard coal-smudged skin, and his eyes are plain brown. For being so thin and long, his nose is wide and large. Then, he gets closer, and I actually see his face, his eyes, his creepy smile.

It's Hannel's friend.

"You're Evin?" he asks. His voice gives me chills. I nod.

"I'm Chesnit," he says. He gives me a smirky smile.

I give a slight nod, and then we board the lift for the Tunnel Room. Dirk is on this lift, and, of course, so is Hannel. Chesnit immediately goes and stands by Hannel. I look at Dirk quickly, trying to see if he has any feelings about Chesnit, but he's looking at the ground. I look back to my new partner and find that he's scooting back over to me. The door to the lift closes as he reaches me again.

"I was a searcher before, so you don't really need to worry about training me," Chesnit informs me. I look away from him. The lift worker slumps against the lift wall, tapping the metal side- *clink! clink! clink!*- and I want to rip his finger off.

The lift jerks downward in little hops, and the wheels on top of us squeak wildly. Each quick drop makes my stomach churn. I feel breakfast sitting heavily inside me like a rock, and I have to stare at the floor, trying not to think about how we're in a tiny tube high above the floor below us in a jumping, unstable metal box.

Another jerk and I have to stifle a squeal. I resist shutting my eyes, though.

"You okay?" Chesnit asks, and I glance up at him without wanting to. He's looking at me with a mocking smile, and I see Hannel stifling a laugh behind him.

I don't respond.

The lift comes to a squeaking halt, and the worker slides open the gate.

I march off, followed by Chesnit.

We make our way to the bins and find ours. Coden's tools are still in it, but the number outside it has changed. I don't even bother seeing what Chesnit's number is. I don't care, and it won't matter after today. Hesitantly, almost reverently, I lift Coden's things up. I hold them for a moment and then thrust them towards Chesnit. They're his now.

I clip on my belt, making sure the pouch is full of marking tools. Then I grab my lantern.

I lead Chesnit over to the in-charge table.

"NM1448," I say quietly. It's the fat in-charge. Wonderful.

"Welcome back," he mocks, and he holds out a timer for me. I reach to take it, but he drops it on the floor.

I resist sighing but quickly bend to grab it.

"Don't drop your tools!" he shouts at me. I flinch but nod. I strap it on my wrist and then head to the Tunnel. I flick on the lantern and, without even checking to make sure Chesnit is following me, I walk into the gaping hole that is my life.

It takes us about an hour of running (more like hobbling on my part), almost wholly on an uphill slant, to get to where Coden and I had left off yesterday. *Yesterday.* It feels like years ago.

The gold diggers are still working on Coden's gold, but I don't say anything to them as we pass by.

Once we get to the flashing blue light, I say, "You search that side and the ground." Then I aim my lantern on the right wall and begin searching in slow, arching sweeps. I quickly fall into a rhythm of limping and switching sore arms holding the lantern, and I settle into silence and darkness.

It hasn't even been two minutes, and Chesnit is already talking.

"Wouldn't it make more sense for me to search the ceiling?" Chesnit asked. "After all, I can actually touch the ceiling." I can hear the smile in his words, but I don't know if he's being stupid or nice. If he's Hannel's friend, my guess is stupid. Besides, I don't want him to be nice.

"You search the ground and that side," I repeat.

"Okay, boss," Chesnit laughs again. The sound makes my teeth grind.

"So, what's your story?" Chesnit asks after another two minutes. I say nothing. He chuckles a little and says, "That's okay. You don't have to tell me. I was only curious after last night, you know, and everyone knows what happened. Too bad about that kid, though, but that's what you get, I guess. And then being *assigned* to you. Well, I was just bursting with questions, but I get not really wanting to talk about it. When I first got here, I did *not* want to talk about anything, anything at all. Especially since I was already thirteen and had been with my parents until they were killed. Then I was brought here. I can't read, obviously, and my parents never taught me. Not really their fault. They had busy jobs. Honestly, I don't even know if *they* could read. I think mostly I-"

I can't take it anymore. "Seems like you got over not wanting to talk," I say harshly.

"Ha, right?" Chesnit doesn't seem to be taking the hint. "I think you get used to this place after a while. So, chin up, right?"

I stop, confused by his words. He stops with me, and I turn to stare at him in a questioning way.

"What do you mean?" I ask.

"Well, I'm just saying that, with time, you get used to-"

"How old are you?" I ask, folding my arms.

"Fifteen," he says proudly, puffing out his chest a little. "I've been here two years."

"Two?" I raise an eyebrow, and he nods enthusiastically. "How long do you think I've been here?" I stare coldly at him.

"Well, can't have been for too long," he shrugs. "Else you'd know not to mess around with stealing and everything. I'd say less than a year."

I clench my hands, threatening to explode on Chesnit.

"How old do you think I am?" I ask through gritted teeth.

Chesnit seems to feel my anger, and he hesitates and shrugs when he answers, "Uh...maybe fourteen?"

"I'm seventeen, maybe older," I hint. "And I was brought here when I was three." I watch as what I say sinks into Chesnit's mind, his eyes growing wide and his mouth stuck as an "o." I turn and begin searching again, cheeks burning. *I didn't steal anything.*

"That makes you an ancient!" Chesnit says, awe clear in his voice. "I mean, gosh, you're even older than Hannel, and he's been here nearly five years!"

"A what?" I ask, almost tiredly. I don't want to talk to him anymore. He acts younger than Coden, and he's way too full of energy, and I don't like that he is friends with Hannel.

"An ancient! You must have been one of the very first batches of Arrivals! This Mine opened fifteen years ago when the Nation was reborn. You've been here longer than almost anyone! You may even be the longest now! There aren't many of you left," he ends almost sadly.

Then, his face brightens, "What's your number?"

"My what?" I ask, looking at him in shock.

He kind of playfully rolls his eyes and says, "Your number! Here, let me see." He moves toward me, and I instinctively press myself against the Tunnel wall, moving away from him. He pauses, looking confused.

"Come on," he whines, "just let me see!"

He moves forward again, and I turn and continue searching, hoping he will get the hint.

He doesn't.

I see it before I feel it and wheel around, smacking his hand away from my left arm.

"Stop!" I shout at him.

"I just want to see your number!" he laughs, shaking his hand like my slap actually hurt.

"Why does it matter? I'll see it on our crate anyway."

"Then see it then," I sneer.

"Just show me now," he says, and an odd look comes over his face. His eyes go from playful to angry, and I suddenly want to run away.

"No," I say, tugging my sleeve lower, holding it tightly in my hand.

A scowl crosses his face, but then it's gone in an instant. He shrugs his shoulders and says, "Fine, I'll just wait, then." He smiles at me.

Thankfully, he moves back to his side of the Tunnel. I watch him until he turns his back to me and starts searching. Hesitantly, I turn my back on him and raise my lantern, my left arm shaking a little bit.

"Are you scared or excited?" he asks after a moment of silence.

I don't reply.

"Oh, stop," he says, laughter in his voice again, "I didn't mean to make you mad. I was just curious." He sounds all happy again, but that look in his eyes flashes in my mind, and I really don't want to talk to him anymore.

"Come on," he says, "I can't stand the silence. Just answer my question."

"No," I say flatly. I don't look at him.

"Man," he scoffs, "Hannel was right. You are no fun. Why are you so angry? I have to be better company than that little boy."

My stomach clenches, and I'm tempted to hit him in the head with my lantern. How dare he.

"What was his name anyway? Colbert, or something? Anyway, I remember them coming in to grab him, and I just knew it. I *knew* he would do something stupid like that. I mean, steal gold? From here? Idiot. His face, though! Ha! His eyes got all wide and-"

"What was your question?" I ask through gritted teeth. If he's going to talk, I'm not going to let him talk about Coden.

He gives a satisfied laugh, though, like he got what he wanted, but then he says, "Are you scared or excited?"

"For what?" I ask, not hiding the anger in my voice.

"For the Colosseum," he says evenly. "I mean, you have to be close now, right?"

"What?" I ask, not knowing what to think. I finally stop to look at him. He's already stopped like he was waiting for me, a dark smile on his face.

"Aren't you a little excited?" he asks, his chest rising and falling a little more quickly. "I mean, to stand there, in front of everyone, and show them what you can do."

I'm scared of this boy. I don't say anything, not sure what to say. So, I turn back around and search as quickly as I can, not caring if he keeps pace with me. Our pace is off for today anyway, with all this stopping, and we need to hurry if we don't want to spend the night down here. And I will not spend the night down here with Chesnit.

To distract myself, I go over the plan in my mind and say the alphabet Aila had taught us.

*Aila.*

Just the thought of her makes me grind my teeth. I don't know what scares me more: getting Departed, or trusting Aila. Maybe Chesnit wins out of either of them right now.

"Look, I'm *sorry*," Chesnit whines. "I just--"

"I don't care," I say flatly.

"Well, what should we talk about, then?" Chesnit asks.

I say nothing.

"Oh, come on, you can't do all this without talking! How boring!" he laughs, but I don't say anything or make any move that I heard him.

"Come on!" I can hear the smile on his face, but I don't think it's a nice smile. "Tell me something about yourself."

Again, I say nothing.

"Look, we can't work and not talk. That's just stupid."

Silence.

"Fine," Chesnit grumbles, but I can hear something in his voice I don't like, and I peek over at him when I get the chance, making sure he keeps to his side.

Silence settles between us like a wall, and I like it. I don't want to talk. I want to *think* for once. I just hope we all make it tonight, but the tightness in my stomach makes me think we won't. I'm lucky Jinade didn't kill me right alongside Coden, and now, if she sees my face as the face of someone doing something wrong, I'll be dead for sure. I think I'd rather have that than be Departed, but I'm worried for Krin and Hoss.

Time passes slowly, my thoughts and worries are only getting stronger. Then I hear a low rumbling up ahead and see two points of light coming toward us.

A group of three diggers comes up on us, pushing a full cart of coal and dirt on the tracks in the middle of the tunnel.

The boy, the one who spoke to me and the in-charge, is with them again. He sees me and gives me a small nod, still walking, but then his gaze finds Chesnit, and he stops, forcing the other two diggers to stop, too.

"What are you doing here?" the massive digger growls at Chesnit.

Chesnit gives the boy a cruel smile and says, "Hello, Hugo."

Hugo glares at Chesnit. Then his gaze flicks back to me. "If he bothers you, you tell me. Okay?" His eyes are icy but firm, and I just feel myself nodding without thinking. I suddenly don't want Hugo and the other diggers to leave.

"How far ahead are you?" I ask as evenly as I can, trying to make it sound normal.

"Diggers maybe half a day," Hugo replies, "track layers only an hour maybe."

I nod, feeling he understood why I asked. I could outrun Chesnit, I'm sure, and the track layers are closer than the Tunnel Room.

Chesnit says nothing, just looks at Hugo with a blank expression. The diggers finally move on, their cart grumbling as it's pushed. We continue searching, and I refuse to look at Chesnit. Once they're gone, and their echoes have faded into silence, he tries to talk to me again.

"Hugo's an idiot," he says with a laugh. "He never smiles, either. Maybe you two would get along."

I don't say anything.

"He and I Arrived together," Chesnit says. "He's always been big, but size doesn't always matter, you know? Sure didn't help him when his sister died on the train."

"What?" I ask without helping myself.

"Oh ya," Chesnit says, and I can hear how satisfied he is that he got a response from me. "She was coughing and everything, and he tried to hide it. Well, it wasn't really *fair* that he was protecting her. We're all on our own, you know?"

I stop dead in my tracks. "Did you tell the in-charges?" I ask horror in my voice.

He shrugs, a small grin on his face, "She was dying anyway."

I turn and search as fast as I can, trying to put space between us. I will not say anything else to him as long as we're partners, no matter what he says.

Years seem to pass before my wrist timer begins beeping, signaling the end of work. I sigh and stretch my neck, tired. I pull out a blue flashing bulb and stick it in the wall, and then turn and start walking back up the tunnel.

*Tonight, tonight, tonight,* I think, my pulse quickening with each step. With any luck, I won't ever be back in these Tunnels.

265

That thought bounces around in my mind as we hurry through the darkness. I hear Chesnit moving just behind me, but I don't turn to acknowledge him. I'm still furious at him, still scared of him.

We've only jogged a little way before Chesnit starts talking again.

"Are you still mad?" he asks, in a drooling, smirking sort of way. I can hear it in his voice.

I say nothing.

"Huh," he laughs. "Well, you're fun."

I run practically against the very edge of the tunnel wall, and he takes up the middle, swinging his lanky arms back and forth.

"Why don't you sit with me at dinner tonight?" Chesnit asks, beaming me a smile. "You can tell us all what it's like being an ancient."

I don't respond, just run faster.

"Oh, come on," he smiles, and I notice his teeth are crooked. "You and your friends always look so angry. Come sit with me."

I go faster.

He speeds up, too.

His arm brushes my arm again, and I start sprinting. I can hear him behind me, but his footsteps are growing fainter and fainter as I sprint up the tunnel. I hate him. I can't even really explain it, but I hate him.

He won't let me escape him.

"I know there's something wrong with your friend!" he yells at me. "I know!"

I start crying, not being able to stop it. I sprint, faster and faster, racing to get away from him and his horrible words and the terror that he just made me feel for Krin.

Finally, the little circle of light ahead announces the Tunnel Room. I burst through, breath coming in heaving gasps, but then I hurry over to the supply table. I want to get away from Chesnit as quickly as I can. I need to get to Krin.

I drop my searching supplies into the crate and hurry over to the in-charges.

"NM1448," I say, thrusting my timer at the two sitting at the table. They look annoyed, but I don't care. At least the fat one isn't here anymore. They write down my time and miles and then let me go.

I get on the lift and hope it's full enough to go up. It's not.

Chesnit walks over with a few other searchers, and I can hear him talking.

"...an honor to have the Chancellor observe us," Chesnit drones as they get on the lift. I see Dirk in the back corner and move to crowd next to him. But, Hannel is right by Dirk. "After all, how often does he come, and what if he thinks our Mine is the best?" Chesnit sounds thrilled; I want to hit him, but I also don't want to get near him. What if he tells everyone about Krin?

Why hasn't he told anyone about Krin?

"Ya, and what if you don't move fast enough for him?" one of the other searchers chuckles darkly. "What if you do something right, but it's wrong?" He says it loudly, and I look around nervously. It's mostly out of habit, but I don't think the in-charges, if they heard, would know for sure who said it, and why not blame the face of the person accused of thievery?

Chesnit just huffs like he doesn't believe the Chancellor would care about those things, and I see expressions darken as they look at the tall boy. I suddenly think that my partner is not very popular with the other kids. That gives me hope; if he tells other kids about Krin, maybe they wouldn't believe. But he seems like the type of kid the in-charges would at least not fully scowl at.

"Have you not been watching?" the same searcher asks. "Haven't you seen all the Departures?"

"Ya, but those were the older kids who--"

"Anha was 16," a girl in the back says softly. "She was my sister. We came here together two years ago when she was 14, and I was 12. I *know* she wasn't 18."

"Maybe you're wrong," Chesnit shrugs. "The Societal Keepers of the Mine don't make mistakes like that, you must-"

"I'm not wrong," the girl says evenly.

The lift worker finally closes the gate and throws the lever, making the lift shudder and begin moving up. As we start moving, I realize something: Chesnit isn't against the in-charges.

In fact, it sounds like he's on their side. I mean, he gave up Hugo's sister...

"You called them by their full name," I say. The workers around me part a little, so I have a clear view of Chesnit, who is standing by the gate.

"Oh, are you speaking to me now?" Chesnit smiles. "Called who by their full name, *Evin?*"

"The in-charges."

"Well," he shrugs, "they're called the Societal Keepers of the Mine. We're supposed to call them that. They don't like being called in-charges. They think it's rude."

We all refer to them as Societal Keepers whenever they're around, but we call them in-charges behind their backs. You can get in trouble if they hear you call them in-charges, but who cares if it hurts their feelings?

"And being called by a number isn't?" Dirks asks. He pulls up his sleeve on his left arm to reveal slightly less coal-blackened flesh, and on it is a number inked into his skin. I touch mine subconsciously, remembering the pain of getting it scratched into my arm.

"They call us numbers because it's easier to keep track of us," Chesnit shrugs. He sounds so...unbothered by it. "Oh, and Evin, you're NM1448. Told you I'd see it eventually. You were in the first batch of Arrivals." He seems very excited by this. Dirk moves closer to me, and then the lift jostles, and I'm thrown against him. He catches me and helps me get my balance; when I turn back to Chesnit, he looks furious.

I quickly turn my gaze and look to the side, but all that's to the side of me is black stone, black stone separated from my fingertips by a thin wall of chain link. My stomach knots, and my breath catches; I turn away and stare at the floor. I hear Chesnit laugh.

Thankfully, we reach B Level then, and the lift worker opens the gates. Chesnit storms through and walks quickly through the tunnel towards the Open Area. Everyone else gets off after throwing me looks, a few good ones, and a few worried ones.

The boy, the one who I was worried was talking too loud, stays on for a moment after it's only me and Dirk left. He gives a small sigh and says, "Some of the younger kids are like that. Not a lot, but some. He's not that young, but he lived in the cities before he came here. He grew up in the Nation before he was sent here, and he still doesn't get it."

"Then he's stupid," I say.

"I know," he says back. "But he will tell the in-charges about us all if we're not careful. He's your new partner?"

I nod.

"Better try and be nice to him tomorrow," he says softly, then moves to get off.

"I do not want to be nice to him," I reply.

He stops at the lift opening, shrugs, and says, "Well, it's that or be Departed."

"He could tell on you, too," I say.

He smiles a little and then says, "I know. I'd rather get Departed." Then he gets off.

"Chesnit's stupid," Dirk says simply, moving to get off. I follow him. "He and Hannel are friends, but Hannel at least doesn't like the in-charges."

"Kids here believe the in-charges are good?" I ask, not really believing. "There are more like him?"

"I don't know," Dirk shrugs. "I hope not. Hannel was asking about you a lot today, Evin. I don't know why. I didn't say much, I swear." He looks at me with apologetic eyes, and I know he's thinking about what he told Hannel about me before.

"Hannel's stupid," I say, "you're not." Dirk gives me a small smile.

We walk through the tunnel and emerge into the Open Area. There are no in-charges on the Overhang, which feels weird, but I'm glad not to have eyes on me, especially Jinade's. We hurry into the tunnel that will lead to the cafeteria.

"Tonight," Dirk whispers to me as we get in line, and I nod. Just a few more hours to escape or die, and either is better than this darkness. Either has to be better than this.

We get our trays, our food and then hurry to the table. When we get there, I almost scream: Aila is in my seat. She's sitting next to Krin. I hold it in and move to the other side to sit next to Duna. I slam my tray down, but no one even glances at me.

I look at Krin, ready to scowl at her all dinner, but then I see her face. Her eyes are wide and look terrified, and her hands are shaking on the table. She's leaning to one side, away from

Aila, and it looks like she's been crying.

"Krin...?" I say, cold fear sliding through me.

"It's fine," Aila says, giving a tight smile. "My aunt had these. They're called labor pains.

It's normal. We shouldn't worry yet."

"What does that mean?" I ask. "Is the baby coming? You said we had more time! Months!" I whisper, but the panic makes my voice go higher and higher.

"I know what I said." Aila looks at me. "I told you I didn't know for sure."

"Well, what do we do?" I ask. "Is the baby coming?"

"I don't think yet," Aila says, straining to sound normal. She looks at me with wide eyes, and for the first time since she came to the Mine, I see fear in Aila's eyes.

But I don't care.

"You said we had time," I say coldly, seeing pain cross Krin's face as she tries to hold in a scream.

"I don't know everything about this, Evin," Aila scowls back, the smile finally off her face.

"Obviously," I say through gritted teeth.

Krin's face begins relaxing a little, and her breathing slows. I look around to make sure no one is watching, especially the guards.

"Breathe," Aila whispers to Krin. "Just breathe."

"How is breathing going to help?" I snap.

"Stop it, Evin," Duna sighs. "Getting mad isn't helping."

I look at Duna, but she says, "We'll figure it out." Duna isn't crying or scowling at me, which makes me feel like maybe the old Duna is coming back, but I'm still fearful for Krin.

"I heard something," Aila said, "today, while I was in the offices. I heard that the Chancellor has been delayed. That he isn't coming until tomorrow."

"What?" I ask, mouth dropping. I really don't know if the in-charges will leave me alone for another day. And I really don't think I could work with Chesnit for another day.

"So we wait until tomorrow?" Dirk asks, raising an eyebrow.

"I think we still need to go tonight," Aila says quietly, looking around at us. "Even if the Chancellor isn't here."

We all just kind of stare at her; I don't know how to feel. We had been planning on tonight, but now it feels much more rushed, much riskier. The Chancellor was our safety net; when he's here, the guards all guard him.

"We may not get tomorrow," Aila replies. "My aunt had pains like this in the last trimester, but I just...I don't know how far along Krin is!" She sounds strained, worried, but she still smiles like it's no big deal. I can see how big of a deal it is in her eyes.

Krin looks up towards the tunnel opening, and I know she's looking for Hoss.

"Krin, what do you think?" I ask.

"Where's Hoss?" her voice is thick with tiredness.

No one says anything, but we all look towards the tunnel.

"There he is," Dirk says, pointing to the line of workers getting food. We can see the back of Hoss's bulky form, and next to him, another form I think is Hugo, the boy from the tunnel.

Seeing Hugo suddenly makes me remember that Hoss might've told him our plan and that I was going to ask him about it last night. But remembering that makes me remember Coden, and suddenly I want to make sure Krin is safe no matter what.

Then I feel someone sit next to me.

I turn, and I see Chesnit sitting down, beginning to eat his food. We're all silent, staring at him.

"Need something?" Aila asks him sweetly, but, for once, I'm glad for the anger behind her kindness.

"Dinner," Chesnit smiles, and he scoops food into his mouth.

I look at the others, feeling the panic on my face. My breath speeds up, and I suddenly see red around my vision. He said he knows about Krin. What reason does he have to lie? He likes the in-charges. Why hasn't he ratted her out? What's going on?

"I told you to have dinner with me tonight," Chesnit says in my ear, but I can hear the food rolling around in his mouth.

I shrug him away and scoot closer to Duna. She doesn't react.

Then, Hoss joins the table, and behind him, Hugo.

"Up," Hugo says, nodding at Chesnit. "Get up."

Chesnit looks up at Hugo, smiles, and says, "We can sit wherever we want. I want to sit by Evin."

"Get. Up," Hugo growls, pale eyes full of icy fire. I don't look at Chesnit.

"Or what?" Chesnit laughs. "What?"

I watch Hugo roll his eyes, then he reaches over and grabs Chesnit's shirt. He hauls the kid to his feet.

"Up," Hugo growls again, and he shoves Chesnit away. Chesnit scowls at Hugo, but then he picks up his tray and marches away. I don't look at him once he finds a seat at a table near us.

I won't look at him again.

"Sit with us, Hugo?" Hoss asks, sitting next to Krin.

"Nah," Hugo waves him off. "Whatever you guys are doing, I don't want it." Then he marches away and goes to another table. Part of me wants him to come back, but part of me is glad that he, at least, won't be Departed or killed tonight.

"Krin?" Hoss asks panic in his voice, seeming to see Krin now. "Krin, what is it? Aila, what's wrong?"

"I'm fine," Krin says, smiling slightly. She's leaning against his chest, her eyes closed. I think she might even fall asleep.

In a whisper, Aila explains to us, mostly Hoss, what happened. "I found her in the tunnel that leads from sorting to the lifts. She was sitting on the floor, crying. She told me she's been having these pains all day. I think the baby might be coming soon, but I don't know for sure--" she throws a glance at me-- "but I think we should get out tonight, even though the Chancellor isn't here."

"You sure he's not coming?" I ask. She nods.

"But...will she make it?" Hoss asks, his eyes wide.

"It's better than waiting and seeing what happens while we're stuck here," Aila says.

For once, I almost agree with Aila.

"Tonight? For sure?" Hoss says quietly.

"It'll be fine, Hoss," Krin says, not opening her eyes. "I'll be fine. Let's get out. Just like we planned."

But then comes a very familiar sound. My heart skips a beat, and I drop my fork.

I look to the tunnel. Whispers die immediately in the cafeteria as everyone waits for whatever is coming to us. I was desperately hoping they would wait and do this tonight, while everyone is sleeping. Not now. Please not now. All eyes are watching, even Krin has opened her eyes, but she hasn't taken her head off Hoss's chest.

Then, guards come marching into the cafeteria. There's only about ten this time, but five in-charges lead them in. Two among them are Jinade and Head Reader Kevoc.

*Krin.* I peek at Krin and see her squeezing Hoss's hand, eyes forward and wide in fear.

Hoss's face is determined, but I see fear in his eyes.

*Not Krin,* I beg silently. *Please, not Krin. Not now.*

My throat is dry, and my hands are ice cold. I don't dare look at Krin again, or even Hoss. I suddenly wish that I was sitting by Krin. I will never forget or forgive Aila if she sat next to Krin on her last night.

The guards and in-charges stop in the middle of the room. No one speaks or seems to breathe.

Clearing her throat, Jinade raises her chin and says, "As you all know, our beloved High Chancellor was scheduled to come tonight. Sadly, he has been delayed. But, rest assured, he will be joining us tomorrow morning." Huh. So Aila was telling the truth about something. Whatever.

"You were all observed today, and based on those observations, we are going to cleanse the Mine to work at highest efficiency."

*What?* I'm tempted to ask Aila what it means, but I don't.

"When your number is called, you will present yourself to the Head Reader," Jinade thrusts out her hand, and an in-charge sets a clipboard in it before he steps quickly back.

She clears her throat and says, "NM3490."

A short boy stands. He's stocky and looks kind of familiar.

"NM15432." Another boy stands, this one tall and thick, almost as big as Hoss.

"NM11386." All these boys are big. Must be diggers or loaders.

"NM8210." Another boy.

"NM6148." Hugo stands up. He was at the table next to ours. I audibly gasp but quickly place a hand over my mouth to hide it. These boys are diggers, and it's Hoss' team.

"NM4243."

Krin turns and looks up at Hoss. She grips his hand, and I see her nails dig into his flesh.

"No," Krin pleads. "No." It's so soft, so sad.

"I love you," Hoss says quietly. "Don't forget that." In one easy motion, he stands, kisses Krin, and then turns to walk towards the in-charges and the rest of his crew.

"No," Krin whispers again, still facing where Hoss had been. I watch her slowly turn, her whole body shaking, and face the middle of the cafeteria where the diggers are lined up in front of the in-charges and guards.

"No," Krin's eyes flood with tears.

It's pretty rare for entire teams to be Departed at once. My mind flashes to yesterday when Hugo had spoken to the in-charges. He had been rude to the in-charges. I guess they noticed.

"You have all reached the age of entering Society," Jinade says. "Congratulations. You will now be tested by Head Reader Kevoc and deemed worthy to participate in Society or to entertain Society."

Head Reader Kevoc hobbles forward, holding his rolled piece of paper. He coughs--a horrible, grating sound-- and then unrolls the paper. The boys stand before him in a line, and he approaches the first one. "You will each come forward to read from the text," he instructs, "and either be Departed or sent to join Society." He gives a broad, toothy smile, making his gray beard wiggle on his chin.

He gestures to the first in line, the shortest one who I think was the team lead. He steps forward with his head held high, but I can see his clenched fists.

The Head Reader holds up the scroll and points to the words that must be written on it.

"Read this," he says simply, but there's expectation in his voice. I suddenly wonder whether Jinade or Kevoc or any of them ever feel bad about any of this; I doubt it.

"I can't," the boy says, his voice deep and booming. The Head Reader gestures to his right, and the boy steps forward into the grasp of two waiting guards. I roll my eyes; where is the boy going to run to? They don't need to grab him.

Kevoc has each of the boys come forward in turn, and each result is the same.

Hugo, when it's his turn, stands tall in front of the wrinkled old man, looking down at him.

"Read this," Kevoc says.

Hugo is silent for a moment, staring at Kevoc. Finally, he scowls and spits out, "You know I can't, old man."

The Head Reader bristles and frowns, and the guards grip the weapons at their sides.

"You will address the Head Reader with respect," Jinade snaps.

Hugo snorts and turns to look at her. They stare at each other for a few breaths, and then he says, "Of course, Lady Executor." He says her name differently, though. Instead of Eh-XEH-cu-tor, he said Ex-AH-cu-tor. I don't know if it's a big difference.

Jinade's face darkens as she looks at Hugo. She seems furious, so I guess the pronunciation is a big difference.

Hugo gives Jinade a wide smile, nods his head slightly, and then, without being prompted, he moves past her and allows the guards to grab him. Jinade watches him with a cold expression, but she doesn't move. I smile a little; it's nice to see someone go out fighting, even if it was with words.

The Head Reader shakes his head but turns his attention to the last in line: Hoss. The smile immediately disappears from my face.

"Step forward," the Head Reader directs. Hoss obeys, coming to a stop just in front of the old man.

"Read this," the Head Reader points to a section of the text.

I hear Krin suck in a breath and hold it.

"Come on, Hoss," I hear Aila whisper. I desperately hope that Aila's lessons have been enough. I sneak a glance at her face, and I see confusion and fear.

Hoss leans closer to the text and studies it. We are looking at his back, so I can't see his expression.

After a moment, he says, "The...gr...great...people...of...our...uh, um...soc, no, sock, um..."

Gasps sound around the cafeteria. Everyone is waiting, eyes glued to Hoss, including Lady Executor Jinade.

"Sock-i-eti...uh..." Hoss hesitates but finishes with, "will...rise...to the...high-est..of all."

Hoss pauses and looks up; the Head Reader is rooted to his spot, face pale and hands shaking.

"Do I need to keep going?" Hoss gives a slight smile, and I feel the corner of my lips turn up.

Cheers erupt in the cafeteria. It's chaos; workers stand on the tables, others on the benches, everyone claps, and cheers and whistles. I feel hot tears slide down my cheeks: he's done it! My hands hurt from clapping so hard. I've never felt so happy for anyone before. He's getting out of here. He won't go to the Colosseum! I feel like hugging Aila.

The sound makes my ears hurt, but I hope it never stops. For once, for once in my entire life, I just saw someone beat the in-charges!

All the in-charges, including Jinade, look shocked, and they quickly start whispering among themselves. The guards don't quite seem to know what to do. They grip their weapons nervously, seemingly wary of the excited crowd before them.

The image of the guards nervously facing us makes me tingle with excitement.

I look around and let the energy soak into me. All these hundreds of workers who...I stop in my thoughts. I suddenly realize something: we have *power*. Not power in words or weapons, but in numbers. *Hundreds of workers*. There can't be more guards than workers down here, so why are we so afraid? I know the guards have weapons, but if we got together and took down a few guards and got their weapons for ourselves, could we be stopped?

Eventually, the in-charges come to their senses and order the guards in among us. I'm watching them more than I am watching the workers around me. I see the guards charge in and start shoving people onto benches.

But we won't go down.

A kid shoves back, *hard*. The guard stumbles and then raises his stick and strikes the kid across his face, sending that worker to the ground below. The workers around him scream in fury and swarm the guard. More guards come, and they grab kids, hurling them to the floor.

Quickly, I sit. I reach over and grab Krin's hand, begging her not to rise. She doesn't move, though; her eyes are still trained on Hoss.

279

More and more guards pour in from the tunnel, and soon, there are enough black-clad figures moving among us that everyone settles back onto their benches, some rubbing now sore welts on their skin.

But I know we're all feeling the same thing: they may have pushed us back down, but victory hangs so thickly in the air that I can almost taste it.

"Silence!" the Head Reader booms. I'm a little shocked: I didn't know such an old man could shout so loud.

Everyone stops talking and looks to see Hoss still standing before the Head Reader, a small smile on his face.

"Unfortunately," Kevoc says, coughing again, "you did not pronounce the entire phrase correctly. As such, you are sentenced to Departure for the entertainment section of Society."

It takes me a minute to fully understand what the old idiot said.

"Wait," I say, turning to Aila. "What-?"

But others figured it out faster.

"NO!" someone shouts.

"He read it!"

"That's the law! He can read!"

"You can't do that!"

Instead of in celebration, workers start getting to their feet in anger. Anger so hot, I can feel it in my cheeks, my hands, my *blood*.

Tables are turned over, and trays are thrown across the room. Workers are back on guards, yanking them down, pulling at their sticks, shoving *them* to the ground.

I hear cries of pain and anger. I see kids shouting and throwing things. Then I look at Krin.

Krin is still staring at Hoss, but now her mouth is set in a furious line, her chest heaving.

One tear rolls down her cheek.

"Sit down!" Kevoc shouts. "SIT DOWN!"

But we don't listen. Not one of us.

"Let him go!"

"No!"

"He can read!"

The shouts come louder and faster.

One boy gets onto a table and begins throwing the trays everywhere. The workers around him hush, and soon, everyone is looking at him expectantly. Once he speaks, I realize who it is. "You!" the boy, the one I had spoken to on the lifts, points at the in-charges. "You made the law, and now you break it! *You* are not fit for Society!"

The workers begin cheering again, pounding feet and fists. I feel rage, and the urge to *do* something fills me up. This isn't right. We were promised that reading would be freedom, but they *lied*.

The workers begin yelling at the in-charges again, pushing the guards down. At a signal from Jinade, two guards run forward to the boy on the table. They seize him and drag him down by his arms and legs.

"You're liars!" the boy shouts. "You are liars, and liars do not belong in Society! Isn't that right?! Isn't that what you beat into us?!" He smiles, an almost crazy look on his face, as the guards drag him to the tunnel.

Jinade keeps her gaze forward, a smile plastered on her face, as the guards take him out of the cafeteria.

I hear Aila gasp.

The workers still cheer, but then a single sound silences us: a loud boom, and everyone knows it came from a gun.

*I guess they didn't care about making a mess with him,* I think.

281

We sit, my legs suddenly shaky. We go quiet; no more cheering.

I suddenly remember why we're all so fearful of the in-charges and guards.

"Messes are not tolerated," Jinade says, breaking the silence.

Workers frantically begin righting tables, picking up trays, doing their best to get the gray sludge off the floor and walls. Our table never moved. Our trays are still where they should be.

I glance at Aila again, and I see something that makes my stomach twist.

Aila is looking at Jinade, and it seems like Jinade is looking back at her. Aila gives a furious look and then raises her eyebrows in a questioning way. It's the slightest movement, but I think Jinade *shrugs*.

Aila turns and sees me looking. I glare at her, confusion clear on my face. She gives me a smile, but it's hasty and doesn't hide her expression.

She's angry. At Jinade? I open my mouth, but Aila shakes her head and nods towards Krin, who is still gazing at Hoss. I feel my fists shake, but I don't say anything. Krin told me to trust her. I don't, but I have little choice now.

Jinade looks at the guards and nods towards Hoss. Two of the black-clad men hurry forward, grab Hoss's arms, and pull him into line behind the rest of his digging team.

Krin moves like she's going to stand, but Aila quickly grabs her and yanks her back down.

"No!" Aila whispers urgently. "If you stand, they'll know. You'll go too, Krin."

"Let me go! I don't care!" Krin hisses, tears in her eyes.

"Stop it," Aila whispers back. "Think of the baby. Would Hoss want that?"

Krin chokes on a sob but stops struggling and lets Aila rub her arms in comfort. I have to look away from Krin's face; it's too heartbroken.

I watch, still fuming inside, as Hugo and Hoss, and the others are marched to the tunnel. Hoss turns around at the last minute and gives Krin a sad smile before facing forward and marching out of existence.

Once again, Jinade remains behind with a few guards.

"As a reminder that you all must learn your place," she says with a cool smile. "Don't forget: the Chancellor arrives in the morning. Goodnight." Then she turns and goes out of the cafeteria, followed by her guards.

Suddenly, the table feels so small.

Duna looks horrified, Dirk outraged, and Aila worried. Krin is crying freely and silently, but her eyes now have energy, life, *fire*.

"Get us out of here," she speaks the words to Aila but then turns to face me. She places a hand on her swollen stomach and says, "Get us out of here tonight."

# Chapter Fifteen

The worker bell rings. Everyone gets up to go to bed, and we figure we'd better do the same.

I stand, my knees shaking, and wait for everyone else to do move. We circle around Krin, like normal, to hide her massive stomach. She kind of waddles when she walks.

We walk quickly, but Aila hisses whispers at us as we go.

"Get to bed and wait until everyone goes to sleep, and then get up and make for the toilet. Make sure no one is looking at you, and then get into the tunnel. Once you're in the tunnel, wait for the rest of us. Once we're all together, we will get to the Gathering Room and try the Arrival door. We're leaving in two hours. It's going to be fine."

I still don't like it; I don't like having to cross the Open Area, and I don't like going to the Gathering Room since that's where the in-charges marched Hoss's team barely an hour ago. I just don't know how many guards will be there, even at night.

I'm about to say something, just to voice my fears to Krin, but then Duna starts sobbing and drops her head in her hands.

We keep walking, but we're all looking at Duna with wide-eyed expressions. Everyone else starts looking at her, too.

"Duna!" Aila whispers. "Duna, stop! It'll be fine."

"Besides," I scowl, looking around, "you're not coming anyway."

We've crossed the Open Area (I don't dare look up. If I see Jinade now, I might pass out) and have just entered the tunnel that leads to the barracks.

We're one of the last groups of workers going through, and once we get to the split, we stop and let everyone else pass. Some throw us weird glances; we're packed tightly together, and Duna is sobbing after all. I suddenly see a tall figure, and then someone grabs my arm and rips me apart from the rest of the group.

"What are you doing?" the voice asks. My stomach tightens, threatening to spill out what little food I ate tonight. It's Chesnit.

I look up and see him smiling at me, but it's a hungry smile. His eyes flick back to the rest of the group, all huddled together. Duna is still crying.

"What's with her?" Chesnit asks. "I thought the tall girl was the one with that digger. I've seen her in the barracks sometimes."

I pull my arm, trying to get him to let go. He just tightens his grip.

"Hugo's not here," Chesnit says. "Were you and Hugo...?"

I look up at him and roll my eyes. "No," I hiss. "Let me go."

"Evin?" I hear Aila call. She finally notices I'm missing and turns to find me. Her eyes widen in panic when she sees who I'm with.

"I just want to talk to you," Chesnit smiles, yanking me around to face him. "You didn't talk to me in the Tunnels."

"I know," I growl, pulling harder.

"Just talk to me!" Chesnit hisses.

"You're hurting me!" I whisper back. The workers passing us give odd glances, but no one does anything.

"Let her go!" Dirk suddenly appears through the swarm of workers and shoves Chesnit. Chesnit doesn't let go of my arm, though, and his fall pulls me into his chest. He steadies himself but gives me an awful smile. I shove away from his chest and pound on it with my free hand.

"Let me go!" I shout.

Dirk punches Chesnit in the face. Chesnit yells in pain and finally drops my arm. Dirk gently grabs my arm and pulls me back to the group.

"Who is that?" Krin asks, looking over all our heads to see Chesnit leaning against the wall, cradling his nose.

"Partner," I say, heart racing.

"He's Hannel's friend," Dirk says. "Stupid kid."

"I'm going to figure out what you're doing!" Chesnit yells at us, his voice muffled by his hands. "Whatever you're doing, you won't get away with it!" Then he stalks into the boy's side of the barracks.

"We need to go," I say softly, hands shaking.

"Duna?" Dirk says, rubbing her arms. "Duna, what?" She's still crying. There aren't many kids left in this tunnel, but still, she's calling way too much attention to us.

She finally lifts her head out of her hands and looks at us with pitiful eyes. "I...I..." she stammers. She swallows and finally manages, "I did something bad."

We all look at each other, not getting it. I'm about to yell at her for making everyone look at us when she continues.

"I...I t-told the in-charges...about your p-plan," sobs shake her shoulders, and she drops her head.

We stand absolutely silent for a moment.

Then it sinks in. I think I might strangle her.

"What-" I begin, but Aila cuts me off.

"How much?" she asks, her chest rising and falling rapidly.

Duna shrugs and says, "All of it. I told them that there was a group of workers who were planning to escape through the Arrival door sometime when the Chancellor was going to be here.

They said they'd double the amount of guards there..."

I'm going to strangle her. I step forward, but Aila pushes me back with a surprisingly strong shove to the chest.

"Not now," she says. She turns back to Duna. "Did you tell them who?"

Duna shakes her head. "I just told them I had overheard it in the sorting room." She won't look at anyone's face.

"How could you?" I finally spit out.

Duna's lip shakes, and she says, "I thought...maybe...they'd, well...Nolan...you know..."

My cheeks burn in fury. "No," I say. "I don't know. I don't know how you could trade living people for a dead one."

Duna looks at me, her eyes wide and full of tears.

"You gave us up?" Dirk asks quietly.

Duna turns to look at him, desperation in her eyes. "No, Dirk...I d-didn't...I just-"

"You gave us up!" Dirk says, and he quickly turns away.

"Dirk…" Duna reaches out to him. She touches his shoulder, but he flinches away.

"You. Gave. Us. Up!" he spits. She recoils, lip trembling.

"How could you be so stupid?" I stammer out. "Do you really think they'll let you or him go if you turn us in? They'll probably kill you, too! And he might not even be alive, Duna!"

She looks down.

"Evin," Krin says softly.

"No," I scowl. "No! There is no...this is just...*how?*" Krin stood up for Aila, but she can't possibly stand up for Duna, too. That's just stupid.

"But he's not coming until tomorrow," Dirk chimes in. "So we should be okay tonight!"

Duna shakes her head, "They already put more guards in. I had to act like I didn't know everything. I told them I didn't know for sure when...I saw a big group of guards go in this morning."

"How *could* you?" I ask again.

Krin looks thoughtfully down at her swollen belly. She cradles it in her arms, then looks to Aila with fear and sadness written all over her face.

"We need a new way out," Aila says hurriedly. She looks at me.

"The window?" I say the only thought that pops in my head.

"Have to," she says.

"But the lift is loud," I gasp, feeling like I can't breathe. I feel like the ceiling is getting closer. "They'll hear us going up there. We won't make it."

"The Hive," Dirk says, eyes wide.

"What?" Aila looks at him, but I squeeze my eyes shut, imagining leading Krin through the Tunnels.

"There's supposed to be a tunnel in the Hive," I finish for Dirk, "that leads to A Level. We talked about it a little bit but didn't do it because we're not for sure it's there. It's supposed to be so in-charges, and guards can get to the Hive easily to make sure no one is hiding down there or something, but I don't know for sure where it is." I shrug, feeling useless. "Or if it even is real."

"I think I know where it is," Dirk says, "but I'm not sure, either. Hannel wanted to go check it out once, but I wouldn't."

"If it leads to A Level, we could get to the window without using the lifts," Aila says quickly.

"Or we could get stuck in the Hive," I say softly.

"What about the belts?" Dirk asks. "The ones that carry the coal? They go to the loading bay."

"They're shut off at night," Aila reminds us. "And the hole is small. I don't think Krin could fit and crawl through them…" She looks sadly at Krin, who stares at her belly, still cradling it.

"Then it's the Hive," I say, determined. She's not dying here. Not without us trying.

Aila nods and asks, "Evin, you remember where the offices are?"

I nod, but I'm not really sure. I mean, I've only seen it once, and it was for like two seconds.

"But you work there?" I ask, confused why I suddenly need to remember.

"I know," Aila nods. "Just in case."

I look at Aila, and her eyes seem wide and sad. For a second, I forget my anger at Aila and see her as just another kid down here. I suddenly realize what we're about to do and what will happen if we fail.

"This is stupid," I say, not being able to help myself. Krin gives a little whimper.

"How do we get to the Hive?" Aila asks, ignoring me. "We have to get to the Tunnels," I say, "and the Tunnel Room."

"But you said the lifts are loud!" Aila says exasperatedly.

"I know," I say, "but the in-charges won't care if we go down. We just have to say we left supplies in the tunnels."

"*All* of us?" Aila asks.

I shrug, "I don't know what else to do."

"There probably aren't in-charges by the lifts or in the Tunnel Room this late anyway,"

Dirk shrugs. "But there will be guards."

"Well," I sigh, "then we will figure out what to do with them if they're there. Let's go."

"But Evin-" Aila starts.

"There's nothing else, Aila," I say firmly. "We need to go."

She opens her mouth to say something, but then she shuts it and nods. She reaches out and grabs Krin's hand. Then she tugs the girl forward. There is no one left in the tunnel, but we can't stand here any longer. We have to get back to the barracks, so no one misses us and alerts the in-charges.

We all hurry into our tunnels, Dirk being the only one now headed to the right. Aila and Duna moves off to their own bunks, so I take over helping Krin.

"Aila said I had months. It doesn't feel right, Evin. It feels...too soon," Krin says softly as we pad through the bunks. Some girls are still awake, and while I'm grateful they're seeing us, I don't want them to hear us.

"I know," I reply. "I'm sorry."

"No, I'm sorry, Evin," Krin says. "I'm so, so sorry."

I don't know what to say, so I say nothing. We get to our beds, and I help her up. She swings onto her bed, much less gracefully than she used to, and then she settles down with a deep sigh.

"They took him," she says softly when I climb up to my bed.

"I know," I say again. "I'm sorry."

"I have to save his baby," Krin whispers. "I have to."

I heave a sigh of my own and say, "We will."

*Stars shining bright above you*
*Night breezes seem to whisper "I love you"*
*Birds singing in the sycamore tree*
*Dream a little dream of me*

*Stars fading, but I linger on, dear*

*Still craving your kiss*
*I'm longing to linger till dawn, dear*
*Just saying this*

*Sweet dreams till sunbeams find you*
*Sweet dreams that leave all worries behind you*
*But in your dreams, whatever they be*
*Dream a little dream of me*

*Stars fading, but I linger on, dear*
*Still craving your kiss*
*I'm longing to linger till dawn, dear*
*Just saying this*

*Sweet dreams till sunbeams find you*
*Sweet dreams that leave all worries far behind you*
*But in your dreams, whatever they be*
*Dream a little dream of me.*

The voice is back, haunting and echoing around the barracks. I find myself mouthing the words as she sings them, hoping it never stops.

*Stars*, I think, *I'm going to see Coden's stars.* A single tear drips down my cheek as the song stops, but I'm firm; Krin is going to get out.

I have no way to keep time in here, but I wait what feels like an hour. I don't know if it is, but I can't wait any longer. I roll over and see Krin, wide awake, staring at the ceiling.

The sounds of sleeping surround us, and it's time to move.

"You first," I whisper to her.

She nods, then swings her legs off the bed and hops down. She reaches underneath her mattress and retrieves the small, clear stone. Then, I hear her silently padding away. I wait what I count as ten minutes before I hop down myself.

As quietly as I can, I make my way through the bunks to the toilet. I'm hoping if anyone notices me, I don't look nervous. I feel sweat dripping down my back, though.

I reach the toilet and silently open the door, stepping inside. I turn the light on and wait two more minutes before turning off the light and leaving the little room.

The room is silent, and I keep to the edge of the wall, staying in the shadows as much as I can. The tunnel opening is just in front of me, and I slip quietly in. I see the others huddled together just at the split, and I hurry towards them.

Krin is on the ground, head between her knees, Aila standing concernedly over her. Dirk and Duna are leaning against the wall, but Dirk's back is to Duna as she stares dejectedly away. I stare at Duna for a moment, wondering why she's here.

"Why are you here?" I whisper angrily at her.

She looks up at me, tears in her eyes, but doesn't say anything.

Aila smiles sadly and says, "Let's go."

I turn around and lead the way back up the tunnel. We walk quickly, and my heart is pounding. This is the stupidest plan ever, but we have to save Krin. I refuse to look at Duna; I can hear she's still crying, and she should be. This mess is her fault. She shouldn't even be with us.

The opening to the Open Area is just ahead, but that's when I hear his voice.

"Evin!"

I pause and cringe. Slowly, I look over my shoulder.

Illuminated in the dim lights of the tunnel is Chesnit, just standing at the mouth of the boy's tunnel. He waves and practically shouts, "Where do you think you're going, Evin?"

"Go back to bed, Chesnit," I call back. I yank Krin's arm forward, and we continue walking.

"Evin!" Chesnit calls again, and I can hear a satisfied smirk on his face. "Evin, *you* should be in bed!"

We're almost running now, and we get to the Open Area when he starts shouting.

"Guards! Guards! Help!" Chesnit is calling at the top of his lungs.

"Come on!" I call to the others, and we hurry to the tunnel that leads to the lifts. I can hear footsteps all around us, but I don't look. I keep my eyes on the tunnel and my hand around Krin's wrist. She will not leave my side.

We get to the tunnel and race to the lifts.

"She's going to the tunnels!" Chesnit shouts. "She's a searcher!"

We all slide into the lift furthest to the left, and I slam the gate shut. We're all panting, and I throw the lever to the "D" slot. Just as the lift starts sliding down, I see Chesnit and three guards burst into the room where the lifts are. I just see the snarl cross Chesnit's face as he meets my eyes before we're sucked down below the floor.

The darkness seems pressing, but I talk fast.

"We're going to have to split up," I pant. "Dirk, you take everyone through your tunnel and get to the Hive. Take as many side tunnels as you can, and go as fast as you can. Once you're there, wait ten minutes. If I don't show up, get out."

"Evin--" Dirk begins, but then Krin screams.

She drops to the floor of the lift, crying and breathing hard.

"Krin?" I ask, my voice high with panic. "Aila--?"

293

"We can't stop it," Aila says, kneeling down next to Krin. "We just have to go as fast as she can."

I watch as Krin eventually breathes slower, then looks up at me.

"Get us out, Evin," she whimpers.

"I will lead them away. Chesnit knows the Tunnels, but I think I can shake him. *Do not* go anywhere near my Tunnels, got it?"

Dirk nods, and I glance at the others. "You'll have to run. Be as quiet as you can." I look at Krin and see her wide eyes. I give her a nod, and she gives me a ghost of a smile.

The lift groans and creaks all the way down, making the darkness around us ring. I take a deep breath, and then the lift comes to a shuddering halt, making us all jolt a little.

I throw the gate open, and we race to the shelves. I pull boxes down and hand out lanterns.

I can hear another lift coming.

"Go!" I hiss at Dirk, and he leads the others into his Tunnel. Krin tosses me a look over her shoulder as they disappear into the darkness.

I grip my lantern and hurry to my Tunnel. I hear the creak of the lift as it comes to a halt and the gate being opened. I pause at the opening, just long enough for me to hear someone shout, "There they go!" before I dart into the Tunnel.

I move fast, but not fast enough that they won't be able to see me. I can hear the footsteps behind me, but I never turn around. I hold my lantern up high so that they will be able to follow my light as I race through the tunnels. They *have* to follow *me*.

Quickly, I dart to the left to the old Tunnel, the one Coden and I finished just a few days ago. I slow a little until I hear the footsteps following me, and then I speed back up. I can see the bouncing light of their own lanterns behind me, but I try to focus only on the darkness ahead of me.

My breath is coming in gasps, but it's not from running; it's from fear. If they catch me, I'm dead.

I run until I see the side tunnel, and I dart inside. They follow behind me; I know there are at least two of them, based on the echoes in the tunnel.

They're getting closer, but I turn left into a main Tunnel and turn back towards the Tunnel Room. Hopefully, these guards are like most guards, and they don't know how to move in the Tunnels.

I pump my arms faster, the lantern swinging wildly, making the darkness dance with strange shadows.

Fingers graze my shoulder and then grip my arm. They yank, hauling me backward. Without turning around, I jab my elbow backward. I hear a sickly *crunch!* as my elbow connects with something soft and squishy.

"Oof!" the person I hit groans, and my arm is released. I put on a burst of speed. Quickly, I turn left again and find myself in a side Tunnel.

They follow, but they're starting to slow. I allow myself a small smile; I think they're getting tired. After running these tunnels all my life, running doesn't really tire me.

I speed up and turn into my main Tunnel again, heading once again to the Tunnel Room.

I can't see their lights on the walls anymore, so I go even faster.

Finally, I see the Tunnel Room ahead of me. I turn into a side Tunnel just before it and find myself standing in the new part of my Tunnel, the one that is at an upward slant. I move quickly up, going as fast as I can. I will just go straight until I hit the Hive unless the guards somehow find me in here. I don't think they will; my guess is, once they see the Tunnel Room, they'll get out and go find the in-charges. At least, that's what I hope.

My legs are burning, but I keep running. I don't know if Dirk and the others have reached the Hive yet, or how close they are, but I told them to leave after ten minutes, and I meant it.

The Tunnel begins to level off, and I dart into a side tunnel and get into the old part of this Tunnel since the uphill one isn't quite finished.

I hurry on, pushing myself faster and faster. I can't hear footsteps, and I can't see light beside my own, so I start to feel a little better, but I want to get to the Hive as soon as possible.

Even though I know it can't even have been an hour with how fast I've been running, I feel like it's been hours since I entered the Tunnels. However, I know the Hive is just ahead. The air feels cooler.

I finally burst into the massive, empty space that is the Hive, and I hold my lantern up as high as I can, looking around. The Hive, as always, fascinates and terrifies me. I stand with my back to the stone wall, looking at the nothingness in front of me. I can't even tell how big the nothingness is because it's all black besides my tiny circle of light.

"Evin!" I hear a call from above. Looking up and to my right, I see Dirk and the others, lanterns held high.

I wave my lantern and then hurry to the nearest ladder. The Hive is set up with narrow paths cut into the stone, making circle loops around the Hive. To get to levels above or below, you have to use stone steps, what we call ladders, cut into the side of walls. Each step is deep enough to hold the front part of a foot or the fingers of a hand.

Getting to the nearest ladder, I hitch my lantern up my arm using the metal loop at the top of the light. I take a breath and then jump to the steps. The steps are about one foot away from the path, so it's a big jump-step to get to them. I catch the step with my hands and dangle for a moment before finding steps with my feet. I release my breath and begin climbing, keeping my eyes upward on each new step.

Finally, I get to the level where the others are waiting and hop over to the path, hugging as close to the wall as I can.

"You made it," Dirk gives me a smile.

"The guards?" Aila asks.

"I think I lost them, but we need to hurry," I gasp out, leaning against the wall.

"Take a breath," Dirk says.

Aila holds up her lantern a little bit and looks around. Her arm is shaking as she holds her light.

"What did you call this place?" she asks, her voice a little shaky.

"The Hive," Dirk replies.

"Oh," she says. "Oh! It's like a beehive! I get it."

"What's...a beehive?" Dirk asks.

"It's a home for bees," Aila explains.

"Like, the letter B?" Dirk asks.

"No, the bug. It's kind of like-"

"Let's go," I say, pushing myself off the wall. Krin's face looks strained, and I don't want to stay here longer than we need to.

Dirk nods and turns to walk up the path to where the next ladder leads to the path above us.

"We're supposed to walk on this?" Aila asks, pointing her lantern at the narrow path. It's about one foot wide, big enough for one person to stand, shoulder against the wall, feet together.

After that, it's a straight drop.

"It's fine," Dirk calls from over his shoulder. "We do it all the time. Just keep your eyes forward and lean against the wall."

Duna follows Dirk and then Aila, albeit very slowly and shakily. Krin heaves a sigh and then follows Aila. I bring up the rear, but I keep a good hold on the back of Krin's shirt.

We reach where the path ends, and you have to jump for the steps when a sneering voice fills the air.

"Evin!" he calls.

I freeze but then turn slowly to look over my shoulder.

There, one path down, right where I had come out, is a lone figure illuminated by lantern light.

Chesnit.

# Chapter Sixteen

"Evin!" he calls again. He laughs once, high and loud. "What are you doing here, Evin?"

I don't respond.

"Oh, come on, Evin," he calls. "Aren't we past this? Why can't we be friends?"

I hear him start moving down the path.

"Quick!" I shout.

Dirk hitches his lantern up his arm and leaps for the ladder. He catches one of the steps and begins climbing up. Duna follows, albeit shakily, and then it's Aila. She slinks against the wall and says, "You better go first, Krin."

"I can't get around you," Krin pants, holding her stomach.

"You first, Krin," Aila whispers, gripping the wall.

"Ugh!" I grunt. "Get around her, Krin!" I'm too scared to yell at Aila. Krin quickly steps around Aila, leaning against the wall as much as she can. Once she's around, I breathe a sigh of relief and hurry forward, ready to kick Aila up the ladder if I have to.

"Evin…" Krin says, looking up to where Dirk's bobbing light dangles above her. He reaches the next path and jumps onto it. Duna follows him, reaching out to take his hand as he hauls her to the safety of the path.

"Dirk!" I shout. "Krin!"

I see Dirk poke his head over the side and then jump back onto the ladder. He begins hurrying back down.

He gets to where he's waiting on the steps just above where Krin will need to reach.

"Krin," he says, "jump out and grab my leg with one hand, the step with the other. I won't let you fall."

Krin lets out a shaky breath but then takes the short leap into empty space. She lets out a shriek as she reaches the step. She gets a hold of Dirk's pant-leg, but then her feet slip, and she's dangling only by her hands.

"Krin!" I shout, gasping, but I can't move. Aila's blocking the path in front of me.

"Move, Aila!" But she seems frozen to the wall.

"Get your feet under you, Krin!" Dirk says, grunting with the effort of holding himself and Krin onto the stone ladder. He reaches down, holding on with only one hand, and he grabs Krin's wrist. He pulls, and she finally gets her feet onto the steps. Dirk keeps her close to him as they climb up.

I hear rock scraping behind me and turn to see Chesnit climbing onto our path, having made the climb on the stone ladder.

"Aila!" I gasp. "Go!" But she's still frozen, having plastered herself against the stone wall.

"Aila! Climb!" I almost beg.

"Climb?" she pants at me, real fear in her voice.

"Yes! Now!"

"Up those?" she asks, pointing with a visibly shaking hand towards the steps.

"You'll be fine," I say, trying to sound calm despite my pounding heart. "You need to go."

Aila is trembling from head to foot as she slides slightly closer to the steps. She looks out into the empty space and glances down, making her blanche and squeal.

"Evin!" Chesnit calls from behind us. He's going to be here in seconds. I want to shove Aila towards the steps.

Finally, she gets to the edge of the path and reaches out a hand.

"I can't reach," she whimpers.

"You have to jump!" I say.

"I...c-can't!" she whispers.

"Yes, you can! Go now!" I say.

"Evin--"

"Aila, you can do this! Go!" I shove her. She screams and flails but then grabs the ladder steps and holds tight.

"Evin--" Aila starts, but I interrupt.

"Climb!"

"Just two levels up, Aila!" Dirk calls from above.

I turn and see Chesnit is barreling towards me. I take a breath and leap onto the steps, moving up as quickly as I can. I have to get rid of Chesnit.

"Evin!" Chesnit calls from below. I look down and see him standing on the edge of the path, but not on the ladder. "You can't get away from me, Evin! You can't get away from this place!"

Then, he does something I do not expect. He turns around and races back up the path. In a moment, I see his light disappear and figure he must have gone inside one of the Tunnels.

I keep climbing, not daring to stop. Chesnit's a searcher; he knows how to use the ladders and paths. I don't know where he's going, but I don't want to wait to find out.

After hurrying up the ladder, I haul myself onto the path where the others are waiting. Dirk and Duna are standing, watching me jump from the ladder to the path. Krin is leaning heavily against the wall, and Aila is almost sitting on the ground against the wall, arms around her legs. Her breath is coming in wild gasps.

"I think it's just one more level," Dirk says quietly. He holds up his lantern so he can see me. "Hannel said his old partner told him it was on one of the top levels, just above where this year's tunnels come out."

I nod, suddenly out of breath.

"Okay," I say. "Where's the ladder on this path?"

"This way," Dirk nods over his shoulder, then turns and begins walking. Not all ladders are connected, so we have to walk along this path to be able to move up more.

Duna turns without looking at us and walks after Dirk. I hope she's happy.

"Aila," I say, resisting the urge to nudge her with my foot. "We have to move."

Aila gets shakily to her feet, gripping the wall with her hands as she does. She is still trembling and breathing fast.

"You okay?" I ask as we start walking forward.

She doesn't say anything, so I let it drop. I feel somewhat satisfied that I finally found something that Aila is not good at. We pass a Tunnel on this path, and she walks slightly inside of it when she can. I roll my eyes.

We get to the next ladder, and Dirk hops onto the steps. He scampers up, and we all watch his light get smaller and smaller as he does.

Finally, he calls down, "This is it! I think that's really the tunnel! It's three levels up."

"Okay!" I call up. Then, just to the girls in front of me, I say, "Let's do what we did last time. Duna, climb up, and then Dirk will come back down to help Krin. Then I'll help Aila."

Duna nods without turning around and then leaps onto the step. Her right foot slips for a second, and I gasp, but she pulls herself up and starts clambering up the steps.

She gets up the ladder without a problem, and then Dirk comes hurrying back down. Krin is still leaning against the wall.

"I don't think I can do it, Evin," Krin almost sighs.

"You can do it," I tell her. But she doesn't look good. "For Hoss."

Krin takes a steadying breath, and then she heaves herself out onto the ladder, reaching up for Dirk's leg again as she does so. He reaches down and helps her get her footing, and then they climb up.

"Your turn, Aila," I say.

She turns and looks at me with huge, terrified eyes.

"Aila, come *on*," I say, unsuccessfully keeping the impatience out of my voice. I mean, *Krin* did it. "You did it before!"

"I can't," Aila gasps, clutching the wall. "I...can't."

I roll my eyes. "Aila, we don't have time for this. This is the only way. Come on!

"I...can't," Aila sniffs. "It's t-too h-high." Her voice is barely a whisper.

Sighing, I say as calmly as I can, "Aila, I will be right below you. You. Will. Not. Fall." Aila, still clinging to the wall, looks at me, nods, wipe her nose on her filthy sleeve, and then turns to face the stone steps.

Aila gasps when her feet leave the safety of the path. Her feet kick out wildly, but her hands manage to grab a step once again. Then, she scrambles and gets her feet onto one as well. She begins climbing, but slowly.

I look up past Aila to see the small circle of light where everyone else is waiting. It does look a long way up.

Taking a deep breath, I jump onto the ladder. I find hand and footholds and wait for Aila to move up some more. She goes slowly, her whole body shaking and audibly crying.

Aila reaches up and pulls herself to the next step, but as she brings her foot up, it slips on the step. She lets out a curdling scream as her leg dangles in between the two steps. I quickly reach up and put my hand under her foot, making it so she can stand on me. I push her up slowly, and she eventually gets her foot on the next step. She freezes, sobbing.

"It's okay, Aila," I say. "That happens sometimes. It's fine. I got you."

"I can't..." Aila cries.

"Yes, you can," I reply firmly. "You have to."

"Evin!" Dirk calls from above. "Look out!"

I turn to my right to see a light emerging from the tunnel Aila had sort of walked in. It's close enough to the steps that I can see the cruel smile on Chesnit's face as he finds me on the ladder.

"Aila!" I shout, not being able to help myself. "Go!"

Aila turns and sees him, too. "Ah!" she cries, but she does start moving faster. It's not fast enough, though; Chesnit is already almost to the ladder.

"I told you I know these Tunnels, Evin!" he laughs.

"Go, Aila!" I almost cry myself. Aila moves up another step, but it takes her so long to get a hold. She just doesn't have the instinct; she can't move on the ladder like searchers and diggers can.

By the time Chesnit reaches the ladder, my foot is within his long reach. He shoots out a long arm and clasps his hand around my ankle.

"Ah!" I cry out. I try to kick my leg free, but his grip is too tight. His fingers are so long that they wrap all the way around my ankle.

"Where do you think *you're* going?" Chesnit sneers, tugging on my leg. I grip the step as hard as I can, groaning with the effort of not letting go.

"Evin!" Aila cries, looking down.

"Go!" I shout. "Climb!" Aila begins moving up again.

"You're not going anywhere!" Chesnit laughs. "You're *my* partner!"

"Let go!" I growl, kicking my leg as hard as I can.

"I'm taking you back!" Chesnit says. "I tried to be your friend, Evin. I *wanted* to be your friend. But if I can't, then the in-charges can have you! They'll reward me!"

"Stop it, Chesnit!" Dirk yells from above, but I know he can't do anything: Aila's still on the ladder, but she's made it almost a whole level up.

"They'll make me one," Chesnit says, his voice disgustingly excited. "Once they hear what I've done, I will be with them!"

"That's what you want?" I ask. "To be one of *them*? You're stupid!"

"There would be nothing better," Chesnit says, still pulling. "I will help rule this Nation."

"You're dirt!" Aila screams from above. "You're dirt, and you always will be! The in-charges won't care that you found us. They'll care you were down here when you weren't supposed to be!"

"No," Chesnit laughs. "No."

"They'll think you're stupid for trying to help them!" Aila continues. "We're nothing to them. *You're* nothing to them!"

"You're wrong!" Chesnit laughs. "They will reward me! They're on their way now! I left markers all through the Tunnels. They'll be here any second." He gives my leg a hard tug, and I cry out, begging my fingers not to let go.

"They're going to Depart you!" Aila sobs.

"No!" Chesnit roars. While still keeping his grip on my ankle, he jumps from the path and onto the steps. "I will make them see! I will make you *all* see!"

I summon what strength I have left in my arms and push off from the steps and go down as hard as I can with my free leg. I feel and hear a squishy *crunch* as my heel connects with Chesnit's nose. I hope it hurts just as much as when Dirk hit him.

"Ah!" he screams, but he doesn't release me. He climbs up, two steps at a time; he finally releases my ankle but wraps his arm around my waist.

"I've got you," he says, his voice low and throaty.

"Let go!" I shout, trying to kick him again, but he shoves me into the wall, knocking the air out of my chest.

"Let her go, and you can come with us!" Aila calls from above, her voice full of desperation. "Please! Let her go, and you can come!"

"No," Chesnit says firmly. "She's coming with me. You can come with me, Evin. Come with me." He says it quietly, so quietly it's only for me.

I shudder but hiss out, "NO!"

"We'll see."

And then he pushes off from the wall, taking me with him.

I scream as we fall backward, dropping into empty space. I thrash against him, but then he twists, and we crash onto a path, Chesnit landing heavily on top of me. We roll, and Chesnit slides off me toward the path's edge. He yells as he begins to drop out of sight, hand shooting out to grab my shirt as he falls.

"NO!" I scream as he pulls me forward. I heave backward, trying to keep from going over the edge. I claw at the dirt, dig my heels in, but I keep inching forward.

"You're coming with me!" Chesnit screams at me, only his head and shoulders visible over the edge.

"Evin!" the others wail from above.

I growl and pull back, scooting until my back touches the wall, but that allows Chesnit to crawl back over the edge. He releases my shirt so he can pull himself up.

"They're going to reward me," he scowls, eyes full of fire. His nose is puffy, making his face lopsided and shadowed. His smile hangs loose and horrible on his face. His eyes are bloodshot and look black in the darkness. His face is full of dark blood that's still gushing out of his crooked nose. "You'll see. I'll be one of them. Come with me." He grins cruelly at me. "You think they're really your friends? They're nothing. They don't care about you. Come with me."

"Never," I scowl, and then I kick Chesnit in the face once more.

He grunts and then gasps as the force of the kick sends him backward over the edge and down into the darkness. He screams wildly, his scream getting fainter and fainter, and then it abruptly stops.

I sit against the wall, panting, sweat rolling down my face, but I can't look away from where Chesnit's face had just been.

"Evin!" Aila screams from above. "Evin!"

"I'm fine," I call up, voice cracking. I still gaze at the empty darkness. Finally, I tear my eyes away, but Chesnit's bruised face seems plastered before me. "I'm coming," I call up, but I don't know if they hear me. There's some sort of ringing sound echoing around the Hive, almost like the worker's bell.

I jump onto the ladder and hurry up to the others, getting off as quickly as I can.

Krin is sitting on the ground, leaning against the wall. Duna looks at me with wide eyes full of tears, and Aila is crying, hugging her arms to her chest.

As soon as I drop onto the path, Aila races to me and throws her arms around me.

I take a step back, confused, and wriggle out from Aila's hug. I give her a weird look, but she just keeps crying, reaching out to me.

"I thought he was going to kill you!" Aila sobs, wiping her eyes with her blackened hand.

"Okay," I say, giving her a somewhat disgusted look before turning to the others.

"He fell?" Dirk asks.

I nod but then turn towards the empty air and vomit. I wipe my mouth with the back of my shaky hand and then turn back to the others. Thankfully, no one says anything.

"What's that sound?" I ask, rubbing my ear.

"What sound?" Dirk asks.

"It sounds like the worker bell," I say.

"There's no sound, Evin," Aila says softly. "You're probably in shock."

"Okay," I say. I don't know what that means. "Chesnit said the guards are on their way. Let's go."

Dirk kneels down and helps Krin to her feet. He gives Duna a cool look, but then he edges around her on the path so he can lead. Duna drops her head but follows him.

Dirk leads us along, holding his lantern high. Duna seems to shuffle oddly as she walks like she can't quite figure out if she wants to keep going. I don't care. I really don't care how she feels.

The path begins to be smoother and wider, almost wide enough that three of us can walk next to each other. Aila moves forward and puts an arm around Krin's waist. Krin gives her a tired smile, and I feel suddenly like we need to move faster.

Finally, we reach what must be the guards' tunnel. I'm simultaneously relieved and terrified that it's real.

We stop before the gaping mouth before us. There's no door, just a dark "O." Even though I know it's just another tunnel, I feel like it's a strange place, a place where we shouldn't go. My stomach flips, and I worry I might vomit again.

Krin groans and reaches out for the wall to steady herself. Aila murmurs something to her while we all just wait quietly. Even though I know it's a bad idea, we have to go into this tunnel. For Krin. We have to get out of here, and this is our only chance, and that baby deserves a chance. I have to give that baby a chance. If I don't, then I'm basically saying that what the Nation and the parents who don't want their kids are doing is fine. Kids deserve a chance, no matter where they're born or who they're born to.

"This is it," Dirk says. Krin's able to stand up again, but I shoot her a worried glance. She puts a hand on her back to steady herself and lets out a long sigh.

No one says anything for a moment. It's as if we all know something bad is going to happen once we enter this tunnel.

"Let's go," I say, nodding to Dirk.

He nods, then lifts his lantern and walks into the tunnel. Duna follows, head down and arms folded tightly across her chest. Aila and Krin go next, Aila still supporting a waddling Krin. I pause at the entrance and turn back. I let the emptiness of the Hive wash over me once more, and then I dart into the tunnel behind the others.

# Chapter Seventeen

The tunnel is wide and smooth, and the walls look like they were shined when this tunnel was formed; I can kind of see our reflections on them as we pass. It's wide enough that we can all walk next to each other, but Duna lags behind us. The only sound coming from her is the occasional whimper or sniff.

"How much farther?" Aila asks, her voice barely more than a whisper.

"I don't know," I shrug. "I've never been here before."

"Where does it go again?" Aila asks.

"I don't know," I say, trying to keep the annoyance out of my voice. "I've never been here before."

"Most of the diggers and searchers think it goes to A Level," Dirk whispers back, "but they're not sure, either. Most guess it's a tunnel for guards, though."

"Wonderful," Aila grumbles.

"Better than the lifts," I remind her.

"What if it's not A Level?" Aila asks. "What then?"

I shrug and say, "We'll see." All I can think, though, is how stupid this is. And Krin is kind of swaying as she walks, looking exhausted.

We walk on, our footsteps echoing and familiar to me. I never thought I'd be happy to be back in a tunnel. I just wish it wasn't this tunnel.

Then, there's a door.

It's large and painted white, so it kind of glows in the darkness even before our lanterns illuminate it. The door is almost as wide as the tunnel itself, and there's a small doorknob on the right side about halfway down.

310

We all stop before the door, looking up at it. We look nervously at each other but then

Dirk nods toward the door.

"Okay," I whisper, and I reach out for the doorknob.

It's cold in my hand, and it turns without a sound. I pull on the door, and it glides seamlessly open. The whole white door isn't actually what opens, but a much smaller door, only big enough for one of us at a time, opens.

A cool, fresh blast of air rushes to our faces, and I blink because of the brightness coming at us.

I squint and lower my lantern to see the room that lays before us. At first, I almost thought the door led outside because of how bright it is, but once my eyes adjust, I see that the room is just sparkling clean and lit with bright lights. There are beds along one side of the room with white sheets and fluffy white pillows; the floor is sparkling, polished stone; the walls are painted white and spotless, and the ceiling is lit with rows of bright string lights. These lights aren't the usual, tunnel-dim, but they're very bright, and the bulbs are big and clear. Somehow, the lights seem to make the room look cleaner.

"Whoa," Dirk says, mouth agape.

"It's so clean," Krin says, reaching out and touching the crisp wall.

"So this is what cleaners do," Dirk chuckles a little.

"Some cleaners," Aila says.

"Stupid job," I grumble. "What is this room?"

"Must be where they sleep," Aila says.

"Who?" Dirk asks. "In-charges or guards?"

"I think guards," I say, pointing. Looking around, there are big holes in the walls hung with rows and rows of black clothes. There is an opening in the room, and I see it leads to another room just like this one, filled with clean beds. Suddenly, I realize something.

"We need to go," I say, pushing them all forward.

"What?" Dirk asks, still looking around,

"This is where the guards sleep, and there are no guards. It's nighttime. We need to go. Chesnit already said they are on their way. If there's not a single guard here, where do you think they'll be coming soon?"

Duna sighs and says, "Remember? They're all in the Arrival room. Waiting for you."

"Well, Evin's still right," Aila says. "We need to go."

I don't know if I like Aila agreeing with me, but I'm at least glad it's moving us in the right direction.

We move quickly down the long room, eyes open and ears perked for any sign of a guard, but the room is deserted. And that makes me very nervous.

"Where do you think this ladder goes?" Aila asks.

I turn, not having noticed that the others stopped. Aila was staring at, well, I don't get how it's a ladder. The only ladders I know are the ones in the Hive, the ones made of stone steps cut into the wall. This ladder isn't built into the wall. It hands down from the ceiling and is made of...metal? Each step is made of a circular rod-type-thing, not a block of stone. There's empty space between each step, and it leads up to some sort of a hatch in the ceiling. The ladder is in the middle of the room, and we all gather around it.

"Should we try this way?" Aila asks. She reaches a hand out and grabs one of the steps.

"I'd rather look for a door..." I say, not really sure about this ladder.

"A door might only lead to B Level," Aila says. "The ladder at least goes up, which is what we want, right?"

I scowl at her but then stop as Krin gives a little squeal.

Krin suddenly doubles over, clutching her stomach. She leans against one of the beds and groans, squeezing her eyes shut.

"Krin!" Aila gasps and goes to her side.

Duna, Dirk, and I just stand there, not sure what to do, eyes glued to Aila and Krin.

"Deep breaths," Aila says calmly, patting Krin's back.

Krin takes shaky breaths that come out in short gasps, but it seems to relax her face a little.

"That's the worst one yet," Krin whimpers, still bent over.

"Take two minutes-" Aila starts, but I interrupt.

"We don't have two minutes, Aila-"

"Take two minutes," Aila shoots me a glare. "Krin needs to rest for a minute."

"Fine, then we're going to look for a door," I say.

"Fine," Aila scowls at me.

I roll my eyes, but Duna and Dirk and I scatter. We go through archways into other rooms full of beds and black clothes. The room I enter looks exactly the same, and there's no door. I go back to the main room.

"I don't see a door," Dirk shrugs.

"Me neither," Duna mumbles.

"So...the ladder?" I ask, looking at the thing that leads to the ceiling.

Krin is back to standing, kind of cradling her stomach with both hands. She gives me a weak smile.

"I'll look," Aila says. She steps onto the ladder and hauls herself upward. She seems much more sure of herself on this ladder than the one in the Hive, but then again, if she fell off this one, she'd land on the floor. She reaches up, twists a handle on the hatch, and pushes it slightly open. She peeks through it and looks around.

"Where does it lead to?" Dirk calls up to her.

"A Level!" Aila whisper-shouts back down triumphantly. "Right next to the lifts, kind of to the side and behind them."

Dirk smiles at all of us, and I can't help but smile in return; we're right where we need to be!

"It looks empty," Aila says excitedly, lowering the hatch slightly so she can look back down at all of us.

"Of course it does," Dirk grumbles. "We know where all the guards and in-charges are."

He shoots Duna a nasty look that makes her shrink back.

"But some are on their way here!" I remind them. I'm not defending Duna, but I'm grateful for the distraction. If some of the guards are in the Gathering Room and the others are in the Tunnels, maybe we have some time.

"Let's go fast," Dirk says, nodding at the ladder. "You first, Krin."

Krin nods and steps forward.

But then we hear it: shouting.

It's coming from the Hive, from the other side of the big white door. Shouting and footsteps. Lots of them.

"Oh no," I whisper, hands going cold.

"Already?" Dirk asks, not really to anyone.

"Come on, Krin!" I yell, pushing her up the ladder. "You've got to get up there!"

Krin pants as she moves up the thin steps, body shaking. I just hope she doesn't slip. Eventually, Krin makes it up to where Aila is waiting.

Aila pushes open the hatch, climbs through, and then reaches down to help Krin.

"They'll know," Duna puts a hand to her mouth. "They'll know where we went. Look at the floor. Look at our footprints!"

"Not if we hurry!" I snap back. "Get up there, Dirk!"

Dirk moves forward to the ladder, but then Duna looks at us, face suddenly full of life.

She runs back down the room.

"Duna!" I call, but she doesn't react. Instead, she starts dragging a bed in front of the big white door.

"Get going!" she shouts at us. She grabs another bed and starts hauling it to the door.

"Go," Dirk says, shoving me towards the ladder now. Fine. *I* don't need to be told twice. I grab the closest step and pull myself up. I look and see Krin is almost all the way through the hatch, and I speed up.

I look back down to see Dirk with one hand on the ladder, but he's facing Duna, who has successfully stacked two beds on top of one another to block the door. The shouting outside the door is loud now, and then the door shudders. The weight of the beds only allows it to open a few inches, but it makes me jump.

"Come on, Dirk!" I call down.

Dirk looks up at me with heartbroken eyes but a smile on his lips.

"Go," he says, barely audible. "We'll be right behind you."

"Dirk!" I shout, but even in my ears, it sounds like pleading.

"I can't leave her," he says softly. Then he jumps off the ladder and runs to the door. He grabs the nearest bed and helps Duna lift it onto her impressive four-high pile.

The door is shoved open another inch. The shouting is even louder.

"Evin!" Aila calls. "Come on!"

315

I'm at the hatch now, but I can't look away from Dirk and Duna.

"Evin!" Aila reaches through and grabs my arm. "Come on! Dirk said they'd be right behind us!"

I look up at Aila.

"We could help-"

"We've got to help, Krin," Aila says, her voice slightly shaky. "She needs to go now."

"But, Duna...Dirk..."

"Made their choice," Aila says firmly. "Now come on."

I look one last time to see Dirk and Duna stacking another bed, but the door is shoved hard from the other side, open almost wide enough for a person to squeeze through.

Aila pulls on my arm, forcing me to turn away and climb through the hatch.

I emerge in a deafeningly quiet tunnel to see Krin leaning against the stone wall, panting and groaning. Aila shuts the hatch behind us, but not before we hear one sound, one all-too-familiar sound. A sound that crushes my heart harder than anything I've seen: a gunshot.

# Chapter Eighteen

"No…" I gasp, looking at the hatch, hoping that Dirk and Duna will suddenly burst through it. "NO!" I cry, lunging for it.

Aila catches me around the waist and hauls me away from it.

"You can't do anything!" she says fiercely.

"I could've helped them!"

"You would've been killed, too!"

"You don't know they're dead!" I sob, fighting to get to the hatch. I feel hot tears rolling down my cheeks, making my vision go blurry.

"Evin, no! We've got to go. Now! They'll be coming! We don't have much longer!" Aila says, but then I see her expression change like she caught herself.

"Much longer for what?" I ask, staring at her with all the fury I have.

"I...no-nothing!" Aila stammers, standing up and moving over to Krin.

"Aila," I reach out and grip her arm tightly, squeezing. "I saw you and Jinade."

Aila freezes, her back to me, but she doesn't look at me. Krin looks at her and then looks at me.

"Say something, Aila," I say.

"We don't have time for this, Evin," Aila sighs. Then she turns to face me. "We have to--"

I punch Aila in the face, sending the girl reeling backward on the ground.

"Evin!" Krin gasps, moving to help Aila.

"Tell me the truth!" I say, chest heaving. "I never trusted you." I step forward, hand curled into a fist.

"Evin!" Krin says, stepping in front of me and putting a hand on my shoulder. She gives a little shove, but I don't care. I keep moving.

"Evin! No!" Krin gasps. "Please! Let's just get out first."

"How can you trust her still?" I ask, looking pleadingly in Krin's eyes. "We just left Dirk and Duna!"

"We trusted Duna," Krin says softly.

"Don't...Don't--" but I can't think of any more words. I sink to my knees and put my face in my hands. "You don't know they're dead," I whisper. *How many more?* I think. *How many more will die here?*

I feel Aila's hand on my shoulder, and she says, "There's nothing you could have done. They made their choice, and we still have a chance because of it."

"Don't touch me," I grumble, slapping her hand away.

"Fine," Aila says. "But we need to get going."

"Why?" I sneer. "You going to turn us in, too? Hand us over so you can go back to your family and have birthdays and parties and whatever?"

"Then why did you agree to this?" Aila asks, gesturing around us. "Why come if you obviously don't trust me?"

My cheeks burn, and I mumble, "Krin needs you."

Aila's face softens, and she says, "We're going to get Krin out. I promise. Come on." She turns and heads up the tunnel, up towards the door that leads to the Field.

I sigh, exhausted and angry and hurt, and rise to my feet. I'm still crying, so I quickly wipe my face. We quickly walk up the wide, clean tunnel. I realize how loud we were when we came through the hatch, and I suddenly feel worried that everyone in the whole Mine heard us. I keep waiting for the hatch to be thrown open and our backs to be filled with bullets.

"Here's the door," Aila says, hurrying over to the right side of the tunnel. She puts her fingers against the wall and seems to be feeling it, roving it over with her fingertips. Then, she pushes against the stone, and we hear a soft click.

I gasp, amazed that that worked. Really, I'm amazed we got this far.

There could be anything on the other side of this door-- guards, in-charges, *Jinade*--but we have to go. There's nowhere else to go now. Not for me, not for Krin, not for the baby. We have to go into this room.

I'm shaking so hard I almost wonder how I'm even standing up straight, but I watch as Aila pulls the door open, barely wide enough that she and I can push our eyes against the opening.

The room beyond the door is completely dark and empty. There are walls separating tables, cushiony chairs, and things that look like tiny trees in pots. The walls form little boxes. Each box holds a chair and a small table. The lights are off, so I can't see too far into the room. It smells nice, though; the Mine normally smells musty, earthy, and kind of stale. This room, though, almost tickles my nose. It looks so clean and odd that I almost forget we're in the Mine.

The guards' room was kind of the same, but at least those walls and the floor were still stone.

This room looks...soft. There isn't a fleck of dirt or coal anywhere.

But it's still empty. And I'm uneasy.

"This can't be right," I say softly. "Where are all the in-charges? We weren't going to come this way because of all the in-charges."

"You want to wait until someone comes by and ask them?" Aila almost spits. "Come on. The windows are over here, on the left side. We're wasting time."

I raise my eyebrows, surprised at her harsh tone, but I pull the door open wide enough for us to squeeze through. Once Krin is inside, I step in and push the door shut. The latch clicks, and the door slides into the wall seamlessly.

We make our way into the room. I'm relentlessly uneasy.

"What is all this?" Krin asks quietly.

"They're cubicles," Aila says. "Kind of small offices. The in-charges are all over something in the Mine, and they keep track of us all and all the gold and coal up here."

"Looks boring," I say.

"Looks clean," Krin says.

Then we see the window. It lets in a bright sheen of silvery light that falls softly on the floor below. There are actually a few of them lining the upper part of the wall. My heart speeds up, knowing I might see Coden's stars. The thought makes me smile and forget my terror for a moment.

We move to stand just under the closest window. It's high up the wall; I don't think I could touch it even if I jump, and it looks *barely* large enough for Krin. It'll be tight.

"How do we get up there?" Krin asks, holding her stomach.

I look around and see a table in the corner. I go to it and drag it over, so it's under the window. I notice as I pull it that there are now coal smudges all over the soft ground. I almost laugh thinking of how disgusted all the in-charges will be when they see dirt in their rooms.

The table is in place, and I climb on. Standing on my toes, I can just reach up and touch the window, but I would have to jump to get out, and Krin can't jump.

I climb down from the table and go get one of the cushiony chairs. I pick it up, take it back to the table, and heave it on top with a grunt. I climb back up and find my face level with the window. Smiling, I climb back down.

"Okay," Aila says, "so we need to--"

Then we hear the creaking, grinding, groaning of the lift in the tunnel. Even through the walls and the shut door, we can hear it.

"Quick!" I hiss. "They're coming!"

Aila's eyes go wide, and Krin clutches her stomach protectively.

"Aila, go!"

Thankfully, she doesn't say anything back. She quickly climbs up the table and the chair. She pushes against the window for a moment, and then it pops open. She jumps a little and gets her legs under her, so she's sitting on the window. Then, she silently drops from view.

"It's not a long drop!" Aila calls softly from outside. "It's on a hill just outside the fence!"

"Okay," I say, "go, Krin."

Krin nods and starts climbing up, but slowly. My heart is hammering. In-charges or guards could be here any second.

Then, she doubles over, face contorted in pain.

"No!" I hiss out, not meaning to.

Krin holds in a scream I know she desperately wants to let out. She puts her face in her hands. I reach up and rub her back, not sure what else to do.

"Uh...breathe!" I say, trying to think what Aila normally does.

"What's happening?" I hear Aila call from outside.

I hear voices in the tunnel outside!

Almost tripping I turn so fast, I hurry back to the door and slide a table in front of it. The table isn't that heavy, though, so I stack a chair on top.

Not even a breath later, the latch clicks, and the door pops open, but it stops before it's even open an inch.

"What the--" I hear.

"What's this? Who's in there?!"

Two voices. Sounds like in-charges.

I race back to where Krin is still kneeling on the table.

"Krin," I beg, "you have to go! Please!"

She takes a steadying breath, her eyes full of tears, and then she rises.

"Evin," Krin says, standing on the chair, "I can't do this. I can't lift myself up!" Her voice shakes, and there's panic in her eyes.

"It's alright," I say. "Here!" I climb up and stand on the table. I hold my hands together and let her put a foot in them. Then, I heave her upward. She gets one leg on the window, and then I lift until she has the other one.

"Go get guards!" one of the voices outside shouts.

They're shoving against the door. I resist turning around to see.

"Drop!" I hiss at Krin.

She takes a breath and slides out of the window. I hear a soft *thump*.

"Come on, Evin!" Aila whispers up at me.

I climb onto the chair, hands on the window, but I pause. I can feel the fresh air on my face, I can smell the trees and the grass, but it feels wrong. My heart is racing; I'm inches from freedom, but I can't make myself go through the window.

"Evin?" Aila calls, almost pleadingly.

If I go out this window, the guards or in-charges or whoever is outside the door will see the table and chairs and the coal footprints, and they'll know. They'll know how we got out, and we'll be caught in seconds. Krin can't run. How far could we get before the guards catch us?

"Open this door!" the in-charge outside the door yells.

"Evin, it'll be fine!" Aila calls like she knows what I'm thinking.

"They'll catch us," I say. "They'll catch up."

"No, they won't!" Aila sounds panicked. "Just come down!"

But I can't get myself to jump out the window. I've lost Coden, we all lost Hoss, and Dirk and Duna. My list of people is dwindling...and Krin *has* to escape.

I make up my mind, and the tears fall freely.

"Run!" I call down to them, choking on the word.

"No-!" Aila cries, but she's cut off as I reach out and pull the window closed, shutting myself back into the Mine, into the darkness.

I realize suddenly that I didn't look up; I didn't see the stars. My heart drops.

I turn to face the dark offices. Whoever is outside has stopped shoving against the door, but I don't waste any time.

Quickly, I hop off the table. I pull the chair off and replace it, and then I slide the table back where it goes. I can't do anything about the footprints.

I hear footsteps stampede to the door. There's more shouting, directions from in-charges, and then there are loud bangs against the door. I see the table I put there get shoved forward quite a bit.

I dive behind a wall, behind a *cubicle*, or whatever Aila called them.

They shove into the room, angry and shouting.

"What is the meaning of this?"

"Who's here?"

"Footprints! Workers! They must be workers!"

"Where did they go?"

"Guards, search the place!"

I dart around the corner of the cubicle I'm in and hurry into the next one. This whole room seems to be a confusing maze of walls and tiny rooms. I'd rather be in the Tunnels.

As quietly as I can, I keep creeping around corners further back into the offices. Eventually, the guards and in-charges seem further away. I just hope there's another door back this way.

Right...left...left...I keep moving, trying to picture these offices as just a cleaner version of the Tunnels I'm so used to running. I automatically keep track of the turns, just like I would in a Tunnel, thinking I might be able to hide and find my way out later.

I can hear them all yelling, but I can't tell what they're saying. They're all shouting at the same time, so I can't hear if the guards are getting any closer to me. I just keep moving as quickly and quietly as I can.

I make another left turn and then come face-to-face with a big door, but this door is solid black metal. It reaches from floor to ceiling. I don't know where this door goes, but it has to be better than turning around straight into a pack of in-charges and guards.

The cold handle turns in my hand, and I begin to pull the door open quietly, not wanting anyone behind me to hear, but then it's suddenly pushed open by a force on the other side.

I get bumped back a little, disoriented. I straighten and face the doorway. Three people stand there. Two are guards, dressed in black, holding large, shining guns. The person between those two guards has a very familiar, very cold face: Lady Executor Jinade.

# Chapter Nineteen

Jinade looks stunned, her eyes wide, as she takes in who is standing before her.

"What are you doing here?" Jinade asks. I expect the cold, commanding voice I'm used to, but the Lady Executor actually sounds surprised and somewhat...fearful.

But, then Jinade waves her hands, and the two guards rush forward. They each grasp my arms and hold them tightly.

My heart drops, but at least they're not focused on the window.

The lights overheard turn on as the in-charges and guards begin filing back to where we're standing.

"Lady Executor!" one of them shouts.

"What's going on?"

"Who's this?"

"Is that a worker?"

"Keeper Adams," Jinade says, the coldness in her voice returned full force. "Step forward."

A thick, fat man with almost no neck steps forward hesitantly. He has a nervous smile on his face, and he keeps pulling his collar away from his neck that doesn't exist.

"Lady Executor?" he asks.

"Explain *this* to me, Adams," Jinade says, turning her icy stare from Adams to me. Adams fiddles with his gray suit, trying to stretch the fabric away from his waist where it seems to squeeze his massive girth.

"I apologize for this--" he gestures at me-- "thing. I assumed, when you so swiftly caught the others, that that was the end of this nonsense."

Jinade turns her attention back to the fat man, eyes narrowing. I see him squirm under her glare.

"Nonsense?" she asks, stepping forward slowly. "Nonsense, Adams? Is this not the very nonsense you're supposed to keep at bay, Adams? Are you not employed by this great Nation to make sure there is no *nonsense*? It would seem there was a great deal of nonsense tonight, don't you think, Adams?"

He's sweating. Great beads fall down his flabby cheeks, around his mouth, and down his chin.

"And why, Adams, did I have to step in and catch this *nonsense* after it had made its way to the guards' rooms? How did all this *nonsense* get so far?" Jinade's tone is calm, but her eyes are fire.

Jinade suddenly stops moving toward Adams and turns back to me. The guards have a painfully tight grip on my arms, and I'm almost glad they're holding me so tight because it's holding me up. Jinade glares at me, and I feel my knees go weak.

She walks up to me slowly and then stops just in front of me. In one fluid motion, without blinking an eye, she slaps me hard across the cheek.

Dots pop up in my vision, and the edges go black. I gasp in pain. It's the same cheek as before, the night she took Coden, and I think it rattled my teeth. I slowly get my vision to return to normal, and I look back at Jinade.

She smiles, cold and cruel, and then grips my cheeks in her hand, squeezing hard, making my eyes water. I want to bite her, but I can't open my mouth. Suddenly, any fear this woman brought out is turned to hatred. She killed Coden, took Hoss from Krin, makes our lives miserable every day, and now she doesn't even have the decency to kill me without hurting me further.

Jinade continues to squeeze, and I think my eyes might pop out of my head. Her nails dig into my cheeks, and I feel blood dripping down. I stare at her, though; I decide I won't look away anymore.

"Lady Executor..." Adams whispers out, looking from Jinade to me.

Jinade drops my face and turns to him. My cheeks burn, and my eyes are still watering, but I don't look away.

"Adams," Jinade says, folding her hands in front of her, "this is unacceptable."

"My Lady, if I could just explain--"

"Explain what?" Jinade smiles at him, and he cowers. "Explain your incompetence? Perhaps you are unfit to serve the Nation. I can only imagine what our beloved and wise Chancellor would say if he had arrived on time. Did that cross your mind, Adams? What do you think he would say?"

Adams seems to shrink before her, mouth agape.

"No, no, Lady Executor," he stammers, "I...I just...no, I--"

"Can't form a thought?" she sneers. "Much like these workers."

The other in-charges begin to slowly edge away from Adams, throwing him disgusted looks. I almost think it's funny that the in-charges fear the same thing we workers do.

"I think we should be grateful, Adams," Jinade says slowly, moving toward him again, "that this did not happen when our beloved Chancellor is here. Don't you feel grateful?"

Adams bows his head and gives a tiny nod.

"Kinn," Jinade says, and a tall, older man steps forward. He has gray hair and looks evenly at Jinade. "Kinn, I do believe that you are up for a promotion, and it seems we have a recent opening in Security and

Discipline. Would you mind very much escorting Adams here to my office? Pick up a few guards on your way and wait for me."

The man, Kinn, nods and reaches out to grab Adams' arm. He pulls, and Adams goes without resisting. He doesn't even look up as he's pulled away from the circle of in-charges.

Jinade turns to address the group of people before her.

"Let us be thankful this was dealt with quickly," she says, "but we must ensure it never happens again. In the meantime, I would suppose our tricky guest here misses her friends terribly. So let's let her rejoin them, shall we?" There are snickers and dark chuckles around the room, and I feel cold dread inside. What "friends" are she talking about? And how will I be joining them?

"Petron, Kaleb, please accompany these guards to the loading bay where they will take care of this little problem. The rest of you, you're dismissed." Jinade nods at them and then moves through the crowd back up through the cubicles. They part around her like they're desperate not to be touched by her.

Two in-charges step forward, both scowling at me.

One picks up a clipboard and grabs a pen from the desk behind him.

"Number?" he asks me, pen at the ready.

For a moment, I'm confused. What does he want? I can't seem to think straight.

The other in-charge rolls his eyes and then gives me a good slap across the cheek. Still burning from Jinade's hit, this one makes me whimper.

"Number?" the clipboard in-charge demands again.

"NM1448," I gasp out, eyes swimming with tears.

He scribbles it down and then turns to head back up through the offices.

I don't have it in me to fight. There's no use; I'm tired, so tired. And I don't know if Aila and Krin got away. What if they were caught and none of it was worth anything? What if not even one of us made it out, even after everything we just went through?

I hope they made it. I hope Krin has the baby, and she raises it with love. I hope Aila teaches the baby to read and that they live somewhere where it's safe.

The guards carry me back through the offices, and my gaze drifts to the window. Maybe I could catch a glimpse of the stars. Why didn't I take one second and look up?

We're back through the door and in the tunnel. The in-charges turn to the right and the guards drag me along. I let my feet dangle; I don't want to walk for them anymore.

No one speaks a word as we reach the staircase. Instead of heading to the left, we turn to the right. Down, down, down the steps we go. Each step hits my feet and makes my toes scream in pain, but I still don't move my legs.

We go through the door I've only ever heard about, and my stomach begins twisting; I suddenly can't breathe. I've accepted that I'm going to die, but I don't think my body has.

The door opens into a large room, but it's dim. There's only a single light bulb dangling from the center of the ceiling. I can see carts and carts full of coal in here and some empty ones.

On one side of the room, I can see a chute with the same type of moving belt the sorting room has. This must be where the coal is loaded to be transported. This is the loading bay.

I'm confused. Why aren't we outside?

To my left, I see a massive archway in the side of the wall, and it leads to some sort of large tunnel. Coming out of the tunnel are huge tracks, like those the carts are pushed on, but bigger. To the right, all the way across the room is another archway-tunnel. I wonder if one of these tunnels leads outside.

I notice this room is full of guards. Looking around, I see one stationed about every ten feet. They are barely distinguishable from the walls, but they're there, like menacing statues guarding the darkness around them.

The in-charges stop in the middle of the room, under the lightbulb. The clipboard in-charge begins scribbling dutifully on his paper, avoiding my gaze at all costs. The other in-charge moves to the side of the room, where there is a long, low bench. He opens a drawer on the bench and reaches inside. He pulls out some black cloth and something long and silver.

The in-charge comes back and hands the black cloth to one of the guards.

The guard drops his hold on my arm to take it. It never even crosses my mind to fight or try to run now. What's the point?

The guard takes the black cloth and holds it up. I get what it is now. I'm heartbroken; I just wanted to see the stars, just once.

"No-!" I start, but it doesn't matter.

The cloth makes my breath hot, and I find it hard to get enough air as they force me forward. Knowing that the hood hides my face, I let the tears come. I cry for Coden, for Hoss, for Duna and Dirk, and for myself, for the stars. I cry silently, the tears coming hot and thick down my cheeks. My heart is hammering in my chest as if it's determining to get in as many beats as it can before it's over.

We walk across the room. I think I hear a door opening and more footsteps entering the room, but I don't know. And I don't really care. My thoughts are far away. I try to imagine that I'm happy, that there are people around me who care about me. Immediately, I picture Coden sitting next to me and pointing out the pictures in the stars; I picture Duna and Dirk laughing; I picture Hoss and Krin, looking so happy just being together. We're all together, under the stars.

I cry harder, picturing that.

Suddenly, they force me to a stop, pulling on my arms, so I jerk backward. The guards kick the back of my knees, making me lunge to the ground. They grab my shoulders, forcing me to kneel.

I can't control the panic in my breath; I know I'm dying for a reason. I just hope death isn't all darkness. I lived in darkness; I can't stand to die in darkness.

They keep me kneeling for a long time; my knees are cold and sore. Then, I hear something loud and mechanical split the silence. It sounds far away, but it seems to be getting closer. The ground is rattling below me. It almost sounds like the machine is breathing. And then the machine screams, making me jump. I think it's a train.

Then, I feel something cold and hard shoved up against my chest. I suck in a breath, waiting. There's stabbing pain. And then...nothing.

I wake up, not sure how long it has been. I'm in a small, dark room, and the ground beneath me is hard and cold, covered in something pokey and somewhat smelly.

I sit up, rubbing my hands together to try and get them warm. Every part of me feels stiff and cold.

Suddenly, I remember what happened. I gasp and feel my chest. It feels sore, but certainly not from a gunshot. I don't think. At least, I don't think I'm dead.

Panicking, I look around to see that one wall of this tiny room is made of metal bars. I can see through the bars into a hallway, and then directly across from me is another room with bars on one of the walls. There's a figure inside that room.

I slide to the bars and press my face against them, squinting in the low light. The figure across from me is large and is leaning against the far wall, facing toward me. I can tell it's a boy; he's huge. He's just outside the light, his face still in shadow.

He seems to notice I'm staring at him, for he slides closer. I gasp as he rests against the barred wall, putting his face between two bars so he can see me.

"Evin," Hugo says, giving me a slight nod.

I can't respond. I can't stop staring at his face. I know it's him. I can see the familiar icy blue eyes under a thick layer of coal smudge.

"Hugo…?" I ask, my eyes searching his face, trying to put the pieces together.

It's just beginning to click for me, and I feel the panic rising up like vomit in my throat.

"Hugo," I ask, dreading the answer but needing to hear it. "Where are we?"

He grunts and says, "Welcome to the Colosseum."